YAR IT

Spark

Books by Amy Kathleen Ryan

Glow
Spark

Spark

AMY KATHLEEN RYAN

MACMILLAN

First published in the US 2012 by St. Martin's Press

This edition published in the UK 2012 by Macmillan Children's Books
a division of Macmillan Publishers Limited
20 New Wharf Road, London N1 9RR
Basingstoke and Oxford
Associated companies throughout the world
www.panmacmillan.com

ISBN 978-1-4472-0805-1

1 3 5 7 9 8 6 4 2

A CIP catalogue record for this book is available from
the British Library.

Printed and bound by CPI Group (UK) Ltd, Croydon CR0 4YY

For my father

It is error alone which needs the support of government. Truth can stand by itself.

—Thomas Jefferson

PART ONE

Pride

All men make mistakes, but a good man yields when he knows his course is wrong, and repairs the evil. The only sin is pride.
                                    —Sophocles

Escape

Seth Ardvale wasn't aware of what woke him; he only remembered the fading dream of a rumbling sound that shook his bones. He sat up on his lonely cot in the brig, deep in the bowels of the Empyrean, and rubbed his eyes. He listened for voices. Sometimes he could catch hints about what was going on from the chatter of his guards, but there was no sound at all.

This isolation was part of his punishment, along with the lights being kept on twenty-four hours a day. Seth had come to accept that it might be a very long time before he was out of the brig. If Kieran Alden stayed Captain of the Empyrean, Seth might never get out. He supposed he deserved imprisonment, not just for the failed mutiny he'd staged against Kieran. He deserved to be here because of who he was. "I'm my father's son," he said aloud.

The sound of his own voice startled him. He *hated* that he'd begun talking to himself, but that was how to survive solitary confinement. He had long, internal conversations, and he always imagined talking to the same person: Waverly Marshall. He would close his eyes and see her on the other side of the bars to his cell, sitting on the floor, her hands wrapped around an ankle, chin leaning on her knee. The conversation always picked up where they'd left off a month before, after he'd asked her to get him out of the brig. She'd only looked at him, a haunting hesitation in her deep brown eyes, the rest of her lovely features smooth and expressionless. He knew her well enough to see she didn't trust him.

"Get me out of here," he'd said, pleading, a hand on one of the cold bars between them.

She'd looked at him for a long time before finally saying through a long, exhaled breath, "I can't do that."

And she'd gotten up and walked away.

Could he blame her? He'd staged a mutiny against her boyfriend, Kieran Alden, had thrown him in the brig, withheld food from him, and, some would say, tried to kill him. It had all made sense to Seth at the time; that's how crazy he'd been. The *time* had been crazy. Out of nowhere the New Horizon had attacked the Empyrean, taken all the girls, and caused a containment leak in the reactors that ended up killing Seth's father. But that didn't excuse him. All the kids on the Empyrean had lost parents or were separated from them; all of them had terrifying responsibilities to run the ship without a single functional adult on board. Among them, Seth Ardvale had the lone distinction of acting like a sociopath.

"Maybe that's what I am," he whispered, then covered his mouth with his hand.

Waverly had been right to walk away.

But he still imagined a million different things he could have said to get her to stay. "You're right. You shouldn't risk it," or, "I understand you can't betray Kieran," or simply, "Don't go."

Then he'd imagine how she would look as she turned back to him, how he might make her smile or even laugh. How she'd tuck her hair behind her ear just before glancing away again—a small, demure gesture that pierced his heart every time she did it.

But he'd said nothing that day. In his shame he'd let her leave.

If he ever did get out of here, he'd show her he could be a good person. It didn't matter that he could never have her. He just couldn't stand the thought of her thinking badly of him. And maybe, just maybe, he could help her, too. Because whatever had happened to her on the New Horizon had pulled her downward, bent her back, hollowed out her eyes. If he could see her again, he'd take nothing from her. He wanted nothing. He just wanted to help—be a friend.

Seth curled himself into a compact ball. He felt eavy and lethargic. The sound that woke him must have been a change in the engines, another increase in the ship's acceleration in a vain attempt to catch up with the New Horizon, where all the parents were being held hostage. It would never work, Seth knew, but he would never have a say in the decision-making process again. He would always be a pariah.

"Sleep, sleep, I can sleep," he whispered. It sometimes helped. "I'm just a body, I'm not a mind. I'm a body that needs to sleep."

Then he heard the whine of the ship's intercom, and Kieran Alden's voice: "Evacuate to the central bunker!"

The alarm light in the corridor started twirling in blue and red.

Seth threw aside his bedclothes, ran to the bars of his cell, and yelled down the corridor, "Hey! What's happening?"

No one answered.

"You can't leave me in here!" Seth stepped to his right to try and get a look down the corridor between the cells, and tripped over a plate of bread and miso spread that had been left for him. He saw only rows of cold iron bars, and shadows. "You have to let me out!"

In his panic, Seth pulled helplessly on the door of his cell.

It slid open easily.

He stared, dumbfounded, and took a stealthy step outside and looked down the corridor.

There was no one.

Slowly he crept down the passageway, past Max Brent's cage, which also hung open and was empty. He went to the door that led to the outer corridor and listened, then inched it open.

Down the hall, a booted foot was sticking out of the maintenance closet. Seth approached cautiously, his eyes on the boot, looking for the slightest twitch that would send him running, but the boot didn't move. He nudged the door open and saw his guard, Harvey

Markem, lying on the floor. Seth leaned over him, his ear to unmoving lips, and waited until a warm puff of air escaped them. A clotted mass of blood showed from beneath Harvey's wiry red hair. Seth took the boy's walkie-talkie off his belt and pressed the call button. "Hello?"

From the other end he heard only static.

"I need medical assistance down here," Seth said, and listened.

No response. He looked at the many channels and frequencies, trying to guess which one would reach Central Command. But he didn't have time to go through them, not if he wanted to escape, so he dropped the walkie-talkie on the floor.

Seth started down the corridor, telling himself Harvey would be all right. When he reached the stairwell door, he turned again and looked at the foot. It hadn't moved, not a centimeter. What if Harvey was bleeding in his brain? What if he died?

Sighing, Seth went back to the closet, dragged Harvey out, pulled the boy into a sitting position, then draped him over his shoulder in a fireman's hold. When he stood up, the pressure of Harvey's weight seemed to squeeze all Seth's blood into his face, and he broke into an instant sweat. Swaying with the strain, he started down the corridor again. Harvey was big anyway, but with the additional inertia from the Empyrean's increased speed, he felt as if he were made of wet cement.

Seth's legs shook, and for a moment he considered taking the elevator up, but he'd be spotted by the security camera immediately, and if the doors opened to a group of people, there would be nowhere to run. So Seth struggled up the stairwell, where there were no cameras, sweat pouring down his face and pooling in the hollow at the base of his ribcage.

"Jesus, Harvey," he groaned. "What do you *eat?*"

The stairs were endless, disappearing into a bleak vanishing point above. He had to get Harvey to the central bunker, which was so many flights up Seth didn't have the energy to count. That's where everyone would be during an emergency, and it would be the only place Harvey could get any help.

Twice Seth sank to his knees. But if he left Harvey in the stairwell, the boy could die there, so he kept on climbing, every step painful.

When he heard voices, he knew he was close. The last few steps were torture, but Seth threw his weight forward and forced himself up, knees popping, spine bent. He paused to listen at the doorway and heard two girls talking in the hallway outside the central bunker.

"Did they come back?" said a squeaky little voice on the other side of the door. "Are they coming to get us again?"

"If they are, panicking won't help." This sounded like that freckle-faced little spitfire, Sarah Hodges.

"What if the hull blew up?" the little girl fretted.

"If the hull blew up, you and I wouldn't be here," Sarah said.

Slowly, Seth lowered Harvey to the floor and bent over with his hands on his knees to wait until his breath came back. When he was sure he could run, Seth rapped his knuckles on the door and took off, sprinting down three flights of stairs before he heard Sarah Hodges calling into the stairwell, "Hey! Who's there! Oh my God, Harvey!"

Seth had covered another five flights when he heard footsteps coming after him. He only needed another four flights and then he'd be home free. "Please, please, please." Seth repeated the word in his mind, pushing away the pain in his limbs, sending his exhaustion outside of himself so that he could run.

When he finally reached the level he needed, he gripped the door handle. As quietly as he could, he swung the door open and slipped through it, then pelted down the corridor and ducked into the nearest doorway.

Immediately his senses were filled with the fresh, loamy air of the rain forest. God, he'd missed this. The humid air moistened his prison-dry skin as he ran through the coconut groves, past the lemon trees, where he turned into the undergrowth of the Australian species. He dove into a stand of eucalyptus and huddled there, his heart pounding on the wall of his chest, hands wrapped around his ankles, and he listened.

Not a footstep. Not a whisper. He'd escaped! Until he could find out what had gone wrong with the Empyrean, he would wait here.

Now that he was safe, he grasped the strangeness of what had happened. Someone had let him out, but who? Probably whoever had caused the explosions had also let him out; the two events couldn't be coincidental. Whoever it was had probably caused the explosions as a smoke screen for his release.

His mind turned to Waverly. She'd never hurt Harvey or endanger the ship, but she could have found a way to let Seth and Max out. Then Max could have been the one to hit Harvey over the head and cause the explosions. Would Max do a thing that vicious?

When they'd shared a cell, Seth had listened to Max rave about all the things he'd do to Kieran Alden when he got out of the brig, how he'd lie in wait for him and pummel him, or use a knife, and then he'd go after his pencil-necked little friend Arthur Dietrich, and that traitor Sarek Hassan. The more he heard Max's sick revenge fantasies, the more Seth wondered why he'd ever chosen the boy as his right-hand man.

Yes, Seth decided, Max was capable of endangering the ship and the mission to serve his own selfish purpose. Someone needed to find that son of a bitch before he did any more damage. But that wasn't the only reason to find Max.

Whatever Max had done, whatever those sounds had been, Kieran would surely blame Seth for the whole thing and would likely use it as an excuse to keep him in the brig forever. If those booming sounds were bombs, and Seth was blamed, everyone would believe he was a traitor.

And what would Waverly think of him then?

Seth had only one choice: He had to find Max and turn him in. He had to prove to Kieran, Waverly, and everyone else that he had not done this.

And somehow, he had to do it without getting caught.

Hero

Waverly was in her quarters, brewing a pot of tea before she had to go to the cornfield to work on a busted combine. She'd never thought of herself as a mechanic, had never planned for it as her profession, so every day was a new exercise in guesswork. She'd chosen this job because it was one of the few positions that didn't require her to talk to anyone. Besides, no one else wanted to do it. She had cuts and scrapes all over her hands from using unfamiliar tools, and she found the work so challenging that she had little time to think about anything else, and even less time to remember.

Still, whenever she closed her eyes, burnout images would appear on the dark screens of her eyelids: the congregation of the New Horizon all dressed in black, swaying to gentle guitar music; the glowing face of Anne Mather speaking to her flock; the lab where they'd operated on Waverly, taken the most essential part of her to create their next generation of apostles; the horrible red gash in her leg where Anne Mather's cronies shot her; having to abandon her mother and the other parents trapped in a cage, where Mather could do anything to them she wished; the red burst of blood when she shot the man who'd stood between her and escape.

When she'd become a killer.

"I don't think about that anymore," she said into the empty room, and covered her eyes with the flat of her hand. No one else on this ship knew what she'd done. She hadn't told anyone about the most singular event of her young life, the moment in time when she stopped being Waverly Marshall and instead became a killer. She was a stranger in her own home.

When the disturbance came, it was so distant at first she might have missed it—a slight shaking of the picture frames on the wall, the barely audible groan deep in the metal of the ship.

She sat up. Something wasn't right.

Then, so deep she felt it in her chest—an explosion.

Her teacup jumped in its saucer, spilling black tea over the rough wooden table.

She bolted out of her chair and ran into the corridor, where dozens of panicked kids were emerging from their quarters, crying and clutching dolls to their chests. Melissa Dickinson was standing at the end of the hallway, surrounded by little boys and girls. She was a petite girl, barely taller than the children she cared for so tenderly.

"What's going on?" Waverly had to shout over the din.

"I don't know," Melissa said. Usually placid, her hazel eyes darted around anxiously. "Boys, girls, stay close!" she called down the hallway. Like magic, the children gathered together, all eyes on her.

The ship's intercom crackled, and Kieran's voice came over the speakers, calling the entire crew to the central bunker.

Every conversation halted; silence loomed over the children as they stared in alarm at Melissa.

"To the elevators, everyone!" she called, and herded them toward the central elevator bank. Melissa was only twelve years old, but she'd taken charge of the orphaned children who were too young to help with the running of the ship. Every day she dutifully reported to the nursery, where she and various helpers played games and planned lessons to keep the kids occupied. At night, Melissa's story hours had become quite famous on the ship, and even some of the older kids came to the library, where she read to everyone from books like *The Wind in the Willows* or *James and the Giant Peach*. Then she tucked each and every child into bed in a group of apartments at the end of the hallway, leaving all doors open in the night so that she was only a whisper away. It was no wonder all the little children loved her. Even Waverly found Melissa's presence comforting.

"Are they coming back?" asked Silas Berg, a boy of six with a knack for voicing everyone's fears in the most straightforward way.

"No, Silas," Melissa told him firmly. "The New Horizon is millions of miles away. And we're not in the nebula anymore, so they can't sneak up on us ever again."

"I'm scared," whispered Paulo Behm as he wove his small brown fingers into the sash of Melissa's bathrobe.

"I am, too," Melissa said, and she stroked his cheek with the backs of her fingers. "But we're all going to stay together, right, Waverly?"

Waverly nodded and tried to smile reassuringly at the children.

"Don't ask her," piped up squeaky little Marina Coelho. "She's the one who left our parents behind."

"If you could have done better, why didn't you?" Melissa said. The words were firm, but her tone was gentle. "Why was it Waverly's job?"

"She's fifteen!" little Marina squeaked, as if that explained everything. "She's the oldest girl, so it was her job."

"She had no choice but to leave when she did," Melissa said angrily, and shot an apologetic glance at Waverly. "She and Sarah rescued us all. I think Waverly is a hero."

"I don't," Silas spat with little-boy contempt. "No one thinks that except you."

Melissa shook her head in exasperation as the elevator opened for them, and everyone stepped on in a scraggly herd.

Waverly turned her back on them to face the elevator doors, but she sensed their accusing stares on the back of her neck. She felt a small body pressing against her leg and glanced down to find Serafina Mbewe looking up at her, her hair two puffy pigtails hovering like clouds over her dainty face. Waverly used to babysit Serafina, who was four years old and deaf. Waverly tried to smile, but turned away too soon and Serafina shrank away. *I should be there for her,* Waverly thought. *But it hurts too much.*

The elevator opened to a chaotic central bunker, an immense room with rows of bunks along the walls and emergency lights hanging from the ceilings. At the end of the room was a large galley where communal meals could be prepared. Kids huddled in groups along the walls, sitting rigid on cots, talking in hushed voices. Waverly tried to ignore the angry stares from a group of girls led by Marjorie Wilkins, a preteen girl with knobby knees, who had an obvious crush on Kieran. Marjorie was a vocal supporter of Kieran, and she would goad anyone who didn't attend his services.

"What did your friends do this time?" Marjorie spat at Waverly as she walked past.

Waverly knew she should ignore her, but she couldn't let this go by without answering. "I don't know who you mean."

"I mean the people you left our parents with," Marjorie said. "They must be your friends, otherwise why would you have left our families there?"

"Would you rather grow up on the New Horizon? Maybe I should have left you there, too," Waverly said, and tried to face her down with a cool stare, but the girl wasn't in the least intimidated.

"Everyone thinks you're a coward," said Millicent, Marjorie's little sister. Both girls had lost their father in the shuttle-bay massacre, but they were holding out hope that their mother was still alive on the treacherous sister ship, the New Horizon. These girls were the most vocal critics of Waverly's failed rescue attempt. Waverly was racked with guilt every time she saw their mean-eyed glares. Because she *should* have tried harder. It didn't matter that Mather's thugs were shooting at her. It didn't matter that they'd winged her shoulder. She should have stayed just a little longer and made that lock give way. The parents would have spilled out of that cargo container and overwhelmed Anne Mather and her thugs. They could have piloted the shuttle back home, and everything would be okay. If only Waverly had stayed another few seconds, or a fraction of a second, instead of turning coward and running. And she'd never have gotten away at all if the crew of the New Horizon hadn't turned against Anne Mather at the last moment and helped the girls escape.

Waverly tried to tell herself that if she hadn't run and at least rescued the girls, Marjorie and her sister and all the little ones might have ended up as reproductive slaves on that ship. They'd have their eggs stolen and put into surrogate mothers, and they'd have to watch their babies be raised by strangers. That's what they'd done to Waverly, Sarah, and all the older girls. But it seemed useless to try to tell Marjorie that. She didn't want to listen.

The only thing that could help now would be for the parents to get away themselves. For days, then weeks after the girls' escape, everyone on the Empyrean had waited, hopeful that the civil unrest the girls had left behind on the New Horizon would lead to the release of their parents. As their hope dwindled, Waverly found more and more kids glaring at her as she went about her duties. Sometimes she didn't even want to leave her quarters.

"I tried my hardest," Waverly said to Marjorie, but she

heard the weakness in her voice.

Marjorie curled her upper lip in disgust. "That wasn't good enough, was it?" she said with a bitter scowl.

"No," Waverly said, meeting every accusing eye in turn. "It wasn't."

They had nothing to say to that, but she could feel them scowling at her as she walked away.

This is why I hide under tractors and combines, Waverly thought bitterly to herself. *No one can see me. No one can say anything to me. And I can just be alone.*

Only the teenage girls who'd had their eggs stolen like Waverly understood why she had to run. Alia Khadivi, Debora Mombasa, and Sarah Hodges were all sitting on a bunk at the far end of the room, and Waverly wove through the crowd to get to them.

"Did that bitch Marjorie say something to you?" Sarah asked, sending a hard glance in the girl's direction. Sarah was compact and intense, and every emotion she had skitted across her freckled face with unmistakable clarity.

"Don't worry about it," Waverly said. "Do you know what's going on?"

Sarah shook her head. "Everyone thinks we're being attacked again."

"The New Horizon is nine million miles ahead of us," Waverly said.

"I know," Alia said through pursed, deep pink lips. Her long, thick hair draped over her shoulder in an ebony cascade. "Maybe Seth got out."

"No," Waverly said instantly. "Seth wouldn't do anything to hurt the ship."

"You better hope the problem *is* Seth," Debora said

with a grim laugh. She ran her fingers nervously through the tight curls in her black hair. "Because if it isn't him, it's the New Horizon."

Waverly sat down on the end of the cot next to Sarah. She wanted to reach out and take her friend's hand, but she didn't want to act like a scared little girl.

"I wish Kieran hadn't hidden all the guns," Alia said. A practical girl, Alia had taken on the task of trying to harvest as much produce as possible from the family gardens, which had become sorely neglected in the last few months. She and her volunteers brought endless baskets of fresh fruit and vegetables to the living quarters, and often they would work together in the ship's galley to make enormous pots of vegetable stews for the younger children to eat. Alia rarely betrayed emotion, but now she jiggled her foot inside her red silk slipper, making the cot the girls sat on tremble.

"They'll have to follow me out an air lock if they want to take me back there," Waverly said. She tucked icy hands under her thighs.

"Don't talk like that," Sarah said automatically.

"Why not?" Waverly said.

She felt Debora studying her for long moments with her luminous eyes before finally saying, "You got us off that ship. No one could have done better. You know that, don't you?"

"I don't want to talk about it."

"Don't pay attention to Marjorie and those idiots," Sarah said.

"I don't," Waverly said coolly, but she knew Sarah didn't believe her.

In the center of the room, a girl named Megan Fuller

held up a hand, calling everyone to attention. Megan wasn't classically pretty, with her over-plump cheeks and scraggly brown hair, but her smile lit up her face beautifully. "Let's all gather around, everyone!"

"Oh God," Waverly said. "Will they ever give it a rest?"

"It makes people feel better," Alia said with unexpected equanimity. "You have to admit that."

A surprisingly large number of kids gathered around Megan. People bowed their heads as she prayed in a singsong: "Dear God, guide our leader, Kieran Alden. Whatever happens tonight, please protect us from our enemies until the day you reunite us with our families, either in this life or the next . . ."

"It's a nice thought, seeing our parents again," Debora said distantly. Shortly after arriving back on the Empyrean, Debora had learned that her parents died in the shuttle-bay massacre. She was brave about it, but she hardly mentioned them, and she seemed to prefer the company of the small herd of sheep and goats she took from field to field throughout the ship, watching them graze with empty eyes. "I feel my mom talking to me at strange times."

"I used to talk to my dad after he died, when I was little," Waverly said, remembering those sad, lonesome nights. "Just as I fell asleep."

"Maybe Megan isn't so wrong to pray, then," Alia said.

Waverly looked at Megan, who held her hands over her head as she prayed aloud. She knew the girl was a great supporter of Kieran; whenever he entered a room she stared at him with a heaven-struck look on her face. It made Waverly sick. "She sounds like Anne Mather."

"You know," Debora said, an edge of impatience in

her voice, "not every religious person is like that woman, Waverly."

"I didn't say that."

"You don't have to," Debora said, her eyes on Waverly's knees. "Anyone can tell it's your attitude."

"I thought you didn't like Kieran's little cult, either," Waverly said, knowing she was getting defensive but unable to help herself. "After Anne Mather, how could you?"

Debora shrugged, sullen. A hunk of her springy hair moved into her eyes, and she impatiently jammed it behind her ear. "Megan isn't Anne Mather. Neither is Kieran. You of all people should know that."

Sarah and Alia looked at Waverly with sympathy but dropped their eyes to the floor rather than join the discussion.

Waverly opened her mouth to protest, and shut it again. *I didn't overreact,* she told herself. *Kieran is dangerous.*

But Anne Mather was worse. And maybe she *had* found a way to sneak up on the Empyrean. Maybe she was boarding the ship with her thugs right now.

Waverly doubled over, leaned her forehead against her knees. *I won't go back there,* she promised herself. *I'll die first.*

The Burdens of Leadership

From his simple podium, under soft yellow stage lights, Kieran looked out over his congregation. The numbers had dwindled over the weeks, as the crew became increasingly demoralized, choosing to sleep in on Sundays rather than bother to attend. Now Kieran was left with about half the crew—the true believers—and they stared at him with light in their eyes.

"I know we had high hopes that increasing our acceleration over the last month would bring us closer to the New Horizon and our parents . . ." He swallowed. Suddenly these words sounded like defeat—the opposite of what he'd meant to write last night. Kieran smiled, and some of his congregation leaned forward in their seats. He caught the eye of a little black-haired boy in the front row chewing on his bottom lip.

"We want the battle to begin," Kieran said with a confidential tone. "But I must ask you to be patient. We'll catch up to them when God wants us to, and not before."

That was all he'd written; they were the last words on the portable reader in front of him. But the energy in the room still hung suspended, waiting to be released.

"We *will* catch them!" he said, and raised his arms over his head, fists clenched. "The deaths of our loved ones *will* be avenged. We'll triumph over our enemies and land on New Earth with the memory of victory in our hearts!"

His congregation jumped to their feet, chanting, "Kyrie Eleison! Kyrie Eleison! Kyrie Eleison!" It was an ancient benediction, in Greek, that meant "Lord, have mercy." It also happened to be the origin of Kieran's name, and he knew it was no accident that his congregation yelled this at the end of all his sermons. He smiled humbly and held up his hands to speak over the din: "Thank you! Thanks! Everyone!" But they just kept on cheering.

Was it wrong for him to love this?

Not so long ago, he sat on this very stage on trial for his life. Seth Ardvale and his thugs had orchestrated one sham witness after another, and for a while, it looked like the crew of boys wanted to throw Kieran out an air lock. He still had nightmares about it and awoke swimming through damp sheets, screams caught in his throat.

Now they loved him. Now they cheered, and he was safe.

But he never forgot that the tide could turn against him once more.

Suddenly a deep, roaring boom seemed to hit Kieran in the middle of the chest. He staggered. The floor under him rumbled, and the wooden podium seemed to dance away from him. Several crew members cried out, holding on to their chairs. The curtains on the stage of the auditorium swayed.

"We're under attack!" someone screamed.

"Get to the central bunker!" Kieran cried. He catapulted himself off the stage and took off running down the aisle, pumping his legs as hard as he could, though the floor swayed in front of him. He moved so fast he was stepping onto the elevator for Central Command before the first of them even reached the hallway.

He hit the com button in the elevator. "Sarek? Arthur? What's happening?"

"I don't know!" came Arthur's panicked voice over the speaker. "I don't know if there was an explosion, or—"

"Where's the New Horizon?"

"They're still way ahead of us! I don't think it's them."

The elevator was moving with agonizing slowness, and Kieran punched the metal wall next to the intercom speaker. "Could they have sent an attack force in a shuttle?"

"Without our sensors picking them up?" Sarek put in. "Impossible."

Sarek and Arthur were good officers, but they were only thirteen. What if they missed something? What if the more-experienced New Horizon crew had fooled them somehow? If so, where would they attack first?

"Check the engines!" Kieran shouted into the intercom as the elevator doors opened. He sprinted down the hallway, his heart pounding painfully, his breath out of control.

An even larger tremor moved through the ship, and he fell against the wall. "Oh God," he said under his breath as he righted himself and lurched to Central Command.

"Seat belts!" he yelled into the room.

Arthur and Sarek buckled themselves in. As he strapped himself to the Captain's chair, Kieran made a ship-wide announcement, ordering the entire crew to the Central Bunker, then swiveled to face Arthur, who looked shaken. "What have you found out?"

"The engines are operating normally," Arthur said. His glasses slid down his sweaty nose, and he jammed them up again. "The computer is acting like there's no change at all."

"Coolant? Reactors?" Kieran barked.

"All fine. I can't find anything wrong!"

"No problems in the hull, either?"

"No!"

"The nav system isn't showing a problem, either," Sarek said, shaking his head.

"What is it? What's happening?" Kieran asked. His entire body shook, and he grabbed the plastic arms of his chair with clawlike hands as he stared out the blast shield at the sky.

And he noticed, along the edge of the large square portholes, the stars were winking out, one by one. He collected himself with a deep breath.

"Those weren't explosions. They were thruster

bursts." Sarek and Arthur looked at him blankly until he added, "We're turning. Check the nav system again, Sarek," he said grimly. "Manually this time."

Sarek shook his head, impressed. "You're right. Those were thruster bursts."

"Can you correct our course?"

"I'll just reengage the nav system," Arthur said. "The course will correct itself automatically."

"At least we're not dealing with a decompression," Kieran said with intense relief. He pressed the com button on the arm of his Captain's chair. At first he'd been nervous to make ship-wide announcements, but now he liked the knowledge that his voice was filling the entire vessel—his whole world. "Attention, crew. We are not under attack. I repeat, we're not under attack. Those disturbances were unexpected thruster bursts, nothing more. We are safe, and the New Horizon is as far away as ever. You can go back to what you were doing."

Kieran turned to Arthur. "How did this happen? The nav system should have prevented this."

Arthur looked at the computer screen in front of him, flipping through the ship's intricate control programs with mechanized efficiency. Something caught Arthur's eye, and he squinted, reading the computer language. "Someone tampered with the programming." He looked at Kieran, wide-eyed. "Sabotage."

For a moment, no one in Central Command spoke or moved.

"Call the brig," Kieran said quietly.

Sarek whirled back to his com display, a hand on his earpiece. "Harvey? Are you down there? Can you give me a status on our prisoners?"

No answer came.

"Check the vid display," Kieran barked. He *knew* it! He knew in his bones Seth had done this somehow.

Sarek flipped through the various views of the brig, both inside and out. "I can't see anyone down there," he said, defeated.

"Send down a team of Command officers," Kieran said, but he knew what they'd find. Harvey Markem injured or dead, and Seth Ardvale gone. Kieran's pulse quickened, and a cold sweat chilled his skin. "How did Seth do this?"

"I don't know," Arthur said as he fast-forwarded through video images of the brig. "The last thing the video shows is Harvey sitting in his chair where he's supposed to be. Then the screen flickers, and suddenly you just see an empty chair. No recording of an attack or Seth leaving." He turned around to face Kieran, his features narrowed with concern. "So the video surveillance system was disabled *before* Seth escaped."

"Someone on the outside helped him escape," Sarek said ominously.

A frigid dread moved through Kieran's limbs. By himself, Seth Ardvale was dangerous enough, but with a crew of followers? He'd nearly killed Kieran once. He could do it again.

"Arthur, can you call up the visitor logs to the brig?" Kieran said on impulse. "See if anyone has been down there lately?"

Arthur tapped at the keyboard in front of him, scrolled through a list of names reflected in green lines of text in his glasses. His boyish face was thinning out, taking on the harder angles of a young man. He looked serious, and burdened. "They're all just people authorized to bring meals, and . . ." Arthur looked at Kieran in surprise. "Waverly Marshall visited Seth about a month ago, before we put him in isolation."

Kieran felt as though he'd been turned to stone. Arthur and Sarek looked away, embarrassed.

"Get her. Bring her here," Kieran said, but before Arthur could react, Kieran got out of his chair and marched out of Central Command, calling over his shoulder, "Never mind."

People were still hovering in the central bunker in groups, talking in whispers about the thruster bursts. The little ones were pale and quiet; the older kids were red faced and angry. Kieran scanned the crowd until he found Waverly in the corner of the room talking to a group of girls huddled around her, among them Sarah Hodges.

Kieran marched up to Waverly. "We need to talk," he said, his voice tightly controlled.

The girls all looked at him, alarmed.

"What's wrong with the ship?" Waverly said. She sat on a cot, her body hidden by a shapeless white tunic, hair pulled into a hasty ponytail. She looked like she'd just rolled out of bed. Naturally she'd chosen to sleep in rather than get up early to attend services. It didn't surprise him, considering they weren't even talking to each other, but it still hurt. And plenty of kids were following her lead.

"Come with me," Kieran said to her, and took hold of her elbow.

She jerked from his grasp but stood. "I'll see you

later," she said to Sarah, who stared at Kieran with distrustful eyes.

Kieran led Waverly through the crowded bunker and across the hallway to his office. The large oak desk, the leather chairs, the multicolored Persian rug, the small oval portholes looking to the stars—all was the same as it had ever been, but Kieran had stopped thinking of it as Captain Jones's office a long time ago. It no longer even smelled like the old man's pipe tobacco; it had taken on the aromas of Kieran's spiced teas.

"What's *wrong*, Kieran?" Waverly demanded as he closed the door behind them.

"Why did you visit Seth Ardvale in the brig?" Kieran said, his voice a slow simmer. He nodded toward the chair facing his desk and took the Captain's seat.

She watched him warily, eyes wide.

"Waverly, answer me."

"I wanted to get his side of the story," she said, her mouth set in a stubborn line.

"He tried to kill me. Doesn't that matter to you?"

"Of course it does. But we've known Seth since we were babies, and I just can't imagine—"

"Where have you been over the last two hours?"

This got her attention. "Kieran, you don't think I had anything to do with—"

"Answer my question." His harsh tone clearly humiliated her, and for a moment he wasn't sure she was going to answer him.

"I was in my quarters." She gave him a wounded look. "How can you—"

"No, Waverly, how can *you*?"

"There's suspicion on me because I went to see Seth?

Last I knew, he's entitled to visitors and medical care. And a trial, incidentally."

"Put yourself in my shoes. My fiancée, or ex-fiancée"— he stumbled here but regained his composure—"goes to visit my worst enemy. How would you feel?"

Waverly softened at this and reached for his hand. He pulled away.

"Kieran, I'm *confused*. You have to give me a chance to understand everything that happened while I was away."

"If you ever loved me you should believe me without question."

"That's not who I am. I'll never be that kind of woman."

"Then you can never be my wife."

The last time they'd spoken, they'd said everything to each other except these final words. Now, with the truth hanging between them, Kieran realized that he'd known already for a long time: He and Waverly were over for good.

For long moments she stared at him, expressionless, then she turned on her heel and started toward the door.

"Waverly, wait," Kieran said. "I'm sorry."

She looked at him skeptically.

"Please, come sit down. Okay?"

Slowly she walked back to the chair across from Kieran's desk and sank into it, her feet planted on the ground as though she planned to bolt back out of it again. She was still lithe and graceful, he couldn't help noticing, with those long, sturdy legs and her delicate wrists that always seemed so heartbreakingly small and beautiful to him.

"You're right. It's not fair to accuse you." Kieran threw up his hands. "It's just . . . so much has changed, and we're all catching up to it. I don't know what to believe anymore."

She bent her gaze toward the floor. "I know."

"But whatever happens," he said, "we've got to keep up a united front."

Her eyes snapped to his. "What do you mean?"

"You don't know how fragile things are. If I lose my influence over the crew, if they start playing hooky and doing all the other things a bunch of scared kids are liable to do, you know what will happen, don't you?"

"The ship will die," she said quietly. For the first time, he thought he saw a hint of remorse in the curves of her face. He made note of it.

"You're the de facto leader of the girls."

"Not anymore," she said ruefully.

He ignored this. "I need your support if we're going to keep this crew eating and breathing clean air." He stood, walked around the desk, and put a hand on hers. "Will you promise to support the policies on this ship?"

"What I say doesn't matter to anybody as much as getting our parents back." She tilted her head in a tentative way, watching his reaction. "Some people think you're hanging back from the New Horizon because you're scared."

He pulled his hand away from hers. "It's unsafe to go faster."

"Not everyone believes that." She watched him, seeming unsure whether to continue. "Some think you don't want the adults back, because then you'd have to give up your command."

He stared at her, shocked. No wonder attendance at services had dwindled. Half the crew didn't trust him.

"What do *you* say?" he asked, wishing it didn't still matter to him, wishing he could keep himself from glancing at her perfectly formed rosebud lips.

"I don't know, Kieran," she said sadly. "Since you, Sarek, and Arthur hardly tell people what's going on, how am I to judge the situation for myself?"

He shook his head. "Are you saying this to hurt me?"

"I'm saying this to *help* you." She threw up her hands in frustration. "People are scared and they miss their parents."

"And I bet you haven't even tried to help."

"What am I supposed to do?"

"Back me up instead of undermining me."

"I haven't said a word against you."

"You don't have to! The other kids can tell you don't agree with the way I'm doing things. They're following your lead! That's how you undermine me."

She stared at him for a long time, as though trying to read his mind, then seemed to decide. She stood and extended a hand. "I won't lie for you, Kieran, but I won't betray you, either, if that's what you're worried about."

Their palms met. Already her hand felt unfamiliar, larger than he remembered, the skin rough from her work as a mechanic. And her eyes—she'd darkened from the inside out. She'd changed.

He studied her, unsure of what she was saying. "Okay . . ."

She smiled sadly at him, then turned and left the room, closing the door quietly behind her.

Kieran sat in the Captain's chair feeling as though a

fundamental part of him had been scooped out. They'd always known each other. They'd always been friends, until they'd become more. He couldn't have imagined this distance. He sat thinking for a long time, measuring his options, until finally he pushed his com button and summoned Arthur into his office.

"Kieran, people are talking," Arthur said breathlessly. "Did you reprimand Waverly in front of—"

"Who do you trust, Arthur?"

"What?" The boy looked at him, bewildered.

"Who among the boys would you trust to do something and be discreet about it?"

Arthur stared at Kieran, fingering the seam on his woven trousers, his toes twitching in their sandals. "Philip Grieg."

"Who?"

"He's nine years old, I think. He never talks to anyone."

"Oh yeah." Philip was that quiet boy with black hair that hung in his face, and the kind of steady gaze that was unnerving if you tried to smile at him. But he came to the ship's services without fail and always sat in the front row, raptly fixed on Kieran's every word. He'd be loyal.

"Bring him here."

"Now?"

"Yes, right away."

Arthur turned to go, but he looked at Kieran over his shoulder as he closed the door. Soon two short knocks sounded, and Kieran stood. "Come in."

Philip glided into the room in the feline, small-boned way he had, and Kieran realized that he was the perfect choice for this assignment.

"Hi," Philip said. His eyebrows twitched with excitement. Kieran had never singled him out before, and clearly this meant a great deal to him.

"Philip," Kieran said gently, for he felt that a careless word from him could hurt this boy. "Can you do something and never tell anyone about it?"

Philip hugged a cloth teddy bear to his chest. God, he was young. He stared at Kieran as though he'd already forgotten the question.

"Philip, I asked you a—"

"Yes. I can be quiet," the boy mumbled through glistening lips.

"If I tell you to follow someone, can you do it without being seen?"

The boy shrugged. "What do you want me to do?"

Kieran leaned back in his chair and stared at Philip, who lowered his gaze to the floor, though he seemed to be listening with all his heart.

"Philip. I think Waverly Marshall might be doing something she shouldn't be doing, and I need you to follow her, watch what she does without being seen, and tell me everything. Can you do that?"

"What if she sees me?"

"You have to make sure she doesn't. Can you do that?"

"Probably, but . . ." The boy held his teddy to his nose and inhaled the scent. Kieran wondered if it had been sewn by the boy's mother, who'd been killed in the shuttle-bay massacre. "*Why* do you want me to do it?"

"I think it's better if only I know why. Is that okay?"

"I guess."

"Do you know where Waverly's quarters are?"

"Yes."

"I want you to find an empty apartment nearby and hide there early in the morning so that you can follow her all day long. Can you do that?"

"That sounds creepy," the boy said. One fine black eyebrow lowered, and he looked at Kieran skeptically.

"It's not creepy if you're doing it for a good reason. And I have a very good reason to keep a watch on Waverly."

"Okay," the boy said.

"So we're going to keep this between us, aren't we?"

"Yes."

"And you're not going to tell any of your friends?"

"I don't really have friends," Philip said softly.

"Good," Kieran said, then he heard himself. He got up, walked around the desk, and lowered himself to one knee. "I'm your friend, Philip."

The boy's eyes widened.

"I'm your friend, and what you're doing is very important. You might even save the ship. You'll be a hero."

This brought a smile to the boy's wan face. "Okay."

Kieran went to his desk drawer, found a small walkie-talkie, and handed it over. "You can call me on this and tell me what Waverly does. I'll want to know who she talks to and where she goes. Take notes if you have to."

"Okay." Philip took the handset but paused, confused. "But isn't Waverly your girlfriend?"

Kieran opened his mouth, closed it. He had to take a few even breaths before he could summon an answer. "No. Not anymore."

"Oh. Okay," Philip said. When he turned and walked out, Kieran saw how bony his shoulders were, how skinny his little legs. He seemed fragile.

Only six months ago, asking a child to perform a duplicitous task like this would have been unthinkable, and Kieran shook his head at how much had changed since the attack by the New Horizon that had killed almost all the adults, leaving the kids to run the ship themselves. If he thought about it too long, his heart raced and his breath came too fast.

He made a fist. He was doing what he *had* to do. If Seth was tampering with the thruster controls and endangering the crew, if Waverly was helping him, he absolutely had to know. He had two hundred and fifty lives in his hands, and it was his job to protect them, no matter how uncomfortable it made him feel.

He was at war. He must never forget that.

The Trail

Seth woke with a fuzzy mouth and a sore spot in the middle of his back. After he heard Kieran's announcement about the thruster misfires, he'd been able to relax, but he'd slept no more than an hour, maybe two. He shouldn't have slept at all. It was past time to leave. He stretched the muscles in his legs and back, horribly sore from carrying Harvey up all those stairs. Slowly, Seth crept along a mossy path until he reached some peanut plants and dug up as many peanuts as he could carry, then tucked himself into a nest of ferns to eat, thinking as he cracked dusty shells in his fist.

What he needed was a way around the surveillance system.

He considered what he knew about it. The cameras

were on twenty-four hours a day, but the central computer only recorded when the motion detector on each camera was activated. This was the obvious solution to reducing the sheer amount of video hours recorded every day all over the vessel. Could there be a way to alter the software controlling the motion detectors?

An idea struck him, and he knew what he had to do.

He sprinted for the door that led to the central corridor and listened for voices, then slipped out and ran as fast as he could to the stairwell on the starboard side of the ship. This stairwell was rarely used, because it ran along the outer hull, and even with the ship's insulation, it was deadly cold. Seth gritted his teeth as he bounded up several flights to the section of the ship that contained the living quarters. Shivering uncontrollably though he was sweating, he paused outside the door to the habitation level to listen for people.

All was quiet. The ship was so underpopulated since the attack, it shouldn't be a surprise the corridor was empty now, but it felt strange to Seth—haunted. When he finally slipped through the door and into the warm air, his frozen skin tingled. He ducked into the maintenance closet around the corner from his old quarters, well out of sight of his front door, for surely it was being watched. The closet smelled of ammonia and the sludgy grease on the various power tools. He prayed under his breath as his fingers ran over the paneling at the back wall, and sighed with relief when he found his old secret hatch.

Years ago, his father had shut him into a closet for mouthing off. After several desperate, hungry hours, Seth had finally pulled away the paneling from the rear wall and found a passageway that ran behind all the apartments. The passage was meant for the plumbing, wiring, and ventilation that kept the apartments going, but it was large enough for a thin boy to sidle along. Seth had never told anyone about it because he was worried his father would find out and punish him. He was thankful for his silence now. No one would suspect him of traveling this way. Best of all, he knew that there was no surveillance camera pointed at the maintenance closet, so he could enter it without fear of detection.

He slipped into the small passageway, which was barely wide enough to admit him, now that he was fully grown. If he sucked in his belly, he found that he could squeeze himself between the dozens of wires that hung in his way, and he could wriggle his legs over the plumbing pipes and ventilation ducts. Each time he stepped over a large pipe meant for a toilet, Seth knew that he'd passed one apartment. When he'd passed twelve of the large pipes, he knew he was home.

He jiggled the paneling loose with his fingernails. It came away with a jerk, and Seth stumbled into his father's closet. Immediately he was surrounded by the scent of the old man, a sour odor that had always reminded Seth of rancid lemons. He fought his way through the clothes and opened the closet door, almost tripping over the pile of dank laundry in the middle of his father's bedroom floor. He caught himself on the desk and paused to listen for signs of life. But no, the apartment was empty, and eerie.

A hundred dreary memories threatened to take hold, but he forced himself into motion. He gathered up his father's portable com system. Folding the screen against the keyboard, he tucked it under his arm and turned to re-enter the passageway.

Negotiating the passageway was twice as hard now that he carried the computer, but Seth took his time, pausing to rest his sore muscles every few minutes. The grimy, smelly maintenance closet was a relief after the cramped passage, and he stopped to stretch his muscles, trying to work out the kinks between his ribs.

He was ready to open the door and leave when he heard voices outside in the corridor and paused to listen, his heart in his mouth. Had they traced him here? Maybe Kieran had found him on the video! But no. It sounded like two little girls on their way to the central elevator bank.

"Did you see the way Kieran took Waverly to his office last night?"

"Maybe it's true. Maybe they really did break up."

"I don't believe it. Not with the way she still looks at him."

Seth's stomach knotted up, and for the thousandth time he wished he didn't love her. She'd never be with a brute like him, and he should let her go. He'd been telling himself this for years and he knew it was true, but he still couldn't make himself give her up. Maybe he was stubborn; probably he was just stupid.

Besides, there's no such thing as love, he told himself, remembering the wolfish way his father used to look at his mother. *When a husband can kill his own wife, you know it's just a fairy tale.*

This brought Seth back to the safe place he knew, the one where he didn't need anyone, where no one would ever depend on him, where he'd never get close enough for anyone to see the darkness inside him. For people like Seth, there was no such thing as uncomplicated love or friendship, and he was better off alone. So was everyone else, especially her.

Seth heard the elevator doors slide open for the girls, and their voices faded away. He slipped out of the closet, sprinted to the outer stairwell, and ran up the stairs two at a time to the shuttle bay. He peeked in through the window to see only the lifeless forms of the shuttle craft and OneMen that lined the walls, then slipped through the doorway and into the bay.

It felt crowded with spirits. Both shuttle bays had been the scenes of such death and loss, he was pretty sure the crew avoided them. He didn't like being here himself.

Seth ducked behind the shuttle craft and jogged to the com station near the air-lock control panel. He fired up his father's portable computer and hooked into the ship's computing system via the universal port, hoping that his father's passwords had not been changed. As head pilot of the Empyrean, Mason Ardvale's level of computer access would have been second only to Captain Jones's. Mason probably wasn't officially *supposed* to allow his passwords to be automatic, even on his own computer, but before the attack, everyone had been lax about security.

"Come on, come on," Seth whispered.

The computer flashed an access screen to the ship's central computers. Seth held his breath and waited for his computer to automatically log on to the ship's system. If it did, he was home free. If it didn't, he'd have to drop the computer and run like hell.

The screen winked once and flashed the words "Access granted."

"Thanks for being such a slacker, Dad," Seth muttered under his breath. As quickly as he could, he located the software that controlled the surveillance system and scanned the lines of code that governed the motion detectors. It took him almost fifteen agonizing minutes to find the code that he needed, and when he found it, his jaw dropped.

Max must have already altered the code. He'd made precisely the change that Seth had intended, disabling the motion detection software, but leaving the cameras themselves intact. Impressive, given that Max was an idiot. Then again, if he could tamper with the thrusters, he ought to be smart enough to do this.

Ought to be. But *was* he? It didn't sit well.

Seth shook his head. It must have been Max who had done all this. No one else had a motive.

Seth folded up his father's computer, tucked it under his arm, and jogged out of the shuttle bay. He disappeared into the outer stairwell again, but he crouched on the landing. At least now he didn't have to worry about keeping one step ahead of the video surveillance.

This might give him the time he needed to find Max. Where would he go to hide?

If Max was smart he'd go someplace out of the way and lie low, but Max was stupid and was ruled by petty appetites. During Seth's brief stint as ship's Captain, more than once he'd reprimanded Max for being drunk while on duty. Max had even broken a little boy's arm pulling him away from the blades of a combine. If Max had been sober, he probably could have saved the kid without hurting him. Seth had let it go at the time but lived to regret it later.

The first thing Max would probably want after getting out of the brig was alcohol. The distillery wouldn't be such a bad hiding place, actually, because distilling grain alcohol would be the last thing Kieran Alden would allow the crew to do. Probably no one went there.

Seth took the stairs two at a time until he reached level 7, then sneaked into the corridor just outside the granary bays. There was no one in the corridor, but he could hear the voices of people working to harvest the wheat. A film of dust from the harvest had drifted through the doors to coat the floor of the corridor. Seth slid along the wall and ducked into the distillery, painfully aware that he was leaving footprints. He must be leaving traces of himself everywhere.

The sharp smell of alcohol stung his nostrils and made his eyes water. The lights were dim in this small room, which resembled a factory. Masses of tentacle tubing snaked along the walls and over the ceiling. A complicated system of beakers and carafes covered the metal countertops. Seth paused, listening, and he saw droplets still clinging to the spigot of the gin still. Gin was Max's poison of choice. He was definitely here.

"Max," Seth whispered, "it's me, Seth."

Nothing stirred, but Seth could sense him here, listening.

"We're in the same boat, Max. It's not like I'm going to turn you in," Seth whispered. "And I don't want to hide out together, either. I just want to talk."

Still no answer.

Seth crept down the narrow passage between the countertops, eyes on the floor. When he reached the end of the room, he found a circle of what looked like crumbs.

"Max, come on. We can help each other."

"I don't need you," a gruff voice muttered.

Seth turned and saw Max crouched inside a stainless steel cabinet, bleary eyed, head wobbling on top of his meaty neck. Max was only fourteen but he was as physically powerful as a grown man.

"Jesus, you're drunk." This was going to be easy.

"Just celebrating."

"What if you need to run?"

"They won't find me."

"If they do, there's nowhere to go. You'll be trapped."

Max thought about it for a minute, his bloodshot eyes swimming in their sockets, then finally eased himself out of his cabinet. When Max stood, Seth was assaulted by a strong odor of gin and stale perspiration. "Where sh-should we go?" he slurred.

"Somewhere we can talk," Seth said, and grabbed hold of the idiot's elbow to steady him.

"Wait," Max said, reaching toward the row of bottles that lined the shelves above him.

Seth jerked him away from it and pulled him to the doorway of the distillery. When he was sure the way was clear, he pulled the weaving Max along the corridor to the outer stairwell and dragged him down several flights until they reached the orchards. The trees would be in their winter dormancy by now, so there would be no reason for anyone to come here. Seth pulled Max into the back corner behind a thicket of blueberry bushes. The boys crouched on the cold soil, hands tucked under their arms for warmth, and Seth waited for Max to catch his breath.

Max didn't look good. There were bluish circles under his eyes, and the skin around his mouth seemed especially pale.

"You doing okay?" Seth said, though he felt no sympathy. He deftly turned on his father's computer and enabled the audio recording software. He'd been worried about doing this in front of Max, but the boy was so drunk, he didn't notice.

"Got a cramp in my gut," Max said, and doubled over.

"That was a good idea, those thruster bursts," Seth said casually. "Created a nice diversion for us."

"Yeah," Max said absently.

"How did you do it?"

"Do what?" Max gasped, massaging his middle.

"How did you program the thrusters to misfire like that?"

Max looked at him in surprise. "I thought *you* did that."

"Come on, Max. Level with me. Who am I going to tell?"

"Seriously. I figured you must have done it. I wouldn't know how to do a thing like that."

Seth searched Max's face and saw that he was being truthful. "What about the surveillance software?" Seth asked, though he already knew the answer.

"What about it?" Max said irritably.

Who, then? Seth wondered. "Did you see who let us out?"

Max held his stomach, eyes screwed shut, panting. "No. I woke up when I heard the door to my cell click open, but they were already gone."

"And Harvey?"

"Didn't see any guards," Max said.

"Any ideas about who might have let us out?"

"Waverly was the only one who came to visit you," the boy said through a grimace, hands massaging his middle. "No one came to see me."

"That's true," Seth said haltingly.

Max doubled over, wincing, and Seth waited while he

puffed and moaned. After what seemed a long time, Max leaned back again. "Oh, that was bad."

"So what are you going to do?"

"You think I'm going to tell you anything?"

"Fine." Seth got up to leave, regretting that he'd wasted his time trying to talk to this moron. "Don't follow me."

"Wait," Max said weakly. His hand gripped his stomach again, and he leaned up on one elbow. "You know, I think I'm sick."

"You shouldn't drink."

"I think it's something I ate . . ."

"Rotten food?"

"Bread and miso spread someone left for me. I grabbed it on my way out." He doubled over and vomited up a foul-smelling greenish liquid. His head lolled backward; his lips were turning blue.

"God, Max. You *are* sick."

"No kidding," Max said, then his head swung back on his neck, farther than seemed physically possible, and suddenly he was snoring violently. Seth felt Max's pulse at his wrist; his heart was racing.

Seth had seen food poisoning. He'd had it several times. This was something else, something serious.

"Max!" Seth held the boy's head upright to straighten out his airway. Max opened his eyes. "We can't stay here!" Seth stood and pulled on Max's arms. Nodding, Max tried to get his feet under him, but he stumbled into Seth's legs and back onto the ground, lolling, boneless. He obviously wasn't going anywhere under his own power.

"Damn it," Seth spat. After a moment's consideration, he jogged to the doorway and checked to make sure the corridor was still clear, then jogged back to Max and heaved him up over his sore shoulder. "I can't believe I'm doing this *again*!"

Max was even heavier than Harvey. Seth felt his vertebrae practically scraping together as he lurched onto the main path of the orchard and hurried to the central elevator bank. Already his legs were shaking from the strain. There was no way he could carry Max all the way up to the infirmary.

He put Max down outside the elevator doors and shook him until he opened his eyes. "Max! I'm sending you to the infirmary so they can pump your stomach."

"No! They'll put me back in the brig!"

"Max, listen to me. You've been poisoned."

Max's head hit the wall behind him with a thud, and he started snoring again. Seth shook him. "Max! You have to stay awake for one more minute, okay? When you get to the infirmary tell them you've been poisoned. Can you do that?"

Max waved Seth away and cuddled against the wall.

"Max!" Seth reared back and slapped him across the face.

Max's eyes flew open, and he looked at Seth in surprise.

"Stay awake. For one minute. Okay?"

"Yes! Jesus!" The boy rallied, straightening his back and shaking his head. He was awake again.

When the elevator arrived, Seth dragged the boy into it and pressed the button for the infirmary level before jumping back into the corridor. As the doors closed, he said again, "Remember to tell them, Max!"

Max nodded at Seth as the elevator doors closed between them.

Seth jogged for the outer stairwell, his mind racing. All along he'd thought the thruster misfire had been a diversion Max had set up to hide his escape from the brig. But what if their *escape* was the diversion? What if the misfire, and pushing the Empyrean off course, what if that was the real point, and whoever did it wanted to cast blame on Seth and Max?

Who would *do* this?

Seth disappeared into the freezing air of the outer stairwell.

He never knew that by the time Max Brent's elevator reached the infirmary, the boy had lost consciousness.

That night he was deep in a coma.

By morning, Max was dead.

Galen and Eddie

Waverly dragged herself back to her quarters after a long day taking apart a tractor engine, looking for the reason it wouldn't run, finding nothing, and putting it back together again. She'd gotten nothing accomplished, but it had taken all her mental power, and that's all she wanted.

With nothing else to do and nowhere to be, she went back to her empty apartment. The door closed behind her with a final-sounding *thunk*. She hung her tool belt on the hook by the door. One day the heavy tools would pull that hook right out of the wall. Repairing it would give her something to do at home other than brood . . .

. . . And wonder where Seth Ardvale was. Surely he would contact her eventually? If he did, she should know ahead of time what she would say to him, how she would act. But her mind was a blank. Too much had happened. She didn't know Kieran anymore; she didn't even know herself. Who could say what this new Waverly would do if Seth Ardvale came knocking?

After she got dressed for bed, she made herself a cup of chamomile tea, then went into the living room to drink it. She lovingly touched her mother's abandoned loom, paused for months now on the same aqua-colored stripe of an elaborate wool blanket, half-finished. The wool smelled earthy and clean, and the rough texture was comforting against the tender skin of her wrist.

"You'll finish it," she whispered, and set her tea down on the dining-room table, where she knew it would leave a ring. She didn't care. There ought to be some proof that a human being was living here.

She went into her pitch-dark bedroom and plopped onto her mattress, stared at the black outline of the Raggedy Ann doll that had sat in the rocking chair opposite her bed since she was a baby. The doll used to frighten her when she was a little girl. She never liked toys that were meant to be children; there was something morbid about them. But now the doll was Waverly's favorite thing to look at as she fell asleep, because her mother had made it for her.

Waverly screwed her eyes shut, tried to block out her last conversation with Kieran, the dark way he'd looked at her from over his tented fingers. They'd reached a sort of détente, but she saw the calculating way he watched her leave his office. Some strange alchemy had changed him into someone who placed her on the outside, in the enemy camp, as if he'd never known her at all.

But then, hadn't she come to feel that way about him, too?

It was useless; she'd never sleep like this. She got up and went into the master bedroom, where she turned on the light. Her mother's double bed had remained rumpled and unmade ever since the day of the attack. Looking at the messy room helped Waverly believe that her mother would come back someday to straighten the bedclothes, hang her nightgown on the hook by the door, put her rouge and lip balm in the top drawer of the dresser, dust the framed picture of Waverly that hung on the wall.

She wished she could talk to her mother about Seth. Regina Marshall had always been a warm, accepting person, and she'd never approved of Waverly's skeptical nature. She would likely say that Seth was just an angry boy who lost his mother and had to live with Mason Ardvale, which would be enough to spoil anyone's mood. Seth had learned his lesson, and his being out of the brig wasn't going to put anyone in danger, not even Kieran.

"He's a good soul," Regina had once said about Seth. "He's just misunderstood."

"That's what I think, too," Waverly said into the empty apartment.

The closet door stood open, and Waverly passed a hand through her mother's clothes, stirring up her sandalwood scent. Regina's black sweater hung askew on a hanger, and Waverly put it on, rubbed the cashmere against her arms.

On the top shelf of the closet was the box of family photos that Regina had squirreled away, always intending to make an album but never getting around to it. "I could do that," Waverly mumbled. "I could make the album and surprise Mom when she comes home."

She'd have to sort through all their family photos, put them in order, pore over the memories. She wouldn't have room in her mind to think about Kieran or Seth or any of the terrible things she'd done. Nothing had ever sounded so comforting.

Waverly got the stepladder from the kitchen, pulled the box down, and marched into the living room to sit on the sofa.

There were dozens of photos, ranging over Regina's infancy and childhood, through her teenage years, and then on to the time she dated and married Waverly's father, a handsome man with a wide smile and deep-set brown eyes. Waverly's baby pictures showed a happy little girl with rosy cheeks. Waverly especially loved an image of her parents holding her as a wild-haired toddler. She set it aside; she'd make a frame for it and put it on her bedroom wall.

One picture at the bottom of the box caught Waverly's attention, and she pulled it out. It showed her father as a young man, the gray just beginning at his temples, standing with Captain Jones. The two men looked as though they'd just shared a private joke; the Captain had one beefy hand on Galen Marshall's shoulder, fingers flexed as though he meant to steer him somewhere. Galen was laughing, his chin tucked into his chest, teeth glistening. They stood in a large white room that looked familiar to Waverly, and she realized that it was one of the labs, probably the botany lab where her father had worked. Waverly turned the photo over.

Galen and Eddie, discovery of phyto-lutein, was scrawled on the back of the photo, again in Regina's hand. Waverly had seen this photo before, of course, but she'd never lingered over it, never wondered why it appeared to have been crumpled and flattened out again, why the edges of it were frayed, showing the white paper underneath the glossy image. And she'd never turned it over to read the caption, or if she had, she hadn't really noticed it. Waverly set this photo aside, too, and went back to sorting through the others, arranging them in chronological order.

As she worked, though, her eyes kept trailing back to the image of her father with Captain Jones. Something about it nagged at her. A part of her didn't want to think about it. She wanted to fix up this album, lose herself in a project, feel better. But Waverly had never had much success at switching off her mind, and the wheels turned until she identified what bothered her about it.

Never once had her mother referred to the Captain as Eddie. He'd always been the Captain, or Captain Jones, and the name had always been spoken with a cool reserve. But on the back of the photo Waverly's mother had identified the Captain as Eddie, as though he were a good friend. Even more odd, Regina had always said that she and her husband had been far from the Captain's inner circle, outsiders who were happy to be kept out of decision making. But the photograph had captured a definite familiarity between the Captain and her father. Clearly the men had been friends. The most troubling thing, though, was that Waverly had never known her father had anything to do with the discovery of phyto-lutein, the drug used to stimulate the women's ovaries and create the next generation of the Empyrean crew. Her father had been a botanist, not a fertility specialist.

But of course, phyto-lutein must have come from plants. Where else did any medications come from? And if her father had been part of the team that discovered the miraculous compound, why would Regina hide it? It didn't make sense.

Waverly looked pensively at her mother's old com station, which was draped with scraps of material that had overflowed from the sewing table next to it. She cleared away the fabric and turned on the computer. A smell of burned dust filled the room, and Waverly realized that this machine had not been used since well before the attack.

Waverly searched back through the ship's logs, cursory records of every day since the beginning of the mission almost forty-three years ago. She scrolled to the date of the air-lock accident that had taken her father's life and read the entry.

Air lock 252 malfunctioned during routine maintenance mission to repair particulate damage to radio antenna 252. Dr. Galen Marshall, Dr. Melissa Ardvale, Dr. James McAvoy were sucked out of the lock in resulting explosive decompression.

That was all?

It was the most serious accident to have occurred on the Empyrean. There ought to be more written about it.

Her fingers hovered over the keyboard, poised to start a search for any and all information about the accident, but this was precisely the sort of thing she didn't want to think about, so she tucked the strange photo under a pile at the bottom of the box. Waverly spent the rest of the night sorting through old photos, arranging them in piles until her eyelids were impossible to hold up.

The next moment, it seemed, she awoke on the couch surrounded by photographs. Her limbs felt loose and weak, her head bleary. Her stomach rumbled from emptiness, and she stood and stretched.

She frowned as she looked over the piles she'd made, then quickly stuffed them into the box in no particular order. With everything going on, the last thing she needed was to be digging around in the ancient past. Besides, she needed a good breakfast. She had a tractor to repair in the cornfield—probably a busted gear shaft—and then she had to change the lubricant on three separate combines, all in different parts of the ship. It was a lot of work, and she was already tired. Plus, judging from the stress in her knees and the ache between her shoulders, Kieran had ordered another increase in acceleration. The excess gravity was getting to everyone, but no one complained. More than anything they wanted to catch up to the New Horizon and get their parents back. If they had to wear out their joints in the pursuit, so be it.

As she dressed, her mind turned back to that photo of her father with Captain Jones, and that cursory report about her father's death. It seemed as though details about the accident had been covered up, by Mason Ardvale, the Captain, even her own mother. Waverly left her quarters in a fog, walked with arms folded, head down, gaze on her own feet, remembering something Seth Ardvale had said to her before the attack: *Friends of Captain Jones lead complicated lives.*

She was so preoccupied she never saw the slip of a boy who left the doorway opposite hers to follow her down the corridor.

The Past

Kieran stood over the lifeless form of Max Brent, staring at the drawn, cold face. The boy looked as though he'd been molded from gray plastic. Deep circles ringed his eyes, and his purple lips were pulled back in a mask of pain. A film of dried spittle had collected in the corners of the corpse's mouth, and the artificial gravity pulled on his skin so that it collected in wrinkled bunches at the base of his jaw. He was being kept in one of the small private rooms in the infirmary, away from the eight-bed main room where most of the patients were. The few adults who had survived the original attack were kept apart, too, in the long-term care unit, so sick from radiation poisoning they couldn't be a help to anyone. If Victoria Hand, the one surviving nurse on board, could have helped, would Max be alive now?

"What happened to him?" Kieran asked, looking away, horrified.

"I don't know!" cried Tobin Ames, who'd been charged with running the infirmary. "It's not a sickness, I don't think. I can't find any holes in him, either."

"Could it be poison?" Arthur asked from behind Kieran. Arthur had taken one look at Max's awful visage and backed away in dread.

Tobin nodded, overwrought. There'd been plenty of death on board the Empyrean, but no one ever got used to it. Tobin looked like he hadn't slept all night, and he chewed his cuticle as he stared at Max's body, clearly tormented that he hadn't been able to save him.

"You did the best you could, Tobin," Kieran said.

"I can't even figure out how Max got *up* here," Tobin said. He ran his fingers through his wiry light brown hair, making it stand on end. "Someone put him on that elevator."

"It'll be easy enough to find out," Arthur said. "I'll just check the video for that elevator on all the levels."

"Also look for evidence of Seth poisoning him," Kieran said.

"Where would he have gotten poison?" Arthur said.

"There's a maintenance closet on every level," Kieran said. "Maybe a cleaning solution?"

"Yeah," Tobin said. "I'll check the ingredients on those, see if they match Max's symptoms."

"Which were . . . ?"

"Blue fingernails and lips. Convulsions. Coma." Tobin shook his head. "I thought it was alcohol poisoning. He smelled like it, anyway. I used charcoal to try to treat him. It took me two hours to figure out how to do it! The manual was really confusing. If I'd been faster . . ."

"You don't know that," Arthur told him. "It's not your fault."

But Tobin didn't seem to believe it.

"Even real doctors lose patients sometimes," Kieran said.

Tobin nodded and marched back to his office, distracted and burdened.

Kieran tapped Arthur on the shoulder. "Let's go." Kieran and Arthur left the infirmary and stood outside the elevators to head back to Central Command. Kieran felt light-headed and wondered if he looked as disturbed as Arthur, who swallowed as though trying to keep from throwing up. Kieran wondered if Arthur was remembering that awful night, months ago, when the two of them had cleared the bodies out of the port-side shuttle bay. Kieran shuddered.

"It doesn't make sense," Arthur finally said as the elevator doors opened and they stepped on. "Why would Seth let Max out of the brig only to poison him?"

"He tried to put me into an air lock, or did you forget about that?" Kieran snapped. He realized he was trembling. Was he angry, or afraid, knowing that his enemy was on the loose? He pressed the button for Central Command, tried to calm down. He'd be no good to anyone if he panicked. *I can handle this,* he told himself.

"I'm just trying to make sense of everything," Arthur said softly.

"I'm sorry," Kieran said, and put his hand on his friend's shoulder. The pressure of running the Empyrean was starting to get to him, and he found himself snapping a lot lately at people who didn't deserve it. The elevator doors opened to the busy corridor, and the boys headed for Central Command. On the wall just to the right of the door Kieran saw a stick-figure drawing of a figure with wavy, trembling arms and a grimace of fear on its face. Underneath, the caption read, *Our fearful leader, Kieran Alden.*

Kieran felt his palms grow cold. He heard whispers behind him and turned to see a couple of little girls watching him. When their eyes met his, they pretended to be talking about something else.

"Clean this up," he said to Arthur, then went into Central Command. Sarek turned in his chair to nod hello. "Any luck tracing Seth through the surveillance system since last night?" Kieran asked him.

"Actually, I wanted to talk to you about that," Sarek said, pivoting back and forth in his swivel chair. "I haven't been able to see *anyone* on the vid system for the last eighteen hours."

"What do you mean?" Kieran settled himself in the Captain's chair.

"I mean all the system seems to be recording is empty corridors and ag bays. If someone were to look at our vid logs for today, they'd think this ship was deserted."

"That's odd," Arthur said, taking his seat near the windows. There were dozens of chairs and com stations arranged in a crescent beneath the large square portholes, all of them empty except for the stations occupied by Arthur, Sarek, and Kieran in the Captain's chair at the head of the room. "Seth must have disabled the motion detectors."

"Damn it." Kieran punched the air. "I knew if that son of a bitch ever got out . . ." He faded into a brooding silence.

"Kieran." Arthur leaned toward Kieran over the back

of his chair. "You have too many friends. It won't happen again."

Kieran didn't have to ask what Arthur was referring to. "I never could have imagined them turning against me the *first* time."

They'd just stood by as Seth injected Kieran with some paralyzing drug and slammed him in the brig. And as Kieran lay starving in that small, cold cell, had any of them come to his aid? They'd all been too afraid of Seth and his thugs to try to help Kieran. And now *they* were calling *him* a coward!

"Okay, so what now?" Arthur said patiently.

"Call up the Command officers," Kieran said to Sarek, who turned to make the announcement.

The Command officers were a detail of a dozen boys, all older than thirteen years, whose overt job was to keep the crew on task throughout the day and keep the peace when fights broke out. But they had a covert assignment as well. They reported any untoward activities to Kieran, kept him apprised of the mood among the crew so he'd always be aware of any malcontents. They were armed only with batons. Kieran didn't want any guns in use on the Empyrean and had scoured the storage bays for all the weapons and locked them away in a secret place only he knew about. The stockpile felt woefully small, though, and he suspected he'd missed some of the weapons in his search. But if he couldn't find them, probably no one could.

Except Seth.

"Arthur," Kieran said. "Help me work up a list of suspects to be taken in for questioning."

"*Suspects?*" Arthur's eyes widened. "So if we find out who let Seth out, we're going to throw them in the brig?"

"Well, yes," Kieran said, trying to sound calm. "That's

what you do when people break the law."

Arthur swallowed audibly. "What law?"

"What?" Kieran regarded Arthur with a studying eye.

"What law was broken by letting Seth out?" Arthur said, visibly cowed but steeling himself. "Specifically?"

"It's illegal to release someone from the brig without due process."

"Okay." Arthur leaned his chin on the back of his chair. "But it's illegal to keep someone *in* the brig without due process. You never held a trial for Seth."

"What are you saying, Arthur?" Kieran barked. "That I should let Seth wander around after he tried to kill me?"

"I'm saying that if you're going to start questioning people and throwing them in jail, you can't be seen to be making up the law as you go along."

"Is that what you think I'm doing?"

"No," Arthur said, but he cast a nervous glance at Sarek, who stared stubbornly at his screen.

"I seem to remember you suggesting I get rid of Seth not too long ago."

"That wasn't a suggestion. That was . . ." Arthur fingered the padded edge of his station.

"What?"

"I wanted to see what you would say."

"And did I pass your little test?"

"You did, like I thought you would." Arthur leaned forward, elbows on his knees, palms pressed together, all his energy focused on Kieran. "I remember you saying you thought Seth was bluffing when he threatened to throw you out an air lock."

"He might have been, but I'm not willing to bet my life on it."

"It's just that right now the crew believes in you

because they think you're a good guy."

"Okay."

"If you start putting people in the brig, you need a solid reason for why you have the authority to do it."

"Arthur, are you proposing we try to run an election in the midst of all this?"

"I think it would protect you."

"I don't. We're in pursuit of the New Horizon, and we've got a dangerous person loose on the ship."

"If you're elected Captain, Seth's supporters couldn't say you have no legal right to lead."

Kieran wanted to scoff at this. Much had always been made about how the Empyrean was a democracy built on humanist values. But the elections had always seemed more like a formality, because Captain Jones and the same people on the Central Council had always been reelected since the mission began. People talked about democracy, but what they really liked, Kieran always thought, was consistency. Maybe this crew of kids had other ideas, though. "Is that what people are saying, Arthur?"

Arthur only looked at Kieran, mouth closed.

"I can't handle an election right now, Arthur!"

"I could take care of it for you."

"Not now, Arthur." Kieran leaned back in his seat, tapped at the edge of his com screen. "We can run this investigation without accusing anyone. We won't mention Seth at all. We'll get a picture of where people say they were, compare stories, and see if anyone's lying."

"Makes sense," Arthur said. "But I still say—"

"I know what you say," Kieran said, irritated.

His Command officers began filing in one by one and stood in a semicircle along the curved wall of windows that looked out to the constant night sky. Matt Allbright was the de facto leader, partly by virtue of his being the oldest, having just turned fourteen, but also because he wasn't afraid to take initiative. He had a quick glance, and he seemed to think before he spoke, and when he did speak, his words were forceful and well chosen. He even looked like an officer, with his broad shoulders and straight bearing and the way he fastidiously kept his hair cropped close to his head. Still, Kieran was never sure he could absolutely trust Matt, or any of the guards for that matter. They were in a position of power, and he knew how easily power could be abused. That's why he'd chosen boys who, even if he couldn't be assured of their character, were at least predictable. None of them were particularly creative thinkers. Even Matt had a plodding kind of intelligence—careful, linear, and purposeful. He seemed incapable of deceit.

"What I am about to tell you does not leave this room," Kieran said to the officers, who all stood straight like Matt, listening. "Someone tampered with the video system the night Seth escaped. I want you to try to find out who."

"Excuse me, sir." Hiro Mazumoto rubbed his hand over the faint shadow of whiskers that grew on his boyish chin. "Are you saying we were sabotaged by a member of our crew?"

"By Seth Ardvale, obviously." Kieran walked along the row of officers. They stood at attention, shoulders back, hands clasped behind their backs. Kieran liked the discipline it conveyed; it made him feel authoritative. "But we know he had help.

"What I want you to do," he continued, "is to move out among the crew, listen to conversations, keep your ears open. Matt?"

The boy's head snapped to attention.

"I want you to organize a detail of several teams to scour the ship for signs of Seth. Where he might be camping, what he might be planning. Finding him and his accomplices is our top priority."

Matt nodded.

When the officers had all filed out with their new orders, Kieran noticed Arthur brooding in the corner. He knew Arthur was right about the election in principle, but practically speaking it would be a huge mess, because it wouldn't just be about holding an election. He'd have to hold trials, too, not only for the people who released Seth but for Seth himself. There would be no way to avoid giving Seth his say in front of the entire crew, and Seth could be very persuasive. The whole thing could blow up in Kieran's face.

"Whoa," Sarek said from his com station. He pulled his headset off and turned, his dark eyes round with surprise. "We're being hailed by the New Horizon."

"What?" Arthur said.

Kieran stood up. "Who is it? Who's calling?"

"Anne Mather," Sarek said in awe.

All three boys froze, staring at the flashing red light on Sarek's com station. Kieran felt weak limbed. He'd tried to contact Anne Mather almost daily to demand the release of the prisoners, and all his hails had gone ignored. Why should she contact him now?

"Send the link to my office," Kieran said quietly, and stalked out of Central Command, down the corridor to the Captain's suite, where he sat at the desk and put on his headset with trembling fingers. He took several deep breaths, then flicked the switch to enable the signal.

His vid screen flickered to the image of a plump, middle-aged woman with abundant white hair swept into a bun on top of her head. She wore spectacles on the tip of her nose, and she had smooth skin, though her features were careworn. "Whom am I addressing?" she asked with clipped words.

"Kieran Alden," he said, trying to sound authoritative.

"I'm Anne Mather," she said with a cool smile.

"What do you want?" Kieran said, his eyes on the porthole that looked out to a thick coating of stars in a black sky. He did not like looking at her. She was too poised, too confident. And her smile disgusted him.

"There are no adults I can talk to?" she asked innocently.

"No. You slaughtered our crew."

The glib smile fell from her face, and she bowed her head. "You'll never believe me, but I didn't expect so many of your crew to be in the shuttle bay. I thought loss of life would be minimal."

"It wasn't," he said bitterly.

She blinked as though his glare burned her eyes. "You probably want to know why I called."

He only stared at her, waiting.

"We saw that you veered off course last night. I'm calling to see if you need assistance."

"How kind of you," Kieran said, his eyes snapping to hers. "But we're doing just peachy back here. How are you?"

"Ah, I miss that. Teenage sarcasm." The woman chuckled. Kieran wished he could shatter her teeth for her. "I see you've increased your rate of acceleration to catch up to us. That's going to have physical consequences for your crew, I hope you know."

"We're young." Kieran grinned. "It'll only make us stronger."

"It'll cause edema, circulation problems, and it'll wear your joints out faster than you might imagine. And those are only the symptoms we know of."

"I'm betting that my crew can take it longer than your crew."

"It won't work. You know I can't let you catch up to us only to attack us. We need some kind of understanding before I let you near us."

"Then put our parents on a shuttle, send them back to us, and we'll let you go."

"I would do that if I didn't know a thing or two about human nature."

"What's to know? You'll be on your ship and we'll be on ours, just like before."

"And when we get to New Earth? What then?" She raised one eyebrow.

"Pick a continent."

"I have a responsibility to the people of this vessel and our way of life."

"You mean attacking people and kidnapping them? That way of life?"

"That's what I'm afraid of, Mr. Alden. Your anger. I can hear it in your voice, see it on your face, that you want to kill me and my crew for what we did." She clucked. "That kind of vitriol can last generations. It could lead to a culture of warfare on New Earth. Remember the Middle East on Old Earth? I don't want something like that to be my legacy."

"You should have thought of that before you attacked us."

"I had just cause." Her calm veneer dropped to show a

core of rage underneath. "You're Captain now; you have access to the ship's records. Find out for yourself how we were sabotaged and provoked. I'm sure Waverly Marshall told you—"

"I'm not going to play games with you," he said. He felt nauseous even talking to her. "Release our parents and you won't have to deal with a violent confrontation."

"I can't do that until we settle our differences. We need a treaty."

"You want to call the shots."

"I want assurance that my crew and our descendants will be safe once we reach New Earth."

"Fine. You have my word. We won't attack you."

"Not good enough. I want the truth to come out about Captain Jones and the past. Only then will you understand why we had to do what we did." Her tone was plaintive, friendly, even, but her expression was flat. "I want you to do some research, Mr. Alden."

"You're giving me *homework*?"

"When you and I can have a frank, honest discussion about the past, then we can begin to discuss the transfer of hostages."

"Or I could simply catch up to your ship, board you, and take them by force."

The slight smile in her eyes flickered out, replaced by hardened steel. "If you think a bunch of kids can overcome a seasoned adult crew, you're deluding yourself."

"It's only to my advantage if you think I'm insane," Kieran said, and severed the com link.

But a text message came through on this computer with a video attachment:

These are records of communications between myself and Captain Jones, from the years when both ships struggled with infertility. You can verify their authenticity by comparing them to your own files and video logs. When you've watched them, hail my ship, and we can resume negotiations. Until then, I'll receive no communication from you.

Kieran stared at the file name: *Sabotage.*

Lies.

He stored the files on a data-dot and put it in the bottom of his desk drawer. He would not watch them. He refused to be manipulated by that woman.

He heard a beep and picked up the walkie-talkie he kept on his belt.

"Hi, Kieran!" Philip's little boy voice called. He sounded excited and happy. Kieran knew that this assignment had done wonders for the boy's outlook. There was no better therapy than being useful.

"Hi, Philip, buddy. What have you turned up?"

"Waverly spent all night alone in her quarters. She didn't even go visit Sarah this time. She looks really tired. Today she was working on a tractor engine in the cornfield. She changed a tire with some help from a couple guys. She hurt her hand with the wrench . . ."

"Less detail is okay, Philip. Did she go anywhere unusual? Talk to anyone? Mention anything about Seth Ardvale maybe?"

"I can't always hear her. Mostly she talks to other mechanics about work. The rest of the time she's quiet and alone. She seems sad."

Kieran's heart hurt, and for a moment he thought of her as the old Waverly, the girl he loved.

"Okay, Philip. Keep on her. You holding up okay?"

"It's easy."

"And you're sure she hasn't seen you?"

"She doesn't notice hardly anything. Like she's always thinking hard about something and not looking around."

"Okay, that's good. You're doing a great job. I think I'm going to promote you to deck officer when this assignment is through."

"That would be great!" Philip squealed.

Kieran severed the link and looked at the drawer that held Mather's data-dot. She wanted a treaty, she said. But she was holding all the cards. He might have little choice other than to play her game. But for now, he'd let her wait. He tapped his intercom link to Central Command, and Sarek answered.

"Sarek, increase our acceleration by another two percent."

"The crew is already complaining," Sarek said. "People are getting backaches."

"We've got to catch up to that damn woman."

"Okay," Sarek said, tired.

Soon Kieran felt the extra pull on his body. When he stood, he had to lean against the desk, panting. The extra gravity was exhausting, but it had to be even harder on the older New Horizon crew. Maybe he could wear them down this way, make Mather see reason and let the parents go. If not, he didn't know what else to do.

He was in his quarters undressing for bed when the intercom from Central Command buzzed. "Yes?" Kieran said, not bothering to go to his com station for the video link.

"Kieran," Sarek said. "The New Horizon has increased their acceleration by two percent."

Kieran leaned his forehead on the wall. "Did we gain on them?"

"No," Sarek said. "What should I do?"

"Keep up the new speed. We'll try to wear them down."

"Okay," Sarek said, and hung up.

When Kieran pressed the off button on his intercom, he noticed his hands were weirdly swollen. He squeezed the pads of his fingertips, which felt like over-full balloons. Edema, Mather had said.

Already it was happening.

He crawled between his sheets, buried his face in his pillow, and prayed. "God. Help us, please?"

But the voice in his mind—that hard-to-hear whisper in the dark that had first come to him when he was starving in the brig and had been with him ever since—only said what it always said to him: *I already am helping you.*

How? he asked desperately as he twisted against the mattress beneath him.

You will know your path when you see it, the voice said.

He knew the voice was telling him to trust himself, and he tried to believe he was equal to the task before him. He had faith in the voice but not enough to keep from being afraid.

Clues

Seth huddled in a corner of the conifer bay behind the juniper bushes. The heat lamps were programmed for springtime, but it was still only a chilly fifty degrees, and he shivered. For the moment, this was the best hiding place. Two hours before, he'd heard a couple of Kieran's guards enter the bay, and they'd strolled through it, peering between the needles, looking for him. He lay perfectly still, not even allowing himself to breathe until they'd disappeared behind a stand of Douglas fir. Since then there'd been no one, and he'd had some time to think about who could have caused those thruster bursts. Who would *want* to send the ship off course?

Considering that everyone on board, even the

orphans, desperately wanted to recover the captives being held on the New Horizon, only one possibility made any sense: There was a stowaway from the New Horizon on board.

Seth rubbed his palms against his arms, letting the friction warm him. The first step to finding the saboteur would be to figure out how he was able to program the thruster misfires, which could only have been done from the well-populated Central Command or from the radioactive engine room.

Seth could never get within a mile of Central Command, but it was unlikely the saboteur had operated there, unless the culprit was Sarek or Arthur, or Kieran himself. Unlikely. That left the engine room, if Seth could only get down there. The entire section had been sealed off to control the radiation, so the only way into the engine room would be through an outer hatch. The main problem: The engine room hatches had been designed to vent gas, not for ingress. They were barely large enough for an adult man to fit through the opening. But getting there was only half the battle; the entire area was flooded with radiation. He knew that OneMen were equipped with radiation shields and oxygen. If only the engine room hatch was big enough to fit a OneMan! Seth leaned back, his arm behind his head, and thought.

OneMen were really glorified space suits. They were bulky because of the outer metal shell, the oxygen tanks, and the rocket packs on the back. But inside each OneMan was an inner sleeve that served as a second layer of protection. If that could be removed from the bulky parts of the OneMan, the wearer would easily fit through the engine room hatch.

It was worth a try.

Seth got up, brushing off juniper needles, and crept to the empty corridor, his father's portable computer tucked under his arm. When he was sure no one was around, he sprinted to the outer stairwell, up seven levels for the starboard shuttle bay, and slipped through the doorway.

The shuttle bay was eerily quiet. Here was where the majority of the Empyrean crew members had met their deaths, and it felt like a tomb. The visors of the OneMen hanging along the walls were as eerie as death masks.

He went to the nearest OneMan and, using the automated system, lowered it from its housing and removed the helmet. He plunged his hand between the soft fabric and the hard shell. The fabric looked metallic and it felt like flexible plastic, but Seth knew it was an advanced carbon polymer modeled after the fibers of a spider, the strongest filament known. It was perfectly airtight and lined with micron-thick lead. It would protect him from the engine room radiation, and once he'd disconnected himself from the air tanks, there'd be at least a few minutes worth of oxygen within the suit for him to breathe, enough to get a look around, but not for much more.

He released the connectors that held the envelope in place and pulled it out by the collar. It looked like a silvery jumpsuit. Seth pulled it on, and the remarkable fabric stretched to accommodate his long frame. Fitting the helmet over the envelope, he heard the automatic click sealing him inside. His ears popped reassuringly when the pressure seals engaged. He climbed into the outer-shell OneMan, leaving the lower connections between the shell and the fabric envelope open so that when the time came, he could simply leave the shell.

He was ready.

"The engineers designed something well for a change," he muttered.

He engaged the thrusters to lessen the weight of the vessel, turned on the oxygen from the tanks, and walked with ponderous steps over to the smaller air lock that was meant for OneMen. Once inside the air lock, he felt as though he'd stepped into a coffin. The heavy metal doors slammed closed behind him, and he jumped inside his suit when the air lock cleared itself with an explosive rush.

He felt the metal shell of the OneMan expand with the pressure difference. Now all Seth had to do was open the outer doors, and there'd be nothing between him and the rest of the universe.

He'd never admitted this to anyone, but space walks terrified him. He'd had to perform several after the damage Kieran had done to the atmospheric conditioning plant. Seth had acted as foreman, teaching the other boys how to use the complex tools, showing them where to make the repairs. The entire time he'd been quaking in his suit, covered with cold sweat, his heart racing. When he looked in any direction in space, there was nothing between him and eternity. The feeling of his own smallness before all that vast, empty cold made his bile rise.

It would be even worse this time: No one knew he was going out here. One wrong move could send him spinning away from the ship, and there'd be no one to come looking for him.

He couldn't let himself think of that.

"I'm not afraid," he told himself with a shaking voice, took a deep breath, and opened the outer doorway.

The door yawned open to the awful blackness of space. The stars were crisp pinpoints, so thickly strewn in places that they looked like foam. They were so far away. Seth swallowed bile.

"It's just the sky," his father had said once, when Seth admitted he was afraid to try flying a OneMan. "If you were on a planet, it'd be the same thing. No walls. No windows. Nothing but nothing above your head."

Seth had only nodded at this because he didn't want to say anything stupid, but in truth the thought of walking a planet's surface gave him a terrible feeling of vertigo. If he could live his entire life on the Empyrean, he probably would. Because now, standing on the edge of the air lock and looking into eternity, he was utterly terrified.

"Don't piss yourself, Ardvale," he whispered ferociously.

He took a deep breath and stepped off the air lock platform.

And he was falling! Not falling; he was being left behind by his home ship, the rivets and portholes and gunmetal coating of the Empyrean dissolving into a terrifying blur of grays and blacks as the ship sped forward without him. Seth helplessly waved his arms— *Oh God, oh God*—before he remembered his thrusters. He pressed the throttle and screamed as his vessel jerked toward the Empyrean. Quickly he backed away from the huge ship, avoiding a crash by less than four feet.

His gorge rose. For a moment he was paralyzed with terror, but he forced his eyes open and swallowed bile as he scrabbled with the attitude, pitch, and yaw until he flew in a parallel course with the great ship.

He punched at the thruster controls, and finally he was accelerating at the same rate as the Empyrean, and the illusion of falling ceased. He found himself hovering near a porthole, and looked in to see that he'd fallen to the level of the rain forest bay. He had several more levels to go before he reached the engine room at the bottom of the ship.

Seth eased back on his rear thrusters just enough to move slowly down the gray landscape of the Empyrean. He kept his eyes on the hull, focusing on the rivets that lined each slab of sheet-metal skin, and then the small valley between the domes of the sewage and the water-purification systems. He floated over what seemed an infinite row of portholes, and he checked each one for a human face, but no one looked out as he passed. He should have been happy no one saw him, but instead he felt irrational disappointment, and that made him realize how alone he was.

He shut out this thought and turned his suit toward the port side. He could sense the bottom of the Empyrean looming at his feet like a horizon. He saw the hatch to the engine room below him and reached for the thruster control, but he fumbled and instead engaged an attitude thruster.

His body rotated madly, and he was falling once more, sailing over the hull in a mad spin. The pink nebula they'd left behind loomed in his vision, ready to swallow him whole.

Did he scream?

In a panic Seth tapped the emergency tether and a

cord shot out, aimed for the Empyrean like it was supposed to be, but he was spinning, and the cord wrapped around his waist, shortening with every turn. As he was pulled backward, he stared at the immense nebula, so silent and dense. It had enveloped the Empyrean for four years, rendered the ship essentially blind and deaf, allowing the New Horizon to sneak up for a surprise attack. Now it looked so calm, and he caught his breath as he gazed on the arms of magenta gas spreading away from its center, the shades of bluish gray tucked into pockets where the gas was most dense. He'd hated it when they were inside it, but now he could see that it was beautiful.

I'm going to live, he told himself. *I won't die out here.*

The enormous rear thrusters of the Empyrean swung into his field of vision, and Seth jammed the joystick forward, aiming for them, knowing that he could be caught in the exhaust and incinerated instantly. He already felt the heat on his face, and a slick layer of sweat coated his skin. "No, please," he whimpered.

Stiff with terror, he pushed his vessel as fast as it would go toward the hull, holding out the clawlike grippers of his suit, praying under his breath, "Come on, you bastard, you son of a bitch. Let me live."

He felt his grippers contact the hot metal of the exhaust tunnels, and activated the magnetic arm, which clamped on to the hull.

Seth didn't know how long he clung to the outside of the Empyrean, gulping air, gritting his teeth, willing himself not to break into a million pieces and cry like a baby. His heart flung itself against his rib cage again and again.

"You're not dead," he said savagely to himself. "Don't be such a goddamned coward."

Sweat poured into his eyes. He checked the temperature gauge in his helmet; it flashed a red warning signal. The last thing he wanted was to release his grip from the hull, but he had to or he might burn up. He rotated the arm until his thrusters were pointing downward again, careful to get the angle just right. Then he engaged the thrusters until he felt the familiar g-force on the soles of his feet.

"One, two, three," he whispered, and the grip released.

As slowly as he could, Seth guided the OneMan back to the starboard side and found the engine room hatch again. He lowered himself over the hatch controls, attached his tether to the hook by the door, and, with a badly shaking hand, hit the manual release lever on the small hatch.

An explosion of debris caught him in the face. He lost his grip on the door and he was blown backward.

I'm dead, he thought with detachment, but when he had the courage to open his eyes, he saw that his tether had held and that he was hanging over the engine room hatch.

"There shouldn't have been any air in there," Seth said aloud. "Dad vented it the day he . . ." He couldn't finish the thought. His voice was shaking, and he took four deep breaths to try to steady himself before this next, terrifying part. "You're going to do this fast," he said to himself.

He called up the command to release his helmet from the outer shell of the OneMan, but his finger hovered over it.

"I'm not going to die," he said to himself, then repeated it, more firmly. "I won't die."

He enabled the command, and the outer seals released with a hiss.

The absolute cold of outer space hit him like a bucket of liquid nitrogen, and he forgot how to breathe. His mind felt flattened. *I can't do this,* he told himself, but somehow he slithered out of the metal cavity, holding on to the ship with one aching hand. He left the shell hovering from its tether outside the engine room as he pulled himself through the doorway, and then he closed the hatch behind him.

It was just as cold in here as it had been outside. Seth took four agonized, jerking steps toward the computer array and, with hands that shook so hard he could barely control them, found the command to repressurize the room.

Air rushed around him, enveloping him in warmth. He collapsed into a chair, huddled in a ball, helpless against the mad spasms in his muscles, and waited for his mind to turn back on.

But he couldn't wait long. Already the air inside his suit was overmoist and stifling. He'd have to be quick.

Teeth still clacking, he took his first glance around. Somehow it was surprising that the lights still worked and the signal buttons still blinked on and off. Everything appeared to be working, but even with the blowouts, there would still be a fine coating of radioactive particles clinging to every surface. To breathe them in would significantly shorten his life. Someday this room would have to be meticulously cleaned with specialized equipment. Until then, it was a no-man's-land. Any maintenance to the engine would have to be done from the outside; Kieran better hope that pushing the engines so hard wouldn't result in total engine failure. Seth shook his head in frustration. For a smart guy, Kieran frequently acted like a fool.

This room was where Seth's father had spent his last few days, working in radioactivity without a protective suit, desperately trying to save the ship after the sabotage by the New Horizon attackers. "You were a bastard," Seth muttered, "but you found a way to die a hero."

Cringing against his muggy recycled breath, Seth walked to the aft side of the room and looked over the metal floor, which was marred with patches of dried blood, and into the corner near the door where he found dozens of discarded ration containers. Others like them must have been what hit him in the face when he opened the hatch.

Seth leaned over the pile of garbage and poked through it with the toe of his boot. Some of the containers still looked moist.

Someone must be camping out down here. But how, with all this radiation?

Seth went to the tool cabinet, where he located a Geiger counter and took a reading, gasping in surprise when it showed radioactivity levels within normal range. Several more readings confirmed it.

How? Cleanup after a radioactive event was arduous and highly technical. Someone must have vacuumed up every last bit of dust from the instruments, the floor, the ceiling, the portals. The entire place had to have been wiped down. The air filters would have needed changing, the room would have had to be hooked up to the air ventilation system again—the list of tasks was endless, and the job would have been dangerous. There was no way Kieran would risk an inexperienced crew to come down here for cleanup.

That left one possibility: The saboteur had done it.

Seth took a deep breath, disengaged his helmet, and slowly pulled it off. He drew in a single, tentative breath. So far so good. The air was fresh and smelled pure. The suit itself felt damp against his skin, which gave him a chill, so he took off the entire thing, folded it, and put it with his helmet by the hatch.

He went again to the pile of garbage in the corner and poked through it. Some of the food scraps looked fairly fresh. He found a stack of uneaten rations in the corner cabinet. In the janitor closet he found blankets and a bedroll on the floor, along with grav bags of water. Someone *was* camping out down here. He must have fled when the decompression alarm went off.

A chilling thought came to Seth then. What if the saboteur was still here? How long had there been a vacuum in the engine room? Seth had repressurized quickly, so the saboteur would have been exposed to the vacuum of space for only ten or twenty seconds. Was that enough time to kill someone? Maybe not. If someone had been in here, that person might still be alive, and maybe even conscious.

He rushed to the tool cabinet, chose the heaviest wrench he could find, and held it tightly in his sweaty palm, eyeing the doorway that led to the reactor rooms. There was a port reactor and a starboard reactor, and each of them sent power to the thrusters and the rest of the ship. It was possible that someone could hide within the housing for the reactors, between the tubes of metal, or down among the snaking pipes for the coolant system. Seth took two deep breaths and opened the door for the port-side reactor.

The room was dark, and Seth switched on the light. He felt claustrophobic here, because the immense room was packed with hundreds of rods of plutonium, deep pools of deuterium, and endless tubes that circulated the coolant. The turbines made a nagging, humming sound that tickled the inside of Seth's ear. He climbed up onto a large metal box that must house one of the coolant control systems and looked around the huge room. There were a million hiding places here. He'd never be able to find the saboteur this way.

Suddenly his ears popped, and he heard a loud creak coming from the door to the reactor room, as though it were being pulled against its seals. He ducked down and waited, but there was no other sound or movement.

He went to the door and looked through the glass peephole. The engine room looked just as it had, but when he tried to pull open the door, it felt as though a thousand-pound weight was holding it in place.

He was trapped!

He pounded on the door, yelling, when a blinking message on the com screen to the right of the door caught his eye. "Repressurize main room," it said.

What?

Seth selected "Yes," and he heard a great whoosh of air. Suddenly the thousand-pound weight against the door was gone.

He ran back to the engine room, and stopped dead in his tracks.

His helmet was gone! So was the silvery inner sleeve, taken from where he'd left them by the hatch! Seth ran to the hatch porthole and looked outside to where he'd tethered his OneMan. That son of a bitch had stolen it! He must have slipped out of the starboard reactor room when Seth was looking for him on the port side.

That must have been how he'd survived the decompression, too. He'd been in one of the reactor rooms, behind a pressurized door.

Seth kicked at one of the chairs in front of the control desk, and it went rolling across the room. He picked up the wrench and slammed it against the metal wall again and again, swearing, sweat stinging his eyes. When his rage was spent, he stood panting, a grimace on his face. He'd been so close to catching that bastard!

Whoever he was, he was sure to do more damage. Seth had to get a warning to Kieran.

Seth climbed up to the surveillance camera above the control desk and pointed it at the corner of the room, where he gathered a pile of the empty ration containers. Next he found a pad of paper and a heavy black pen, and wrote in block letters, saboteur from the new horizon on board, has been camping here. radiation levels are now normal.

He doubted Kieran would believe him, but he had to try.

He went to the emergency lever on the wall by the door and, bracing his feet so that he could run, pulled it down. An alarm pierced his ears, and he knew it would sound throughout the ship.

Now all he could do was run.

Official Investigation

"You haven't been attending services lately," Kieran said to Sarah Hodges. He leaned back in his desk chair, pressed his fingertips together, and studied the girl.

Sarah glowered at him, twisting in her seat. Her hair was greasy, pulled back into a ponytail, and her fingernails were cruddy. She'd been assigned to dig up stray potatoes for the last few days, a task no one liked. Kieran had thought his offer to switch her to combine duty might have loosened her tongue, but she'd remained as uncooperative as ever.

"Don't you like services?"

"I guess not," she said flatly.

"Why not?"

"They remind me too much of that woman."

"I'm nothing like her."

"How do you know? You've never met her," she sneered.

Yes I have, he almost said, but he didn't want his conversation with Mather to be known yet. He still hadn't watched the vid files she'd sent, and he hadn't heard from her again or tried to contact her. Right now, he was focused on finding Seth Ardvale before he could do any more damage.

Kieran leaned his elbows on his desk, and the chair creaked under him. The milky scent of red bush tea hovered in the air. "Where were you on the night the thrusters misfired?"

"I was in my quarters. When I heard your announcement I went to the central bunker. Waverly was there with me."

"That's what she says."

"Looks like we have our story straight," she spat.

"What is that supposed to mean?"

"It means that people don't like being questioned as though they were criminals."

"That's not my intention, Sarah." Kieran sighed. She was only the third person he'd interviewed, after Sealy Arndt and Tobin Ames, who'd both been early supporters of Seth. Word was already getting around. He'd have to write his sermon for this Sunday very carefully, find a way to get people back on his side. "It's not that I think you had anything to do with the thruster problems—"

"Oh, isn't it?"

"I'm just trying to get a picture of what happened that night," he said, though in fact his suspicion of her was more acute than ever. She was Waverly's friend, and she seemed like the type of recalcitrant person who would sympathize with Seth. But right now, he needed to get her guard down. "You might have seen something without realizing it. It's the only place I can think of to start."

This was intended to mollify her, but she folded her arms over her chest and stared stubbornly at him.

Suddenly the lights in the room flashed, sending weird shadows over the bust of Harry Truman that stood in the corner of the office. An alarm shrieked through the ship.

"Oh my God," Sarah said. "What is that?"

"Stay here," Kieran said as he shoved back from his desk and bolted for the door. He ran down the corridor to Central Command, aware of Sarah's footsteps behind him. When he got there, he found Arthur and Sarek leaning over a vid screen, looking baffled.

"What happened?" he asked.

"Someone pulled the emergency alarm in the engine room," Sarek said.

"Why?" Kieran started toward his chair but stopped cold. "Did you say *the engine room*?"

"Yeah," Sarek said, visibly shaken. "That was after two decompressions a few minutes apart. I thought they were instrument malfunctions, but now . . ."

"Look." Arthur pivoted the vid screen toward Kieran.

It showed a pile of what looked like ration containers, and a sign in bold letters. Kieran read it, shaking his head. "But that room is flooded with radiation!"

"Not according to the note," Arthur said, but he didn't appear to believe it.

"The repair crew *did* vent it before leaving," Sarek said thoughtfully.

"Yes, but there'd be residue!" Kieran insisted.

"I know," Arthur said. "It's strange."

"Well, someone has definitely been living there," said a female voice.

All three boys turned to see Sarah Hodges looking at the vid screen over their shoulders. She returned their gazes with a cool stare.

"What are you doing here?" Kieran asked her, annoyed.

"This is my ship, too," she said. "I can be here if I want."

"This is a restricted area," Arthur said.

She glared at each of them in turn. "The more you guys act like you're in charge, the less people trust you."

"Can you run back the image?" Kieran said, ignoring her for the moment. "Did the camera see who pulled the emergency alarm?"

"I've tried that," Sarek said, and ran the video back. The image showed the engine room control panel, then instantaneously flashed to a view of the pile of trash.

"Weird," Sarah said pensively. "The opposite should have happened."

"What do you mean the opposite?" Kieran said.

Sarah looked at Kieran defiantly, keeping her mouth closed.

"Something is wrong with the motion detectors," Arthur said. "We're working on it."

"I know exactly what's wrong," Sarah said with a smug smile.

All three boys looked at her and waited.

"Oh, I'm not telling *you* what it is."

"*How* do you know? Are you in touch with—" Kieran almost named Seth, but bit back the words. "Did someone tell you about this?"

"No, it's just obvious what the problem is. I'm surprised you guys haven't thought of it."

"Sarah," Kieran said in a dangerously low voice. "You tell me what you know."

"I will, when you stop acting like this ship is your own personal cult."

Kieran stared at her insolent face so hard he thought he could light her freckles on fire. "Throw her in the brig."

Arthur looked at him, surprised. "Kieran—"

"Do it!"

"You're a rat!" Sarah yelled as a bewildered Sarek called two guards into Central Command. Sarek mumbled orders to them, and they flanked Sarah, dwarfing her by over a foot, but they didn't intimidate her. "I'll make you regret this!" she snarled at Kieran as one of them took hold of her elbow.

"How did Seth get down there?" Kieran barked at Arthur, who stared at him, wide-eyed. Sarah could still be heard swearing and yelling all the way to the elevators. "Arthur! How?"

"I don't know," Arthur said quietly. He wouldn't look at Kieran directly, clearly very upset. "That whole level is sealed off."

"Sarek?" Kieran said.

Sarek engaged the security software and searched the com system data on the different doors and bulkheads that had sealed off the lower levels to contain the radiation. "Nothing has changed," he said. "The elevators are all still sealed."

"What about the stairwells?" Arthur asked from the corner of the room.

"Check them individually," Kieran said with a sinking feeling.

Sarek scrolled through the many doors on the lower levels. "There it is. The starboard stairwell. It looks like someone manually opened the seal."

"How did we not see that?" Kieran asked angrily.

"It's not like I have nothing else to do!" Sarek snapped.

"Where are the radiation suits?" Kieran barked.

"The infirmary, I think," Arthur said, his tone blank, his face unreadable. Kieran could see Arthur didn't approve of what he'd done to Sarah, but right now he didn't care. "You can't go down there."

"If the seal is broken, the damage is done," Kieran said bitterly. Seth Ardvale should be thrown out an air lock for this.

Kieran ran down to the infirmary, where he found Tobin Ames and Sealy Arndt talking. The rest of the ward was empty. The eight surviving adults, bedridden and weak with radiation sickness, had all been moved to the long-term-care unit next door.

Both Tobin and Sealy looked at Kieran warily. "You going to question me again?" Sealy asked.

"No, Sealy," Kieran said with a sigh, then added, "I really just thought you could help with the investigation. Seth must be behind the thrusters—"

"That bastard can rot in the brig for the rest of his life, for all I care," Sealy said, looking at Kieran angrily. "But I'm starting not to trust *anyone* who thinks he's in charge."

"I'm doing the best I can," Kieran said, wounded. Everything had been going well until the girls got here. Now everything felt out of balance, like he could lose control at any second, and the crew might erupt into the same insanity that nearly got him killed once before. "Where did you guys put the radiation suits when the patients came in?"

Tobin pointed to a cabinet in the corner of the room, and Kieran opened the door. The suits were smelly with body odor and filthy, almost unwearable.

"Didn't you guys ever clean them?"

"We hosed them down as best we could and ejected the dirty water. That's all we had time to do."

Kieran chose the least-offensive one and slung it over his shoulder.

"Where are you going?" Tobin called after him.

"None of your business," Kieran called back, and marched to the starboard elevator bank. On the ride down, Kieran put on the suit. He zipped up the leggings and the bodysuit, pressed all the seals closed, but waited to put on the helmet. The faceplate was grimy, and he wiped at it with his fingers, which left a nasty brown film under his nails. Then he put on the rank helmet, wrinkling his nose against the odor.

Kieran's heart galloped when the elevator doors opened to the level above engineering. He took the stairs down one at a time until he reached the doorway to the engine room, at the bottom of the ship. The noise from the engines seemed to beat against his eardrums, and he could feel the power of the thrusters vibrating the soles of his feet. Slowly he approached the doorway, which looked like any other doorway on the ship. The steel bulkhead doors that had sealed off the room had indeed been manually cranked open. He took a deep breath and opened the door to the engine room.

For months he'd thought of this place as a tomb, and he didn't like being here. Kieran went to the tool cabinet for the Geiger counter. He checked the reading, which amazed him. He hesitated, but finally took off the helmet and breathed in the comparatively fresh air. Then he shed the entire disgusting suit and kicked it into a corner.

Kieran went to the pile of trash and sifted through it. The containers looked to be in different stages of rot, some of them completely desiccated, some still moist and recognizable. He counted them and figured that there were enough containers for a person to subsist for more than a week.

Seth had only been out of jail for two days.

Kieran sat on the floor, staring at the pile. Unless all this was staged—and he didn't think it had been—it hadn't been Seth camping out down here. Kieran's blood ran cold when he thought of the possibilities.

With renewed urgency, he got up and looked through all the cabinets, and then he went into the huge reactor rooms and walked their perimeter, looking for any more clues. He found none. He was fairly certain that whoever had been spending time down here wouldn't come back, not now that the alarm had been pulled, but he'd station a team here to be on the safe side. He shook his head angrily. He thought he'd find more, some clue about what had happened during that thruster misfire, and he was disappointed.

Kieran walked back to the elevator bank and pressed the call button, deep in thought. It was Seth who had pulled that emergency lever, he felt certain of it. Seth knew something, and for some reason, he was willing to risk revealing himself to send Kieran a message. Was he taunting him?

The elevator bell rang and the doors opened, but on impulse Kieran instead headed for the starboard stairwell again. It was the least-used stairwell on the ship. Without his radiation suit, it was uncomfortably cold here, and therefore seldom used. Besides, there were no surveillance cameras. This could be how Seth was traveling.

A frigid burst of air met Kieran's face. The stairs were made of metal mesh, and they rose several hundred feet above his head, all the way to the prow of the ship. Kieran held his breath and listened for footsteps. Even if Seth were ten stories above him, Kieran would be able to hear him. Or maybe Seth hadn't gone that far.

On a hunch Kieran went up to the storage bay and entered the enormous room. Here, hundreds of shipping containers were stacked ten deep, waiting to be deployed when the ship reached New Earth. In this silent room, surrounded by these mammoth containers, he realized it had been a long time since he'd wandered the ship on his own. He used to do this all the time, just head off without a destination, walking around, saying hello to people he ran into, stopping to help Mrs. Dunnow dig up some parsnips or to feed the trout with Mr. Aims. Now the ship felt so empty.

For the first time in a long time, he allowed himself to think of his parents. If he ever saw his mom again, he'd tell her everything that had happened, all the things he'd done, and she'd wrap him in her arms and say, "You did everything you could. No one could have done better." His father would pat him on the shoulder, the kind of smack that hurt just a little bit, to make him feel tough, and he'd say, "I'm proud of you, son."

"I'm proud of you," Kieran murmured to himself, trying to sound like his dad.

A sound tugged at his ear.

He stopped. Listened.

Had he just heard something? A surprised intake of breath? The scuff of a shoe?

Footsteps! Someone padding across the floor!

Kieran ran toward the sound. Now that he was running, the footsteps were louder, as though the other person had given up being quiet. He ran past several rows of containers, then the flash of a human shape caught his eye.

Seth! He knew it instinctively even before he could take in the dirty blond hair and square shoulders.

Seth was running away, a heavy-looking bag strapped over his shoulders. It was weighing him down, but he was still fast. Kieran took off after him, running as hard as he could. But he was slow.

He knew he'd never fully recovered from his month of starvation in the brig, but he was surprised at how hard it was to run for even a short amount of time. His heart already hurt, and the extra gravity pulled at his limbs, making his whole body sluggish. He had no speed. Seth got smaller and smaller in the distance. Kieran's vision clouded, and he thought he might faint. He slammed his body against a container in rage, ignoring the pain in his shoulder.

"Stop!" he screamed helplessly.

To his amazement, Seth stopped. Slowly he turned around.

The two boys looked at each other, and Seth started walking back toward Kieran. The arrogance of that! Just strolling back the way he'd come, so confident he could outrun him. Finally there were no more than one hundred feet separating them. Seth stopped and glared at Kieran through those cold blue eyes.

Kieran wanted to tear him apart, but his fingertips were tingling.

Seth's eyes darted around. "You're alone?"

There was no point in pretending. Kieran could only manage a couple words at a time between gulps of air. "I came . . . to look at . . . the engine room."

"It wasn't me camped out down there," Seth said.

Kieran took a step forward and collapsed against the container. Seth took a step back, reached for something in the bag he carried, but he didn't pull it out. Kieran thought he knew what it was.

"How did you . . . get out?" Kieran asked, though he was choked for air.

"I woke up and my cell was open."

"Liar."

"If you're not going to believe me, why ask?"

Kieran stared at Seth, unbelieving. This was the guy Waverly couldn't resist visiting in the brig. This lying, conniving bully.

"Look," Seth said. He pulled his hand out of his bag and held it up in appeal. "You need to listen to me, Kieran, okay? This is important."

Kieran didn't even blink.

"I think there's a stowaway from the New Horizon on board. He must have come on Waverly's shuttle. Or he's been here all along, since the first attack. I don't know. He's the one who let me out, to make you think it was me tampering with the thrusters. He's dangerous. You need to find him."

"Don't tell me what to do," Kieran said, disgusted.

"Kieran, this isn't about you and me anymore. You get that, don't you?"

"I think you're lying."

"I'm not. You know I'm not. Why would I undermine the mission, or endanger the ship? All I've ever wanted to be was a deck officer."

"Then why did you stage a mutiny?" Kieran demanded.

"It wasn't really a mutiny, Kieran," Seth said gently, almost kindly. "You weren't the Captain."

Again, Kieran said nothing. He was furious that Seth was trying to be the bigger man, to reason with him, after all that had happened. The hypocrisy was disgusting.

"You can't catch me today," Seth said. His hand went to the strap of his bag; he shifted its weight on his shoulder.

"I'll catch you soon," Kieran gasped.

"You can try."

Seth turned on his heel and started to jog away, but he stopped and turned. His hand went to the back of his neck, and his eyes darted around the floor between them. "Look," he finally said, "I'm sorry. About how I treated you in the brig. I think I was sort of . . . blaming you for what happened to my dad."

"You tried to kill me."

"I wouldn't have gone through with it."

"You know that for sure?"

Seth only looked at him with a haunted expression.

"I'll never let you take this ship from me again," Kieran said. He pushed himself away from the container to stand on his own two feet. "I'll die before you sit in the Captain's chair."

"I know that."

"And you can never have Waverly," Kieran said, trying to think of the most vicious thing he could say. "She'd get bored of you. You're too . . . primitive for her."

Seth darkened at this, and the corners of his mouth pulled down. For a moment, it looked as though he might cry, but instead he turned a corner toward the starboard side and was gone.

Kieran sat down on the floor of the storage bay and waited for the tingling to leave his fingers. This had never happened to him before, but then he hadn't tried running since his month of starvation. Something was wrong with him. But that was the least of his worries.

Seth probably wasn't lying about the stowaway. He hated Seth but not enough to let go of his reason. Seth wanted power, and he'd know the last way to get it would be to delay the pursuit of the parents by tampering with the thrusters.

Kieran kicked himself. He should have realized this sooner. There was a saboteur from the New Horizon on board, and Seth was looking for him. If Seth brought the saboteur to justice, he'd be a hero. And Kieran would look like a fool.

Unease spread through Kieran like fever.

Maybe it wouldn't be so terrible if the crew went on thinking Seth was a saboteur.

Kieran stayed in the storage bay for a long time, weighing his options. When he could walk, he went to the port-side elevators and directly to Central Command to call in the Command officers for a meeting.

PART TWO

Power

Nearly all men can stand adversity, but if you want to test a man's character, give him power.
　　　　　　—Abraham Lincoln

New Rules

Waverly lay under a combine, tugging at a stubborn bolt on a leaky battery pack, when she heard the crackle of the ship's intercom. Her hands felt heavy and swollen from the increased gravity; her whole body felt sluggish. She rested her head on the fragrant soil, staring at the undercarriage of the machine while she listened.

"This is Kieran Alden. Please stop what you're doing and pay attention, as this might be the most important announcement I'll ever make."

Waverly rolled her eyes. Since taking over the ship, Kieran was given to hyperbole. She supposed that's what got people to listen to him.

"We have reason to believe," Kieran said, "that there is a terrorist from the New Horizon on board."

The blood drained from Waverly's face. Waverly heard several people cry out. Two girls who had been changing the oil on a tractor held hands, staring at the intercom speaker, wide-eyed. Waverly pulled herself out from under the combine and stood up to get a better listen.

"It now seems clear that Seth Ardvale is working with him."

"No way," Waverly said, but closed her mouth when several people shushed her.

"We think Seth worked with the terrorist. Together they murdered Max Brent and sent the ship off course with those thruster bursts. We have reason to believe that they have armed themselves with guns."

Several people gasped in alarm, and Waverly heard frantic whispers exchanged.

"What's more," Kieran said, "the terrorist must have come aboard the Empyrean on the escape shuttle piloted by Waverly Marshall."

Waverly had to lean on the tractor.

"With this in mind, I am instituting a new rule designed to make certain every crew member is safe and accounted for. Services will be held daily, and attendance is mandatory. Report to the auditorium every morning at eight o'clock, when we will perform a head count and make announcements, as well as begin our day with some reflection, prayer, and community. We have to band together, folks. Now is not the time for divisiveness or faulty commitment. We need to trust each other if we're going to get through this.

"Thank you for your attention. Please carry on with your duties."

Waverly dropped her wrench. She realized she'd been

holding her breath, and she opened her mouth for air.

There'd been a stowaway on her shuttle? She and the rest of the girls had lived on that shuttle for nearly a month, waiting for the Empyrean to emerge from the nebula so they could make contact. The girls had been all over that shuttle, going stir-crazy, trying not to think about the ever-shortening pile of rations in the cargo hold. Where could a stowaway have hidden all that time?

She should have searched that shuttle, torn it apart, looked under every maintenance panel, crawled through every conduit. She couldn't believe she let this happen!

Now Kieran and everyone else on the ship had one more reason to hate her.

Waverly threw down her work gloves, ignoring the angry glares coming from the others—angry pubescent kids looking for someone to hate. She took off at a dead run. She tore through the wheat field, kicking her knees up, pounding through the ankle-deep soil until she reached the port-side elevators. She slammed the call button with the heel of her hand and then angrily punched the wall, once, twice, until something in her wrist popped.

The elevator opened to an empty corridor. Waverly hardly felt her feet touch the floor as she ran between the ghostly rows of OneMen to the shuttle she'd brought here. She'd never wanted to see it again, but now she ran up the ramp and into the cargo hold.

It smelled terrible. She remembered again their terrifying journey back home from their captivity on the New Horizon. The shuttle was meant to be occupied by ground crews on New Earth during the early days of the terraforming projects, so they were equipped with water and air recirculation, as well as rations, but they were ill suited to deep-space travel. They had only rudimentary systems for coping with zero gravity, which made proper waste management and food consumption nearly impossible. The cargo hold was a disgusting mess.

She climbed the stairs to the passenger area, which was even worse. Discarded ration containers littered the floor, and the seats were in various stages of recline. She remembered the crying, the pleading, the endless questions: "How much longer? The Empyrean is out there still, isn't it, Waverly?" And the worst questions of all, repeated endlessly by practically everyone: "Why couldn't you save my mommy? My dad? My uncle? Why did you leave them behind?"

She could show them the bullet wound on her shoulder all she wanted, but she could never make them understand what it had been like.

An image of a man dying as blood blossomed red on his shirt. Dying because of her.

"I don't think about that anymore," she said aloud.

"Hello?!" A male voice, one she didn't recognize.

Waverly jumped. Someone was in the cockpit. Her heart kicked into overdrive and she took one step backward, but then Arthur Dietrich looked out the small doorway and smiled. "I thought you might come. When you heard the announcement, I mean."

Waverly said nothing. She watched Arthur. Waited for him to say something, because she couldn't.

"I'm glad you're here," Arthur said. He turned back to the cockpit and beckoned to her with one hand over his shoulder. "Any ideas where he could have hidden?"

Waverly slowly walked toward the cockpit to find

Arthur sitting in the copilot chair. *That's where Sarah sits,* she thought irrationally, but held her tongue. The screen in the center of the control panel flickered, making shadows over his round face. He was watching a video recording of the few minutes before the shuttle took off from the New Horizon.

"I didn't even know there was a camera on board," Waverly said.

"It turns on when the engines warm up, and records shuttle takeoffs and landings. In case there's an accident."

"Oh right."

"I can't see when the stowaway got on," Arthur said. "Could it have happened before you got to the shuttle bay?"

"Sarah brought the girls. I came last."

"Oh yeah, there you are." Arthur pointed at the screen, and Waverly saw an image of herself—a skinny, desperate girl limping through a crowd of benign-looking women. She was wild-eyed, her hair a nest of snarls, blood dripping down her arm. She moved like a wounded animal, pointing her gun at anyone who came near.

"God, Waverly," Arthur said, and looked at her, shocked. "I had no idea—"

"Don't." Waverly held up a hand, and quickly Arthur turned back to the video.

"There! What's that?" Arthur pointed at the cart of supplies being rolled toward the shuttle by a group of women. The Waverly on the video screen watched the women suspiciously and then slowly walked toward the shuttle, the muzzle of her gun pointed into the crowd.

It made her sick to see it. What had she become? Was she still frozen inside like that?

Was she still a killer?

"Do you think someone rode in on that cart?" Arthur asked her.

"No way," she said, jarred back to the present. "It was full of food, and that other cart? See there? That's full of water. There was no way a person could have fit."

They watched the screen a few minutes more as the women backed away from the shuttle when the engine's exhaust flared. The shuttle eased inside the air lock, then it moved out and pulled away from the New Horizon, which grew smaller and smaller until it disappeared into the black sky.

But the New Horizon is still out there, Waverly reminded herself. *It didn't disappear. And she's waiting for us. Because she has what we want, and that puts her on top again.*

"Wait," Arthur said. "I thought there was . . ." He ran the recording back, and they watched the image of the New Horizon shrinking away, until Arthur hit pause. "There!" He pointed at a dim, blurry dot floating in the frozen image, just above the New Horizon.

"What?"

"A OneMan. That's a OneMan!"

Waverly squinted at the screen, and Arthur hit play again. The dot drifted up from the New Horizon and sped toward the shuttle. Quickly, the OneMan sank out of view below the border of the screen, but it was unmistakable.

"He tethered to you. He reeled himself in. And then somehow he got on board and hid."

"How? When?"

"He must've used the small air lock in the cargo hold."

Arthur got up from his seat, beckoning to her over his shoulder, and the two of them went down to the cargo hold. At the aft side there was a man-size hatch with a tiny porthole in the door. Arthur and Waverly peered through the scratched glass to see the face mask of an empty OneMan peering back. "You guys didn't notice this here?"

At first Waverly was too stunned to speak, but she regained her voice to say, "I think I looked in there once, just to see what was inside. The OneMan was facing the other way, so I could only see the back of it." She shuddered. She'd looked right at the stowaway, hiding in that suit, and she hadn't seen him. "I thought it was standard to keep a OneMan in there."

Arthur nodded. "I would probably have thought the same thing."

"He might have even slept in there, spent his time in there."

"Logical. It would get claustrophobic, but if he kept the air valves open, he could have stayed there almost the whole time."

"Yes," Waverly said. "Oh God, Arthur!"

He put a hand on her shoulder and waited for her to look at him. "Waverly, *we* should have thought of it, too. We should have searched the shuttle, quarantined it. Hell, we should have jettisoned it."

She nodded. She could see why Kieran liked Arthur so much. He was kind.

The two walked down the shuttle ramp, and Arthur pressed the button to raise it up again. Waverly watched as the evidence of her frightening passage home disappeared behind the door.

"I have something I need to tell you," Arthur said as they crossed the empty shuttle bay. The OneMen hanging along the wall seemed to lean away from their hooks, heads bent, as though trying to eavesdrop. Waverly didn't like looking at them. It reminded her of how many people *weren't* on the ship. "You're going to get upset."

He had her attention now. "What? What are you talking about?"

"First I want your promise—that you won't do anything right away. You and I will think about what to do, and we'll come up with a plan, and we'll execute it. We're not going to let our emotions get the better of us, okay?"

"What happened? Did he capture Seth?" Suddenly the rest of Kieran's announcement came home to her. "There's no way Seth would work with the stowaway, Arthur! No way! Kieran was wrong to make that announcement."

The panic in her voice seemed to give Arthur pause, and he looked at her, his brow furrowed.

She bowed her head. Arthur might be kind, but he was loyal to Kieran. She must remember that.

The two walked through the doorway and into the corridor. Arthur closed the shuttle-bay door behind them. "Waverly, Sarah was mouthing off to Kieran earlier."

"Oh God."

"You need to understand, though. Sarah was really goading Kieran on, implying that she knew something about Seth's escape. She said she knew why our surveillance system isn't working, but she refused to tell us. So Kieran—"

"He threw her in the brig."

Arthur nodded.

Waverly shook her head. Her anger made her fingers tremble. Every heartbeat was painful. "God, Kieran."

"Here's the problem as I see it," Arthur said. "If Kieran was *really* Captain, he'd have every right to arrest her for insubordination."

"But he's not really Captain."

Arthur nodded.

"And you want to hold an election to give him that power?"

"It might help with the crew's attitude. If he were really Captain, Sarah might have been more cooperative."

"Or Kieran might have been even more of an uncontrollable bastard."

To this, Arthur said nothing.

"So what do you want to do about it?"

Arthur didn't pretend to think about it; he'd clearly already considered what he wanted Waverly to do. "I want you to talk Sarah into telling you what is wrong with the surveillance system, so then I can talk Kieran into letting Sarah go. That way they can both back down and still save face."

Waverly sighed heavily. "Have we all lost our minds?"

"Kids aren't meant to deal with this kind of stuff."

"Adults are no better," Waverly said ruefully, thinking of the way Captain Jones and Anne Mather had both seemed to have their adult crews hoodwinked completely.

"So you'll do it?"

Waverly nodded.

"And you won't run at Kieran?"

"I think it's best if we avoid each other for a while."

"I'm thinking tomorrow morning would be a good time to visit Sarah," Arthur said.

"No, I'm going now." She started toward the elevator, but Arthur stopped her with a hand on her shoulder. She turned to see him biting his lip anxiously.

"I just wanted you to know, it wasn't my idea for Kieran to phrase it that way. In the announcement."

"What way?"

"When he said the stowaway was on the shuttle piloted by Waverly Marshall."

She stared at Arthur as his meaning sank in. Of course. By mentioning Waverly in the same sentence as the stowaway, Kieran was pinning responsibility for the stowaway's presence on her. "I hadn't thought of that."

"It was kind of a dirty trick, I thought," Arthur said, embarrassed.

"Yeah." Her voice sounded disaffected and cold.

"He's under a lot of pressure . . ." Arthur began.

"Don't even tell me," Waverly said, shaking her head, and strode off to the starboard elevator bank, leaving Arthur behind. When the doors opened, she marched in and punched at the control panel. It was a long ride down to the brig, and the more she thought about everything Kieran had done, the angrier she got.

The elevator opened to the deepest level of the ship, and Waverly headed toward the brig. The noise of the engines was especially loud down here, and she wondered how Seth had been able to stand it night after night. But then, she supposed, you could get used to just about anything if you had to.

She heard voices when she turned onto the corridor to the brig. Boys' voices, mostly, and then a shriek that sounded like Sarah.

Waverly broke into a run, all Arthur's admonitions forgotten. When she got to the brig, she stopped to listen for Sarah. There were over a dozen cells here in a long line of steel bars that stretched ahead on either side of her. She heard voices on her left and took off running. In the third cell down she found Kieran standing over Sarah, who was sitting on the metal cot in the middle of the cell, surrounded by boys, looking enraged.

"Sarah, I've got a ship full of kids to protect, and I don't have time to play games with you."

"I'll tell you if you let me out of here!" Sarah growled through her teeth.

Kieran reared back, hand raised, shaking from anger. He looked like he wanted to slap her.

"Stop it!" Waverly screamed. She barreled past two guards who were standing in the doorway. "What are you *doing*?"

Kieran looked at her as though replaying the scene in his mind and considering how it would look. But he recovered quickly. "Get out of here, Waverly."

"No! I won't let you do this!" Her voice sounded hoarse and panicked.

Kieran grabbed Waverly by the elbow, but she jerked away from him. "You're a monster! I don't know you!"

"Waverly," Kieran said softly, and dragged her out of Sarah's cell by the arm. She pulled against him, but his grip tightened painfully and he jerked her out of the brig, her feet skidding as she tried to claw at him with her free hand until he caught her wrist. Once they were in the corridor he backed her into a corner and pressed against her with his weight, his eyes on hers. His face was swollen with the edema caused by the increased gravity, and she could see the tiny capillaries under the surface of his skin. Once he'd been so handsome, but now he looked hideous to her.

"Waverly," he said softly. "I wasn't going to hurt her. I was just angry."

"Yeah, right!" she spat.

"It's true. Come on, you know me. I'm not a bully."

"You *weren't* a bully before you made yourself Captain."

"Look." He shoved a finger in her face. "I've got a terrorist on this ship killing my crew. I don't have time for Sarah's stubbornness. She knows what's wrong with our surveillance system, and she won't say what it is."

"The more you treat her this way, the less she'll want to help you!"

"What do you suggest?"

"Reason with her, for God's sake!"

"You want to try it?" he said. It sounded like a rhetorical question, but he raised his eyebrows hopefully.

"You'll let her out if she cooperates?"

"Of course."

"I'll try," Waverly said coldly. "If I have your promise you won't threaten anyone on this ship again, no matter what."

She jerked away from him and marched back into the brig. The two guards, Harvey Markem and Vince Petrelli, looked over her shoulder at Kieran. Harvey wore a filthy bandage over his forehead, but otherwise he seemed as sturdy as he always had. Vince was just as big as Harvey, but their faces were still those of young boys. They must have received a nonverbal signal from Kieran, because they stepped aside for Waverly, and she went into Sarah's cell.

The girl looked shaken but strong. She stared at Kieran with pure hatred, but when Waverly knelt in front of her, she softened.

"Sarah, if you know how to fix the surveillance system, you have to tell them."

"Why?" the girl spat.

"You *know* why. Because there's a stowaway from the New Horizon on board, and we need to find him."

"There's a *stowaway*?" The girl's eyes grew so wide her irises were ringed by a circle of white.

Waverly turned to Kieran. "You didn't *tell* her?"

"I made the announcement an hour ago," Kieran said, confused.

"Well, I didn't hear it," Sarah said. "Because you didn't turn the speakers on in the brig! Idiot!"

Kieran bristled, but Waverly held up a hand in warning. The best thing for Sarah right now was to keep Kieran from losing his temper.

"Sarah," Waverly said. "If you have some insight—"

"I'll tell you what you need to know," Sarah said, but not to Waverly. She was looking at Kieran, her eyes like marble. "If you let me out of here."

"I'll let you out of here," Kieran said, "*after* you tell me."

Sarah turned to Waverly again and sighed. "Can you untie my hands?"

Waverly walked around the girl and saw that her

hands were bluish red, the cord pulled so tightly that her fingers had contorted into claws. Waverly shook her head, even angrier, but said nothing as she picked apart the knot, pulling on it until it loosened and Sarah could lift her hands to rub the raw skin.

"They reprogrammed the software controlling the motion detectors," Sarah said with a sneer.

"That's not it," Kieran said. "We checked the code. It's untouched."

"It would be easy to miss. All they did was reverse the software commands. Now the cameras *stop* recording when there's motion, and *start* recording when there isn't any. The opposite of what they're supposed to do. They probably just had to change around a few characters. Check it again. That's got to be it."

Waverly could see Kieran felt foolish. This was so simple, he should have been able to figure it out immediately. He certainly shouldn't have needed to threaten someone.

"Now I'm going home," Sarah said, and stood up from the cot.

Kieran shook his head. "When I say you can."

"What!" Waverly shrieked.

"You still need to spend some time in the brig for the way you delayed the investigation," Kieran said to Sarah.

The girl shook her head, her mouth set in a grim line across her hard face. "Kieran Alden, you're nothing but a liar."

"I didn't lie. I said I'd let you out of here. Just not right away."

Waverly was frozen with rage. She thought if she allowed her body to move, she would scratch Kieran's face. Instead she sat next to Sarah and stared at this boy she'd loved for so long, the boy she'd thought she would marry. Now she despised him.

"Let's go," Kieran said, and motioned to the guards to follow him out of the brig. He turned to look back at Waverly, who remained in the cell, still staring, unbelieving.

"Waverly," he said. "Let's go."

She shook her head. "As long as Sarah stays in here, I'm staying, too."

"I can have you removed by force."

"If you want to prove me right about you." Though anger was churning inside, her voice was steady and low. "You're just like Anne Mather. You've turned into a petty little version of her, and you're only going to get worse until you see the light."

"Fine," Kieran said. He nodded at Harvey, who briskly stepped forward and locked the cage. Sarah took Waverly's hand, and the two girls sat close.

"Three square meals," Kieran said to the guards, and left the brig.

Unofficial Investigation

Seth sat on the floor of the conifer bay, dismantling pine-cones, munching on the nuts that were nestled between the spines. He felt like a damn squirrel, but he knew he needed protein more than anything, and at least the nuts provided that.

He kept going over that announcement again and again. Kieran had sunk lower than he'd thought possible, saying Seth was working with the stowaway. He'd known Kieran might try something like this, but it still stung to know the entire shipful of people now suspected him of treason. "Well played, Kieran," Seth muttered.

He picked up another pinecone and pulled off the dry spines, picking at the small nuts. The only way Seth could redeem himself now would be to catch the bastard himself. As he nibbled on one of the small, sweet nuts, he tried to think like a saboteur. What would be his next move?

It seemed likely he'd try to hobble the ship, but without access to the engine room, that would be difficult. He might use a OneMan to disable the engines from the outside, but that would be impossible to do without some kind of explosive device. If the saboteur had been a stowaway on Waverly's shuttle from the New Horizon, it was doubtful that he'd been able to bring along any weapons. That meant he'd have to make a bomb from scratch.

Where would he find the materials for an explosive?

Seth leaned back, letting the carpet of pine needles crackle against him. He didn't know anything about making a bomb. The only thing he could think of was to check the labs, where there were all kinds of chemicals.

He brushed himself off and jogged out of the conifer bay, welcoming the warm air that enveloped him in the corridor. He went to the outer stairwell and opened the door to go through, and was shocked to hear voices a few levels above him. Quickly he backed out of the stairwell and crouched just outside the door to listen.

As the voices got closer, he could hear two boys talking boisterously about what they'd do to the "terrorist" if they ever caught him. Their footsteps came louder and louder, until they were just on the other side of the door.

Then they stopped.

"Do you smell that?" This sounded like Troy Halderson, a strapping thirteen-year-old.

"Smell what?"

"Like the world's worst BO."

"Dude, I was going to say something, but—"

"I showered this morning."

"Well, you smell like a chicken coop."

They rounded the bend in the stairwell and went down to the next level. Seth smelled his own shirt and made a face. He couldn't stay hidden for long smelling like this. Fortunately there were showers at the back of the labs in case of chemical spills. They'd be no-frills but they'd work.

Seth waited until the voices of the sentries faded away. Without making a sound, he inched open the door and slipped into the stairwell. He slinked up the metal staircase quickly, hugging the wall, and crept to the chemistry lab. He kept his eyes and ears open, but the entire level seemed to be completely empty.

He slipped inside the lab and locked the door behind him.

He was shocked by the first thing he saw—a counter heaped with dozens of empty boxes. The surface was covered with tracings of a white powder that Seth didn't recognize, along with empty liquid-nitrogen cartridges. Seth looked in the sink, where he found several empty beakers, the insides coated with a corrosive brown muck. He sniffed at them and coughed.

This stuff might have been left by the saboteur! He had to get a message to Kieran, but he couldn't without his father's portable com station, which he'd left in the conifer bay. And he still needed that shower. A very quick one.

He jogged for the shower stalls at the back of the room. God love scientists, there was even shampoo. Seth wanted to lose himself in the feeling of the hot water on his skin, but he made himself count off the seconds until he reached one hundred, scrubbing furiously, and then he turned off the water.

Seth dried himself off with a lab coat, then riffled through the lockers until he found a clean shirt and pair of pants hanging from a hook. He almost ran out of the room, but on second thought, he went back and gathered up all the clothes from the lockers. He even found a hand-knit sweater. It was too small, but it would help keep him warm in those frigid stairwells and in the conifer bay. With the small pile of clothes tucked under his arm, he walked toward the door, his mind on his message to Kieran.

"Dear Saint Kieran, deliver us from evil," he muttered under his breath, and chuckled.

He was reaching for the doorknob when he was hit from behind.

His head slapped the metal door in front of him. For a second he forgot how to breathe, but he kept his feet and turned to face his attacker. He only saw a metal chair swinging toward his head. He ducked, but not in time, and a sharp edge of the chair cut his scalp.

He blinked, thinking at first he'd gone blind. His eyes were flooded with sticky, hot blood. He wiped it away with his right hand while reaching for his attacker with his left. Seth felt wiry hair and grabbed on to it, swung around with all his strength, and slammed his attacker's head into the wall, then again.

Trying to see through the blood in his eyes was like looking through a reddish film. He saw a hulking shape buckle and roll forward, then he felt the full force of a shoulder ramming into his gut.

His wind exploded out of him and he fell onto the floor, kicking blindly, struggling to recover his breath.

Helpless on the floor, Seth rolled to his side and covered his head with his arms. Savage blows crushed him. A hard boot sole crashed into his rib cage once, twice, sending shards of pain deep into his chest. The light in the room faded.

The light in Seth faded.

He blacked out.

When he came to, Seth expected to find himself in the conifer bay. But instead of pine needles there were metal countertops above him, fluorescent lights blurring in and out of focus. He had no idea how he'd gotten here.

"What happened," he whispered.

No one answered.

He was lying on a stone cold floor. He forced his eyes open. He was hurt, hurt so badly. Slowly he unwound himself, checking his legs, his joints, his arms—all intact. He sat up.

A stabbing pain seared through his chest.

Oh, it *hurt*!

Couldn't breathe. Fractured rib. Maybe two.

He forced himself to take small even breaths, then pulled himself to his feet, swaying, and looked around. He was in one of the labs, and he was wearing strange clothes. He limped to a mirror. His face looked like a Halloween mask. He had a bruise under his right eye, and streaks of blood covered his face. He turned on the overhead light and poked through his hair at the cut on his scalp. Four inches, and deep, oozing blood. He'd need stitches.

The last thing he remembered was eating pine nuts, thinking about how to get close to the stowaway . . .

I guess I found him, Seth thought grimly. *No way*

Kieran or his cronies would have done this to me. If they'd been the ones, I'd be in the brig right now.

He peeled off his bloody shirt, one he didn't recognize, and turned, wincing against the pain in his ribs. His entire right side was a pattern of bluish bruises. As bad as he looked now, he knew he'd look ten times worse in the morning.

He needed help.

He limped to the door and listened, then slipped out and struggled down the corridor toward the port side—a long walk. This level was little used, but he was still lucky not to happen upon anyone. Once he was inside the stairwell he paused, trying to breathe, hoping he didn't have a punctured lung. He'd gotten beat up plenty, but now he understood all those times his father had said, "I'm only giving you forty percent, son."

"I love you, too, Dad," Seth muttered, then remembered where he was, and paused to listen. He thought he heard footsteps below him, but they were far away, near the rain forest level or maybe lower.

Seth held tightly to the handrail and slid down the stairwell, letting the wall hold some of his weight. His thigh ached where he'd been hit, but his leg still felt strong enough to get him there, if he didn't pass out from his horrible, pounding headache.

He took it slow, until he reached the level where the living quarters were, then he listened at the door.

What if she doesn't help me? he thought, holding a hand against his side. *She will. When she sees me, she'll let me stay.*

The corridor on the living level was quiet, but someone might come any second. He had to be fast. Struggling against the pain, he forced himself to walk quickly though his ribs screamed. The pain was bad enough to turn his vision red, or was that the blood in his eyes? He didn't know. If he didn't lie down soon he'd pass out.

He mustn't be seen entering her place, so he headed for the maintenance closet down the hall from her quarters. He glanced around the hallway, looking for surveillance cameras here, but like on the level where his quarters were, there was no camera pointed at the maintenance closet. Once inside, he found a putty knife in a dirty bucket and pried away the back wall. He stuck his head into the passageway. It looked identical to the narrow space behind his father's apartment. Squeezing into it, agonized, sweat pouring over his face in rivulets, he sidled along, counting pipes until he was almost certain he'd found Waverly's quarters. He pried away the back wall and fell into a closet that smelled of sandalwood, then fought his way through the hanging clothes and into a dark room.

He listened. The apartment sounded empty. He'd never been invited into Waverly's quarters, not since a birthday party when they were five. What if he was in someone else's place?

"Waverly?" he asked timidly. He even *sounded* injured, his voice thready and weak, pinched with pain. When no answer came, he said more loudly, "Waverly?"

He crossed the hall to the other bedroom and turned on the light. There was a huge Raggedy Ann doll in a chair in the corner, and over the twin bed a picture of a woman standing in a field of flowers, a parasol over her shadowed face. A black sweater lay draped over the back of a chair, and Seth picked it up to smell it. Waverly. This was definitely her quarters.

He stood in the darkness, catching his breath. His heart pounded against his cracked ribs, feeling as though it were chipping away at the bones, displacing jagged shards one beat at a time. He wanted to lie down so badly.

But no. He couldn't. Not before he stitched that cut closed.

He hobbled into the bathroom and looked in the mirror. The gash in his scalp yawned apart like an open mouth nestled in his hair, bloody edges thick and floppy. Butterfly bandages wouldn't do it. If he didn't force it closed, it would certainly get infected.

He knew he should wait for Waverly, let her do it. But he couldn't bear the thought of letting another person anywhere near the savage cut. Not even her.

For once, Seth let himself cry as he limped into the living room to Waverly's sewing table. He chose what looked to be strong black thread and the thinnest needle he could find.

"Four stitches, that's nothing," he told himself with a shaking voice. "One, two, three, four, done." He found an antibiotic solution under the sink in the bathroom, and cotton swabs and a patch of gauze that he could tie over the cut.

Back in the bathroom, he looked at his reflection, trying to measure the boy in the mirror: *Are you strong enough to do this?* His blood had congealed into grooves in his forehead and along the natural folds of skin around his mouth. He thought this must be what he would look like as an old man, and he stared. Maybe he'd already become an old man. Maybe all this had made him old.

He shook his head. "Don't go crazy yet, Ardvale."

First he trimmed the hair away from the edges of the

cut with a pair of scissors, as close to the skin as possible. He'd have a bald patch, but that didn't matter. Next he dabbed at the cut with the antibiotic. It stung all the way through his core, and he nearly passed out. He wished for something gentler, but he knew the only place to find that was at the infirmary. So he had to endure the deep, physical hurt of the solution in the underlayers of his skin until he was sure that the cut was clean. Even if it wasn't, he couldn't take the pain anymore.

"I can do this," he said as he held a flame to the needle, then threaded it. "I'm a tough son of a bitch," he said as he pinched the end of the cut closed. "This is nothing. People have gone through much worse."

Still, he held the needle in position for a long time, just staring at it, knowing that the longer he put it off the worse it would be. He had to just get this over with so he could go to sleep. But the simple act of piercing his own flesh wasn't, in fact, simple. He had to overcome every instinct in his body forbidding self-injury. And the fear of the pain. How bad it would be. How horribly it would hurt.

"Doesn't matter," he told himself in the mirror. "You don't want to die from a little cut, right?"

He jabbed the needle through the skin on his scalp, and screamed. He couldn't help himself. The pain was excruciating, but he forced himself to pierce the other side of the cut, the needle entering the raw bloody skin underneath. Tears streamed down his face and plopped into the sink in red rivulets. But with shaking fingers he managed to tie off the first suture as tightly as he could stand.

Then he threw up. He hadn't even noticed feeling sick. The spasm took him by surprise, wrenching his ribs, grinding the bones against one another. He cried out, holding his side, his forehead on cold porcelain. He didn't remember falling to his knees, but somehow there he was, on the floor, sweat pouring over his face.

How was he supposed to do another one?

It took him much longer to build up the courage for the second stitch, but when the needle finally pierced his skin, it didn't hurt as much. Somehow his body had numbed the cut, and he thanked God for that. Each successive stitch hurt less than the last, but he was shaking uncontrollably, and his breath came in jagged, rasping heaves.

The cut needed six stitches after all. They were uneven, jagged, very ugly. But the wound was closed. Seth forced himself to dab at it again with an ointment-soaked cotton ball, then he tied a piece of gauze over the cut and down under his chin. He'd look ridiculous when Waverly got home, but that couldn't be helped.

Seth bent down and drank from the bathroom tap, deep gushes of water flowing into his mouth. Then he rooted through the medicine cabinet until he found aspirin. He chewed on four tablets at once, knowing how little it would do for his pain.

He needed sleep. His legs shook under him, and his torso felt soft and wobbly. He had to lie down right now.

He crossed the hallway to a dark room, not even sure where he was going, and saw in front of him a messy bed. He groaned and hobbled forward until his knees touched the mattress, then he fell, trying to protect his ribs with his arm. The cool sheets enveloped him, and he descended into a fitful sleep.

The Shepherd

"Thank you all for coming," Kieran said to his congregation. This was the first service since he made the rule requiring attendance, and he was pleased with the results. Almost the entire crew had come. Arthur was in the back row, quietly taking down names to find out who wasn't here, though he'd balked at the duty. Kieran looked at the faces in the crowd, trying to gauge how many he'd have to win over. Almost all of the older girls were staring at him with open contempt, angry about Sarah and Waverly's incarceration. They must have heard about it from one of the guards. Even some of the boys looked at Kieran distrustfully, but he still had allies. And the front rows were full of his core supporters, the kids who would stand by him no matter what. He hoped that number would increase with this sermon. His life might depend on it.

He shut out the memory of that sham trial that Seth had arranged. Kieran had been half conscious, starved, weak, and sick, and he'd listened to false charges against him enumerated by boys he'd once called his friends. He remembered the coldness in some of their eyes, the way they leaned forward in their seats when Seth mentioned execution. He'd been a slab of meat to them, a bit of trash to be thrown out an air lock. Seth had convinced them of this once, and it could happen again, unless Kieran consolidated support for himself by whatever means necessary.

"By now you've heard that Sarah Hodges and Waverly Marshall are being held in the brig. I bet some of you are pretty mad about that. Well, I'm mad about it, too. I want to make it clear that they were not arrested to settle a personal score. They were put there for obstructing an investigation into a series of incidents on this ship that gravely endanger us all. No single crew member will ever be allowed to endanger us or our mission. You have my word on that."

He looked at the faces again. Many looked at him with distrust, but they were listening. They hadn't shut him out. That was as good as he could hope for. He could see from the nodding and thoughtful expressions that he had almost full support among the boys. He bowed his head.

"I didn't ask to be forced into a position of command at so young an age. I would have liked a lot more years to learn how to run this ship. But we don't have the luxury of time. Right now our parents are in the hands of our enemy, and who knows what they suffer? My number-one priority is getting them back, and protecting all of you while we do it. I know I've made plenty of mistakes, but haven't we all? We've had more combine breakdowns in the past six months than we had in the previous five years. That's because our maintenance crews and our drivers are all making mistakes. Well, I make mistakes, too. And I'm sorry for every single one of them."

Now even more faces in the crowd had softened as people remembered their own mistakes along the way. Not so many scowls.

"This brings me to Seth Ardvale. He escaped on the same night as the thruster misfire, which makes him a person of interest. He may even lead us to the terrorist, but only if we can find him. Already the terrorist has killed one of us and tampered with the ship's navigation system. I implore you, for the safety of everyone in this room, if you know anything about Seth's whereabouts, please come forward."

Kieran looked around. Now his congregation wasn't thinking so much about Sarah and Waverly, not with a dangerous terrorist on the loose. (He had chosen that word deliberately.) Already most of the older girls seemed more afraid than angry, and all their eyes were on him.

"A confrontation is coming. We need to stand together against our enemies. Until now, I'm not sure we *have* been standing together. I hear about a lot of complaints, misgivings, people questioning rather than trusting." Kieran slammed his fist into his palm. "This cannot go on! If we don't present a united front to our enemies, we can't prevail. They're older, they're more experienced, and they outnumber us. When we finally catch up to them and demand the release of our families, if they sense any discord on this ship, any doubt or bickering, they'll use it to their advantage. But if we present a united front, sure in the justice of our cause, I promise you we *will* prevail. Not only because we're younger, we're stronger, and we're smarter; we'll prevail because we stand on the side of the good and the just, and they stand on the side of evil. And all through history, if you look, good always triumphs over evil."

He could see their eyes lowering as they thought about what they knew of Earth's history, and then they raised their eyes to him again. He had them. They believed in him. How could they not? The truth was naturally persuasive. It spoke to their souls, massaged away their misgivings, defused their anger, negated strife. If ever he doubted he was doing God's will, today was proof that he was doing what he was supposed to do, what his creator *wanted* him to do. He was meant to lead this ship into the future. He knew it.

"Will you join me? Let's set aside our differences and unite in a common purpose. Let's make a covenant, right here, right now. We are a single people, united!" He raised his fists over his head and lifted his face to the lights above. "And we'll never let them tear us apart!"

His voice echoed over the room, and his congregation answered with a burst of cheers. His core believers raised their fists, pumping them in the air, chanting, "Kyrie Eleison!" It was slow at first, but little by little, the other kids joined in, too, chanting this benediction and cheering. He felt the thunder of their voices in the drum of his chest, and he smiled down at them. God was on his side, after all. How could he fail?

He was safe once more.

Dissident

Waverly stood when Arthur came to release her and Sarah from the brig the next day. He looked ashamed as he flung the metal bars aside. "You're free to go," he mumbled, his eyes trained on the floor.

Sarah bolted out without even looking at him, but Waverly lingered.

"Do you know what I found him doing to her?" Waverly said, her voice at full boil. "He was threatening her—"

"I heard," Arthur said quietly.

"He's out of control!" Waverly yelled.

Arthur held up a hand. "He didn't hurt her."

"That doesn't justify ..." she began, but was too furious to finish.

Arthur pressed his lips together and glanced nervously at Matt Allbright, who stood in the hallway with hands clasped behind his back, obviously listening. Arthur beckoned Waverly to follow him out of the brig, and the two started off down the corridor toward the elevators. Once they were out of Matt's earshot, Arthur grasped Waverly's arm and spoke softly into her ear. "I agree Kieran was out of line, but Sarah was, too."

"She acted like an idiot," Waverly admitted. "But we can't threaten people! Or throw them in jail without a trial!"

"I agree." Arthur spoke out of the side of his mouth. "Did you hear Kieran's sermon yesterday?"

"I couldn't *help* hearing. He had it blaring in our cell."

"Then you know he has basically painted you and Sarah as collaborators with the terrorist."

From Arthur's neutral expression, Waverly couldn't tell if he was threatening her or trying to warn her. "We can't let this go on, Arthur."

"We're all doing the best we can," Arthur said, sounding exhausted. He pressed the call button for the elevator as he licked at the sweaty fuzz on his upper lip. "I know you're mad at Kieran. I am, too. But let's be careful."

"As in 'Please don't incite mutiny'?" Waverly said as the elevator doors opened and the two stepped onto it. She noticed Arthur watch as she pressed the key for the habitation level. Was he sent here to see where she went? "Kieran keeps too many secrets. A Central Council would help with that."

"Do you want to be on it?" Arthur asked, his face impassive.

"No. But I'm going to be."

Arthur tilted his head. "You know what his supporters will say about you, don't you?"

"That I support terrorists?"

"Yes." Arthur's face darkened. "And that you're the one who was supposed to rescue the parents, and you failed."

Waverly felt as though she'd been punched in the gut, but maybe Arthur was right. Maybe she couldn't get elected at all.

"Look," Arthur said, appealing to her through his eyeglasses, with magnified blue eyes. "It's not like I haven't thought about an election."

The elevator doors opened, but Waverly stayed put, looking at Arthur with sadness. After their talk in the shuttle, she'd thought she had an ally, someone who was her equal. Now she wasn't sure what to think about him.

"Good-bye, Arthur," Waverly said as she stepped off the elevator. Arthur seemed to want to say more, but only nodded as the doors closed between them.

She walked down the corridor deep in thought. When she reached her door, she punched in her lock code without looking at her fingers and walked into the living room.

Immediately, she knew something wasn't right. In the dark room there was an earthy smell that didn't belong. Someone was here. She picked up the cricket bat that she kept by the door and cautiously turned on the light. She blinked her eyes, unable to believe what they were showing her: a man lying on her couch. A man whose face was a mass of bloody bruises and swollen features, leaning up on his elbow. She tried to find a scream inside of her, but she was paralyzed.

He opened his mouth and spoke: "I'll leave if you want me to."

"Seth," she whispered, dropping the bat. "Seth, oh my God."

"I needed someplace safe."

She locked the door behind her and ran to him, knelt on the floor, put her hand to his swollen forehead. A sloppy bandage, blood-soaked, covered the top of his scalp. "What *happened* to you?"

"I think I met our stowaway," he slurred. His lower lip was split and swollen like a purple balloon. "Nice guy."

Seth told her that he'd woken up in the lab and had come here for help. He didn't remember much about the attack itself. She could see just talking was a strain for him; he was in a great deal of pain.

"You have to get to the infirmary."

"No, please." He reached for her hand, closed his fingers around hers, squeezed. "I can't go back to the brig."

His face was so swollen he was barely recognizable, but when Waverly brushed her fingers against his cheek, his skin felt cool.

"I don't think you're running a fever. No infection, anyway."

"Do you have any pain meds?"

"I think so," Waverly said, and went into the bathroom to look. She found a bottle of strong medication that her mother had used for her migraines, and a pang went through her. *What if Mom gets a migraine on that ship?* She blinked back tears and went back to the living room.

"Here," she said, and meted out three pills to him,

which he swallowed all in one go. "Your face looks like hamburger," she said.

"We can't all be beauty queens," he said without skipping a beat. Despite his injuries, he seemed happy to see her.

She hid a smile and went to the kitchen to fill a small basin with warm soapy water, then sat on the coffee table next to him and, with a damp washcloth, began wiping the blood off his face to reveal a gray, peaked complexion.

"How did you get out of the brig?"

"The stowaway let me out, I'm pretty sure."

"What?" She was so surprised she dropped the washcloth, and it landed on his chest. "Why?"

"I think I was his decoy."

"Kieran thinks I let you out."

"That making trouble between you two?"

She shrugged. "We broke up awhile ago."

"I'm sorry," he said sincerely. "If I had anywhere else to go . . ."

She tried to read his expression, looking for any evidence that he was glad she and Kieran had split. She found none. His face was consumed with pain. "Can you sit up enough to undress?"

"Time for my sponge bath?" He managed a smirk.

"You're lucky I don't throw you out with the trash," she said, but she held the washcloth, waiting.

He sat up, groaning, and wriggled out of his shirt, which was caked with blood. She gasped. His chest was mottled with ugly bruises and abrasions. "What did he *do* to you?"

"Gave me a bear hug," he said with a groan.

Quickly and efficiently, Waverly passed the soapy cloth over his shoulders, down his back, across his abdomen, and along the ridges of his ribs, taking special care around an evil black bruise at his side. She knew he was looking at her as she worked, but she wouldn't meet his eyes. She couldn't. She was too aware of how quickly she was breathing. It was perfectly natural to be helping him, and yet she felt awkward. She heard him breathing, too, could see the rise and fall of his rib cage. His scent was sharp but pleasant, like pinesap, and she caught herself taking it in as she scrubbed his torso clean.

"And now for the lower half," he said straight-faced.

She only handed him the washcloth. "I'm going to see if I've got anything that will fit you."

She went to her mother's room and turned on the light, then cried out in dismay when she saw the bloody sheets. "What did you *do*?"

"I'm sorry," Seth said, sounding mortified. "I didn't know what room I was in. I came in here when I realized."

"That's my *mom's* bed."

Bottom lip quivering, Waverly walked past the soiled bed and went to the closet, where she found a pair of her mother's sweatpants and an old shirt of her father's that Regina had kept. Waverly went back into the living room and handed the clothes to Seth. He stood shakily to dress but collapsed on the sofa again with a whimper.

"You're really hurt," Waverly said.

"I am aware."

She resisted the urge to brush his hair out of his eyes, and instead sat in the armchair with her hands in her lap. "What does the terrorist look like?"

"All I saw was the blood in my eyes." He lay back, his eyes on the ceiling. "I woke up in the chemistry lab. I went there for a shower, I think."

"What would he be doing in the chem lab?"

Seth sat up suddenly, winced, and collapsed back onto the couch. "I can't believe I forgot," he said breathlessly.

"Forgot what?"

"I found a mess in the lab. I think he was making something." He hit the couch cushions with a fist. "How did I *forget* that?"

"Making what?" Waverly asked.

His eyes snapped to hers. The two looked at each other for a long moment.

"Better tell Kieran," Seth finally said, resigned.

"Okay," she said, doubtfully. "What do I say?"

"You're a smart girl," Seth said, eyes closed. "Lie."

Waverly walked out of the apartment and down the corridor, rehearsing under her breath. When she reached the corridor for Central Command, she passed a group of preteen girls, led by Marjorie Wilkins. As Waverly passed by, Marjorie took a bracelet from a small basket she wore over her arm. "Do you want to show your support for Kieran by wearing one of our bracelets?" the girl said. There was no smile behind the offer. The rest all turned to see what Waverly would say.

Waverly felt the girls' challenge and was annoyed. "No, thanks."

"Because you're a collaborator?" one of the girls shot back. She had thin red lips that stretched across her face like a slash.

"Collaborator with who?" Waverly said, arms crossed.

"Seth Ardvale," Marjorie said, squinting meanly.

"Everyone knows you're helping him."

Waverly felt the air go out of her, but she made her face blank. *There's no way they could know,* she told herself. "That's ridiculous."

"Everyone knows you went behind Kieran's back to visit Seth in the brig."

"That's nobody's business but my own," Waverly said. She tried to pass them, but one of Marjorie's friends, a stubby little pip-squeak named Melanie, blocked her way. With a crooked grin, she shifted her gaze meaningfully to the wall to Waverly's right.

Waverly saw her name written there with an arrow pointed toward a picture, and though she knew she shouldn't give them the satisfaction, she took it in. It showed a stick figure with long flowing hair on her knees in front of another stick figure with a large erection. Underneath was the caption *Traitor plus traitor equals true love.*

"Who drew that?" Waverly demanded.

Marjorie only shrugged her shoulders. "It was there when we got here."

Waverly looked at each of them in turn. They stared back with insolent smirks on their faces. Waverly felt hunted, transparent. *They're just kids,* she told herself. But how many of the crew thought this way about her?

She shouldered her way through them and marched to Central Command to ring the buzzer. The door slid open for her almost immediately, and she looked back at Marjorie, who was obviously jealous that Waverly could walk right in.

Inside, Kieran stood up from the Captain's chair and

looked at her as if watching for sudden moves. Arthur visibly stiffened.

"I won't take up much of your time," Waverly said to Kieran coolly.

Kieran indicated a chair. "Have a seat."

Waverly sat down in one of the chairs near Kieran. "I was in the chemistry lab yesterday, and I saw something that seemed out of place. It's been bugging me ever since, so I thought you should know."

"Okay . . ." Kieran said slowly. He wove his fingers together and waited for her to go on.

She realized she had no idea what Seth had seen exactly. "I think it's better if I show you."

Kieran regarded her for a moment, then stood. "Let's go."

"Maybe we should bring some guards," she said shakily.

Kieran went to the cabinet in the corner of the room and took out a can of mace. "We'll be fine," he said.

She wanted to insist on more protection, but she knew it would look odd if she did.

It felt strange to be walking down a corridor with Kieran like in the old days. He pressed the button for the elevator, casting glances toward Waverly. She pretended not to see, tried not to show her fear.

The lab level was dark, and Kieran went to a control panel and turned on the lights, then the two of them padded down the corridor. Waverly was afraid to breathe too loudly. When they reached the door to the lab, Kieran walked confidently in.

The lab looked as immaculate as ever. Every surface gleamed bright stainless steel. The sink was spotless and dry, as though it hadn't been used in weeks. All the trash cans were empty. Waverly looked around the room desperately for some sign of what Seth had been talking about. But there was nothing.

"What did you see?" Kieran asked, his eyes on her face, his voice quiet.

"I— It looked like a science experiment," Waverly fumbled. "Beakers and test tubes . . ."

Kieran looked around the spotless lab. "Where?"

"On the counter." She could feel her face redden and pretended not to notice that Kieran was studying her.

"Where on the counter?"

She pointed to a random spot by the sink, and Kieran walked over to it. "When did you see this?"

"I don't know. Yesterday morning," she said, kicking herself. How stupid could she be? Each of her lies was more obvious than the last.

He walked back to stand next to her by the entrance, his eyes on her face. "Are you in contact with Seth Ardvale?"

Her throat closed, and she stared at him, her mind racing. "Really, Kieran?" she said, feigning anger to cover her fear. "That's where your mind goes?"

"This morning we found a video record of him leaving this room yesterday, looking pretty beat up. When we came down here, this lab was clean. How else would you know about it if he didn't tell you?"

"Well, I haven't seen him," she said, and stared at Kieran, defying him to contradict her. She watched his face, waiting for some sign that he knew Seth was in her apartment, but when Kieran dropped his eyes, she knew he'd only been guessing.

"All I need to do to find out if you're lying is check the video log."

She kicked herself for not thinking of that, but it couldn't be helped. The best thing was to change the topic. "Why are you pretending Seth is working with the terrorist?"

Kieran's mouth tightened. "It's the most logical explanation right now."

"Seth would never work with anyone from the New Horizon, and you know it."

"He's capable of anything, Waverly," Kieran said quietly and very condescendingly. But he was lying. From his guilty manner, she could see he didn't really believe it.

"He's not a traitor," she spat.

"He turned on his Captain," Kieran said, voice raised.

"You're not the Captain!" she yelled. The metal walls around her rang with her voice. "You've never been elected!"

"You agreed to support me!" he shouted with a finger in her face. "Now you're just being irresponsible. If the leaders of our vessel seem to be quarreling, that's bad for morale."

"Without an election, Kieran, there *are* no leaders."

Kieran's lips flitted together and apart, the way they did whenever he was nervous. "There hasn't been an election on this ship for decades," he said breathily. "And with a terrorist running around—"

"You're using the terrorist to gain political points, Kieran. And that's just . . . just . . ." She felt tears welling in her eyes, but she furiously squinted them away. "I mean how can you say Sarah and I—"

"She helped them *hide*! By defying me she gave Seth and the terrorist time to—"

"She didn't know about the terrorist!"

"She knew about Seth. Everyone did."

"And you're using him as a scapegoat." She sliced the air with the flat of her hand. "You're turning the whole crew against him."

"Keeping the crew united against a common enemy is one way to protect them. If you were in charge, you'd see—"

"That's just the thing, Kieran. You're the only one who thinks you're in charge."

"You want to try it? See how easy it is?"

"I intend to."

She left him looking blank-faced and small.

As she walked down the corridor to the elevator, she didn't see the tiny boy watching her through the glass of the stairwell doorway. She didn't see him slip into the corridor as she stepped onto the elevator, and so she didn't know that she was followed back to her quarters, and as she closed the door, the small shape slipped into the apartment across the way.

The Girl

Seth understood his stay with Waverly would be ending, even before Waverly returned and told him that Kieran had guessed he'd contacted her, and that he couldn't stay beyond tonight. He also understood that there wouldn't be anything between them, but he couldn't deny his giddy happiness at being handed a bowl of hot chicken soup and a crusty roll by the beautiful Waverly Marshall.

"I don't like kicking you out," she said, her large brown eyes trailing over the bruises and scrapes on his face.

"The pain meds were really what I needed," he said, sitting up. It was amazing how much better he felt already. "One more night on your couch, and I'll be fine."

Their eyes met, and for a long moment, Seth wondered

what she was thinking. There was no seeing past her stony gaze.

"How about I drop off food for you. Would that help?" she asked as she dipped a crust of bread into her soup.

"Sounds too risky," Seth said.

"It's not like I could get in worse trouble with Kieran, or the rest of the crew for that matter."

"The rest of the crew? What for?"

She paused, her head down, gaze remote, as if the topic were too painful to discuss. Finally she said, "They're mad I left the parents behind on the New Horizon."

"If you did, so did they."

She shook her head. "No. I should have—"

"Waverly," he said sternly. "You chose between rescuing a bunch of little kids who can't help themselves, and a bunch of adults who can. You did the right thing."

"But—"

"No!" he said, and stared into her eyes until she looked up at him. "No one has the right to criticize you for what you did. No one. You have to believe that, inside of you, or they'll keep coming at you."

She looked at him for a long time, thinking about what he said, before finally nodding. "You're right."

"I usually am."

Her eyes moved slowly, from her bowl, to his face, to his hands, to her bowl. She showed him very little, but he could still see she felt uncomfortable, and he liked what it did to her. She was vulnerable this way.

"Anyway," she said, her voice stronger now, "about some food for you. We'll work out four or five drop-off places and the times. I don't think anyone would figure it out."

He was tempted, especially after the soup, which was salty and spicy and perfectly balanced. But he shook his head. "I've put you in enough danger already."

"It's not like Kieran would have me executed."

"I know," Seth said, leaning up on one elbow. "But I don't like thinking of you in the brig."

"You act like you have a say in what I do," she snapped. She seemed upset from her talk with Kieran, but he knew better than to ask her about it. The last thing he wanted to talk about was Kieran Alden. "I'm going to leave you meals whether you want me to or not, so you might as well get the benefit of them."

"What if someone notices you?"

"I'll just leave the food where no one ever goes. The observatory, for one. There are lots of abandoned places like that."

"Okay," Seth said doubtfully. "If I can't stop you, go ahead."

Waverly smiled nervously at him, then went into the kitchen, and she soon came back in with a small plate heaped with cookies. "Want one?"

"I'll have four," he said, and took a handful, leaving her a single cookie.

She looked pointedly at him. "Don't be shy."

"Okay." He grinned, and took the last one, too.

She snatched a cookie back from him and sat on the couch near where his feet were, her thigh pressing on his toes with a comforting kind of pressure. Seth wondered if she was as aware of the contact as he was, but she seemed a million miles away. The look of concentration on her face created furrows between her eyebrows as the light from the lamp winked tiny pinpoints in the globes of her eyes.

"You once said something strange about Captain Jones," she finally said. "Right before the attack."

"Yeah." His voice was husky, and he knew that he was looking at her in a way that could not be mistaken.

If she noticed, she pretended not to. "You said his friends lead complicated lives."

"Yeah." His throat tightened.

She leaned toward him. "Were our parents murdered?"

He sat up, wincing, and wrapped his arms around his knees, leaning close enough to smell the lingering trace of shampoo on her hair. But what she wanted to talk about was ugly, so he leaned away again and pulled himself together. "What do you know?"

"Nothing, but . . ." She brushed cookie crumbs off her hands. "Can I show you something?"

She didn't wait for an answer. She went to a box hidden behind a large loom, pulled a single photograph from it, and handed it to Seth. It showed Waverly's father as a young man, the gray just beginning at his temples, standing with Captain Jones, looking as though the two had just shared a private joke.

"So?" Seth asked her.

"Look," she said, and turned the photo over to show writing on the back: *Galen and Eddie, discovery of phyto-lutein.* "That's my mom's handwriting," Waverly said darkly.

Seth looked at her, not comprehending.

"Never once has my mother ever called the Captain by his first name." She sat back on the couch, her eyes on Seth's, deadly serious. "She's never *said* so, but I've always felt that she hated him," she said, then seemed to hear herself. "Hates, I mean."

Seth nodded. "Do you think your mom knows something?"

"Yes, I do."

"Why would she lie to you?"

"To protect me," Waverly said, without a hint of doubt. "That's not all, though. Seth, I've combed through the ship's public logs. Hardly anything was written about it. They said the accident was caused by a malfunction in the air lock that had come from a faulty installation."

That didn't sound right. "If the problem occurred at installation . . ."

"It should have shown up the first time the air lock was used."

"Then the thing to do is find out how many times that air lock was used before—"

"Thirty-five times that air lock was opened, all without incident. I looked through all the maintenance logs since the Empyrean launched."

"It's not evidence, but I agree it sounds strange." Seth sighed. He didn't want to think about this. For so many years he'd protected Waverly and his father from the truth getting out, but maybe his hiding the truth was only tormenting her. As for his father, nothing could hurt him now.

"I can't find anything more," she said. "Not without sneaking into the Captain's suite and reading Captain Jones's private log."

"You think you'll find anything there?" Seth said ruefully. "You'll just find more of the same lies."

"Lies," she said thoughtfully, studying his face. He dropped his eyes. "You know something."

"I don't know anything for sure." He leaned the side of his head on the back of the couch. "Just some things I remember from when I was a kid."

"Tell me," she said, and put her hand over his. "Please, Seth."

He could only look at her small hand on his larger one. He froze lest she take her hand away, until finally she did take it away and leaned back, waiting for him to begin.

"All I have to go on is a conversation I overheard between my dad and the Captain when I was four years old. I was supposed to be taking a nap, but they woke me up." Seth closed his eyes, letting the memory come back to him—the thing he never let himself think about that was nevertheless always there.

The anger in his father's voice had woken him, and he'd sat up and rubbed his eyes with pudgy fists as the two men stood in the next room hissing at each other. Seth toddled to the doorway and sat on the floor, arms wrapped around his knees, listening through the crack in the door.

"She had nothing to do with it," Mason Ardvale had rasped to the Captain. "She couldn't do a thing like that."

"Mason, I'm sorry. I don't know what to say."

"There's nothing *to* say. You can just leave."

"I wouldn't make an accusation like this without evidence." The Captain had pulled a data-dot from his pocket and walked to the computer terminal in the corner. The two men were quiet for a long time. Seth peeked into the room and saw them leaning over the vid screen, their faces awash in blue light. His father's face was a block of impassivity, but his expression changed incrementally to one of shock, and then profound grief.

"We have to ask her about this," Mason Ardvale had cried. "There might be some explanation."

"What could possibly justify this?" the Captain had said evenly, his eyes fixed on the younger man's face as he leaned over him, one thick hand on his shoulder.

"Give her a chance to explain!"

"She'll have her chance," the Captain had said.

Seth's father wouldn't look at him, and the big man had seemed to recognize it was time to go. Captain Jones lurched out the door on his clumsy legs, his bearded chin tucked in to his chest like a man who knows he ought to look sad.

Mom was in trouble, of that much Seth had been certain. But when his mother came home that evening, covered in crop dust from the wheat fields, her husband was darkly quiet, and when she asked him over dinner what the matter was, he cleared his expression and said with a smile, "Oh, just looking forward to having some time off."

So Seth had decided Mom wasn't in that much trouble after all.

How much time passed? A week? A month? Seth didn't know. But later, when Seth was in the nursery, playing alone with blocks like always, an alarm sounded through the ship, red lights flashing. Seth dropped the blocks, covered his ears, and began to scream. The teachers took him by his shoulders and held him as he kicked at their shins. The other children had stared, and some began to cry.

"I remember that," Waverly said, jarring him into the infinitely lovelier present. "I didn't understand why you were so upset."

"I still don't understand it."

"Because you knew." Waverly put a hand on his

shoulder. "God. Seth, you knew your father had something to do with it!"

"I didn't know that for sure, and I still don't." He spoke more sharply than he meant. She pulled away from him. He softened his voice. "What I mean is, I don't understand how I knew at that moment that my mother was dead. But I sensed it. It was like one moment I was playing with those stupid number blocks, and the next there was a huge hole in my life."

Seth had never told anyone this before, but he found that once he let himself form the words, a weight lifted away from his center. He wanted to pour all his stories into Waverly, let her have anything she wanted from him. "Maybe you're right on some level, though. Maybe I'd expected something to happen, from the way Dad watched her when she wasn't looking. He'd smile when she looked at him, but his smile wiped away the moment her back was turned, and he looked at her like . . . I don't know . . . like a predator looks at something it's going to kill. I *knew* that look, even at that age." Seth raised his eyes to Waverly's. She watched him steadily, accepting every word without judgment. "He wanted to do her harm."

"But why?" Waverly asked, tears pooling in the corners of her eyes. "Why did they kill my dad?"

Seth could only shake his head. "I don't know *what* they did to make the Captain so mad."

"Mad enough to kill." A tear slid down her face. Without thinking, Seth held the back of his finger to her cheek and pulled the tear away from her skin, pressed it with the pad of his thumb. He never took his eyes from her face.

"Do you remember your dad?" Seth asked gently.

"Only little flashes," she whispered. "Sometimes I wonder if I invented the memories from things my mother has said."

"I know what you mean."

"You had it worse than I did. At least my one remaining parent was nice to me," she said, then checked herself and looked into his eyes.

"You knew?" he said, feeling cold. "The way Dad treated me?"

She dropped a beat, watchful and hesitant, but then she said, "Everyone did."

"And no one did a thing to stop it," he said, even colder.

"He was Captain Jones's best friend," Waverly said, but seemed to realize she was making excuses. "No. You're right. It's wrong that no one stepped in to help you."

"Amazing the things people get away with when they're powerful."

Waverly nodded, then leaned the side of her head against the back of the couch. Her eyes had the liquid quality of sleep, but he didn't want to stop talking. He wondered if this was some rite of passage, whispering your parents' secrets.

He'd always thought telling the truth about his father would feel like a betrayal, but actually it felt, for the first time, like he was being loyal to himself.

"Seth," Waverly said. "I need to know the truth."

"I don't know how that's ever going to happen."

"I don't, either. But I'm going to make it happen."

She looked so determined, so strong, he wanted to kiss her. He thought that he could take her by the shoulders and press his mouth against hers, test her, see what she did. If she were any girl other than Waverly Marshall, that's what he'd do. But one wrong move with her . . . He didn't want to think how it would hurt if she rejected him once and for all.

Still, she'd cried in front of him. Had he unlocked her, too?

He watched her face, but she only looked back at him, examining his features as though she was still undecided about whether she could really trust him.

She's not yours, he reminded himself. *She can't be yours.*

"Well, you must be tired," she said with an apologetic smile.

Don't go, he wanted to say. But he nodded.

"Come on," she said, and held out her hand to him.

His heart leapt, but then he realized she was only helping him stand up, letting him lean on her. She took him slowly into her mother's bedroom, where he saw she'd changed the sheets. "You're too hurt to sleep on a couch," she said.

He turned to her. He knew his face was showing too much, that she could see everything he was feeling right there on the shape of his lips.

"Good night," she said, and turned to go to her bedroom. She looked back at him as she closed the door between them.

"Good night," Seth said to the empty hallway.

Attack

Kieran looked out over his congregation, beaming. The auditorium had never been this full even on a Sunday, not even after he'd made attendance mandatory. Nearly every seat was filled. Even Waverly was here, sitting in a middle row wearing a blue dress, looking up at him. Something in her manner was difficult to pinpoint. Apologetic? Guilty? Maybe she felt bad about their conversation and was here to make amends.

He felt particularly energized about his sermon. His voice felt clearer, his words stronger, his feeling more joyful and open. He was going to reach them. He knew it.

"Do you ever think about how you came to be on this ship instead of back on Earth, trying to scratch out a living from a planet turning into desert before your eyes? Do you ever ponder the vast set of circumstances that had to happen, in just the right order, for you to be among those chosen for the most important mission humanity has ever seen?"

He cleared his throat, his eyes on the straight wooden edge of his podium. He brushed the sides of it, feeling the firm wood under his hands. It felt solid and true.

"Some of you might remember Arthur Dietrich's story. Do you? How his parents had to travel all the way across the Atlantic Ocean on a two-bit freight ship? The ship's engine broke down five hundred miles off the coast of Greenland because of poorly refined gasoline, and they floated on the waters of the northern sea for six weeks, distilling their own water and eating only what they could catch with their fishing nets, until finally a cruiser came along and towed them into Nova Scotia. Then they had to hitch rides on the cross-continental railway, riding on the tops of railcars that weren't meant for people, freezing at night and roasting under the sun during the day, until finally they made their way to Chicago, where they had to pass a grueling series of aptitude tests and prove their education level time and again, until finally their names were entered in a vast lottery. But it doesn't end there. No. They weren't chosen in the first round; did you know that? Their names were filed away as alternates, and they almost went back to Germany in defeat. After all, the mission was set to launch in only two weeks. But they decided to wait, and you know what happened? The people chosen ahead of them were killed by raiders in a random attack only four days before the Empyrean launched. That's how Gunther and Edith Dietrich were chosen as engineers for the Empyrean crew.

"Think about that for a minute. Think of all the things that could have gone wrong, but didn't." Kieran held his hands up in a gesture of wonder. "Some people might call it chance, but my heart tells me that chance doesn't explain it. And think about the other stories you've heard, all the crew members who had to fight tooth and nail to be included on this vessel. Your parents. Mine." He could see them thinking back, looking into the past as they sat in their chairs, expressions of concentration on each and every face. "For me, there's only one conclusion. We belong here. This ship is our destiny. There's a vast plan for each and every one of us. And everything we do is a fulfillment of that plan. Each of us is doing just what we're meant to do, just precisely the way we're meant to do it. That is how I know in my heart that we will not fail."

He paused, long enough to hear the echo of his voice ringing through the auditorium. Nothing felt more wonderful to him than these moments of silence during his sermons, when he could feel the presence of God in the room. He felt so much love, so much rightness. He was glad Waverly had come to see it. He looked at her now, her beautiful oval face and her huge eyes, the way they fastened on him. She was thinking hard about something, he could see. Was he reaching her?

"Can you feel it?" he whispered into the microphone, then paused, waiting for the utter silence of his rapt crowd to filter through the air. "Can you feel the power of this message? I hope you keep feeling it, all day long. I hope you go on feeling it, until we can meet again tomorrow morning to renew our faith once more."

Now came his favorite part. He stepped aside from the podium, lifted up his hands, and shouted to the crowd, "Now it's time for you to speak! Please step forward with your cares and concerns!"

He was shocked when Waverly stood up without hesitation.

"I'm concerned that we haven't held an election yet," Waverly said, looking right at him. "This ship is supposed to be a democracy. We need a Central Council immediately."

Every word was a chip of ice.

But her comment was only the beginning of an avalanche. Sarah Hodges stood up from the middle of the congregation, fixed her angry eyes on him, and said with a nasty grin, "I'm concerned that Kieran keeps all the information to himself. We've got a terrorist on board, and we need to know what's going on."

Kieran opened his mouth to speak, but then Melissa Dickinson rose and called out in her small voice, "I'm concerned that Kieran Alden is throwing people in the brig without a Justice of the Peace approving it."

He was in a nightmare.

Kieran stared at the three of them, paralyzed, until Waverly cleared her throat.

"Kieran has been doing an admirable job," she said loudly, turning to address the entire congregation. "But he was traumatized by the attack, just like the rest of us. How can we expect him to shoulder the burden of governing this vessel all by himself? He needs some time off." Her eyes met his, and she said clear as a bell, "With that in mind, I nominate Sarah Hodges to run against

Kieran Alden in a general election for the Captain's chair."

"I nominate Waverly Marshall for the Central Council," Sarah Hodges called out.

Suddenly the air was filled with voices, all calling out names to fill posts on board the ship.

This had been orchestrated. They hadn't come to hear his sermon. They'd come to attack his government.

"Wait now! Wait!" he screamed over their heads. He hadn't meant to sound so angry, but at least it shut them up. All two hundred and fifty kids turned to look at him. "How can we run an election while we have a terrorist on board?"

"We can get it done in one day," Waverly shouted over the crowd. "If you're reelected, by tonight you could be briefing your Central Council and they could start sharing the burden."

He hated her for putting it like that, as if she were doing him a favor.

Sarah Hodges started handing out slips of paper. She had hundreds of them in a packet, and the kids in the congregation took them eagerly. Kieran looked at Waverly, who looked right back at him, not a shred of remorse on her face. The last bit of admiration he'd felt for her flew away, and he realized that those lovely large eyes, that heart-shaped chin, those high cheekbones, that honey-colored skin—all made up the face of his enemy.

"This is a schedule for debates between the nominees," Sarah Hodges yelled into the crowd. "At the end of each debate we can vote for our favorites. In a few hours we'll have a Central Council. Then this afternoon we can elect a Justice of the Peace, and this evening the two Captain nominees can have their debate, so you have time to prepare, Kieran."

"I don't need time to prepare!" Kieran said angrily.

"Good," Sarah said happily.

He stared at her insolent grin, shaking his head in disbelief.

But as he looked out over the crowd, he began to see how eager they all were. The kids were milling around, excited, reading the schedule, talking among themselves. Never had they looked so animated. They *wanted* this.

If he tried to prevent an election, he'd lose the Captain's chair for sure.

"I defer to the will of the crew," Kieran said loudly, to make sure everyone heard him. With a mean smile, Sarah handed him a schedule. He went to his office to think, leaving behind the sound of excited voices all talking at once.

He rested his head on his desk and closed his eyes. He was being tested.

Kieran breathed deeply, tried to calm down.

I need to have faith, he told himself. *If this election is part of His plan, I just have to trust.*

But what if I lose? he thought.

I won't, he told himself. *I am meant to be the Captain. Otherwise, what has all this been for?*

He was calm and ready to face down his opponents by the time he went back to the auditorium, where the debates were about to begin.

There were about twenty-five crew members sitting on the stage, all vying for a position on the seven-member council, all of them eager to have their say about how they would help improve the way the Empyrean was run. Kieran bravely endured criticism after criticism, most of which was based on a poor understanding of the capacity of the crew and the ship.

Adam Mizrahi made the most ridiculous suggestion in his bid for a Central Council seat. "We could catch up to the New Horizon tomorrow if we just punched the engines as hard as they'll go."

This was met with a robust round of applause from the younger kids, but Kieran could see the older kids, who understood the health effects of the added gravity, were less enthusiastic.

Arthur Dietrich, who was also a nominee, stood and faced Adam. "Aside from the effect that would have on our bodies, we can't push the engines any harder than we're doing right now without risking a collision with a deep-space particle that could rip through our hull. It's right there in the *Piloting and Navigation Manual,* if you'd bother to look." This quieted the crowd, and Arthur turned to face them. "There has got to be at least one person on the Central Council who is familiar with the workings of the ship, and is up to date on all the latest information about the terrorist and our plans for confronting the New Horizon. That person is me, if you'll vote for me."

Arthur looked meaningfully at Kieran, and he knew that Arthur would serve as a trusty go-between. Kieran hoped he'd be elected.

Then Waverly raised her hand to get the attention of the crowd. "I have more experience than anyone dealing with the command structure of the New Horizon, and I'm familiar with the political situation on that ship as well as the physical layout. I have expertise that would be invaluable to the Central Council as we plan our attack."

"You left our parents behind!" yelled a small girl in the back, one of Marjorie's cohorts. Several other girls raised shrill voices in agreement as Marjorie smiled from among them.

"If I did, then so did you," Waverly shot back, her eyes flashing.

This seemed to cow them. But some of the boys weren't satisfied. "You didn't even try to find out who's still alive!" shouted a boy of twelve. Kieran knew that his parents were unaccounted for.

"Do you have a bullet hole in you?" Waverly asked angrily, pulling her shirt collar over to expose the ugly red welt on her shoulder. "I got this trying to save our parents. I'd have done it, too, if there hadn't been bullets flying everywhere."

"You left them there!" called out Marjorie Wilkins. Though she was one of Kieran's fiercest supporters, he'd never really liked her. There was something about her sneering face that hinted at an ugly little soul.

"It was *my* plan that got the girls off that ship, along with Sarah Hodges. Samantha Stapleton gave her life so we could free ourselves," Waverly said, her eyes trained on Marjorie. "If there are girls sitting in this audience today, it's because of *us*."

No one seemed to have anything to say to that.

Once the debate was finished, the crew members all lined up at the back of the auditorium and entered their top seven choices for Central Council into a computer, which tallied up the numbers immediately. Kieran had a few friends on the council. Arthur had been elected, along with Tobin Ames, or "Doctor Tobin" as the kids had begun calling him, and Harvey Markem, a Command officer. Harvey's bandage was gone from his head, and he looked perfectly healed. Waverly was voted in by a slender margin, along with some kids who would be more likely to side with her: Alia Khadivi was a loyal friend of Waverly's; Melissa Dickinson, the girl who took care of the little kids, was always defending Waverly from her detractors; and Sealy Arndt had been Seth's hotheaded crony. Kieran's heart sank. His supporters would be in the minority on the council. Arthur would have to be very persuasive in debates.

After what seemed an endless debate between five candidates for Justice of the Peace, the crew narrowly elected twelve-year-old Bobby Martin. Kieran tried not to show his disapproval of the choice. Bobby had an unpredictable personality, and Kieran had never been sure of his loyalty. It seemed crazy to let legal decisions rest on the shoulders of a boy who didn't even have to shave yet. The problem was, all the older kids were already saddled with responsibilities as guards, Central Council members, or in Central Command. They'd run out of teenagers to run the ship.

Kieran sent an angry glare in Waverly's direction and was surprised to see her already looking at him. He nodded at her, since no matter how he felt, it looked like he'd be working with her. But he knew she could see his fury through his placid surface. He'd never been able to hide anything from her.

When all the debates for the lower positions were finished, Waverly walked onto the empty stage and took hold of the microphone. "It's time for the debate for the Captain's chair. I'd like to invite Sarah Hodges to the podium."

Sarah walked to the front of the room, swinging her arms, looking as though she were preparing for a physical fight. She took hold of the microphone and smiled hatefully at Kieran before beginning. "As you know, several days ago I was imprisoned in the brig without due process. I was threatened and I was branded a traitor. If you don't vote for me, something like that might happen to you. Kieran Alden isn't Captain of this vessel. He's a dictator, and it's up to all of us to stop him."

Kieran shook with anger as he listened to slander after slander from Sarah. He was alarmed to hear himself spoken of with such hatred, but when he looked out over the crowd, he saw many skeptical faces watching her. The more she talked—about how she'd speed up the pursuit of the New Horizon and how she'd execute Anne Mather and her Central Council for what they did—the less she sounded like a leader, and the more she sounded like an angry, scared little girl who didn't have the slightest idea of what she was up against. Though the end of her speech was met with applause, Kieran knew he could do better.

When he took the podium, Arthur, who was standing at the back of the room, led such a round of cheers that instantly Kieran felt more confident.

"That certainly was an interesting story Sarah Hodges told you about me," he said, trying to sound amused rather than furious. "I call it a story because none of it is true. I put Ms. Hodges in the brig because she withheld vital information that could help us find Seth Ardvale and the terrorist. I care about getting our parents back, and I care about keeping this ship running, but there's one thing I care about even more: keeping you alive. If there are maniacs running around killing our crew the way they killed Max Brent, then don't you think I'd better stop at nothing to find them and bring them to justice?"

Arthur whooped in the back, which triggered a chorus of cheering and whistles.

"Look," Kieran said, then waited for the applause to die down. "I know I haven't been a perfect Captain. I've made mistakes. Just like you, I'm a kid doing an adult's job. Even though there have been problems along the way, I'm confident that I've done the best job anyone on this ship could have done."

Another round of applause. Already the crowd sounded more excited than they had for Sarah's speech. She sat in the front row, scowling up at Kieran as she gnawed at a fingernail.

"Even more important, we shouldn't change leaders in the middle of this thing. I've been at the job already for several months. I know what's involved. I understand this ship. To change leadership when we're under a serious threat could be disastrous, not only for the ship, but for our rescue mission.

"All these are good reasons to elect me to the Captain's chair," he said humbly. "But I've got one more reason that I think supersedes them all." He paused for effect, looking out over the crew, who all looked at him, some with skepticism, but most with interest and hope. "No one has my vision for the future of this vessel. I took a bedraggled, dysfunctional crew and got us running this ship. Look at how far we've come! But I can't take credit for it. I believe we've been able to rally together because we've finally accepted that we have a common purpose. Together we're building an ethos for our future, and I am honored beyond words to be the instrument for fulfilling our destiny as the creators of the next world."

Now there was a thoughtful pause before the applause, but when it finally began, it was loud and prolonged. Kieran nodded. He felt certain now that he'd be elected.

The voting took a matter of minutes, with each crew member dropping small ballots in a box. Tallying the votes by three independent counters went quickly, too, and they did the counting right on stage. Sarah watched the process with squinty eyes, casting furious glances in Kieran's direction. He tried to look confident as he sat in the front row, but he couldn't stop himself from worrying. What would he do if he were no longer Captain? He wasn't sure life would have the same meaning for him anymore. He *had* to win.

You will win, said the voice in the back of his mind.

He sat up straighter. Where was his faith? If he was truly meant to lead the Empyrean to New Earth, the way he believed, then of course he would win. He shouldn't fear.

When finally the three counters—Harvey Markem, Alia Khadivi, and Melissa Dickinson—approached the microphone, the murmuring conversations in the room died away, and everyone looked at them expectantly.

Harvey cleared his throat, his face bright red under his orange hair. "Sarah Hodges won ninety-one votes. Kieran Alden got one hundred and forty-nine. Kieran Alden is—"

Harvey's voice got lost in the crackle of applause and

cheers. Kieran stood, and the applause rose to a crescendo as he mounted the stairs to the stage and walked to the podium. He couldn't help smiling. When he looked down at Sarah, she was sitting with her arms crossed over her chest, scowling. Waverly was sitting a few rows behind her, looking unsurprised.

"Thank you, thank you," he said with a smile, holding up his hands for them to quiet. After a while the cheering died down, and people sat to listen to his speech. "First off, I'd like to thank Waverly Marshall for calling this election."

Waverly watched him, impassive. If she heard his sarcasm, she didn't let on.

"I just want you all to know that I'll continue to lead this ship . . ." Some people in the back coughed, and he waited for them to quiet. But then several more kids in the back started coughing, and some of them stood up, their hands covering their faces.

And then they fell down.

His speech forgotten, Kieran watched as the sickness seemed to spread from the back of the audience forward. More and more kids were grimacing, choking, doubling over, tears streaming from their eyes. It moved toward the stage like a wave. "Evacuate!" Kieran cried into the microphone. People in the front rows stared at him blankly. "Evacuate immediately!" he screamed. "Exit through the front doors! There's some kind of gas! Go!"

It seemed to take hours for them to stand up, look around, see the crew members falling down in the back, grasping at their necks, struggling for breath, before they began to understand.

The auditorium erupted into chaos.

Kieran looked over the crowd, first for Waverly, who was holding two little girls, one on each hip, running awkwardly for the nearest exit. Next he registered Sarah Hodges, who was pulling a little boy behind her, covering her nose and mouth with the collar of her shirt.

Then he saw Arthur.

He was lying on his back, spread-eagled in the middle of the aisle.

Kieran didn't think. He dove.

He swam through the crowd, pushing against shoulders and sweaty foreheads, fighting through them to get to Arthur. Twenty feet to go. He couldn't see him through the crowd slamming him backward—an endless stream of terrified, tear-streaked faces rushing at him down the aisle. Kieran felt a horrible, caustic sting in his throat, his eyes, his stomach. And the taste was like orange juice that had sat out too long. He thought he would vomit, but he realized he shouldn't breathe it in. He clamped his mouth closed, willed himself not to inhale. He plunged against the current of fleeing kids— ten feet more—and he thought he caught a glimpse of yellow hair on the floor. Then he lost Arthur completely, but he walked forward blindly, until he stepped on him.

He reached for Arthur's hand, missed, then made a desperate swipe again, and this time made contact with his leather belt. Kieran wrapped his fingers around it and pulled until he could get his other arm underneath Arthur's waist, and then somehow, he didn't know how, he lifted the boy over his shoulder and began to run.

His lungs ached. It hadn't been twenty seconds since he started holding his breath, but the strain of carrying

Arthur made every muscle in his body cry out for oxygen. He fought the instinct to gulp air, and instead focused his eyes on the door, which was at least seventy feet away. He groped, blinking tears out of his stinging eyes, feeling along a row of seats with his legs until finally the door was in front of him.

He threw his weight against it and staggered into the corridor, which was full of sick kids, coughing kids, crying kids. He limped to the elevator, wheezing, barely able to breathe. His throat felt narrow and swollen, and he felt hemmed in by all the kids who had piled into the elevator with him. By the time the elevator opened to the madness of the infirmary, Kieran's vision had turned gray. Panicked kids were packed into the waiting area, and there wasn't a free chair or bed to be had. He gently set Arthur down on the floor and stood up to find Tobin.

He felt a wave of vertigo rise like bile from his stomach.

A loud crack resounded through the crowded room, quieting the crowd as people looked around for the source of the noise. Kieran realized it had been the sound of his own head hitting the metal floor. He hadn't felt a thing.

The Central Council

The day after the attack, the ship felt eerily quiet as Waverly walked the corridor to Central Command. The crew had been badly scared, and most of them stayed hidden in their quarters, many of them shirking their duties to do so. She still had a sore throat, and her eyes stung from the toxic gas, but she was unscathed compared to some other people. Several kids, including Kieran and Arthur, had been badly affected and were receiving oxygen therapy in the infirmary. Beyond that, few details had been released.

Waverly turned the corner and saw that more graffiti had been added to the walls outside Central Command. There was a drawing of the Central Council, all seven members, and in front of them, on its hands and knees, was a figure Waverly could only assume was meant to be her, looking ready to perform any number of lewd acts.

The first thing she'd do as a Central Council member would be to clean up this damn hallway.

Waverly took a deep breath, made a fist, and knocked on the door of Central Command. She heard the whirring of a video camera, and looked up at the empty black lens trained on her. Sarek Hassan's voice crackled through the intercom, "What is it, Waverly?"

"I'd like to use the com system to call a meeting of the Central Council." This was an excuse. There were other places she could make an announcement from, but she wanted to know what was going on.

There was a brief pause, then the door slid open to Central Command looking dark and empty without Kieran in the Captain's chair and Arthur in the number-two spot near the portholes. Of the usual command crew only Sarek remained, seated at his spot at the main com board. Matt Allbright, Kieran's chief henchman, stood behind Sarek, looking over his shoulder at the com screen.

"Who's doing that graffiti?" Waverly asked, trying to sound nonchalant.

"Whoever it is wears a black hood over their face," Sarek said, sounding annoyed by it himself. "Anyway, it's the least of our worries."

"Which station should I use for the announcement?" Waverly asked.

Sarek nodded toward the Captain's chair. She sat down in it, put the headset on, and engaged the system. "Attention Central Council members, this is Waverly Marshall, and I'm calling a meeting. Please report to the council chamber in five minutes."

She stayed seated and looked across the aisle at the

screen that so absorbed Sarek and Matt. It was a view of
the corridor outside of the auditorium. They must be
looking for video evidence of the terrorist planting the gas.

"Did the cameras capture anything?" Waverly asked.

Sarek jerked his head toward her angrily but seemed
to calm down when he saw she was looking at the screen
with grave concern. "Not a single image on any camera
has ever caught him."

"He must be disabling them somehow," she said.

Sarek looked at Matt, whose face was impassive, then
grudgingly said, "He is." He fast-forwarded the image to
a completely white screen that lasted for several seconds.
"We think he's shining a laser into the lenses of the
cameras as he passes by. We'd seen this white screen
several times before we realized what it was."

"So you've never gotten his image, not once?"

"Not anything we can work with," Sarek said darkly.
"All we know is that he's big."

He flicked the screen, and a shadowy image of a
hulking figure in a hooded jacket appeared frozen, arm
upraised, a device in his hand pointed toward the camera.
The hood cast a shadow over his features.

Waverly shook her head, though she knew it didn't
really matter. Any stranger on board would obviously be
the terrorist, and any crew member would instantly
recognize him. So why was he bothering to hide himself?
"How's Kieran?"

"He'll be fine in a day or two. So will Arthur."

"Has anyone been able to figure out what that gas
was?"

Sarek shook his head. "Nothing we had in our stores.
He must have made it in the lab. We think it must be like
the kind of stuff used in crowd control back on Earth

during the Water Wars. Not lethal, but it's incapacitating."

"Why would he do that?" Matt said in his deep baritone. "Why not finish us off?"

"It's a warning," Waverly said. "He's trying to scare us. Next time he'll use something worse."

Matt and Sarek looked at each other.

"What?" Waverly asked them. "Guys?"

Matt stared stubbornly at the screen. Sarek avoided Waverly's glance.

"There's a Central Council now," she told them, "and I'm on it. If you're withholding information from me, I can sic the Justice of the Peace on you for obstruction of an official investigation."

Sarek held up a hand. "Okay. There was a note." Sarek raised his eyebrows at Matt, who pulled a key from a chain around his neck and went to a cabinet behind the Captain's chair. From it he pulled a red metal canister, the kind used by farmhands for drinking water. It was wrapped in a clear plastic bag.

"We found this in the lighting booth at the back of the auditorium."

Waverly took it from him. Fastened to the canister was a note written in bold black lettering:

ATTACKS WILL INCREASE IN SEVERITY UNTIL YOU SIGN A PEACE TREATY WITH THE NEW HORIZON.

"Peace treaty?" she said. "How can we sign a peace treaty if they won't even answer our hails?"

Sarek's expression darkened but he said nothing. Waverly filed this away for later. Now wasn't the time to press him.

Waverly pushed the bag at Matt, who took it from her.

The note had the kind of twisted logic Anne Mather used. Those words were probably dictated by the woman herself.

"I want to know everything you're doing to find that bastard," Waverly said to Matt. "Come with me."

"*Now?*"

"You're making a report," she barked. She didn't care about how bossy she sounded. "When Matt comes back, Sarek, I want you to come tell us what you know, too."

Sarek looked at her doubtfully, but she stared him down, and he finally gave a terse nod.

She marched out of Central Command and down the long hallway to the chamber, where she found the rest of the council already waiting for her. The council chamber was a domed room—one of the few rooms in the vessel with an almost panoramic view of the starry sky—so it was one of the few places where the nebula they'd just finished traversing was still visible. It was huge, pink, with tentacles that spread away from its center. It looked vaguely like a squid. She shuddered and turned away from it.

Alia Khadivi sat at the table twisting her big turquoise ring around her finger, her enormous dark eyes glistening in the lamplight. Tobin Ames sat with his hands woven together behind his neck, and he watched Matt cautiously through his overgrown brown bangs. Melissa Dickinson, Sealy Arndt, and Harvey Markem lined the other side of the table. The two huge boys dwarfed mousy little Melissa, but she seemed unaware of the effect and smiled shyly at Waverly, who took the seat they'd left open for her at the head of the table.

"Thanks for coming," Waverly said. "Unfortunately, Arthur Dietrich is too unwell to be here, but I'll catch him up later. Matt Allbright is here to report on the progress so far in the investigation to find the terrorist. Matt?" Waverly swiveled her chair to face him.

At first Matt stared at the center of the table, seeming tongue-tied, but he cleared his throat.

"The fact is, we have very few leads. There is no clear video trace of the terrorist, so we can't learn where he's living, how he's getting supplies, or whether he's in contact with the New Horizon."

"Well," Waverly said. "You have the white screens he's leaving behind. You can follow his movements that way."

"Maybe," Matt said, "but it's hard to search for a white screen that lasts for only a second or two. We'd have to fast-forward through days' worth of video, and we'll probably miss a lot of them. Instead we're concentrating on trying to learn if he's in contact with Anne Mather."

"Are you monitoring outside transmissions?" Waverly asked.

"There are ways to encrypt transmissions to make them sound like background radiation. So far we're not seeing anything like that originating from the ship, but we've got to assume that he has superior technical knowledge to us."

"Have you physically searched the ship?"

"We go out on patrol every single day in pairs."

"And do you randomly change the timing of where you go?" Waverly asked.

Matt looked at her, blank.

"If you want to catch him, your movements have to be unpredictable," Waverly said, surprised Kieran hadn't thought of this. "Also, you shouldn't be talking or making any sound. If he can hear you coming, he'll be able to get away easily."

Matt nodded, but he was clearly perturbed at being shown up. He looked at Waverly mistrustfully, and she figured he shared Kieran's attitude about her.

Alia leaned forward, a finger raised. "Have you located any campsites where he might be staying?"

"Other than the engine room and maybe the lab, we haven't located a single trace of him. We think he's being more careful now, never staying in the same place twice." Matt paused awkwardly, obviously hesitant to go on. The council waited in silence, all of them seeming to have the same instinct Waverly had, not to push him, not to ask for too much or he might clam up. "Actually, we've found a few spots, but all of them appear to be where Seth Ardvale has been camping."

"Where?" Sealy asked forcefully.

"The conifer bay, the rain forest bay."

"How do you know those campsites belong to Seth and not the terrorist?" Melissa Dickinson asked, seeming embarrassed at the sound of her own voice.

"Because we can backtrack and find video of Seth going there and leaving."

"Then why haven't you caught him?" Sealy demanded. Ever since his fistfight in the brig with Seth, Sealy had it in for him.

"There's so much video footage to go through," Matt said. "The surveillance system isn't designed to search for fugitives. It's really there for investigations into accidents or crimes that happen in a particular spot at a particular time, see. There are cameras all over the ship recording every crew member. We have to wade through all that material to find video of Seth."

"You should be focusing on the terrorist," Waverly said a little too quickly. She ignored the curious glances sent her way. "How many people do you have on patrol?"

"With six pairs of us, we're able to cover the entire ship every day."

"That's not enough people," Waverly said, throwing up her hands. "You need more Command officers."

Matt ducked his chin. He didn't respond, which Waverly took as tacit agreement.

"Matt, I want you to get new recruits. Double your force. And when those search teams head out, they should include one experienced boy and one less-experienced"—she had a moment of inspiration—"girl. Recruit from the older girls. There's no reason the Command officers should be all boys."

Matt clearly didn't like this idea, but he held his tongue.

"That's a good idea. I will volunteer," Alia said with a smile at Matt.

"Me too," Melissa Dickinson piped up, this time without hesitation.

"Matt, is there anything else you want to add?" Waverly asked. She felt she'd pushed him around a bit, and tried to make it up to him with a softer tone. "We'd appreciate anything you could tell us."

Matt's jaw muscle worked for a few tense moments, but finally he came out with, "Kieran is a good leader. He's done a magnificent job."

"Thank you, Matt," Waverly said with a smile. "Can you send Sarek in next, please?"

After Matt left the room, Waverly looked around the table at the council members. Melissa's quick glance belied her placid expression; she seemed to have a fiery soul underneath her waifish, quiet exterior. Harvey Markem was gnawing at a cuticle, his eyes trained on the center of the table. He had a thick smattering of orange freckles across his nose, and though he was brawny from his work on the farms, his face had the softness of a little boy's. Next to Harvey, Alia looked like a Moorish princess, with her thick long black hair and olive skin. Waverly was glad to have her quiet strength on the council. Sealy was staring darkly out the window, his wiry light brown hair standing up in messy whorls. Waverly thought it strange he was elected to the council at all, considering he'd been one of Seth's main henchmen. She hoped his election meant there was an undercurrent of sympathy for Seth among the crew.

Everyone straightened in their chairs when Sarek came in looking sullen and wary. He didn't even wait for any questions; he just marched to an empty chair, sat down with a *thunk,* and launched into a speech.

"Look, I've been working with Kieran for months in Central Command, and he's the only one who could have pulled this crew together." He looked around the room at each person in turn, but he rested his eyes on Waverly for the next part: "I know some of you have doubts about his religious side, but I think after so many kids lost their parents, they needed something like that. Otherwise they would have just sunken into despair."

Waverly looked thoughtfully at Sarek. She realized how intelligent he was, and she even felt herself being persuaded a little. She found it within herself to say, "You're probably right about that, Sarek."

He looked at her with surprise, then his forehead creased with tension. He looked as though a small battle were raging within him. Maybe he wanted to talk to the council, but his loyalty to Kieran was stopping him. She'd have to be gentle with him.

"Is there anything you'd like to report?" she asked softly.

He shook his head doubtfully.

She studied him and took a shot in the dark. "Any news from the New Horizon?"

His eyes darted up, and he seemed to hold his breath.

"Sarek, you have to tell us anything you know," Waverly said. The rest of the council watched him, waiting for him to speak.

"About two weeks ago . . ." he began. He closed his mouth again, his eyes on his hands, which were clenched together on the table in front of him. Finally he took a deep breath and said, "Anne Mather hailed the ship, and Kieran had a private conversation with her."

Alia gasped at hearing the name. Melissa Dickinson blanched. Waverly wiped a damp palm on her soft cotton pants.

"Do you know what they talked about?" Waverly asked quietly.

"She wants a peace treaty," Sarek said, looking shamefaced. "She wants Kieran to watch some videos about something to do with Captain Jones, and then she'll discuss releasing the hostages. I mean . . . our parents."

The room was silent with anguish.

"And has Kieran . . ." Waverly said, then took a deep breath to steady the shaking of her voice. "Has Kieran complied with Mather's wishes?"

"I don't know," Sarek said. "He hasn't talked to her since then."

"That you know of?"

"I have full access to the central com station on this vessel. No transmission occurs without my being able to find out about it."

"And since the attack in the auditorium?" Alia asked.

She seemed just as upset as Waverly felt. Hearing mention of Mather's name seemed to bring it all back: the strange puritan customs, Mather's coded language, being drugged, having her ova harvested without her consent. It was the kind of violation that never heals. "Have we heard anything more from Anne Mather?"

"No," Sarek said, "but . . . I wouldn't be surprised if we did hear from her soon."

The council received this with grave silence.

"It seems Mather has given us an opportunity," Alia ventured. "We have been pursuing the New Horizon for months with no progress. Perhaps if we seem willing to play her game, we could get close to her."

The rest of the council looked at her.

"I think that's what Kieran was trying to decide," Sarek said.

"All on his own," Waverly said bitterly, then wished she hadn't. Sarek looked at her distrustfully. She needed to keep comments like that to herself if she wanted his cooperation.

"Do you have those videos?" Sealy asked. His gray eyes were trained on Sarek. Clearly he was less forgiving of the secrecy Sarek had participated in than the other council members were. Hearing his forceful tone made Waverly realize she was angry, too. She should have known Mather had contacted Kieran. The whole crew should have known.

"I saved a copy of Mather's transmission," Sarek said.

"We're going to need to see it," Harvey Markem said. It was the first time he'd spoken. Because Harvey had been one of the guards watching over Seth in the brig, Waverly hadn't been sure of where his loyalty lay—with Kieran or with the council. Now it seemed clear that he was willing to stand up to Kieran. "Can you get the video for us so we can watch it?" he asked Sarek.

For the first time in a long time, Waverly felt hopeful. This council was exactly what had been needed all along.

"I'm not sure I can do that," Sarek said slowly.

"What?" Melissa Dickinson squeaked. "If you have anything at all that might bring us closer to our parents, you've got to give it up!"

"Kieran kept it to himself for a reason," Sarek said. "I've already said much more than I think he would want. I won't do this to him."

A general outcry sounded in the room, but Waverly held up a hand. "Hey, hey! Wait!" The protests died down, and the council looked at Waverly. "Sarek's right. Kieran is the elected Captain, and we should respect his authority."

All doubt about her seemed to wipe free from Sarek's face, and he even smiled a little as he looked at her. She had his trust, at least for now.

"Kieran should be well enough soon that we can get his permission."

"I don't want to negotiate with that woman," Alia said, her velvety voice suddenly cold and rigid.

"We're not giving her a single thing she wants," Waverly spat fiercely. "But we can make her think we're willing to play by her rules."

This seemed to catch everyone's full attention, and the room grew even quieter, so that Waverly's next words carried extra meaning.

"We'll act like we want to work with her," Waverly said grimly. "Then we'll kill her."

The Observatory

Seth missed Waverly. He was curled up against a warm exhaust vent in the atmospheric conditioning bay, letting the heat permeate the terrible ache in his ribs. He needed a soft bed and warm meals, but he'd get none of that. Waverly had been dropping off sandwiches and cold salads for him daily in their designated spots. Yesterday she'd left him a chicken sandwich and some plums just inside the door on level 15 of the outer starboard staircase. The meal had nearly frozen solid by the time he picked it up, but he was grateful for it nonetheless. He could subsist on what grew in the biosphere bays, but none of it satisfied him for long.

His stomach rumbled. Only another few minutes before she left him some dinner in the observatory. It was a domed glass room, so it was always pretty cold, and no one ever went there—a good place to store food. He should try to rest until it was time to go.

But he couldn't turn off his mind. He couldn't stop thinking about the stowaway. There'd been some new attack, he knew. He'd caught little snatches of conversations, whenever crew members passed by his hiding places. Though he didn't know the details, it was clear the crew seemed even more scared than before. He wished he could make sure Waverly was okay, but the only indication of her well-being was the meals she left for him. Maybe with the next one there would be a note.

He closed his eyes and tried to sleep. An image of Waverly passed before him, the way she smiled at him, never an open smile, more like the smile of someone who is trying not to smile. It was his goal to get a real smile out of her someday. He wanted to see what she looked like when she was happy.

She was probably on her way to the observatory with his food right now. The observatory had always been where the kids on the Empyrean went for dates. The view was the same as out any porthole, but it was a quiet place where couples could have a little privacy in the darkness. Did it mean something that Waverly had chosen it as a drop-off place? He told himself no. The observatory had been all but abandoned, now that there were no adults on the vessel and the kids could go anywhere they wanted to be alone. The only reason anyone would ever go there now would be for maintenance on the forward sensor array, which hardly ever needed maintenance at all.

Seth opened his eyes.

In a flash, he knew how the stowaway was

communicating with the New Horizon.

The forward array was the long-range detection device that helped the nav system make course corrections to avoid objects in space. It worked by sending out high-density electromagnetic bursts and recording when the light was reflected off an object. It could be easily modified to send out and receive encrypted voice signals. The main controls for it were in Central Command, but there was a manual station in the prow of the ship meant for maintenance.

And that was located in the observatory.

The more Seth thought about it, the more certain he became: Using the forward array was the only way the terrorist could be communicating in secret with the other ship. There was *no* other way. The terrorist could probably spend all day in the observatory, waiting for messages, without ever being discovered.

And Waverly was headed there right now.

Seth was suddenly filled with a horrible feeling of dread. He had to get to the observatory *right now.*

After listening at the outer stairwell door for sentries, he jogged up several flights until he reached the prow. His breath came hard, and it made his ribs ache awfully, but the only thing he cared about was making sure Waverly was safe. The corridor was quiet, and Seth was stealthy as he tiptoed to the observatory door.

He couldn't shake the feeling that he was too late.

"Don't be paranoid," he said under his breath.

He peeked his head into the dark room. He heard nothing, saw only the rows of theater seats arranged in a semicircle, pointed toward the domed glass that formed the walls of the room. How ridiculous of the engineers back on Earth to think this room would see any real use!

The monotony of the view made people avoid looking out portholes, because it reminded them too much of how far they were from Earth and its constantly changing sky. Instead, the crew turned their eyes inward, toward the plants and animals, reminders of a planet they'd left behind decades ago that they'd never see again.

Seth tucked himself behind a row of seats and watched the door. The room smelled musty, and the air had the close, dead quality that comes from being shut up for too long. Probably Kieran was conserving power by only running ventilation to areas of the ship seeing heavy use, not a bad idea considering the engines had recently been at the point of meltdown. In fact, much as he hated to admit it, Kieran wasn't doing that bad a job . . .

Seth froze. He heard something. *Did* he hear it? Or did he *sense* it? Something behind him, close. Maybe the faint stir of air exhaled. Maybe the smallest whiff of another body.

He turned half a degree before an iron arm clamped around his neck.

"I don't know how you keep finding me, you little shit," snarled a hoarse voice. Seth tried to pull the arm away from his throat, but the man's strength was brutish. He wedged Seth's neck into the crook of his elbow, closing his windpipe. Seth could feel the blood supply to his brain being squeezed off, and he blinked his eyes against red spots. "This time I'm going to have to kill you," the voice said softly, caressingly. "I'm sorry, kid. It's not personal."

I'm going to die, Seth thought distantly. His face felt swollen with blood, and his throat was clamped shut. He tried to pull the man's arm away from his windpipe, his legs twisting underneath him. But already he felt his mind growing small, his limbs weak, as the blood supply to his brain trickled to a stop.

Then he heard the click of the door latch.

Waverly.

With his last bit of strength, Seth twisted his body away from the door so the man wouldn't see her. He wrapped his hands around the meaty arm to relieve some of the pressure on his throat and drove all his weight downward, pulling the man into a stooped position.

Run, he thought at her as he felt petals of nothingness blooming inside his skull. *Please run away.*

He heard the sickening *thunk* of metal meeting bone, and the hold on his neck loosened.

"You little bitch," he heard the man growl. "You killed Shelby."

Seth felt himself falling, and he was on the floor, unable to move or open his eyes. He heard Waverly yelp with surprise, and then he heard her gurgling.

He's strangling her.

He thought it like he might think of a scientific fact. Nothing travels faster than light, and Waverly is dying.

I'm on my hands and knees, he realized. He was wobbling there as spots covered the dark room. He took a ragged breath through a badly swollen throat and somehow managed to get one foot underneath him, then the other. When he stood, the room tilted, but he caught himself on the back of a seat and staggered toward the sounds of Waverly being choked.

On the floor in front of his left foot was a heavy wrench, the kind used for loosening the bolts on a tractor tire. From Waverly's tool belt, he decided. There it was, the belt, fastened around her tiny writhing waist, screws and bolts spilling out of it as her legs twisted helplessly on the floor. The man's bulk blocked her face as he knelt over her, leaning his weight into his hold on her neck.

Rage rose in Seth, and he forgot about the weakness in his limbs and the way the room twirled. He picked up the wrench, took two steps toward the man, and swung with all his strength.

The tip of the wrench peeled a flap of skin off the man's skull, and he turned around, surprised.

Never before had Seth seen features twisted in such an ugly way. The man's nose was wrinkled, his eyes red-bleary in the dim light, his teeth were gnashing, and spittle glistened at the corners of his mouth. Seth swung the wrench again, but the man leaned away, and Seth missed. He felt the wrench being pulled from his weak fingers.

The man swung back, grimacing, holding the wrench high above his head. If that wrench met Seth's skull, he would be killed. He took a step back, and another, until he felt Waverly's warm legs under his feet, and he sank down on top of her, covering her face with his hands. *She's dead,* he thought for one terrifying instant.

Nothing had ever felt more beautiful to him than when her breath warmed his fingers.

He waited for the blow, but it didn't come. Instead he heard a cry of surprise, and when he looked behind him, he saw a massively humpbacked creature wrestling with itself. The man screamed and dropped the wrench, pulling a now-bloody hand to cradle it against his body. The man turned slightly so Seth could see his back, and he knew what he was looking at:

A tiny boy was fastened to the man, his legs wrapped around the waist, spindly arms around the muscular neck, clinging for dear life as the man clawed at his back with his good hand. The boy screamed bloody murder and said in words barely recognizable, "You killed my mom! You people killed my mom!"

"Seth," he heard whispered. He looked down to find Waverly looking at him, gasping. "Help him," she managed to say before fighting for another breath.

Seth took up the wrench again and stood up shakily, just as the man backed the little boy into the cold glass of the dome, hitting hard. The boy's head slammed into the glass, and he groaned once, then fell limp onto the metal floor. The man looked down at him in astonishment and had just turned back around when Seth swung with every ounce of strength he had left. The wrench made solid contact with the brute's temple, and he looked at Seth with stunned, watery eyes.

The wrench vibrated in Seth's hand like the clacker of a bell.

The man collapsed first to his knees, his eyes still open but vacant, a line of drool rolling down his chin. Then he fell facedown onto the floor and lay there, twitching.

Seth was on his knees again, he realized, though he didn't know when he dropped the wrench and crawled to the com system at the back of the room. The button was four feet off the ground, so far away he didn't know how he could reach it. He lifted his right arm despite its leaden weight and found the emergency call button with the flat of his hand. The screen flickered to life, and Seth saw Sarek Hassan's shocked face staring at him.

"Help," Seth croaked through his swelling throat.

He heard Sarek's voice barking orders at someone. Help was coming. He wanted to crawl back to Waverly, but there were too many red spots, and she was so far away. So he lay on his side, closed his eyes, and waited for them to come.

PART THREE

Justice

Revenge is a kind of wild justice;
which the more man's nature runs
to, the more ought law to weed it
out.

—Sir Francis Bacon

Recovery

Kieran's headache seemed too huge to contain in a single skull. The pain was throbbing outward from the infirmary and into the black emptiness beyond the porthole above the head of his bed. A little girl with a minor cut on her finger wandered in and showed it to one of Tobin's helpers, who took her to one of the curtained areas to clean it for her. As she passed by the foot of Kieran's bed, she smiled shyly. Once again Kieran questioned why the designers thought to put most of the infirmary beds in the large main room, facing the door, in full view of anyone who might come in. It was humiliating to be so sick in such a public place.

"Come on, tough guy. Ready for some morphine?"

Tobin Ames asked again, a callused hand on his wrist, taking his pulse.

"Go ahead." Kieran finally nodded, and watched as Tobin expertly prepared a hypodermic and plunged it into the vein in Kieran's elbow. The pain ebbed away, floated out through the hull of the ship, where it hovered just outside the porthole, watching Kieran, waiting for the morphine to trickle away so that it could come back.

"I don't know why you insisted on waiting," Tobin said, shaking his head.

"Morphine seems too strong for a headache."

"Depends on the headache."

"How can I tell how bad the pain is unless I let the morphine run out?" Kieran said groggily. He hated the morphine almost as much as he hated the pain. Morphine deadened his mind, unsettled his stomach, made him feel confused and weak. It gave him horrible dreams of Waverly cackling at him, Sarah poking him with a long accusing finger, or, worst of all, being trapped in an air lock about to be blown out by Seth Ardvale, who grinned at him through the porthole, his thumb poised over the button. Morphine was better than agony, but just barely.

"You got a pretty nasty dose of that gas, I think," Tobin said. "Either that or you're more susceptible to it than the other kids."

"How are all the others?" Kieran said, waving away Tobin's suggestion that he was fragile. *I am, though,* he thought. *I used to be so much stronger, and now I'm weak. Because Seth Ardvale starved me.*

"Mostly over it." Tobin pointed to his left with his thumb at Arthur, in the next bed over. "You and he are the sickest ones."

Kieran turned to Arthur, who was sipping at a bowl of

soup. Arthur saw him looking and nodded.

"Is your voice back?" Kieran asked.

Arthur shook his head.

"That gas is hell on vocal cords," Tobin said. He shuffled around Kieran's bed in that slow gait of his, his head hunched down between his shoulders in a permanent shrug. "All I can do is give Arthur steroids and hope his voice comes back."

"How do you know to do that?" Kieran asked him.

"How do I know to do anything? I read the textbooks. I watch the training videos."

"Must be awful not being able to talk," Kieran said to Arthur.

The boy shrugged with an ironic roll of his eyes, as though Arthur considered his voice no great loss since he was quiet most of the time anyway.

Kieran lay back. Now that the pain was out of him, he could turn his mind to other things. Waverly was probably doing everything she could to undermine him while he was laid up. That was the real reason he'd wanted to try going off the morphine, to see if he could function if he left the infirmary. If he stayed here as long as Tobin wanted him to, Waverly would have plenty of time to consolidate her power.

She was probably up to something right now.

He threw his covers aside and stood up from his bed, swaying on his feet. He had one hand gripped on the bed railing as he took a tentative step toward the infirmary door.

"Whoa, what do you think you're doing?" Tobin rushed at him, a clipboard in his hand. "Get back in bed."

"I just need to make a quick trip to Central Command."

"Sarek has everything under control." Tobin tried to

push Kieran back onto the mattress, but Kieran resisted him.

"I'm Captain of this ship," Kieran said, blinking. The room seemed to be changing color, from green to blue to red to yellow, flicking through the hues like an alarm light.

"The Captain is supposed to follow doctor's orders," Tobin said, crossing his arms over his chest. He was about to say more, but suddenly an alarm sounded in his office, signifying some kind of emergency, and he ran off to answer it.

Something was going on. Kieran hobbled toward the door, his steps uneven. Only a few of the gas victims remained, mostly younger children who were still asthmatic from the attack. He waved at one little girl, who was sucking on the ear of her stuffed bear as she stared at him. He probably looked drunk to her, but he kept his feet under him, and he walked out the door with as much dignity as he could muster.

He got off the elevator without remembering how he'd ever gotten on it. The hallway to Central Command seemed to pulsate, growing wider then narrower. He had his eyes on the doorway for an hour, it seemed, before he finally reached it. He heard the whir of the video camera checking his face, and then the sound of a bell when the door opened for him.

"Let me know when you get to the infirmary," Sarek was barking into his microphone, then he switched channels. "Harvey! Have you gotten to the brig yet?"

"Almost there," came Harvey's breathless voice. "He's heavy!"

"I'll send a medical team down. But I want him tied up before you let anyone near him." Sarek looked up and, when he saw Kieran, waved him over excitedly.

"What's going on?" Kieran asked. He looked out the portholes, and sure enough, his headache had followed him here. It hovered just outside, pulsing.

"Waverly and Seth caught the terrorist!" Sarek said.

"What? Waverly and *Seth*?" Kieran asked. He swooned for a second and almost fell, but a chair appeared behind him. He looked up to see Matt Allbright standing over him, hands on the back of the chair. He nodded curtly at Kieran.

"He beat them pretty badly," Matt said. Kieran was looking up the boy's nose, at his nostril hairs, which quivered as he spoke. "And that little kid, Philip Grieg."

"He's unconscious," Sarek put in, one hand poised over the earpiece of his headset. "Waverly and Seth are in and out."

"They weren't in the infirmary just now," Kieran said. Or were they? The morphine had made his mind fuzzier than he thought.

"They're just getting there." Sarek bent over his com station when Harvey's voice came back on. "Yes! He's there? Okay, I'll let Tobin know."

Sarek paged the infirmary, and Tobin answered with, "What? I've got my hands full!"

"I need a medic sent to the brig," Sarek said.

"The terrorist waits!" Tobin yelled. "I've got three of our own here, badly hurt."

Kieran must have just missed them. He sat in his chair, dazed. Seth and Waverly, his two greatest enemies, found the terrorist. They'll be big heroes now.

I'm going to look like a fool.

"It all happened just a few minutes ago," Sarek said excitedly. "I don't know how or why, but Waverly and

Seth came across the guy in the observatory."

"The observatory," Kieran said quietly. He used to take Waverly there for dates. They'd huddle under a blanket, looking at stars, kissing. Now she was meeting Seth there. "What were they doing?"

"Looking for the terrorist, I think."

"No," Kieran said, slicing a hand through the air. "They happened on him by accident."

"What do you mean?" Sarek said, confused.

"Seth and Waverly were working together," Kieran said. His voice was wispy thin. "They were meeting in the observatory to bring me down, don't you see? The election was Seth's idea. He's controlling Waverly. They found the terrorist by chance."

"I suppose that's possible," said Matt slowly. "But—"

"Not *possible*," Kieran said with a sluggish tongue. "That's what happened. I know for sure."

"*How* do you know?" Sarek said.

"It's just the way things are," Kieran said. He shook his head to clear it and almost fell off his chair.

"You know, boss, I don't think you're okay to be here," said Matt's floating head, which was drifting over Kieran. "I think you're still sick."

"You all want to bring me down," Kieran said, then took in a sharp breath. "I didn't mean that."

"Take him back to the infirmary," Sarek said to Matt.

"Don't talk about me. I'm not a child," Kieran said, but he felt himself being wheeled down the hallway. He wasn't sure he was sitting or lying down, because sometimes he could see the ceiling and sometimes he could see ahead of him.

When Matt wheeled him into the infirmary, he entered a scene of chaos.

Waverly was lying on the bed right next to his own, and on the other side of Waverly was Seth. Both of them had their eyes closed. Horrible purple bruises covered their throats, and both were taking labored, staccato breaths. Oxygen tubes snaked from tanks by their beds up to their nostrils. Waverly was so pale.

From the adjoining room came a burst of frantic voices. Tobin and two other boys were leaning over a bed, blocking Kieran's view of the patient. All he could see was a pair of small feet shuddering and quaking. "Who is that?" Kieran asked.

"Philip Grieg," someone whispered. He turned to see Waverly looking at him through sickeningly bloodshot eyes. "He saved our lives," she said.

"Take me to him," Kieran said, and Matt obediently wheeled him to the room. Kieran got out of his chair and, leaning on the wall, moved along the back of the small private room until he could see Philip's face.

The little boy's left eye was swelling out of its socket. He was foaming at the mouth, and his limbs were trembling and jerking. Dried blood crusted his nostrils, and hideous moans and growls came from his throat. He sounded monstrous.

"What's wrong with him?" Kieran shouted. He was already scared, but his blood chilled when he saw Tobin Ames, this competent boy who had been acting as ship's doctor, look up at him with a tear-streaked face.

"Bleeding in his brain, I think," Tobin said, then broke down. "I can't help him! I can't!"

"Why not?" Kieran screamed. The morphine suddenly cleared away and he could stand on his own two feet, his entire mind crystallized on a single point: saving Philip Grieg. "What would a doctor do?"

"Drill into his head!"

"Then do it!" The room got quiet, and every eye turned to him. Kieran was calm now.

"You don't understand!" Tobin cried. "Everything I've needed was in the manuals until now! There's no training video for brain surgery!"

"Anyone can see he's going to die if you don't."

"He'll die if I *do*."

"Give him a chance," Kieran said.

Tobin stood over Philip's quaking body, panting, his short neck bulging out at the veins. Finally he said, "Okay. Bring me a shaver and a scalpel, and, uh, iodine. And . . . I don't know. Find a drill."

His two helpers stared at him, openmouthed, until he yelled, "Go! We've got no time."

He went to the sink and washed his hands, scrubbing with a small white brush up to the elbows. One of his helpers put rubber gloves on him while the other wheeled in a cart holding an array of instruments, each one more frightening and complicated than the next.

"We've got to get the adults back," Kieran said quietly to himself. But then he remembered, there *were* adults on the ship, in the long-term care section, still recovering from radiation poisoning. "Is Victoria Hand conscious?" he asked the room at large, but no one answered.

"Turn him over," Tobin said. The boys gently turned Philip's scrawny body, and gasped when they saw the huge bump on the back of his head, swelling out like a grotesque balloon. There must be so much blood in that young skull. Tobin closed his eyes, pushed all the air in his lungs out from between pursed lips, then his helper tied a surgical mask over his nose and mouth. "Everybody out," Tobin said.

"You don't need help?" said his assistant, wide-eyed.

"I can't do this with someone watching," he said.

Matt took hold of Kieran's elbow and drew him out of the room. Matt headed for Kieran's bed, but Kieran planted his feet, pulling against the boy's grip. "Let's check on the adults."

Matt held firmly to Kieran's elbow as the two of them walked past the doctor's office and into the next room, a large space with a row of eight beds, every one of them occupied by the ailing adults. It had been weeks since Kieran had come down to check on them. Two of them were hooked up to ventilators that puffed their chests up, making them look like dolls. Tobin's mother was one of them. No wonder the boy never seemed to leave the infirmary; he was working hard saving other people so he wouldn't have to think about how he couldn't help his own mother. That Tobin was able to keep these adults alive at all showed how intelligent and capable he and his helpers were.

In the far corner of the room lay Victoria Hand, a nurse, the sole surviving member of the Empyrean's medical team. Next to her bed dozed her son, Austen, who had become the de facto nurse of this ward, along with the other children whose relatives were here.

"How is she?" Kieran asked Austen, who straightened in his chair when he saw Kieran. He rubbed sleep out of his eyes with his long fingers and sniffed. "She sleeps like twenty hours a day, and I have to do dialysis on her every day."

"How did you guys know to do dialysis?"

"She told me."

"So she's talking?"

"When she's awake we can ask her questions."

No wonder the medical ward was running so well.

Kieran leaned over her and took her hand. "Vickie? Vickie, wake up."

Her eyelids fluttered, but they closed again. Her skin was puffy, and she looked as though she'd aged twenty years in the last few months. She opened her mouth a few millimeters, and with a soft gush of air, said, "Kieran."

"Vickie, we've got a severe head injury in the other room." Her eyes fluttered closed again, until Kieran knelt down and said loudly into her ear. "Tobin Ames is about to drill into Philip Grieg's skull."

Her eyes flew open, and she focused on Kieran. "His mother will never consent—" she began, but then seemed to remember that Philip's mother was dead.

"If I get you into a wheelchair . . ." Kieran began, but she was already nodding, struggling to sit up. Austen threw his weight behind her and pushed her.

"Mom, are you sure?"

"Yes," she rasped. "Just get me there."

Now that she was upright and the light shone on her scalp, Kieran realized that her hair had fallen out and been replaced with a weak-looking peach fuzz all over her skull. Through her thin infirmary gown, her back showed every rib; she looked as though she were made of sticks.

Austen, biting his lower lip, brought a wheelchair, and Matt lifted Victoria into it. She swooned, and leaned over the side of the chair to vomit a thin, watery substance, which dribbled onto her hospital gown.

"Mom!" Austen cried.

"Just from being upright after so long on my back," she said faintly.

Everyone in the main room of the infirmary stopped

to stare as she was wheeled to Philip's operating room. Kieran could see through the glass door that Tobin was shaving Philip's hair. Victoria picked up a surgical mask. "Tie this on me," she told her son, who bent over her, his features twisted with worry.

"Mask on you," she rasped, pointing at Matt, who quickly tied one around his own face, then he pushed her inside the room. Austen stood back. He clearly didn't want to go in at all.

Kieran watched through the glass of the door. When Tobin saw Victoria, he cried out in relief. Matt wheeled her around so she could get a look at poor Philip's misshapen skull, then he quickly left the room and came to stand next to Kieran. They watched as Victoria pointed at the boy, and Tobin listened closely. Tobin picked up a large swab with iodine on it and began to smear it over Philip's head. Then, with sweat pouring down his face, he picked up the scalpel.

"Tobin is brave," said a voice, and Kieran turned around to see that Seth was watching from his bed. "I could never do that."

"Me neither," whispered Waverly, who was also watching as tears trickled from her eyes.

They seemed much better now that the medicines had a chance to work, though their voices both sounded squeezed.

Kieran stumbled over to his bed, his eyes on Seth, who eyed him back. Seth had lost weight, Kieran could see, but of course that only brought out the definition of his muscles, the finely carved bones of his face. Was Waverly so stupid that she could be taken in by nothing more than physical beauty?

"Matt," Kieran said, and beckoned to the boy with a

finger. Matt leaned down, his back straight, and Kieran whispered in his ear, "Go down and tell the guards in the brig to notify me when the terrorist regains consciousness. No one is to talk to him until I get down there."

"Okay," Matt said.

"And bring back a couple guards with you."

Matt looked stonily at Seth and nodded.

"So I guess I'll be going back to the brig," Seth said, though he couldn't have heard what Kieran said.

"But now you'll get a trial," Waverly said. "Right, Kieran?"

Kieran stared straight ahead, ignoring her.

"Seth figured out how to capture the terrorist," she rasped.

"He modified the forward sensor array to carry a voice transmission," Seth said matter-of-factly. "I can't believe I didn't think of it before."

He sounded so smug, so arrogant. Kieran wanted to choke him all over again.

"How did you two happen to be there?" Kieran said quietly.

There was an awkward silence. Kieran turned to find Waverly looking at her hands, her mouth stubbornly set. She raised her eyes to his and said evenly, "I was bringing Seth food."

"Under threat," Seth put in. "I forced her to do it."

"No one can force me to do anything," Waverly said, glaring at Seth before turning to Kieran. "I was doing it because I didn't think he should go back to the brig after I saw the way you threatened Sarah. I thought he was in danger, so I helped him hide."

"How kind of you," Kieran said, and turned away from her. How disgusting she was to him now.

Soon Matt walked back into the infirmary, Harvey Markem and Hiro Mazumoto trailing behind, looking nervous.

"Matt, Hiro, take Seth to the brig," Kieran said. The two boys looked hesitant, but when Hiro took hold of Seth's arm, Seth took the oxygen hose off his face and got out of bed willingly enough. He seemed shaky on his feet, and he swayed a bit, so Kieran said, "Better bring down an oxygen tank with you." With his free hand, Hiro picked up a tank and walked Seth toward the door.

"Harvey," Kieran said. "I'm placing Waverly under arrest for obstructing justice and aiding a fugitive."

He ignored her hoarse cry of outrage as Harvey reluctantly pulled on her arm. She lay still at first, seeming to consider whether to fight, but finally accepted that she couldn't win. Harvey picked up her oxygen tank and pulled her toward the door.

"Kieran, we're sick," Waverly said. Kieran heard clicks inside her throat when she drew a breath. "We should be here in the infirmary, not in the brig."

"You'll get medical care," Kieran said.

Seth was just about to stumble out the door when he pulled against his two guards, resisting them long enough to look back at Kieran with a murderous glare. "You're no better than I was," he managed to say before they overpowered him and pulled him away.

Once they were gone, Kieran looked to his left to find Arthur's steady blue eyes on him.

"I have no choice, Arthur. You see that, don't you?"

Arthur turned away and hunkered down under his covers. Kieran kept his eyes on the door to the operating room, where Tobin and Victoria were working on Philip. Right now, all he cared about was that little boy's life.

Release

"We're too sick to be down here," Waverly said to Harvey, who dragged her along the corridor. Even to her own ears, it sounded like an excuse, but she *knew* it to be true. The steroids Tobin had pumped into her had revived her, but what about when they wore off? The fleshy insides of her throat could swell together again, and she might suffocate. She needed to be in bed, and she needed medical care. She could see only the back of Seth as he staggered between his two guards; she was afraid he would fall. "Harvey, I'm not kidding. We almost died!"

"I know," Harvey whispered through the side of his mouth. "I'm going to call a Central Council meeting. Sit tight."

He pulled her into the corridor that ran between the cells of the brig. Waverly looked into the first cell on her left to find the man who had nearly killed her lying on the cot, snoring loudly.

"I don't want to be near him." She shuddered.

"He'll never know you're here," Harvey said.

She stumbled, almost fell to her knees when, with surprising strength, Harvey scooped her up and carried her the rest of the way down the corridor and laid her on the cot in the cell at the end of the row, across from where they were putting Seth.

She and Seth would be able to see each other and talk. Kieran wouldn't like that. Harvey and the other guards probably knew it, too. Was this their way of acknowledging Kieran's unfairness?

Waverly lay still as Harvey fixed a tube under her nose and turned the dial on the oxygen tank. She felt somewhat revived.

"You okay?" she heard, and turned to see Seth looking at her, his oxygen already on. The whites of his eyes were red from burst blood vessels, and his skin was gray. Did she look that pale? Were her bruises as ugly as his?

"I'm okay I think," she said, but she was still out of breath from walking down here. "You?"

"I've just been choked by a gorilla, so, yeah. Feeling great."

Waverly looked at the ceiling because she couldn't look at Seth's bruises any longer. She was afraid to close her eyes. She might die in her sleep if her throat closed again.

I'm still scared, is all, she told herself, trying to

calm down. *Sleep will heal me.*

But when she closed her eyes, all she saw was that animalistic face twisted with fury as iron hands squeezed her throat. Every detail of him was crystallized in her mind: his receding hairline, his large, oily pores, his rotten breath, the sweat that had run in streaks down to the tip of his nose, where it lingered, then fell in droplets that splashed on her face, her neck, her hair. Her vertebrae had ground together under his fingers, and she'd heard the crackling of her larynx. She forgot Seth was in the room. She forgot where she was. She was dying, alone with her killer. She'd kicked, trying to twist out of his grasp, but he was impossibly strong, and he was huge.

She'd known fear before, of course, but this terror at the end of her life had been new. It hollowed her out, debased her, turned her into nothing more than airless lungs and bloodless brain. A gray cloud had crept into the borders of her vision, and a voice inside her had screamed, *I'm dying! I'm dying now!*

When she had wakened in the infirmary, she couldn't feel her own body. There were people leaning over her, talking about her, shouting at her, but she couldn't speak to them. She wasn't sure she was in the same space with them. They were the living, and she was dead.

Then she must have turned her head, and she'd seen Seth in the next bed over, looking at her.

I've come back, she'd thought. *I'm alive again.*

After all that, Kieran had sent her down to this cold, comfortless, lonely place. He'd banished her.

He must really hate me.

Waverly shook her head, wincing at the pain in the

base of her skull. She felt tears running down the sides of her face, across the indentations of her temples, into her hair. She'd known Kieran didn't love her anymore. That had been clear for a while, and she'd accepted it. But now he'd become her enemy.

I knew this might happen, she told herself fiercely. She didn't like her own grief. She longed for the time to come when she no longer mourned the loss of her old life, when she no longer cared so much about the future. At some point she had to become hardened so that it wouldn't hurt anymore. She felt parts of herself starting to break, like fibers in a twisted palm frond giving in little by little. What would happen when she finally gave way?

"I'll go crazy," she whispered, and opened her eyes.

She'd lost some time somehow. Had she slept? Someone had turned off the lights. Now her cell was dim, with only a small bulb glowing over her metal sink. The only sound was the hiss of her oxygen tube.

"No you won't," she heard, and turned to Seth.

He was looking at her in the faint light as he lay on his cot, breathing in short bursts that hollowed out his belly. He smiled meagerly.

"Somewhere along the line," she said through the pain in her throat, "after everything we've been through, we'll break."

"Then what?"

She shook her head, then cried out from pain all through her neck, in the muscles and the bones. Her hand flew up to her throat. If there had been someone nearby, a guard or a medic, she'd ask for a pain reliever, but there was no one. "Then," she whispered, "it might be a relief to go crazy."

"Maybe," he said with a shrug. "But you won't."

"How do you know?"

"By now you'd already *be* crazy."

She closed her eyes. Maybe he was right. But she wished sometimes that she could just give up and forget about all the things she felt obligated to fight for. Let someone else worry about it.

"Waverly," Seth whispered.

She turned to look at him.

"There's a bag buried in the conifer bay, in the juniper grove. It's marked with a branch of holly on top. Lots of red berries. Easy to spot if you're looking for it."

She wrinkled her brow. "What are you talking about?"

"If something bad happens, you'll need what's in it."

"What's in it?"

He shook his head. He didn't want to say, so she knew.

"It won't come to that," she said quietly.

He raised one eyebrow at her, and she felt foolish for saying such a naive, childish thing.

The hallway light blinked on, and Waverly heard footsteps approaching. She was surprised to see Tobin Ames come to stand outside her cell. He swayed on his feet, looking utterly spent, and held up a syringe with raised eyebrows. "More anti-inflammatory for the lady?"

"Okay," she said.

He pulled a key from a hook on his belt and turned the lock to her cell. When he crossed the threshold, the lights flickered on, and Waverly squinted against the brightness. Tobin swabbed her shoulder with alcohol and sank the needle into her muscle.

"You're good at that," she whispered.

He didn't acknowledge the compliment, and instead handed her a couple of pills with a cup of water to wash them down. "For the pain," he said.

She studied his face. "How'd it go with the little boy? Philip?"

"You wouldn't have believed the blood," Tobin said. "But now there's room in his head for his brain."

"Is he going to be okay?" Seth asked from across the hallway.

Tobin shook his head. "Victoria Hand says he might survive, but he'll probably never be the same again."

Waverly let out a whimper, and fresh tears ran down her face.

"Hey." She felt a thumb on her chin, and she looked at Tobin. "Cry later, okay? Being upset right now isn't good for you."

She nodded and took deep breaths through her ragged throat.

Tobin left her cell, locked the door behind him, and stood outside Seth's cell.

"You going to let me treat you without any trouble?"

"Why, you scared of me?"

"You could crumble me up like dry leaves," Tobin said frankly.

"Not now, I couldn't," Seth said, and lifted a limp arm to show how weak he was.

"There are four guards at the end of the hallway, and you won't get past them, just so you know," Tobin said, then fitted his key into the lock and entered Seth's cell. He handed over Seth's pills, which Seth swallowed dry. When Tobin administered the shot, Seth winced.

"Wimp," Waverly said.

"Not everyone can have the superhuman strength of a hundred-and-ten-pound girl," Seth said.

"You two are real cards." Tobin yawned like a monster, showing all his teeth.

"Go get some sleep," Waverly told him.

Tobin nodded and shuffled out of Seth's cell. He started down the hallway but paused and turned around. "And just for the record, I think Kieran sending you down here after you caught the terrorist is rubbish," Tobin said, then tilted his blockish head slightly. "Even though, Seth, you were kind of a bastard when you were in charge."

"Thank you for your support," Seth said blandly.

"You were," Tobin insisted, sticking out his chin.

"Yeah, I know!" Seth said irritably.

"Well if you can admit it to me, maybe you can admit it to everyone, throw your support behind Kieran publicly, and this whole thing can end."

"You think that would do it?" Seth said skeptically.

"Worth a try," Tobin said with a shrug before he headed off down the hallway, yawning again. He disappeared into the shadowy hallway between the cells faster than Waverly liked. This place was all cold metal, all unyielding edges, nothing soft or warm.

"Maybe he's right," Waverly said. "Maybe Kieran just needs to know you won't stage another mutiny."

"Oh yeah? And how are *you* going to redeem yourself?"

"Maybe I should apologize, too," she said wistfully.

"So you think you were wrong to help me?"

She turned to look at him and saw a wounded expression in his poor, reddened eyes. "No, Seth."

Saying his name aloud shifted something inside of

her. She thought she saw the change happen in him, too. His eyes softened, his cheeks sank inward, and he bit his bottom lip. If she'd been looking at anyone but Seth Ardvale, she'd think that was the face of someone who was about to cry.

They looked at each other across the hallway until the lights flickered back off. Now that she'd had her steroid shot, her fear of dying in her sleep had subsided, and she realized she was drowsy. Waverly felt her eyelids droop, and she surrendered.

When she awoke, she was looking at the olive-shaped face of Alia Khadivi, watching through the bars of her cell with warm eyes. "Are you well?"

"I'm sore," Waverly croaked. Her throat felt scraped bloody, and it was dry from sleep. "I need water."

"Guard!" Alia shouted down the hallway, and soon Hiro appeared, his features immobile. When Alia pointed at the lock on Waverly's cell, he obediently fitted the key into it and opened the door.

Alia went to the sink that stood against the wall of Waverly's cell to fill a plastic tumbler with water, then knelt by Waverly, very gently lifted her head, and held the rim of the cup to her lips. The water was cold, tasted clean and sweet, and Waverly gulped it down.

"More," she croaked.

Alia patiently brought Waverly several tumblers full of water until her thirst was sated. Then she sat on the edge of Waverly's cot and took her hand. Her dry palm felt sisterly, comforting on Waverly's cold hand.

"I've gotten a court order from the Justice of the Peace to release you. Doctor Tobin is waiting outside with a wheelchair to take you back to the infirmary."

Waverly smiled at her friend. "How did you do that?"

"Very simple." Her ruby lips turned upward at the corners. "Seth was never charged with a crime, so at the time you helped him, he could not technically be considered a fugitive."

"So Seth can get out, too?"

She heard Seth chuckle in the other cell, but she could not see him because Alia was in the way.

"No, because Kieran finally brought formal charges against him."

"And they are?" Seth rasped. He was leaning up on one elbow, but from the way his head weaved, Waverly could see this cost him a great deal of effort.

Alia hesitated, but she turned to Seth, and now Waverly could get a glimpse of him. He still looked gray. The whites of his eyes had congealed into pink puddings, and he licked at his dry lips. He'd gotten worse.

"Kieran is accusing you of attempted murder," Alia said to him.

"Sounds about right," Seth said before collapsing back onto his cot.

"Seth needs medical attention," Waverly said.

"I can see that. I will appeal to the Justice that Seth be released to the custody of the infirmary." She turned again to Seth. "How long can you last?"

"I need water," Seth said. He tried to get up from his cot, but he was too weak and fell back again.

"Hiro! I need to see Seth Ardvale for a moment," Alia said, and Hiro came and let her out of Waverly's cell, then led her to Seth's and unlocked the door. He stood over Seth, one hand on his nightstick and the other on a can of mace that was hooked to his belt, but he needn't

have been so vigilant. When Alia held a cup of water to
Seth's lips, he was barely strong enough to lift his head
off his pillow to drink.

Suddenly an angry voice echoed down the hallway.
"It's pointless to hold me!"

"He's awake," Waverly said, chilled.

"He is a very frightening man." Alia shuddered. "The
way he looked at me when I walked past him. He
recognized me from the New Horizon, I think."

"Do you remember him?"

"No." Alia shook her head.

"When can we question him?"

Alia's expression clouded. "Kieran wants exclusive
access to him."

"He's invoking Captain's privilege to interview the
terrorist?"

"And he's shutting the Central Council out."

"No," Waverly said. Revived by the water, which
seemed to loosen the blood in her veins, she found she
could sit up, though she was very dizzy. "The Central
Council should be there."

"We'll have to get past his guards," Alia said with a
glance at Hiro, whose eyes shifted to look at the wall,
pretending to be deaf.

"We'll get our own guards," Waverly said.

"Do you intend to start a war with Kieran Alden?" Alia
asked, one charcoal eyebrow raised.

"He's the one who started it."

Waverly heard footsteps in the hallway, and Tobin
Ames appeared with a wheelchair. "Ready for your ride?"

"Look at Seth first," Waverly said.

Tobin took in Seth's poor color and labored breathing

and shook his head. "He should have been under observation."

"How's Philip?" Seth asked in a throaty whisper.

"Alive," Tobin said grimly. "If I knew how to run an electroencephalograph I'd tell you how his brain is, but I don't. So we wait." He lifted his eyes to Hiro, who stood staring at the wall. "Let me in so I can see my patient."

Doctor Tobin, indeed, Waverly thought. He'd taken to the role, if not with ease, then with a grim determination to learn fast and execute well.

Tobin shined a light in Seth's eyes and down his throat, then took a syringe from his pocket. "I thought you might need some more of this."

Seth accepted the shot with complete apathy, his body flat on his cot, his only movement his chest as he breathed in and out.

"Seth, I'm coming back down and I'm going to set you up with an IV," Tobin said. "You need fluids and glucose to keep your strength up, okay?"

"You're the doctor."

"I wish I were." Tobin looked at Hiro, who opened Seth's cell door for him, locked it, and finally came into Waverly's cell. Tobin helped Waverly sit up and then, with a hand in each of her armpits, assisted her into the wheelchair.

"I'm going to get you out of here," Waverly said to Seth as Tobin wheeled her away.

"Okay," Seth said, but she could see in his eyes that he didn't believe she had the power.

Waverly leaned to her left, clinging to the arm of the wheelchair as Tobin slowly wheeled her toward her almost-murderer's cell. Her breath came in gasps, and she felt beads of sweat mingle with the tiny hairs at her hairline. She could smell her own fear rising like a mist around her.

Sit up straight. Don't let him see you like this. Waverly straightened and crammed her hands under her thighs, and when she came even with his cell, she made herself look inside.

He sat rigid, his wrists in manacles, his fists like stones on his knees. He was hunched, his head nestled between massive shoulders, and he stared out of his cell from the cave of his heavy brow ridge. As he breathed, his lips puffed out, then sucked inward like a bizarre bellows, and his cheeks quivered with fury when he recognized her. His eyes were black, and they followed her progress past his cell with a steady, fierce hatred. He looked like a man who had never known civilization.

"Stop," she said to Tobin, her fear replaced by anger. "Turn me toward him."

Tobin did as she asked without a word.

"I'm going to make you terrified," she said to the terrorist's meaty face. Her voice was still reedy, but her tone was murderous. He seemed to be looking past her, at the empty air behind her head. "I'm going to make you hurt so bad that you'll tell me anything to make it stop. And I'll enjoy it."

For half a second or less his eyes flickered to hers, and then his gaze was nonspecific again. But she knew she'd gotten to him. She'd given him something to think about so that when she came back here, he wouldn't be so brave.

Talk

Kieran sat on the metal folding chair across from the terrorist, ignoring the last remnant of his headache, which had faded to a nagging soreness since he left the infirmary. The man breathed noisily through hairy nostrils, and he kept his small eyes on Kieran's chest, refusing to speak. The sink against the rear wall of his cell had a leak and made a dripping noise that nagged at Kieran's ear.

"What is your mission?" Kieran asked the man again, but he was met only with numb silence.

Kieran knew from his own captivity that after a long while of being alone, you were willing to talk to anyone, even someone you hated. Maybe he hadn't isolated this man long enough to let the solitude work on him, but he couldn't afford any more time. There might be booby traps laid in the ship. He needed a way into this man's mind, and fast.

"Max Brent," Kieran said, and paused to let the name rest between them. "That was the name of the boy you poisoned. He was fourteen years old. You like killing kids?"

The piggish eyes flickered over Kieran's face.

"And Philip Grieg. He was an orphan who carried his teddy bear everywhere he went. You knocked his head so hard that his brain hemorrhaged. He'll never be the same. You feel good about that?"

This seemed to move the man. His eyes softened a little and he said sadly, "I didn't know he was so little until he was on the floor."

He'd spoken! Kieran tried to hide his excitement and responded with, "And you tried to strangle to death two of our crew members, both fifteen years old."

His eyes darkened at this. "That bitch deserved it."

"Oh really?" Kieran said, forcing his voice to stay cool. "And why is that?"

"She killed my . . . friend. Murdered him in cold blood."

"I know Waverly, and she wouldn't have done that unless she thought he was going to kill her."

"Shelby wasn't a bad man."

"So you think Waverly should have let Anne Mather do anything she wanted to her and not try to get away?"

"After the way your crew sterilized our women," the man said, "your girls owed us."

"What are you talking about?"

"Don't pretend you don't know," the man shot at Kieran with contempt. "You destroyed our women."

"I don't see how that's possible."

"You sent us a bad formula for the drug therapy. You assured us it had been tested and it was safe."

"Did Anne Mather tell you to say that?"

"She doesn't even know I'm here."

"Sure she does. Otherwise why would you have been in the observatory at all, if not to communicate with her?"

"I like to look at stars," the man said flatly.

"You say our crew sent you a bad formula? You didn't test it yourselves before you used it? Seems pretty stupid to me."

"We trusted you!" the man screamed with deafening violence. He jerked off the cot where he was sitting, but the chains around his hands held him back. He glared at Kieran as though intending to kill him.

With half a turn of his head, Kieran made sure that Hiro was still standing behind him, ready with a baton. He let out a quiet, slow breath, calming himself.

"Even if what you say is true, it doesn't give you the right to kill two young boys."

The terrorist's eyes fastened on Kieran's, and he closed his fleshy lips as if resolving to say nothing more.

Kieran stood and motioned to Hiro to unlock the cell door. Let the terrorist stew for a while.

Harvey and two other guards stood in the hallway outside the entrance to the brig, armed with mace and batons.

"No one sees him or talks to him, understand?" Kieran barked at them.

"Sure thing," Harvey said to Kieran, but he didn't look him in the eye for long. He was on the Central Council, and Kieran guessed that already his loyalties were being tested. He thought of moving Harvey to a less-crucial duty, but that might alienate the boy further.

Back in his office, Kieran opened the bottom drawer of his desk. The data-dot with Mather's files was still where he'd left it. He'd thought she would contact him again, try to cajole him into watching the vid files, give him a chance to work on her, but he'd heard nothing from her.

He logged on to the radar system in Central Command and checked the position of the New Horizon. They were about 8.75 million miles ahead. He'd managed to close the gap by a quarter million miles, but at this rate it would be at least a year before he could catch up to them. And then what? If they ever did catch up, his crew would be so weakened from severe edema, muscle strain, and worn-down joints that they'd be useless in a fight. His whole body hurt him, and he could see in the faces of his crew that they hurt just as much.

He'd thought through dozens of ideas for how to attack the other vessel without killing the parents on board in the process. He'd only be able to use the older kids in an offensive—that would be about forty, maybe fifty at the most. They'd have to board the ship and get the parents out by force, but Mather had all the advantages. He'd never be able to sneak up on her; she could monitor the Empyrean's position easily. The battlefield would be her own ship, which she could prepare any way she liked. And worst of all, he and the attack force would have no idea where to look for the parents. The more he thought about it, the more he could see that overt warfare would never work.

Though he had butterflies in his stomach at the thought of what he meant to do, he keyed into the long-range com system and hailed the New Horizon. A woman's sallow face flicked onto the screen, and Kieran said, "I want to speak to Anne Mather."

"I've been instructed to inquire whether you've seen the video files that she sent to you?"

"I haven't had the time. We've been dealing with a terrorist on board our ship."

"I've been instructed to tell you the Pastor is unavailable."

"I just want to ask her a question."

"Until you've watched . . ." The woman lifted her hand to an earpiece and looked again at Kieran with colorless eyes. "One moment, please."

Abruptly, the screen changed to Mather's plump pink cheeks. "Hello, Kieran."

"We've captured your man."

"What man?" she said, eyebrows raised in curiosity.

"The Neanderthal you sent to sabotage our ship? He's in our brig."

"Are you saying there's a member of my crew on board the Empyrean?" she asked, blinking her eyes with surprise.

He watched her, looking for signs of deception. Her gaze was steady and her brow wrinkled, as though she were displeased to learn one of her crew was AWOL. Either she really didn't know about the terrorist or she was a good liar.

"He won't give us his name, but he's a big guy,

heavy features, receding hairline . . ."

"Jake," Mather said under her breath. "Jacob Pauley has been missing from his duties for quite some time. I thought he was depressed and keeping to his quarters."

This was clearly a lie. The New Horizon was just as large and complicated a ship as the Empyrean. Every crew member had vital duties to perform and would be severely admonished if those duties were neglected. No. She must have sent him here, or at least she'd known he was here for a long time.

"I assume you've watched those videos," she said.

"No, and I don't plan on watching them, if you want to know."

Her eyebrows flicked upward at this. "I thought you wanted your families back."

"How do we even know they're still alive? You've given us no proof."

Mather nodded, eyes drifting away from the com screen. "Yes, I suppose that's right. You'd want proof, wouldn't you?" She leaned forward and pressed her fingertips together to make five spikes. "When you've watched the video, I'll give you a partial list of survivor names. As we make progress in our negotiations, you'll get more names."

"I'm not going to let you manipulate—"

"I wouldn't dream of it," she said with a smug smile, and her screen flickered out.

She was hateful, but at least she wasn't pretending to be his friend. Kieran stared reluctantly at the data-dot, afraid of what he was going to find there. He almost shut it back in the desk drawer, but he'd just seen some graffiti outside the central bunker calling Seth Ardvale and Waverly Marshall heroes for capturing the terrorist. Sarek had captured a video image of the artist, who had draped a blanket over him- or herself. It was impossible to even see if it was a boy or a girl. "Do we put our heroes in the brig?" was scrawled in large blue letters across the wall. Kieran's political position was shaky at best.

If he got all the surviving parents back, his leadership would never be questioned again.

Kieran picked up the data-dot, twirled it in his fingers. His insides churned, and he swallowed the last of his spit.

God, what do I do? He pleaded for a sign, but his heart was too filled with doubt, and the way was obscured to him.

With a darting motion, Kieran fitted the data-dot into his com station and turned it on.

Instantly the image of a much-younger Captain Jones appeared, smiling at the screen. His hair was bright red instead of the paper white that Kieran was used to. He was seated in the very chair Kieran sat in now, in front of the Goya painting that was now at Kieran's back. It gave Kieran an eerie feeling of impermanence. The Captain hadn't grown his beard yet, and without it he had hang-dog jowls and a weak, dimpled chin. He looked like a different person. "Anne, you'll never believe it," said Captain Jones.

"Did you find it?" said Mather's eager voice. She wasn't visible on the screen; only the Captain could be seen. "Did you find the formula?"

"Our preliminary trials are astounding! You're not going to believe your eyes!"

"Have you moved on to human trials yet?"

"I'm *talking* about the human trials! The drug stimulates the ovaries; we expected that. But it appears to improve egg quality! We've got embryos!"

"Oh my God! And they're growing?"

"Beautifully, Anne." Captain Jones rubbed his hand over his face, overjoyed. "I'm going to send you instructions for synthesizing the formula."

"Edmond, I'm going to say ten prayers for you tonight!"

Jones paused—a minuscule caesura, a cooling of the expression in his eyes—and then he said, "Good. Thanks. You do that."

The screen flickered to a new image, one of Captain Jones growing out a scruffy beard. He was still young enough that there wasn't any gray at his temples, and his eyes were clear of their spidery veins, but the look of contempt on his face made him seem monstrous.

"How could you do this to us?" cried a tearful Anne Mather. Kieran wished he could see her face. He'd love to see her cry.

"Anne, I'm sorry for what happened; I can't tell you how sorry!" the Captain said. But he didn't look sorry. He looked annoyed. "But to accuse us of purposefully sabotaging you—"

"I rescind it!" Mather cried. "I withdraw the accusation, and no one will ever hear of it again; just please, help us! We don't have much time, Edmond!"

"We have young children on this ship. Their bones are still growing. Our medical team thinks the results could be physically disastrous for them if we increased our acceleration—"

"It would still be only a fraction of full Earth g-force,

Edmond, and you know it! It's no more than their bodies
are designed to cope with!"

"But what about when we slow down again? We have
no way to judge how that would affect their development.
If it was just us adults—"

"You're lying! Making excuses! You don't want to help
us!"

"Anne, I have to think about my crew."

"You want New Earth for yourself so you can create
your sick idea of the perfect society. You don't want us
there."

"Anne," he said, and for the first time, Kieran detected
compassion in his voice, "you know me too well to really
think—"

The video skipped, as though a portion had been
edited out.

"Edmond, there were over five hundred steps for
synthesizing that compound. At the crucial step, we were
given directions that created a poison specifically
targeted to destroy our fertility. What are the odds of
that? How do you explain it?"

The Captain stared at the screen, blank. "I can't
explain it."

"We were sabotaged. It's the only explanation."

"Anne, our kids are more precious than ever now,
don't you see?" the Captain pleaded, his fingers woven
together. "We can't take any chances with their health,
none at all. It could mean success or failure for the
mission."

"You won't be able to have enough kids for the mission,
Edmond, and you know it. We'll need a full complement
when we get to New Earth."

"We can make a full complement if our daughters get pregnant young. I've got my logistics team on it right now."

"Logistics! I'm talking about what's right and wrong!"

"Back to that old discussion, are we? Now more than ever, I think we should acknowledge that morality is relative." Captain Jones leaned toward the screen, and his face loomed. Kieran saw his large pores and the droplets of sweat coating his forehead. "It would be right to help you, Anne, but it would be *more* right to protect our kids, to make certain they make it to New Earth."

"You're condemning us to certain destruction for the *small* chance that accelerating would hurt those kids."

"If that's the way you want to see it . . ."

"All our hopes destroyed," she said, her disembodied voice quivering with despair. "Our future. You're prepared to let that weigh on your shoulders?"

"For the good of future generations."

"You'll be remembered as the first war criminal of New Earth."

For a moment a look of apprehension passed over the Captain's features, but then he shook his head. "No, Anne. No one on New Earth is going to remember this ever happened."

The screen flickered to an image of the present-day Anne Mather, her hair gathered on top of her head in a neat bun, spectacles resting on the end of her well-made nose. "It's my belief that Captain Jones knew about the sabotage, and even approved it. But, Mr. Alden, even if he didn't know, once he learned of it, don't you think that he and the rest of the crew on the Empyrean should have done everything in their power to right the situation? Wouldn't that have been the humane thing to do?"

Kieran shifted uncomfortably in his seat. He'd expected manipulation. He hadn't expected it to be so effective.

"Since your Captain refused, and since we were faced not only with our own extinction but also with the probability that the mission to terraform New Earth might fail, we had no choice but to invade your vessel and take genetic material that could restore our fertility." Anne Mather smiled, her face full of weird joy. "Now we have almost one hundred babies on board our ship, and we've got over a hundred crew members pregnant with more. The mission is safe, now, Mr. Alden. But the future is tenuous. I call on you to bring the truth to your crew, to make what happened known. Even if we are still reviled by you, at least you'll understand why. And I believe future generations from both ships will be able to forgive the mistakes of their forebears and live in peace, side by side, on New Earth."

Kieran leaned back in his seat, wide-eyed, flabbergasted.

Captain Jones had been lying all those years?

He understood why the Captain refused to help the New Horizon, but he couldn't understand the lies. Captain Jones had kept the truth hidden from the Empyrean crew for sixteen years. He'd created a bitter enemy, and he never let the crew know they might be in danger of an attack. Kieran had always loved and admired the man. But now he didn't know what was true anymore.

Nothing could justify the New Horizon's attack and all

that senseless loss of life. But if what Mather claimed was true . . .

He flicked the call button on his com console and hailed the New Horizon. This time, Anne Mather answered directly.

"I trust you have watched the video?" she asked, one thin eyebrow raised.

"Yes."

"And?"

"What do you want from me?"

"An acknowledgment."

"Of what? So far I see that Captain Jones did nothing wrong. He was only protecting his crew."

"Like you're doing? You've accelerated, though he refused to. Have you thought of that?"

This stopped Kieran cold. What about the little kids? Had he harmed them? It was time to drop the acceleration back down, he realized. It hadn't worked anyway.

"I've done what you asked," he said to Mather. "Send me the list."

"All right," Mather said, and the screen flickered off, but a text with five names came through, and Kieran hungrily read them over, hoping to see his mother's name. He did not, but he smiled anyway. He pushed the hail button for Central Command, and Sarek's face filled the screen.

"Sarek, I just got a partial list of survivor names from Anne Mather."

"And?" Sarek said, biting his lip.

"Your dad is on it."

Inmates

Seth lay on his back, eyes hidden under the crook of his elbow. He felt a little easier in his bones, less tired, and he thought Kieran must have dropped the acceleration down. Every part of his body, from his muscles to his joints, even his skin, felt relief. Now if he could only figure out a way out of this torture chamber. However little he weighed, he was still lying on a hard metal cot. And his ears were being tormented, too. The terrorist had been humming an old-fashioned hymn over and over again for hours, and it was driving Seth crazy.

"Hey!" Seth called down the hallway, his injured voice cracking. "Why don't you shut up?!"

The humming stopped for half a beat but started up again, this time in a higher key.

"You trying out for the church choir, asshole?" Seth called, as loudly as his weakened body would allow. "I said shut up!"

"You shut up, you little punk!" the man screamed back, the first words he'd spoken in more than a day.

"Cro-Magnon gains the power of speech!" Seth called. To his surprise, the gorilla laughed.

Seth wanted to get up and get a drink of water, but with all the tubes hooked up to his arm, it was a hassle. Besides, drinking wasn't even necessary. As Tobin had inserted the IV needle into the back of Seth's hand, he'd said, "This will give you all the fluids and nutrients you need right now."

"Why can't I just have a chicken dinner?" Seth had asked weakly.

"Not through that throat, Seth. He hurt you pretty bad. Liquids only." Tobin had lifted up Seth's shirt and taken in the ugly bruises over his ribs, then he'd fingered through Seth's longish blond hair until he found the bald patch where his gash was stitched together. "Seems to be healing okay."

"I guess Waverly told you . . ."

". . . about the beating you got. Yes. How's the IV feeling to you?"

"It's just delicious."

"First this, then some fried chicken and okra, okay? Just lie here and let your body heal."

But lying still was not a skill Seth Ardvale had ever mastered.

His throat was feeling much better, but he still couldn't shout, so, with a metal food tray, Seth banged on the bars of his cell. He heard heavy bootsteps, and Harvey Markem appeared on the other side of the bars.

"Yes?" Harvey said. He was a good deal friendlier toward Seth than he used to be. Seth guessed this was because he'd caught the terrorist; that's why a lot of people were being nicer. He didn't point out to anyone that the terrorist had caught him, too.

"If I have to hear that son of a bitch," Seth said, "why don't you move me where I can see him?"

"What for? The view isn't exactly pretty."

Seth watched Harvey's open face, trying to decide if the truth would get him anywhere. He gave up on a lie, though. He was just too tired, so he shrugged, trying to seem humble. "He might talk to me."

"Why?" Harvey screwed up his face, looking like a little boy for all his impressive size.

"Honor among thieves? Misery loves company? Something along those lines?"

"Oh," Harvey said. He thought it over for a minute, chewing the corner of his mouth, then fitted the key into the door of the cell. "If anyone asks, I moved you as a punishment."

"For what?"

"For being so damn good looking." Harvey leaned over Seth, hooked his arm over his shoulder, and pulled him to a sitting position. "Okay?"

"Yeah," Seth said, wrapping his fingers around the pole to his IV. "Take it slow."

Groaning, Harvey heaved on Seth's arm until he could get on his feet, and then slowly the two swayed out of the cell and into the corridor.

"Did Kieran slow the ship down?" Seth asked.

"Yeah. My back feels a lot better now, too."

Seth hadn't been on his feet in days, and he realized how weak he truly was. He tried to hide it so Harvey wouldn't notice, and appreciated how the younger boy tactfully kept his eyes on the floor ahead of them.

"So," Harvey ventured, "it was you who carried me up to the central bunker after I got knocked out?"

"Yeah," Seth said, puffing.

"That was nice of you."

"Don't think I didn't have second thoughts," Seth rasped.

"Why did you do it?"

"Because you looked pathetic."

"Well, thanks."

Seth felt embarrassed and looked into the empty cells they passed by. Finally Harvey pulled him into the cell across from the gorilla and eased him down on the cot. He gave Seth an apologetic smile as he locked the door behind him, then left.

The prisoner sat on the floor of his cell, leaning against the metal cot. He hadn't stopped humming his precious hymn, his milky eyes fixed on the ceiling. There was a weird, glazed quality to his expression that made Seth wonder if the man was entirely sane. He thought he recognized that look. He'd seen it on his own face many times before. It was the look of having nothing left to lose. The look of someone ruled by impulse because thinking for very long about anything was too painful.

"Mind if I sing along?" Seth asked the guy.

The humming stopped momentarily, but the gorilla picked up the melody again from the beginning.

How do you get someone to talk? Seth wasn't exactly the most social guy; he'd always been jealous of people who could open up and talk about themselves without reservation. It always seemed to make people want to talk back.

"You and your crewmates sure know how to make a great first impression," Seth said, and glanced sideways at the man. "Really excellent attack. Very efficient."

The guy went on singing, staring at his hands, which he held cupped between his bent knees.

"My dad died because of what you and your friends did," Seth said. "And since then I've been on my own. So thanks for that. I've learned a lot about myself."

The man's humming seemed a little quieter, and he was very still, as though he were listening.

"I lost my mom years ago," Seth said, eyes on the ceiling. If he looked at the guy, he knew he'd give away what he was trying to do. "Some freak air-lock accident, they said. When I was four. I don't really remember her. All I've got left are pictures."

"You want sympathy?" the gorilla grumbled.

"Just passing the time," Seth said, trying to hide his excitement that he'd gotten the guy to speak.

"I'm not interested."

"Then don't listen," Seth snapped.

The man went back to humming.

Seth focused his eyes on the ceiling again as he fingered the calluses on his hands. "It's funny the things you miss. Mom used to make the best hot chocolate in the world. It was real creamy, and it made a thick mustache on your upper lip. I'd make a big show of licking it away, too, just to make her laugh. After she was gone, my dad tried to make it for me, but I could never choke it down. When I got older I even tried to make it myself, but Mom did something to it that I guess I'll never discover. Some spice, or extra goat's milk, or something. But her hot chocolate was the best there was. Now, I never touch the stuff."

Somewhere along the line, the humming had stopped.

"She used to laugh a lot," Seth said. He closed his eyes and imagined the sound of his mother laughing, a light giggle that never lasted very long but always made him happy. He loved clowning for her. He used to dance around in his pajamas, kicking up his legs and making faces until she'd give him a kiss. "After Mom died, no one laughed in our house. My dad was a real . . . Well, I hate to speak ill of the dead, but he was the kind of son of a bitch who thinks laughter is a sign of weakness. I guess I take after him there, because I don't think there's a person on this ship who has ever managed to make me laugh."

"Maybe you're just sad," the gorilla said.

Seth was shocked for a second at this apparent compassion, but he recovered quickly. "I guess I am."

"I didn't know you were an orphan."

"Yeah," Seth said. His throat was hurting from so much talking, so he held his breath, waiting for the man to speak.

He waited a long time and had almost fallen asleep when the man finally said, "I'm an orphan." The man said it with a voice so deep it seemed to come from the middle of his broad chest. "My mom died on Earth, before we got on the New Horizon. Dog bite, and we couldn't find any antibiotics for her. Can you imagine that? Something so simple as penicillin, and we couldn't find it! That almost drove me crazy. I think that's why my dad wanted to get on the ship so bad—so we'd always have a doctor."

"What happened to your dad?" Seth asked.

"Liver cancer. When I was twelve."

"That sucks."

"I grew up okay. Folks looked out for me."

"Yeah, you *grew*," Seth said with false appreciation. "How tall are you?"

The man chuckled. "Six two."

"Really? I'd have guessed more."

"How tall are you?"

"Six feet, about."

"You'll still grow some. If you don't get yourself killed first."

"Interesting comment from the guy who tried to murder me. Twice."

"That wasn't personal."

"Sure as hell *felt* personal." For a moment, Seth forgot what he was trying to do. He wanted to scream at the man, throw knives at him.

"Well, I'm sorry," the guy said. He shifted his weight, making the cot he was leaning against creak. He straightened out his legs until the soles of his enormous shoes touched the bars of his cage. "I was just trying to stay alive."

"And you tried to kill Waverly."

"She killed Shelby."

"That your pet sheep?"

"He was my brother," the man said. There was a vulnerable quality to his voice that made him sound boyish. "We weren't related by blood. Our neighbors took me in after Dad died, and Shelby was their son. A lot of kids would be resentful of a new kid in the house, but Shelby, he wrapped his arm around me and said, 'I always wanted a brother.' That was on the first day. I think he felt sorry for me, losing my dad and all, and he wanted to help."

"Sounds like a good guy," Seth said when the gorilla paused.

"He was a *great* guy," the man said defensively. "He had a big crush on Pastor Mather, is all, did whatever she wanted him to do."

"And you didn't?"

"She never paid me much attention," the man said, but Seth guessed he'd *wanted* attention from her.

"So why did she send you here?"

The man turned his head to look directly at Seth, who tried his best to hold his gaze. "What are you trying to do?" the man asked.

"What?" Seth said innocently. "You think I'm a spy or something?"

The man narrowed his eyes.

"Believe whatever you want," Seth said, and turned on his side to go to sleep. He stared at the darkened wall at the back of his cell, the stainless-steel sink, the dented cabinet in the corner. His silence was all pretense, but his eyelids were heavy, and he decided it was best not to press the guy. So he let himself drift off.

He was woken by the grinding sound of metal on metal, and turned to see Kieran Alden sitting down in a chair across from the prisoner. The man looked at Kieran with hooded eyes. Being a tough guy himself, Seth could see that the gorilla's angry posture concealed real fear. Maybe it was a good thing if the gorilla was afraid of Kieran.

"Do you need any additional medical attention?" Kieran asked the prisoner.

Involuntarily, Seth scoffed. Kieran hadn't offered him so much as a cotton ball since he'd been down here. Kieran looked expressionlessly at Seth, then at Harvey, who stood with his hands clasped behind him, watching to make sure Kieran was safe. Seth knew Harvey would have to explain why he'd been moved.

Seth studied Kieran, who seemed smaller somehow. His skin had a greenish tinge, and he squinted against the light in the cell. He didn't look healthy.

"How's your head feeling?" Kieran said to the prisoner, who stared at a spot just above Kieran's shoulder, ignoring him.

"I'll have a medic bring down some pain relievers," Kieran said. "You're going to have to let him take your temperature, too. We need to make sure you don't have an infection."

"What do you care if I'm sick?" the man spat. "You ought to let me die."

"If I did that, I'd lose the chance to talk to you."

"I'm not giving you anything."

"I know who you are," Kieran cajoled. "You're Jake Pauley. Mather told me."

Seth perked up at this. He'd had no idea that Kieran was in contact with the other ship.

The gorilla seemed unsure what to do now. He obviously hadn't expected Mather to reveal anything about him.

"I tried to use you as leverage," Kieran was saying. "Negotiate an exchange. Our parents for you. But Mather told me that she doesn't care what I do with you."

It was barely perceptible, but Seth saw the gorilla's eyes seethe at this.

"She was especially angry when I told her you killed one kid and tried to kill others."

The man's eyes flicked over Kieran, then landed on Seth for a moment before settling back on their nowhere spot, just over Kieran's shoulder.

"So I don't know why you'd want to be loyal to her," Kieran said. "She's a ruthless bitch."

"She's a woman of God," the man said.

"Last I heard, it's a sin to murder innocent people."

"She didn't expect the whole crew to be there," the man started, then clamped his mouth shut.

"In the shuttle bay?" Kieran asked, too eagerly. He waited, but the prisoner said no more. "So she didn't mean to massacre our crew?"

The man sealed his mouth, staring at the wall.

"Then why did she open the air lock in the shuttle bay?"

No answer.

"Jake, what's your mission?" Kieran asked him.

"No mission," Jake said, but then closed his mouth again and shook his head.

"Jake, I need to know. Is my crew still in danger?"

The man refused to answer, just kept staring at the spot over Kieran's shoulder.

"What can you tell me about the location of the hostages on the New Horizon? Jake?" Kieran's voice quivered with impatience now. "They're our parents. We need to get them back!"

Jake just sat on the floor and stared.

Kieran stood up, leaned over him, and pointed a finger in his face. "If you think that I can protect you forever, you're deluding yourself. There are two hundred and fifty kids on this ship who want to torture information out of you, and I'm not going to be able to keep them away forever. Unless I get some information from you that we can use."

"Sorry," the gorilla said, and rolled his eyes upward to

meet Kieran's gaze. Kieran straightened, motioned to Harvey to let him out of the cell, and marched off, glaring over his shoulder, not at the prisoner, but at Seth.

"He doesn't like you very much," Seth said to Jake with a chuckle.

"You neither, I think." Jake laughed.

"Yeah, well, he thinks I tried to kill him."

"Did you?"

Seth tucked his chin, took a deep breath, shutting out the ugly images from that day. "I was just trying to scare some sense into him by threatening to shove him out an air lock."

"Maybe you could have thought that one through a little better."

"Yeah. I think so," Seth said with a crooked grin. He turned on his side, leaned his head in his hand. "Mather didn't send you at all, did she?"

Jake's gaze shifted to the wall of Seth's cell.

"You came here all on your own like a crazy vigilante. You bucking for a promotion or something?"

The man sighed long and hard. "I didn't think it out. I saw the shuttle leaving, grabbed a OneMan. Mostly I wanted to kill Waverly Marshall. I've just been waiting for the right time."

Seth swallowed. At the mention of Waverly, he had a hard time hiding his loathing for this man. "She can be kind of a bitch," Seth said casually. "Kind of stuck up."

"There's families aboard the New Horizon now," the gorilla said distantly, as though he were reciting something he'd thought many times before. "They got to be protected."

"You have kids?"

"No," the man said bitterly. "I don't have no kids."

"But you want to protect other people's kids. That's good, I guess."

"It's what Shelby would've done."

"And you're trying to honor him," Seth said, as though finishing the man's thought. His throat was starting to burn desperately now. He needed to be quiet. "He'd probably like that."

"I hope so," the man said with quiet sadness.

"How did poisoning Max and me figure into that?" Seth said, and when the man looked at him, he held up a hand. "You can't blame me for wanting to know."

The gorilla's mouth lengthened, and he tucked his chin into his barrel chest. "I wasn't sure you two didn't see me when I came in."

"I was asleep the whole time. And Max said he saw nothing."

"I couldn't be sure. I wanted you two as scapegoats, but if you were around to say there was a stowaway on board, I thought that might threaten my mission."

"So you *do* have a mission," Seth said in an offhand way. "And you're just driving Kieran crazy on purpose. I like it."

The man smiled, showing triangular gaps between his teeth.

He thinks we're friends, Seth thought, and lay back on his mattress to sleep. *Stupid son of a bitch doesn't know he's a dead man.*

Clash

Kieran sat at his desk, tapping the wood with his index finger. He leaned forward and jabbed the intercom button for the infirmary. "Tobin? Can you talk?"

"Here, Kieran," Tobin said when the video screen flicked to his image. He looked like he hadn't slept in days.

"Any change in Philip's condition?"

"No. Victoria and I are working on learning the EEG machine. As soon as I understand it enough I'll take a reading and check on his brain function."

"She's helping you?"

"Kind of. She's awake a few hours a day. She can't do much."

"Is Philip breathing on his own?"

"He's still on a ventilator. We're going to try disconnecting him as soon as his other vitals look strong enough."

"Call me when you do, okay? I want to be there," Kieran said, and hung up.

There were so many things to worry about, so many things to fear, but what kept him up at night was the memory of Philip's swollen head, his bulging eye, the way his limbs shook like a marionette's. Kieran should never have sent such a small boy on such a risky task. At the time, it hadn't seemed dangerous.

It got dangerous because of Waverly. If she hadn't been doing things she shouldn't, Philip would be okay.

She was probably meeting with her Central Council right now. At least Arthur had recovered enough to attend meetings, and though he could barely speak, he was able to bring back faithful reports. Waverly wouldn't be able to make a move without Kieran knowing. For now, that threat was neutralized.

Or was it? As he'd walked from his quarters to Central Command, he'd passed an especially vivid bit of graffiti that showed Kieran playing with himself while Waverly and Seth beat up the terrorist. Underneath if the caption read, *Who is our real leadership?* A few days before, there was a picture of Seth behind bars with a caption that read, *This is how we thank our heroes.* Maybe by incarcerating Seth, Kieran had made him a martyr for some people, but what was his alternative?

"Get our parents back," he murmured to himself. "No one can complain if you do that."

He trembled with apprehension, and his breath was quick and unsteady, but he made himself lean forward to log on to the long-range com system, and hailed the other vessel.

Immediately a bland-looking man answered his call. "Empyrean, this is the New Horizon."

"I'd like to speak with Anne Mather, please."

"I'll see if the Pastor is available," the man said.

Kieran didn't have to wait long. Soon Mather's face appeared on his screen. He was heartened to see her looking tired and worn, as though she was being kept up nights, too. "Hello, Kieran. I hope you have good news for me."

"I want to know what your terms are."

"All right," she said, planting her elbows on her desk. "First, I want immunity."

"For who?"

"For me. You might try to paint me as a war criminal, but if you do that to the figurehead of this vessel, you insult everyone on board. Peace cannot exist if we each try to persecute the other side."

"I'll consider it."

She looked at him sharply but continued. "Next, I want to know that when we reach New Earth, both vessels will have a hand in negotiating territories."

"To divide an entire planet among a few hundred people? Do you really think that's going to be a sticking point?"

"We have limited data on ecosystems there, Kieran. There might be very little arable land. I can't have my people stuck in a desert."

"Okay. I can agree to that."

"And I think that representatives from both vessels should take part at least once a year in a congress, hosted alternately by each vessel, or colony, in which information is traded and planetary governance is decided."

Kieran began to realize that he hadn't prepared any terms of his own other than getting the parents back, and that Mather was calling all the shots. "Pastor Mather—"

"Anne, please."

He sighed, irritated by her friendly tone. "I'm going to need you to send your terms over to me in a text document so that I can go over these carefully with my people."

"Your people?" she asked with a smug smile.

"My Central Council," he said, just to buy time. "My crew. It isn't right for me to make all these decisions for them."

Mather leaned back in her chair, regarding Kieran. "You're on good terms with your Central Council?"

"Of course," he said with a tight smile.

She nodded, but Kieran suspected she didn't believe him.

"So the terrorist—Jacob—was feeding you information after all?" he guessed. Why else should she doubt what he said?

Her eyes snapped to his, but her expression didn't move a single micron. "No."

"Because it sounds as if you think you've got information about this ship."

"I'm sorry I gave that impression. No. My doubts about your relationship with your council stem only from my own experience. Like any governing body, they vie for power."

"And you don't want to give it to them," Kieran said.

"They don't always like what I do, but sometimes a

leader has to make unpopular decisions. I would think you'd know that by now."

The two looked at each other for a frozen moment. This woman was uncomfortably perceptive, and she knew just how to say the most unnerving thing. She reminded him of Waverly. But she'd revealed a weakness, hadn't she? *She's afraid of being tried as a war criminal,* he realized. *How can I use that?*

"I'll send you my terms in a text document, Kieran. Take your time to review them, and we'll speak again, soon I hope."

"Wait," Kieran said. "I want a manifest of every Empyrean crew member on board your vessel, or the talks don't move forward at all."

Mather sighed.

"Also, I want each of them to send a video message to the Empyrean, so that we can see their condition for ourselves."

"That's going to take time."

"I want it in twenty-four hours. And they all better be in good health, or I'll make sure you'll be known through all of New Earth's history as the first war criminal," Kieran said, and ended the transmission before she could respond.

Let her stew on that for a while, he thought with satisfaction.

His intercom beeped, and he leaned forward, expecting to see Mather calling him back, but in fact the signal was coming from the infirmary. Kieran answered, and Tobin's tired face appeared on his screen. "Kieran, his eyes are open."

"I'll be right there."

He stumbled through the corridors and down the

stairwell to the infirmary, where he found Tobin leaning over Philip, looking into his oval face. The little boy's eyes were as opaque as coals, staring up at the ceiling without seeming to recognize anything.

"Can he speak?" Kieran asked anxiously.

"Not with that respirator in his throat," Tobin said. "I could try disconnecting it."

"Is that safe?"

"I was going to anyway. It's the only way to see if he can breathe on his own."

"Do it," Kieran said, and stood back while Tobin carefully released a clamp around the hose. The machine above Philip's bed made several alarming beeps, but Tobin switched it off, irritated, and then leaned his cheek over Philip to feel for breath. Kieran saw the small boy's chest rise and fall, then there was an agonizing pause until it rose and fell again. Tobin took several readings, then looked at Kieran, relieved. "He seems okay right now."

Philip's eyes landed on Tobin's face for a moment, watching him speak, but then drifted back to the ceiling again.

"Philip," Tobin said, "I bet you want that hose out of your throat, don't you, buddy?"

The boy closed and opened his eyes, seeming unable to do more. He reminded Kieran of an antique doll owned by Felicity Wiggam, the one girl who had chosen to stay behind on the New Horizon. If she laid the doll on its back, its eyes shut with an unnerving mechanical swivel. *Is Philip still in there?* Kieran wondered.

"I'm going to pull it out in one motion, okay?" Tobin said loudly to Philip as he gripped the breathing tube firmly in his fist. "I need you to breath out when I do."

"Have you done this before?" Kieran asked.

"Quiet," Tobin said. Kieran understood that most everything Tobin did was for the first time, and his only hope of keeping his patients calm was if he pretended total confidence.

Tobin waited until Philip was about to exhale, then, with a swift motion, pulled the tube out of his throat. The boy coughed, little hacking noises that shook his shoulders. When he'd settled, Tobin picked up a spray bottle from the bedside table, gently opened the boy's mouth, and spritzed a fine mist into it. Philip's breath smelled rancid and stale, but Kieran leaned close to him.

"Philip, can you hear me?" Kieran asked, trying to keep the emotion out of his voice. The boy's lips opened and closed, making him look like a fish. Kieran leaned closer to him and put his hand on the boy's shoulder. It felt fragile under his fingers.

The boy whispered a dry, papery word that Kieran couldn't hear.

"Try more water," he said to Tobin, who sprayed a little more into the boy's mouth. Philip mashed his lips together.

"Bright," Philip whispered, blinking his eyes as though a light was being shined into them.

"Dim the lights," Kieran said, and Tobin pushed a pad on the wall, reducing the brightness in the room by half.

"A flash," Philip said, then coughed again. "Flash of light."

"You're seeing flashing lights, Philip?" Tobin asked, concerned.

Philip rolled his head to look at Tobin, but his eyes seemed too far apart, and his pupils, Kieran noticed for the first time, were two different sizes. "The starboard side."

"I think he's delirious," Tobin said. "We should let him rest."

Kieran nodded and began to pull away, but Philip reached for him. Grasping his hand gently, Kieran leaned over the little boy, his mouth level with the curving shell of his ear, and whispered, "Philip, I don't know if you can hear me, but I'm sorry. I shouldn't have put you in that situation."

"They're all through the starboard side," Philip whispered. "In the ceiling."

"Philip. Did you hear me?"

"Oh God." Philip's eyes widened, and he took in a quick, shallow breath. "They'll never forgive us."

Kieran felt Tobin's hand on his arm. "Let's give him a chance to rest, okay?"

"What's he saying?" Kieran asked. He felt chilled, and his heart was pounding.

"He's not conscious," Tobin said apologetically. "I read about this. It happens with coma patients sometimes. He's talking in his sleep. It's gibberish."

"Like he's dreaming?" Kieran asked. Philip's murmurs sounded disembodied, abandoned.

"Kind of like dreams," Tobin said sadly. "He's active and breathing on his own. It's a good sign."

Tobin was being gentle with Kieran. He'd heard his apology to Philip, Kieran realized.

"If there's any change at all, tell me, okay?"

"Right away," Tobin said, nodding. When he turned back to Philip, Kieran noticed that Tobin's shoulder muscles had gotten huge. *He must be lifting patients all day long*, Kieran realized, *to give them meds or help them adjust in bed. It's got to be backbreaking work. He never complains.*

"I think making you medical officer has been the best decision I've made as Captain," he said to Tobin.

Embarrassed, Tobin couldn't seem to bring himself to look at Kieran. Instead, he waved him out of the infirmary and turned his back to write something on Philip's chart. Kieran thought he saw a tear in the corner of the boy's eye just as he turned away. Of all people on the ship, Tobin probably understood the weight of responsibility as much as Kieran did. He made life-and-death decisions, he had to work tirelessly, and he was rarely thanked. If only there was someone on board who could tell Kieran he was doing a good job, too. He longed for some reassurance that he wasn't doing the wrong thing at every step. But he knew by now this wasn't something leaders got from their crew.

Once he asked the voice that visited him if he was doing a good job, and he thought he'd heard what he wanted. But part of him wondered if he'd made it up.

When he got back to his office, he found Waverly waiting for him outside the door.

"We need to talk," she said, her mouth set in a short, stubborn line. Her voice still sounded squeezed, but her bruises had faded to yellow and she seemed healthy again.

"I don't have time right now."

"It'll only take a minute."

He sighed heavily but unlocked the door to his office and stood aside for her. She walked through without thanking him and sat down in the chair across from his desk. He sat in his chair and looked at her, waiting.

"The Central Council wants to see the terrorist," she said.

"I can't let that happen."

"Why not?"

"Security reasons."

"The ship's bylaws say the council has the right to access any prisoner on the Empyrean to verify physical health and state of mind. It's on page forty-two."

"So you're worried that he misses his mommy?"

"You can't legally stop us, Kieran."

He let his eyes trail over to the volume of laws that sat on the top of the Captain's bookshelf. Unlike Waverly, he didn't have the time to study them.

"I'll have to check into this," he said. "Can it wait for a couple days?"

"No."

"You can't just spring this on me."

"I just did."

"When did you become such a bitch?"

It was out of his mouth before he'd even completed the thought. But it was true. She'd become demanding, unreasonable, impossible.

"What did you call me?" Her voice sounded as though it were suspended from a heated wire.

"You're always going where you don't belong, doing things that are none of your business."

"The running of this ship is everyone's business." Her voice cracked with strain. "It's supposed to be a democracy."

"That doesn't make me your errand boy."

"Are you going to let us past your goon squad or not, Kieran?"

"Before you understand the situation? Before you've

gotten any information from me about the prisoner? You just want to rush in there and stir the pot?" He was yelling now. He could feel his face heating up, turning red.

"It's not like you've gotten any results!" She swatted the air with an open hand. "Let us try."

"How do you know he's said nothing?"

"You think your guards don't talk?"

Harvey. He'd obviously made a report to the council. She'd managed to turn one of his most loyal guards. Kieran narrowed his eyes at her. She folded her arms over her chest. Her leg was tapping a jackrabbit rhythm on the floor, which made him grind his teeth.

"You're going to get even more people hurt," he finally said to her, using his voice like a knife, probing for a soft spot.

"What are you talking about?" She'd gone ashen, and her leg stopped its motion.

"If it wasn't for you, poor Philip wouldn't be—" Kieran stopped himself.

"What do you mean? That was random chance! You can't blame me for—" She stopped mid-sentence, her mouth hanging open. Slowly, her eyes turned into two black pinpoints.

He tried to think of something to say that would deflect her, painfully aware that the longer he was silent, the guiltier he seemed.

"You had me followed," Waverly said quietly. "Philip was reporting to you. Wasn't he?"

"No," he said, but he made the mistake of trying to laugh off the suggestion. He couldn't have seemed more inauthentic if he'd tried.

She stood up. "You're a liar."

He pointed a finger in her face. "You gave me cause."

"So you admit it."

"Are you going to stand there and try to convince me that you weren't helping Seth Ardvale? Really, Waverly?" His voice rose to a scream. His ears rang with every word. He'd been taken over, and he couldn't stop himself. "You were on your way to meet him! You didn't find the terrorist! He found you!"

"He almost killed us!" Waverly croaked. "Believe me, I'd rather I hadn't found him!"

"Don't give me that! It's the best thing that could have happened for you politically!"

"You remind me more of Anne Mather every day!" Her voice broke on the last words, and her hand flew to her throat. "You're using your pulpit to brainwash people!"

"I'm keeping them aloft! They'd sink into despair otherwise!"

"Without their messiah Kieran Alden to show them the way?" she snarled. "You're disgusting!"

He swung back, ready to slap her. But he stopped himself.

She stood there, breathing through flared nostrils, her eyes red, hair askew, fists hanging at her sides as though she were ready to tackle him to the floor. They stared at each other, the air between them crackling, until she whirled around and marched out of his office.

Wild Justice

"He said no," Waverly said bitterly as she came back into the council chamber.

The rest of the council accepted this news with grim resignation. Alia and Melissa both smiled sadly at Waverly as she dropped into her seat at the large oval table.

"I should have gone," croaked Arthur.

"No, we need him to trust you, Arthur," Waverly said with a dim smile.

She wanted to cry. She wanted to scream and kick. But she could only finger the device she had secreted in her pocket. *I'll use it,* she told herself. *One way or another.*

Alia was looking pensively out the domed glass ceiling

at the Milky Way, dense with tiny stars. Harvey and Melissa were staring at their folded hands. Tobin Ames seemed troubled by the news and chewed on a cuticle, his eyes off to the side while he thought. Sealy Arndt simply looked furious.

"So," Alia ventured with her velvety voice. "What you're telling us is that we will have to go down there and force our way in."

Harvey shook his head. "Those guards are loyal to Kieran. They're not going to go against his orders."

"So it could get violent," Waverly said with dread. She'd had enough blood.

"What about the Justice of the Peace? Can we appeal to Bobby?" Tobin asked. "If we have the law on our side, let's use it."

"Can we call him in?" Arthur asked.

Melissa went to the intercom and asked Sarek in Central Command to find Bobby Martin. While they waited, Waverly told them that Kieran had ordered Philip to follow her.

"He was spying on you?" Melissa asked, her eyes round.

"Are you really surprised?" Waverly asked.

"Can you blame him?" Arthur croaked, and all eyes were on him. "Waverly, you were visiting Seth Ardvale in the brig. How did you expect Kieran to react to that?"

"Reasonably. I saw him one time!"

"And you were clearly meeting Seth in the observatory," Harvey said, his eyebrows lowered over his wide, farm-boy eyes.

"So we condone spying on our own crew members?"

Waverly spat, then coughed. Her throat still felt scratchy and weak.

"We are all afraid," Alia said simply. "Fear makes people do terrible things."

"Well, it shouldn't go against people's rights," Waverly said stubbornly.

"Ideally it shouldn't," Arthur rasped quietly. "But nothing about our situation is ideal."

Waverly felt chastened, and dropped out of the conversation for a while, until it turned to the prisoner and interrogating him.

"We should have a list of questions for the terrorist," Tobin was saying. "We can't just go in there without knowing what we want to ask."

"He's been in contact with the New Horizon," Waverly said, leaning into the conversation, making them look at her. "He might know something about what's going on there."

"Yes," Alia said. "He might know where the prisoners are being kept."

"And who they are," Melissa Dickinson put in. "Maybe some of our parents . . ."

"And how they're being guarded," said Harvey.

Arthur pulled a portable computer from his satchel and began to type out questions. They were still working when Bobby Martin came in, looking exhausted. His white-blond hair was a messy thatch over his pale blue eyes, which made a shocking contrast with his olive-toned skin. Someday, he could be even more handsome than Seth Ardvale, Waverly thought while she watched him pull out a chair at the council table. For now, though, he was still a boy. Judging from his smell, he'd been spreading sheep manure in the potato field.

"I bet this is about the prisoner," he said, looking at Arthur, who he seemed to assume was the leader of the Central Council. Waverly was irritated by this, but she ignored it.

"We want access to him," she said, using her voice firmly so he'd know he couldn't ignore her. "We want to interrogate him."

"I thought Kieran was taking the lead on that," he said, his eyes darting from one face to another.

"We think we could be . . . more effective," Sealy said. He wove his knobby fingers together and leaned his elbows on the table. "We'll get to the core of the matter a little faster."

"Why do you need me?" Bobby asked, his voice squeaking, making him sound like the young boy he was.

"Kieran doesn't want to grant us access," Alia said.

"And according to the rules of incarceration, we have the right—" Waverly began, but Bobby cut her off.

"Hand me the bylaws," he said, shaking his hand at Arthur, who turned to the shelf behind him and pulled down the volume.

"Page forty-two," Waverly said as Bobby thumbed through the book. He read the section, his pale eyes darting across the page as he sucked on his lower lip. He was silent, the whole room was, while he considered the meaning of the words.

"He can't legally stop you from checking on the prisoner," he said at the end of it.

"Then let's go down there," Waverly said. "Right now, before Kieran can find a way to stop us."

Alia stood up, looking around the room, challenging the others to follow her. Sealy went to the door and ushered Alia out ahead of him, then Harvey and Melissa followed. Tobin and Arthur seemed the most reluctant, and Waverly felt sorry for them. They were both close to Kieran, and they didn't want to create a rift. But that would be Kieran's doing, not theirs. She was last out of the chamber, and she jogged to catch up to Bobby, who was rubbing his grubby hands on his pants.

"I should be cleaner for something like this," he said, embarrassed.

"Remember J.P. Connor?" Waverly said with a fond smile, recalling the slender man, the way he always seemed to be eating a piece of bread. He had died several years before the attack, and the whole crew attended his memorial. Waverly was sad he was gone, but maybe it was a good thing he didn't live to see the attack. He died before, when everyone thought they were on a peaceful mission, when everyone believed they were safe. "He always had grease under his fingernails. You're carrying on the tradition."

"I guess," Bobby said doubtfully.

The elevator ride down was grim. There was a tangy, musky scent to the close air—the scent people give off when they're afraid. Waverly thought absently that she ought to feel afraid herself, but she didn't. She felt eager.

When the guards outside the brig saw the Central Council coming, they both straightened their spines, holding their rifles across their chests. So Kieran had finally resorted to the use of firearms, Waverly noted.

"Access to the brig is restricted," Hiro Mazumoto said, his eyes immobile in their sockets.

Bobby Martin stepped up, pulled something from his pocket, and flashed a badge in Hiro's face. Waverly wondered where he'd gotten it. "I'm the J.P. and I'm ordering you aside."

"Not without orders from Kieran Alden," said Ali Jaffar, his hazel eyes shifting nervously from face to face.

"If you don't stand aside, I'll arrest you both," Bobby said.

"The bylaws state we're to be given access," Arthur said with his gravelly voice, which was still healing. He produced the book of laws, opening it for the guards so they could see for themselves.

Hiro took the book and read the passage, Ali leaning over his shoulder. Neither boy seemed to know what to do.

"We're the Central Council and the Justice of the Peace. You've got two branches of the ship's government standing in front of you," Waverly said. "Kieran's word doesn't stand against all of ours. He's not our dictator."

Hiro sighed, shaking his head. "I wish people could just get along," he murmured, but he stood aside and let them pass.

The brig smelled of rancid sweat. The prisoner was lying on his cot, the crook of his elbow shielding his eyes from the light as he slept. His mouth hung open, showing a ruin of teeth, crooked and brown, as he snored. He sounded like an animal.

"Wake him up," Waverly said to the guards.

Hiro banged on the iron bars of the cell with the muzzle of his gun. "Hey. You've got visitors."

The prisoner rubbed sleep out of his eyes, smacking his thick, stubbled lips, slow to wake, until he saw

Waverly on the other side of the bars, looking at him. Instantly his face hardened, and he sat up, staring at her, murder in his eyes.

"Cuff him," she said, her voice low.

Ali positioned himself outside the cage, his gun pointed at the prisoner's head while Hiro unlocked the door and stepped in. "Stand," Hiro said to the prisoner, who complied, never taking his ruddy eyes off Waverly's face.

"Now cuff his ankles to the feet of his cot," Waverly said.

The prisoner's face shifted almost imperceptibly; Waverly could see he was becoming afraid. Ali handed Hiro two sets of cuffs from his belt, and Hiro fastened each of the prisoner's ankles to the bottom legs of the metal cot, which were fastened to the floor with heavy bolts. The prisoner sat, his legs spread awkwardly, hands behind his back. He was helpless.

"Waverly," someone whispered, and she turned, surprised to see Seth standing in the cell right behind her.

"I thought you were at the other end," she said to him. She didn't want him watching this.

"What are you doing?" He was still hooked up to an IV, and his color wasn't good.

"We're going to ask him questions," she said. She held her chin up, defying him to say something.

Seth cocked his head, studying her. "You're not doing what I think you're doing, are you?"

"Leave me alone," she said, and turned away. She wanted to be the first one in the cell with the terrorist. She wanted to be the one asking the questions.

She stood over the brute, close enough to smell old onions on his breath. She could see beads of sweat on his scalp between the cropped hairs on his head, and she could smell his odor, a sharp reek that stung her nostrils in the place between her eyes. She stood over the man, letting him feel her presence, letting him hate her, until she could find a way through her rage to speak.

"We're going to ask you some questions," she said, her voice shaking, barely within her control. "And you're going to answer them."

He laughed mockingly.

From her pocket she pulled a Taser. She heard murmurs of surprise from the Central Council. Alia watched her searchingly. Melissa stared, her face blank. The Taser was normally used on the livestock if the herd was in a panic and injuring themselves. It had enough power to knock out a billy goat, but the shock wouldn't be enough to knock out a man. It would cause hurt, though—a deep, physical pain in the nerves.

"I didn't agree to this," Bobby said, stepping toward her.

"I want to know if our parents are still alive on the New Horizon," she said to the terrorist, knowing this would stop Bobby, whose parents were unaccounted for.

Bobby hung back, waiting for the man to answer. The rest of the council and even Kieran's guards all seemed to be holding their breath.

"I don't know," the prisoner said.

She jammed the business end of the Taser into his neck and held down the trigger. The man cried out and his body shook, rattling the chains on his cuffs. When

Waverly pulled the Taser away, she saw a V-shaped burn on his skin, and she could smell singed flesh.

"Waverly, don't," Seth called hoarsely from across the way.

"Are our parents still alive?" Waverly said, and pressed the Taser against the prisoner again, but she didn't pull the trigger. Not yet.

Instinctively, he drew away from it, but he said quietly, "I think so."

"Where are they being held?" she asked him.

The man closed his lips, his eyes stubbornly focused on the floor.

"Where!" she screamed in his ear, and pulled the trigger again. She could feel the buzz of the current moving through the device and into the man's body, which shook with spasms deep in his core. He screamed, and his face contorted into a mask of agony. She remembered the way he'd held her windpipe closed, the way he'd looked into her eyes, whispering, "I'm going to kill you like you killed Shelby, you little witch." The way she'd accepted that this was her death, that he was her killer. The hopelessness he'd made her feel. How easily she'd given up. Oh, she hated him.

But she took her finger off the trigger, and his spasms stopped. He groaned.

"Where are they?" she said softly.

"I haven't heard anything new," he said, breathless. "They're probably still in atmospheric conditioning."

"Mather's too careful. She's moved them. I'm sure of it."

"I don't know!"

She zapped him again, and he cried out. When she

released him, he blubbered, "Please don't do that again. Please."

"Then tell me where the prisoners are!"

"They're . . . they're in the sewage plant! The doors are chained closed! You'll need bolt cutters to get them away from there!"

"How do you know that?"

"She . . . she wanted a more permanent place, so they modified the sewage plant. It's probably done by now."

"Is that the truth?" Waverly said warningly, holding the Taser near his eye.

"I swear it." He begged, his blue eyes darting from one council member to the next, pleading, looking for a sympathetic gaze. "It's true. That's where they are."

Waverly looked at Alia, who nodded at her. She seemed to believe him.

"What kind of guard is being kept on them?" Waverly asked, moving the Taser between the knobs of bone at the base of the man's neck, just over his spine.

"A light detail, I think," he said tearfully. "Since you're not on the ship anymore."

"And what's the political situation?" she asked.

"I haven't been there since you have. I don't know anything more than you do."

"You've been talking to them."

"No, I haven't."

She jammed the Taser into his spine and pulled the trigger. This time he screamed, but she didn't stop. He shook, and spittle rolled from his mouth as his head flopped forward and backward. When finally she released the Taser, he was limp, shoulders hunched, head hanging between his knees.

"Water," she said.

Ali went to the sink, filled a plastic tumbler with water, and handed it to her. She poured it over the prisoner's head, and he shook himself awake, grunting. He sounded like a pig.

"You've been in contact with the New Horizon, haven't you?"

Tears ran down his face, but he nodded.

"And what have you learned about the situation there?"

"What do you want to hear?"

"The truth. When we left, things weren't going well for Mather."

"She's still in control," he said, his eyes screwed shut.

"You're holding something back." This time she moved the Taser to his groin and glared right into his face. Tears streamed from his eyes as he searched her expression. He trembled. She felt the muscles of his thighs tense and release under her Taser. "Tell me everything you know."

"Mather doesn't have a good relationship with the church elders. Shelby told me that once. They could oust her any day now."

"Is that the truth?"

"Yes," he whined.

But she pulled the trigger anyway. He screamed, and screamed again, but she held the Taser in place, watching his face as it twisted in agony, feeling the helpless tremor of his legs, the jolts and spasms that rocked his body. He gurgled, and bubbles formed at the corners of his mouth, but still she held on, until she felt a hand on her arm and looked up to see Alia's shocked face.

"He's finished," Alia said. Her face was drained of color, and her lips twitched as she pulled Waverly away from the prisoner, who was sobbing.

Waverly let herself be led out of the cell. Until she tried to walk, she didn't realize how shaky her legs were. She watched as Ali unlocked the man's cuffs and arranged him on his mattress. The man jumped at every touch, every movement, whimpering like a toddler. When Ali laid him down, the man curled himself into the fetal position, moving his hand to his mouth as if to suck his thumb.

The other Central Council members shuffled out of the brig, each of their eyes trained on the floor, making little sound other than embarrassed coughs and the scuff of their shoes on the grimy metal floor. Waverly watched them leave, then turned to Seth, who stared at her wide-eyed, as if he'd never seen her before.

She opened her mouth to speak, but her voice was stopped up in her throat, so she turned to go. She didn't understand her feelings yet. She didn't understand the hollow pit in the center of her chest, the weight that dragged on her limbs, and the gray dark that seemed to cloud her mind. She'd never felt it before.

Later that night, when she couldn't sleep, she understood what she felt was deep, irrevocable shame.

Seth had seen the whole thing.

Hints

Seth lay on his side staring at Jacob, who hadn't moved in hours. The man sat crumpled in his bed, rocking back and forth, singing some unintelligible song under his breath. He'd come unhinged. But it wasn't the behavior that disturbed Seth. What frightened him was what the man said in his sleep, crying out or moaning. At first it had sounded like babble or baby talk, but after a while Seth's ear was attuned to it, and the words resolved into something ominous: "She's gonna burn, Shelby."

Something terrible was going to happen. Something Jake had planned. And Seth had to get a message to someone about it.

"Guard!" Seth croaked, picking up his metal plate and banging on his bars. "Guard! I need help!"

He'd tried this before, but Kieran must have given new orders, because no one came. No one even spoke to him. No one looked at him when they slid his meals into his cell. He felt like an animal in a trap.

"Hey! I need medical assistance!" He tried to scream, hoping that might rouse them. In truth he felt better now that he was eating again, but if Tobin came to give him "medical assistance," he might listen.

"Everyone on this ship is dead." The words were spoken with satisfied smugness.

A chill settled between Seth's shoulder blades.

The voice had been Jake's, but it had a removed quality, as though someone else were speaking through him. His eyes were oddly distant, and his lower lip hung from his face like a piece of flab.

Seth stared at him, his mouth dry. "What do you mean?"

"I mean don't get worked up. Because it doesn't matter anyway," Jacob said. For the first time since he'd been tortured, he turned to look at Seth. His lips pulled back to show his crooked teeth, and his cheeks bunched up under his eyes, which shone in the bright lights of his cell. But it wasn't a smile. It was an effigy of a smile. "Soon, nothing is going to matter."

"Why?" Seth asked. "Jake?"

"You don't want to know. Just trust me."

"What did you do?" Seth tried to sound eager, like a coconspirator, someone who wanted to be let in on the joke. It was a thin disguise, and he guessed Jake could see through it. "The engines. Did you screw up the engines somehow? Or the reactors?"

"Why did you want medical assistance?" Jake asked, suspicious. "You seem fine."

"I . . ." Seth wiped his hand over his face to buy time.

"To get a message out that the Central Council is torturing prisoners, because, you know, I might be next."

"They don't hate you enough."

"I'm not exactly popular."

Jacob only laughed, shaking his head as if to say *Silly boy*.

"Come on, man. Tell me what you've got planned! Who am I going to tell?"

"Why do you want to know?"

"Because I'm bored," Seth said, knowing the urgency in his voice was betraying the lie. "And if these bastards have something coming to them, I want to savor it."

"I want it to be a surprise," Jake said, and smiled that chilling smile.

"It's the reactor, isn't it? You rigged it to melt down."

Jake turned away, uninterested, and went back to singing his eerie, tuneless song. He rocked back and forth, his hands buried in his lap, staring at a faraway point. The torture had been bad, but it hadn't lasted that long, and it had only happened once. It shouldn't have been enough to unhinge a sane person. But then do sane people go around killing kids? Maybe the guy had always been nuts and Waverly's Taser had been the last straw to push him over the edge.

When he stopped singing, Seth said, "You're starting to creep me out."

Jake smiled again. His forehead was shiny with sweat, and his breath, moving in and out of his barrel chest, sounded wet and weighed down by his fleshy throat.

"Shelby wasn't the only one you lost, was he?" Seth said. It was only a hunch, but he had to try something to get Jake to talk.

"My parents. I told you that," Jake said, sounding like

a man who was thinking of something else.

"No. More recently. You lost someone else. Didn't you?"

For a long time Jake sat there as though unaware of Seth's question. When he turned again to look at Seth, there were wet patches on his cheeks.

"All she ever wanted, all her life, was to be a mama," the man finally said. His voice broke, and he buried his chin in his chest. "My Ginny was the only one on the New Horizon who could conceive."

Seth held his breath and watched as the man relived the past, sorrow passing like a shadow over his features.

"The first time we were so happy, and proud. We told the whole crew, and everyone congratulated us. We gave them hope. Pastor Mather even said a sermon about us. She called Ginny the new Eve, and I guess that made me Adam." He straightened as he said this, smiling at the memory.

"I thought there weren't any kids on the New Horizon," Seth said, his voice eerily quiet.

Jake's smile faded away. He glanced at Seth, the kind of look a predator flashes at his prey. "There aren't."

"She lost the baby," Seth said quietly. He almost felt sorry for this fractured, confused man.

Jake buried his face in his square hands. "And another and another and another."

Seth let it rest for a few moments, watching Jake's labored breathing.

"After a while it was like her light went out," Jake finally said, his voice strained. "She stopped smiling, then she stopped talking, then she stopped getting out of bed. I didn't know what to do. I thought she'd get better. But . . ."

Seth wanted to ask what happened to Ginny. He thought he knew.

"I'm just trying to make it right," Jake said into his hands. "All our dead babies. All our babies who never got to be. There's got to be a way to even things out, you know? After what they did to us."

"Killing Max made it right?"

"It was a start."

"Max wasn't even born when all that happened."

"But his dad was," Jake said, his voice coated with misery. "Now his father will know what it's like when your baby dies."

"His dad died in the attack." It gave Seth no satisfaction to say these words.

Jake made no response.

Seth stared at him, at first unaware that he was trembling with rage. The foolishness, the blind idiocy of lashing out for the sake of revenge—it was repugnant. Seth had done it to Kieran, after his father died, punished him for everything that had gone wrong. Hurting Kieran had made Seth feel good for a while, but the feeling soured, and then he'd just wanted a way out of the sickening black maze he'd made for himself.

Now Waverly was wandering a maze just like it. Her face, when she'd pressed that Taser into Jake's neck, grimacing when he screamed, her eyes glistening as she watched the fine tendril of smoke rising from his burning flesh. Ostensibly she'd been after information, but Seth knew what she was really doing. She'd been through too much. Some part of her had snapped. Her humanity had gone on hiatus, and what was left behind was her animal instinct: kill, hurt, maim, survive.

But he knew, just as his memories of what he'd done to Kieran haunted him, Waverly would remember that moment in time when she'd taken leave of her higher nature. There was nothing worse than knowing how deep you could go into barbarity.

This man was even more lost than Seth or Waverly had ever been.

"I used to believe in revenge," Seth said, trying to sound conversational. "I tortured Kieran Alden, punished him for his mistakes, made him suffer. I was a monster. I was only making everything worse, creating more enemies, more hatred on this ship, more reasons for revenge. Look where I am now. Kieran thinks I'm dangerous, and he's right. I *was* dangerous. But now here I am stuck in the brig when I could be helping run the ship. And even if the adults come back and things go back to some kind of normal, I'll never be trusted again. I ruined my life, all because I wanted to make someone suffer."

"I guess he's the one who got his revenge, then," Jake said with a twisted smile.

"All I know," Seth said, trying his best to sound reasonable, "is that I made things worse by being mean when I could have made things better by being kind."

"You're still young enough to believe in fairy tales."

"It's pure logic I'm spouting here, man."

Jake looked at Seth askance, a lopsided grin on his face. "You're the only one I'm going to regret."

"*What* are you going to regret, Jake? What do you have planned?"

"You'll see," he said. The smile was back. That strange, beatific smile on a gargoyle face, and Jake turned away and started humming to himself, that odd melody. Seth stared at him, awash in the most horrid feeling of helplessness he'd ever felt in his life as he listened to the broken man sing.

Damage

Kieran was still seething about his argument the day before with Waverly when he arrived in the brig for another interview with the terrorist. He walked past Hiro and Ali, both loyal guards. They seemed withdrawn and troubled today. When he got to Jake's cell and looked through the bars at him, he saw a man trembling on the floor, lying curled on his side, his hands tucked between his knees, sleeping fitfully.

"Jake?" Kieran said.

The man didn't move.

"Ali!" Kieran called. Ali walked down the hallway, sighing heavily. He was barely able to meet Kieran's eyes.

"How long has he been like this?"

"About twenty-four hours."

"Why didn't you call me?"

The boy stood before Kieran, his mouth open as if to speak, but he was unable.

"Kieran," someone whispered behind him. He turned to find Seth Ardvale leaning on the bars of his cell. Seth looked in Kieran's eyes, desperate and pleading. "I need to talk to you."

Kieran turned his back on him.

"Is he sick?" Kieran asked. The man was covered in sweat, and though his eyes were closed, Kieran could see the bulge of his corneas moving under his eyelids, as though he were deep inside a disturbing dream.

"No," Ali said reluctantly. "The Central Council was here."

Kieran turned to glare at Ali, who shrank away from him.

"What happened?" Kieran growled.

Ali hesitated.

"Kieran," Seth whispered. "Seriously. I need to talk to you."

Kieran took hold of Ali's arm and pulled the boy back to the guard station, where Hiro stood, eyes trained on the empty corridor. "I want to know what happened here, right now."

The guards looked nervously at each other.

"Waverly Marshall brought Bobby Martin down here," Ali finally said, haltingly, "and they said it would be illegal to keep them out."

"Why didn't you call me?"

"We were about to, but . . ." Ali looked at Hiro, who was watching the conversation with worried eyes.

"Waverly started asking him about our parents," Hiro

said. "I forgot about calling you. I wanted to know what he'd say."

"What did she do to him?" Kieran asked with a sinking feeling.

"She used a sheep Taser on him," Ali said, shamefaced.

"Why didn't you call me?" His voice shook with rage, and both boys looked frightened of him.

"We were afraid to," Hiro said. "We knew you'd be mad."

"You were hoping I wouldn't find out."

Both guards looked at Kieran as though they expected to be rapped across the knuckles with a ruler. *They're kids,* Kieran thought. *They're little boys afraid of getting into trouble.*

Kieran closed his eyes and sighed. How could he run a ship with guards who acted like eight-year-olds?

"Give me your walkie-talkie," Kieran spat. Hiro handed his over, and Kieran spoke into it. "Sarek, send two fresh guards down to the brig."

"Are you giving us a break?" Hiro said hopefully.

Kieran laughed as he jerked the keys from Ali's belt, then from Hiro's. He took each of their guns and locked them in the metal cabinet behind the guard desk. "I'm relieving you of duty. You're back on farm work."

Hiro dropped his eyes, seeming to accept that he deserved to be punished, but Ali glared at Kieran.

"If you weren't such a jerk, people wouldn't be so afraid of telling you the truth," Ali said.

Kieran ignored him and went back into the brig. The terrorist hadn't moved a muscle.

"Kieran, please," Seth whispered, reaching for him through the bars. "I know some things that you need to know."

"So tell me," Kieran said without looking at him.

"I can't here," Seth said, his eyes on the prisoner, who was stirring from sleep.

"Jake?" Kieran called loudly through the bars. "It's me, Kieran."

The man didn't move. Quietly, Kieran let himself into the cell, careful to stay near the door in case he bolted. "Jake," Kieran whispered.

The man's eyes popped open, and he gasped as though he were finding himself in the brig for the very first time.

"Jake, I'm sorry. I didn't know they were going to do that to you."

The man's eyes rolled in his head until they found Kieran, then he stared.

"You've got to believe me. Waverly didn't have permission to do that. I'm very sorry."

"No you're not," the man said, sounding tearful.

"I don't believe in torture. I haven't laid a hand on you, have I?"

"Good cop, bad cop. That's what they call it."

"What?"

"One is your enemy, one is your friend." He spoke as though he'd repeated this over and over to himself, preparing himself. "That's how they do it."

"Waverly is no friend of mine," Kieran pleaded. All his work trying to build a bridge to this man was finished. "We're not working together."

The man looked at him, eyes and face blank.

"I'm going to get you some medical attention, okay?" Kieran said.

Jake closed his eyes, shielding them from the light with his hand.

Kieran stepped back out of the cell and locked it behind him.

"Kieran, please," Seth said. "I need to get out of here for a few minutes. Just to talk."

"Go to hell," Kieran said to him, and left.

Once he gave orders to the new guards for a medical team to come check on the prisoner, Kieran went directly to the Central Council chamber. It wasn't until he saw Arthur sitting at the table with the rest of them that he realized his trusted friend hadn't told him what happened with the prisoner, either. When Arthur saw Kieran standing in the doorway, Arthur's face drained of color and he looked into his lap. Soon the rest of the council sensed Kieran standing there, and the conversation trickled to a murmur, then ceased altogether into an embarrassed silence.

"Hello," Waverly said to him. She was the only one who looked defiant.

"I heard you visited the brig," Kieran said.

"That's our legal right," Waverly said, sticking her chin out.

"And torture? Is that your legal right, too?"

Her face changed; he could see she didn't like the word.

"I caused him no permanent harm."

"Not to his body, maybe."

"I did what needed to be done."

"We do not torture on this ship, you once told me," Kieran said, his voice deadly quiet. "You're a hypocrite."

Waverly looked down at her hands, which were wrestling with each other in her lap.

Finally Arthur piped up. "Don't you want to know what we found out?"

Staring at his friend, Kieran felt racked with betrayal. He'd never have thought it possible that Arthur could side with Waverly against him.

"Kieran," Arthur said, "Mather's situation might be politically vulnerable. She and the church elders aren't on good terms."

Kieran wanted to deny the value of this information, but he couldn't. This could be useful.

"Also," said Waverly, "our parents are being held in the sewage plant."

"So what?"

"So it's not a bad place to fight," Waverly said.

Kieran looked at the table and saw that the council was looking at schematics for the New Horizon.

"We're not going to fight them," Kieran said quietly.

The room was quiet as they all looked at him, until finally Alia Khadivi said, "You aren't suggesting that we negotiate with Anne Mather?"

"It's the only way," Kieran said. He met Arthur's eyes, but the boy was unable to hold his gaze and looked instead at the blueprint in front of him.

"She'll trick you, Kieran," Waverly warned.

"She *thinks* she's going to," Kieran said.

"She'll never give us what we want," someone said from the corner, and Kieran looked to see Sarah Hodges scowling at him. Her ruddy hair was pulled away from her face in a sloppy ponytail, and she sat hunched in her chair, glaring at Kieran like she used to glare at the physics teacher. She wasn't even on the Central Council! Why was she privy to this ridiculous meeting and he wasn't?

"You cannot win a battle against Mather's crew," Kieran said.

"With good planning, we might—" Waverly began.

He cut her off. "You say she's so tricky. You think you can beat her in a war?"

"She won't expect—" Alia said, but Kieran cut her off, too.

"I had a front-row seat for the original attack, and I'm telling you, Anne Mather is tactically ingenious. We'll never win a battle on her turf, with her crew. Not without getting a bunch of kids killed. Are you prepared for that?"

His voice boomed, magnified by the glass paneling that formed the domed ceiling. The stars over their heads looked cold and remote.

"You might be right," Arthur finally said. He stood up, leaning one hand on the table. "But we think there's an excellent chance that Mather plans to take over this vessel when we rendezvous. She's hungry for power, and we know that she wants to set up a theocracy on New Earth like the one she has on her ship. Could you live under her rule? Because I don't think I could."

Kieran stared at Arthur, shocked. That Arthur would defy him openly, in front of his political enemies, was unforgivable.

The council seemed to sense the tension between the two boys. There was an awkward pause while they looked from one face to the other, until Waverly stood, too.

"Diplomacy might be a good plan A, Kieran, but we need to be prepared for the worst. That's what we're doing now," she said quietly, making eye contact with each council member. The room seemed muffled, and everyone held their tongues, even Sarah, who looked at Waverly in a studying way.

"So this is plan B? You're saying you won't attack unless my diplomacy fails?"

Waverly looked at each face around the table. Reluctantly, each member of the council nodded.

"Okay, make your little plans," he said to the room at large, but his anger was directed at Arthur. "But I'll have to think long and hard before I give you access to the guns."

"That's okay," Waverly said with a mysterious smile.

This startled him, but he tried not to show it, and whirled on his heel to go back to Central Command before they could say another word.

When he arrived, Sarek looked up excitedly from his com console. "Kieran, we've just received a huge video file from the New Horizon."

"Send it to my office," Kieran said, and ran down the corridor. With shaking fingers he keyed in the lock code to his office, bolted to his desk, and activated the file.

Dozens of thumbnail pictures filled his screen, faces he hadn't seen in months, and a vast well of sadness surged inside him, filling him with longing. He counted them—forty-six survivors.

Only forty-six? Out of over three hundred and fifty crew members? For a time he was paralyzed by the enormity of this, his heart thumping powerfully in his chest, the rest of his body weak. He'd known their losses had been huge, but . . . he couldn't grasp that over three hundred people he'd known his entire life had been snuffed out in a matter of minutes. He relived those awful moments in the starboard shuttle bay, his helplessness in trying to convince people that they shouldn't load the bay full of so many crew members, and then the horror of the air lock doors opening to the vacuum of space, sucking almost the entire crew out to their deaths. Spinning forever in the cold. They'd never stop spinning.

Snap out of it, Kieran.

He took deep breaths until the old feelings of shock and loss subsided, and made himself look more closely at each thumbnail. Now that this moment had arrived, he found he dreaded knowing the truth. If his mother's face wasn't among the survivors . . .

Regina Marshall, Harvard Stapleton, Kalik Hassan, Gunther Dietrich—the faces of his friends' parents popped out at him, and he was relieved by each one. But as he scrolled through the thumbnails, his heart weakened, and he felt hot tears burning his eyelids. She wasn't here. His mother's face wasn't among the survivors. Neither was his father's, but he'd expected that.

At the bottom of the screen was a thumbnail of Mather's face, and he clicked on it.

"These are all the survivors from the Empyrean on our ship, Kieran, except for one," Mather said with false regret. "I'm withholding the video of your mother until you meet us at the coordinates I'm transmitting now."

The screen went blank.

His mother was alive. She was alive! But quickly Kieran saw the other side of this message: His father was not.

He'd suspected for a long time that his father hadn't survived the initial attack. But knowing for sure . . . it made him feel frozen inside.

He couldn't begin to deal with his feelings about it. He wanted to cry. He knew he *should* cry, or scream. But instead he played the videos of the captives, one by one, watching them for signs of duress. All the captives looked well fed and clean though haggard, and all of them spoke to the camera, telling their children how much they loved them, don't worry, I'll be home soon. Don't be afraid.

Harvard Stapleton's video was especially haunting. The man had aged, with deep creases in the skin under his red-rimmed eyes. His voice had changed, too, hoarser, weaker, more plaintive. Kieran felt deep pity for him; Harvard had taped this message for a daughter and wife who'd been dead for months.

"You're strong, Samantha," Harvard said bravely. "I don't fear for you. I know you made it out, and that you're doing all right. But I know you and your mom are worried about me. I'm okay. It's been hard, but they feed us and give us medical care. Physically, I'm fine. The hardest part of this is missing you and your mom. I just can't wait to see your faces again."

Kieran buried his face in his hands and cried for the families destroyed, for the young minds so deeply scarred by what had happened. And for the future. He hadn't given voice to his fears for what would happen next, but he couldn't keep them at bay any longer. How was he going to pull this off? How would he get them back? And even if he did, how could they ever coexist on New Earth with the evil people who had destroyed so many lives?

By the end of the videos, Kieran's mind had settled back into familiar territory. He had things to do, tasks to complete, and he couldn't let his grief get in the way of the job he was here to do. He sent the video files to Sarek with instructions to contact the families of the captives so they could view them. "But don't tell them these are all the captives."

"This is *all* of them?" Sarek asked, incredulous.

Kieran looked at the younger boy's wide eyes in his monitor. "Yes."

Sarek sat shaking his head, mouth open.

"Hail the New Horizon," Kieran said. Sarek didn't move. "Sarek?"

"Okay," the boy said quietly.

Only after the com blinked off did Kieran realize that Sarek had just found out his mother was dead. And Kieran hadn't said a word of condolence.

I'll make it better, Kieran thought, but he felt he'd lost his chance forever to tell Sarek how sorry he was, and to be heard. *I'm becoming hard. I'm not the same person anymore.*

His com link beeped, and he was looking at the hateful face of Anne Mather once again. She took in his dark expression and raised an eyebrow. "This is what I was afraid of. Those videos awakened some demons."

Kieran ignored this. "I've looked at the coordinates you sent and they seem fine. We'll head for the rendezvous point tonight and should arrive within a few days."

"As soon as I've confirmed your course change, I'll send you the remaining file." She moved to sever the com link, but Kieran rushed to speak.

"I've been thinking about your terms for a treaty."

Her eyes flicked to his.

"I can't agree to making you immune to criminal charges," he said.

She leaned back in her seat, eyes narrow. "My people will be very disappointed."

"Oh, I don't think so." He spat out each word like a bitter seed.

Her expression betrayed nothing, but her cheeks grew pale.

"You see, Pastor Mather," he said with quiet vitriol, "I

think there are plenty of people on your crew who don't like what you did to the Empyrean."

"They understand I did what I had to do."

"They understand that you've orphaned two hundred kids?" Kieran said. "Your entire crew would have to be as morally bereft as you are. I think that's unlikely."

For once, she seemed to have no idea what to say; her mouth hung open, and she stared into the screen, her eyes two watery blobs.

"Now you have to decide how much of a hypocrite you're willing to be. Are you going to jeopardize the entire peace treaty on the single condition that Anne Mather be held above the law?"

"I—"

"How is that going to look to your crew?"

"Now wait just a minute."

"How is it going to look in the history books, do you think?"

She was silent, her face frozen as she looked at him anew. *I've surprised her,* he realized. *She's not used to being surprised.*

"All right, Mr. Alden," she said, her cool composure already regained. "You've made yourself heard."

"We're going to start from scratch. I'll be transmitting *my* terms for peace. And we'll begin to discuss how to deal with your war crimes only after every single Empyrean crew member has been returned safely to my ship. Am I making myself clear?"

He hung up on her dumbfounded face before she could respond.

PART FOUR

Spark

It is the flash which appears, the thunderbolt will follow.

—Voltaire

Practice Run

The conifer bay was frigid. Waverly hated coming here when the heat lamps were off, but she needed cover of darkness. She carried a lightweight collapsible shovel under her tunic and strolled between the stands of fir and pine, aware that surveillance cameras were capturing her every move. Though she wore a hooded shirt, she thought she was probably still recognizable from the way she limped. At least her throat was mostly healed. It had been over a week since she'd been choked, and every day she felt stronger.

When she reached the juniper grove, she ducked out of view between the branches and turned on her flashlight, training the yellow circle of light on the floor, searching the ground for a holly branch.

There were fifteen species of juniper here, each represented by several specimens, and it took her a long time to find the holly branch Seth had left between two Rocky Mountain junipers. The place smelled piney and fresh, and though she shivered against the terrible cold, she liked the crisp air on her face. She kicked the holly out of the way and jabbed the blade of her shovel into the hard frozen ground, hacking at the mat of needles and then the cold earth below them. She hadn't thought of how frozen the ground would be, and cursed Seth under her breath as she leaned all her weight into her work. Soon she had a fine film of sweat that made her even colder. It was numbing toil, so her mind wandered back to the same thing it had been stuck on for the last two days.

"Don't do anything stupid," her mother had said in her video. Waverly had watched it over and over again for hours, looking for some hint of her mother's true state. Regina smiled bravely at the camera, and her voice was modulated at an almost cheerful timbre, but there was something off about her. The way her left eye twitched. The way she kept glancing off to the left of the camera, as though seeking the approval of the person taping her. Waverly hadn't known what to expect when Sarek sent her the video file with a note that said Kieran had forced Anne Mather to send these communiqués. Her heart had soared at first, but the more she watched the video, the more she worried. Something in her mother's manner appeared coerced.

All the more reason to get what she came for now.

Waverly's shovel struck something hard about a foot down, and she worked around the shape of the thing, at first chipping the hard dirt away with her shovel, but finally kneeling on the ground and brushing away clumps with her fingers until finally she felt the strap. She pulled on it as hard as she could, prying it out of the ground, until it came loose, and she fell backward, hard.

She put the end of the flashlight in her mouth and opened the zipper, finding exactly what she expected: two dozen guns and countless rounds of ammunition to go with them.

Why had Seth taken these? And when?

She didn't know, and for now she didn't care. Kieran had hidden all the firearms on board the Empyrean, and not even Arthur knew where they were. These were the only ones left.

Waverly hurried out of the conifer bay and into the warmth of the corridors, the bag weighing on her shoulder, the metal guns inside it knocking against her hip with each step. The bag was unbearably heavy, and it slowed her down, but she didn't encounter anyone on her way to the shuttle bay, which was lucky. If she'd run into some of Kieran's goons, she didn't know how she'd prevent them from looking in the bag. She suspected Kieran knew the rescue team would be using guns, but she didn't feel like dealing with any questions.

Arthur was inside their chosen shuttle when she got there, sitting in the cockpit, staring pensively at the control panel as though memorizing the positions of the switches and levers.

"How many are there?" he asked solemnly when he heard her come in.

"Twenty-four," she said.

"More than we need."

"But we'll bring them all. If we have to shoot our way out, our parents can help."

"Good thinking," Arthur said with an audible swallow. Clearly, the thought of a battle unsettled him. He'd barely spoken about his father's video, other than to say he looked thinner and older. But Waverly knew there was a well of concern beneath those two words. Arthur seemed thinner and older himself.

"How long before we reach the rendezvous point?" she asked, taking a seat in the copilot's chair. She couldn't help feeling that Arthur was in her chair—the pilot's seat—but of course after piloting the Empyrean for the last several months, he was certainly able to fly this mission. When the time came, he would wait with the shuttle and Waverly would lead the attack force to liberate the parents.

Arthur shrugged. "I can't get anywhere near Central Command. Now it's just Sarek and Kieran in there, and neither of them is talking to me." The boy spoke hesitantly, as though Kieran's anger made him doubt himself.

"We're doing the right thing, Arthur."

"I just wish we could make Kieran listen to us."

"We've tried that."

"Did we? Did we really try?" His eyes, magnified through his glasses, studied her like two blue searchlights.

"You know him," Waverly said, shaking her head as she put the bag of guns down on the floor. "He's stubborn."

"I don't like double-crossing him."

"We didn't," she said, sticking her chin out. "He knows what we're doing."

"You're stubborn, too," Arthur said distantly.

"When you're right, it's good to be stubborn." She

leaned across the space between the seats and put her hand on his arm. He was still small, but she could feel the muscles of early manhood under her fingers. He was growing up. They all were. "Arthur, are you having second thoughts?"

"I have second thoughts about everything all the time. I have a ruminative mind."

"And do you think we're doing the wrong thing?"

"Our experience with Anne Mather would suggest that we're not."

"But . . ."

"But we're about to act just like her."

Waverly drew away from him, her nose wrinkled in disgust. "You don't know that woman—" she began, but Arthur cut her off.

"She tried to solve her problems with violence. Now that's what we're doing."

"Only if Kieran's plan doesn't succeed," Waverly reminded him.

"Define success," he said.

"What?"

"When do we make the decision that diplomacy has failed?"

"If he gets our parents back, we call off the attack," Waverly said. She could hear the anxiety in her own voice. Arthur was making it complicated; she liked to think it was simple. But of course he was right. Nothing about this was simple.

"What if the exchange of hostages takes more time than we'd like?" Arthur said, suddenly animated. "What if Mather only gives us ten of the hostages? What if Kieran accidentally gives us away?" He swiveled his chair to face her, leaning his head against the back of his seat, his face scrunched into a lopsided shape. "These things are hardly ever all or nothing."

"We'll just have to make those decisions when the time comes."

He sighed heavily. "We'll be in a fog. We'll be scared and confused."

"We'll be brave," Waverly said firmly. She took hold of Arthur's hand and waited for him to look at her. "I'm going to get you through this."

He blinked but said nothing.

"Remember, target practice later," she said to cover the silence.

Arthur reached into the bag and looked at the guns, touching a telescope device attached to the top of one of them. "It shouldn't be too hard with those laser sights," Arthur said. "Seth chose well."

"Laser sights?" she asked, feeling stupid.

"These are for hunting." He picked up a gun and aimed it at the back wall of the shuttle and gently pressed his finger on the trigger. A small red dot appeared on the wall. "See that? That's where the bullet will go."

"That makes it easy," she said, suddenly breathless to be reminded that she might have to kill again. Watch them crumple as their life leaves them in a gush of red. Her mouth went dry, and she swallowed hard. Somehow through all this planning, all this careful consideration, she hadn't really thought about the killing. Surely some people on the New Horizon might die. She wouldn't have time to hesitate, not unless she wanted to give them a chance to kill her first. Arthur was watching her, and Waverly straightened in her seat and gave him a smile.

"It's not fair that you have to go back there," Arthur said.

"Nothing about this is fair to anyone," she said. "But we're going to make it fair again. We're going to get our parents back, and anyone who stands in our way . . ." She didn't finish. She didn't want to hear herself say it.

They were justified to do anything. They'd been attacked, their way of life destroyed, their families split up, their futures stolen—the list of violations was endless. And what about all the videos that *hadn't* come for anxiously waiting kids? Only forty-six videos had made it through, and though a mob of kids loitered outside the door of Central Command round the clock, waiting for more, there was no news. *We're a ship full of orphans,* she thought. And for that, she wanted to kill Anne Mather herself.

She looked forward to it.

She'd been having dreams of running through the corridors of the New Horizon, chasing the guards and matrons and doctors and nurses who had taken so much from her and the other girls. Dreams of their surprised faces as she pulled the trigger and they fell to their knees. The gurgling sounds as they choked on their own blood. The way they'd hold up a hand as if thin flesh and bone could stop a bullet. Or several. Always at the end of the corridor stood Anne Mather, alone and defenseless. She'd hold up her hands prayerfully and intone, "Revenge is the Lord's alone," and then Waverly would pump her full of bullets, each of them exploding into blooms of rosy flesh against the white silk of her robe, spraying her face with a fine pollen of blood.

The old Waverly would have woken from this dream horrified, but the new Waverly found herself smiling when she opened her eyes in the lonely dark.

It's her fault I'm like this, Waverly thought. *She twisted me.*

"I'm going to see if I can find out anything from Sarek," she said to Arthur.

"He won't tell you anything," Arthur said.

"Yes, he will," she said, and left the cockpit.

The ship was just beginning to stir from sleep as she paced the corridor to Central Command. Bleary boys and girls were obediently heading down to morning services. Even after the terrorist had been captured, Kieran still held compulsory daily meetings. She never went, and she still wondered why Kieran hadn't punished her for it. Maybe his forbearance was the final vestige of what she'd once meant to him.

Outside Central Command, Waverly rang the bell for entrance, and waited. She heard the camera pivot toward her, and she looked at it expectantly.

"Go away, Waverly." Sarek's tired voice. With Arthur gone, his duties must have doubled.

"The Central Council has a right to know when we'll reach the rendezvous point, Sarek."

"I'm under orders not to talk to you."

"If you don't let me in, I'll tell Kieran you've been monitoring his conversations with Anne Mather."

"He won't believe you."

"I know details that could only have come from you, Sarek. So let me in."

She waited patiently until the doors slid open.

Sarek looked exhausted, and he smelled like he hadn't bathed in days. Waverly took the seat nearest him and leaned an elbow on the com station in front of her chair.

"I'm sorry to have to pressure you—"

"No you're not," he said bitterly. Sarek seemed tired,

but there was something else about him. His eyes were red rimmed and his voice was husky, as though he'd been crying.

"What's wrong?"

"Nothing," he said quietly.

"You know something, Sarek," she said. "Is this ship in danger?"

"Not any more than usual," he said ruefully.

"You got a video from your dad, didn't you?" she said to Sarek, trying to break through his sour mood. "Maybe you'll get one from your mom, too."

His eyes flicked to hers, and they burned with a fiery rage. It wasn't directed at her, but she recognized it—the helpless rage of loss. He looked away, shaking his head. She could see him clenching his jaw, biting back tears.

"Oh, Sarek, I'm sorry."

He shook his head. "I don't want to talk about it."

She sat with him in silence, sharing the atmosphere of his pain. The whole room reeked of grief, as though it had sloughed off him like musk and left traces everywhere.

"We both have one parent left," she finally said. "And we need to figure out how to get them out of there."

"Kieran told me what you're going to do."

"Good. So when is the rendezvous? I need to know."

"Forty-eight hours," he spat. "Now get out."

"I really am so sorry, Sarek," she said softly.

"I said please leave," he said without looking at her.

He obviously didn't want her there, so she left without another word.

Her body buzzed with fear. Two days before she saw her mother again! She didn't let herself entertain other possibilities.

She met the Central Council and the five other volunteers for the mission in the shuttle bay, where they'd gathered to practice the assault. Plenty of kids had come forward, wanting to help with the attack, but the council had decided to keep the force small for the sake of speed and had chosen volunteers on the basis of age. "Thanks for coming, everyone. I've finally gotten confirmation that the rendezvous is happening about when we expected, in forty-eight hours."

Murmurs rustled through the crowd. Alia, Sarah, and Melissa wore frowns of determination. Melissa's eyes were puffy and red, and Waverly guessed the poor girl had been crying since the videos came through three days ago; she'd had no news from either parent. Sarah, who'd also heard nothing, seemed enraged, and Alia, with her huge brown eyes, simply looked numb.

"Are there any questions before we do our practice run?" Waverly asked.

The team went over last-minute changes to the operation, reviewing their roles and positions. This went on for half an hour, until finally the conversation petered out.

"Any other questions?" Waverly asked.

Alia smiled with quivering lips. Next to her stood Debora Mombasa, with her wild hair and coffee-colored skin, who'd had no reason to expect a video, though the happiness of some of the other kids only seemed to deepen her grief. Sarah Hodges chewed on a lip, looking fiercely around the room. Next to her stood Randy Ortega, a tall boy with a round face and shoulders and large brown hands. He whispered something to Sarah, and she visibly relaxed and gave him a shy smile. Waverly suspected the two had struck up a tentative romance. No one made a move for a question, and after waiting awhile, Waverly began to feel she was stalling.

"Okay then," Waverly said. "I think we all have memorized our plan. So let's get going."

She felt foolish rushing through the empty corridors to the sewage plant, pretending to carry a gun. Alia looked confident as she ran ahead of the group and set up her position at each turn, pivoting around the corner and pointing her gun at an imagined shooter. Sarah brought up the rear along with Randy, running backward. Once they got to the sewage plant, three kids were stationed at each entrance, while a small force of four ran to where they anticipated the parents would be kept, and Waverly fired up the arc welder they'd taken from the machine room. She practiced cutting through a thick steel bolt like the one she'd seen on the livestock container back on the New Horizon. It felt like it took an hour, but when she finished, Sealy said, "Four minutes! Awesome, Waverly!"

The team clapped, but Waverly shouted over them. "We're only halfway done! Let's go!"

They moved back through a different route until they reached the shuttle bay. This was the most dangerous part, Waverly knew, and it would be the stage of the mission that was least predictable. Almost certainly, they'd have to shoot their way out, and Waverly knew that all kinds of things could go wrong. She'd had this same feeling before her escape from Mather's clutches— butterflies in her stomach, a dry mouth, and fear that seemed to take up all the space in her lungs. She'd lost Samantha escaping from the New Horizon. Who would they lose this time?

You can't think about that, she told herself angrily.

You have to believe this will work, or it never will.

In all, the entire practice run had taken a total of nineteen minutes, but she was still nervous. Nineteen minutes was plenty of time for Mather to react.

After the dry run, the council and its volunteers went to the storage bay in pairs and practiced shooting live ammo into a thick piece of sheet metal. She saw joy in their faces when they pulled the triggers, that same weird enjoyment she felt in her blood-soaked dreams. She wondered if they'd still feel that way when they were shooting people instead of dead metal.

When they'd used as much ammunition as they dared, the team said good-bye for the night. Waverly took the guns back to the hiding place on the shuttle. The walk through the ship had an ethereal quality, as though the Empyrean were part of a universe she no longer completely belonged in. The smooth metal walls, the loamy smell of the rain forest level that penetrated even all the way up here, the sound of the air whooshing through the ventilation system, the ever-present hum of the engines—it could all vanish in an instant. Or, even more likely, she herself could vanish without leaving a trace. Every fiber of her body felt vulnerable, each cell aware that a few hours might be all that was left of her life. She wanted the mission to go well; she believed it would. But she had seen what happened to Samantha on the New Horizon. She knew death could happen to her, too.

She should say her good-byes, but there was only one person she really wanted to see, and she couldn't face him. She'd locked away her memories of the way she'd tortured the prisoner in front of Seth, made a tight box in her mind, and she never looked inside so she never had to hear the prisoner's cries again or see his twisted features or recall the damp stink of fear rising from the creases of his body as she stood over him. But she couldn't forget Seth's face as she'd left the brig, the way he'd looked at her with deep regret, as though realizing for the first time that she wasn't the girl he thought she was. She knew she wasn't. No one could be as perfect as that, anyway. But she'd lost something that she hadn't even known she treasured until it was gone. Seth had respected and admired her; now, after what she'd done in front of him, after the way he'd seen her grimace of pleasure as she drove the Taser deep into the man's groin, how could he ever respect her again? How could anyone?

And this time, she had no one but herself to blame.

Still, she wanted to say good-bye to him. She wanted to wish him luck. She wanted . . . She didn't know what she wanted. But she couldn't let him see her. So she left the shuttle bay and went to her quarters. She boiled a mash of grain and beans and ate it without seasoning. Her eyes trailed the words of one of her mother's old mystery novels as she sat curled on the sofa in the shape of a sea prawn. And when she went to bed, she stared into the dark with round eyes, trying to forget Seth, the prisoner, Anne Mather—everything. She tried to forget herself.

The Last Amen

"Thank you all for coming." Kieran looked at his dwindling congregation as he massaged the wooden podium with his fingers. He wasn't feeling inspired for this sermon. He was too afraid.

"Tomorrow morning, early, we are going to meet our enemies for the first time since the attack. This time, I hope, our encounter will be a peaceful one. I know you want revenge. I want that, too. But my job is to keep you safe. That's why I'm making a deal to try to negotiate a peaceful resolution to our conflict. If that doesn't work—"

"Then what?" someone cried from the back of the room. "You'll bend over and kiss their asses?"

Kieran looked up, stunned. He scanned the congregation for the speaker, but with the bright stage lights shining in his face, he couldn't see into the back of the room.

"No," he said. He glanced over the rest of his sermon, realized how bland it was, crumpled it up into a stiff ball, and threw it backward over his shoulder. Some people laughed, and a few people sat up straight in their chairs. "No. If they don't give us our parents immediately, and if they try to board this vessel or in any way make a hostile move, then . . . the Central Council and I have agreed that we'll take back our parents by force."

A whoop issued from the back of the room, and several catcalls joined it, and then suddenly the congregation was on its feet, clapping and hollering for joy. "We'll kill them! Kill them all!" someone screamed over the applause. Several boys started chanting, "Anne Mather's head! On a stake! Anne Mather's head! On a stake!" Soon the entire audience had taken up the battle cry, and the room broke into a frenzy of bloodlust.

Marjorie Wilkins and her sister stood on their chairs in the front row, hands raised over their heads as they screamed their helpless rage into the air. They'd received no video from the New Horizon. In fact, that was probably the source of most of the ire in the room—to see friends get news from loved ones and to go without it yourself. It would be enough to turn anyone savage.

And savage they were. Red faces bawled, clenched fists pumped the air, voices rose in hoarse cries for revenge. Kieran stared, amazed. He didn't recognize them. He had no idea how to talk to them. When he got ahold of himself, he raised his hands over his head and yelled into the microphone, "That's enough! Stop! Stop!"

Slowly the crowd settled down, looking at him expectantly.

"I know you want revenge for what they've done to us. I do, too."

"Damn straight!" Marjorie screamed, and several people laughed.

"Let's skip the negotiations!" a boy yelled from the front row. "Let's get them!"

Several cries of approval answered this.

"We have to be realistic!" Kieran said loudly over them. "We all want to punish them, but in a fight on their turf, we might be the ones getting punished."

"Fearin' Kieran!" someone screamed from the back, and several people started chanting it, first in soft voices, but the volume mounted, and soon the entire congregation was yelling at the tops of their lungs, some of them defending Kieran, most attacking.

Kieran licked the sweat from his upper lip, tasted its salt. He'd been here before, standing in front of a crowd that wanted to condemn him. He'd felt this terror before, and it had almost beaten him.

No, he told himself. *No.*

"Shut up! All of you!" he screamed into the microphone. Ignoring him, Marjorie Wilkins lunged over the back of her seat to swat at a boy who was jeering at Kieran with his tongue hanging out. The boy shook her off, and she fell down. Overtaken with a fresh surge of anger, Kieran's voice trebled in volume as he bellowed, "SHUT THE HELL UP!"

His voice was so loud in the speakers it drowned out the chanting, and the jeers petered out as people looked at him in surprise.

He let them look, waited for the silence to expand to the outer walls of the room. When he spoke again, his voice was even, modulated, quiet.

"If you think for one second that you're going to walk in there, shoot a bunch of adults, and then walk back out with our parents, you're fooling yourselves." He took the microphone off of its stand and jumped off the stage to walk up the aisle, looking at every face he passed. "I saw what they did to our crew in the initial attack, and I'm telling you, we can't beat them that way. Get that through your thick skulls."

A murmur of annoyance spread through the crowd, but he squelched it by yelling over them.

"And you can all go to hell if you think I'm a coward! Tomorrow I'm going to the New Horizon all alone to negotiate with those murderers. They'll be able to kill me on the spot if they want to. And why wouldn't they? I'm nothing to them."

He'd reached the back of the room, which had gone silent. Most of the eyes he met seemed embarrassed, though a few people looked at him with insolent grins.

"I've already told Anne Mather that I'll allow her no immunity from war crimes charges, not on our ship, and not on New Earth, either. She's got reason to get rid of me, but I'm betting my life that she won't."

He found the insolent faces in the audience, and he stared each of them down as he backed up the aisle again toward the stage. Some of them tried to hold his gaze but eventually dropped their eyes. Marjorie Wilkins, her shirt torn and hanging on her lanky frame, looked chastened and sheepish.

"It's time for all of you to grow up. You might want some final showdown like in the storybooks, but this isn't a storybook. This is war. And I can tell you, as someone who watched our families blown out an air lock with my own eyes, war doesn't have a happy ending. Not for anyone."

He took the stairs two at a time back onto the stage and stared out over the congregation, which looked back at him, cowed and quiet. And then he said, "Let us pray."

To his surprise, every head in the room bowed down, even if some were more reluctant than others.

The rest of the service was peaceful, though he noticed a few people walked out. He decided he didn't care about them. Maybe he didn't have the approval of everyone on the ship, but that wasn't what mattered now. Human beings might be thinly disguised savages; that's what the history books seemed to say. But peace was always better than war. He was doing the right thing by trying to talk to Mather, and he wasn't going to let anyone make him doubt himself ever again.

When he'd said the last amen, he walked to Central Command without meeting anyone's eyes and took his post, watching the point of light on the long-range radar screen as it crept nearer and nearer the center. That point of light was the New Horizon, and when it finally reached the center of the screen, he'd be able to look out a porthole and see it looming once again in the sky. Then it would begin.

At bedtime he went alone to his quarters and ate a plain meal of dry bread, cold chicken, figs, and raw asparagus. He chewed without tasting, his eyes on the circle of starry sky framed by his porthole. When bedtime came he lay down with a cool cloth across his eyes. He wanted sleep, but he couldn't stop himself from going over the negotiating points he'd memorized. Though no amount of rehearsal was going to make this conversation easy (Mather was too wily for that), it made him feel better to know what he intended to say.

It gave him some small illusion of control.

In the wee hours, he bathed and put on his best clothes, then went to Central Command to sit with Sarek while he guided the ship to the rendezvous point. Sarek looked like a haggard old man, cruelly over-worked. Once again Kieran felt the loss of Arthur. He'd kept himself from thinking about the betrayal of his most trusted friend, but now he wished he could talk things over with that owlish boy, who would have reasoned through every step in their plan, looking at it from all angles, considering many perspectives at once—a talent few possessed. The only two people he knew were capable of this type of thinking were preparing an attack he'd never approved. Now that he was about to board the enemy ship, though, Kieran supposed he was glad there was a group of kids ready to meet violence with violence, if it should come to that.

"Are you nervous?" Sarek asked him, breaking through his thoughts. Sarek's eyes were ringed by blue circles so dark they looked like bruises, and the skin around his mouth had creased into parentheses—features Kieran had seen only on much older adults. Sarek was working himself into exhaustion, and no matter what Kieran did, no matter how many times Matt Allbright offered to take over for him so he could get some sleep, Sarek would irritably shake his head. Kieran thought he knew why: because sleep was impossible anyway. Until his father was safely aboard the Empyrean, Sarek would stay in his chair.

"Nervous about what?" Kieran asked with a sarcastic smirk.

"Talking to that woman. Going on board that ship."

"Of course I am."

Sarek looked at him pensively. "What about the Central Council?"

"What about them?" Kieran said, annoyed.

"Are they up to this?"

Kieran laughed. "No. But they think they are."

"Well," Sarek said ruefully, "that's half the battle."

"Promise me that you won't open the shuttle air lock for them until you've heard from me that Mather's going to betray us. Can you do that?"

"I've written new encryption codes. They won't be able to leave without me opening the doors from up here."

"Good." The two boys stared at each other, faces blank, until Kieran gathered the courage to say, "I don't know what I would do without you."

"Yeah, right."

"I mean it."

"Shut up," Sarek said.

Kieran wanted to hug him. He was suddenly haunted by the thought that this could be the last time he'd ever see this boy who had stood by him through all these months of struggle. But Sarek wouldn't want a hug. He didn't like sentimentality, and, anyway, Kieran didn't want to think he might die today. That would only make him more afraid. And he couldn't succeed with Mather if he was overcome by fear. So he settled for patting Sarek on the back and saying, "I'll see you soon."

"Yep," Sarek said, and turned back to his screen as if this were any other day.

Kieran walked out of Central Command, past the endless graffiti depicting him as a coward, as a capitulator, as an evil dictator, as a saint. He took the stairs down to the port-side shuttle bay, where he found

Waverly standing outside a shuttle with its ramp down. She was pacing back and forth nervously, wringing her hands. As he approached he saw beads of sweat in the hollow of her neck, and the skin around her eyes was pulled tight. He was close enough to smell her shampoo when she finally noticed him. She stopped pacing and stood in front of him, just two feet away, looking without speaking.

"You guys all ready?" he asked her. His voice sounded strained in his own ears, but the anger was gone from him. Now that the day had arrived when their fate would be decided, everything felt clearer.

"We've practiced ourselves almost to death," she said. "I think we're ready."

"Good." He prodded at the floor with the soft toe of his shoe. "So you'll wait to hear from me?"

"Of course."

"And I don't need to say this, probably, but . . ." He glanced at her, saw that she was listening. There was no trace of defensiveness in her eyes. She was trying to be stoic, as always, but fear ebbed off of her. "You know they'll probably kill me if you try to board while I'm still negotiating."

"Kieran, we'll wait to hear from you."

"I'm trusting you with my life."

"I know that," she said softly, but she looked away.

It seemed there ought to be something more to say, but no words came to him. He turned to go, but she lunged at him, wrapped her arms around his shoulders, and hung on.

He was shocked and didn't move at first, but soon his arms found their natural position, wrapped around her, his hands pressing against the bones of her back. She smelled like he remembered, felt almost like he remembered, though her softness was gone. They held each other like that for . . . he didn't know. It could have been seconds or minutes, until finally she let him go and, wiping at tears, turned and ran back into the shuttle. He watched her go, remembering that terrible day he'd watched her board another shuttle to face a horrible ordeal at Anne Mather's hands. That terrible day he'd begged her to stay, get off the shuttle, don't go. He wanted to beg her to stay now, but instead he turned and walked out of the shuttle bay, the only sound in his ears the scuff of his soles against the cold metal floor.

He walked across the ship to the starboard shuttle bay and the shuttle nearest the air lock doors. When he pushed the button to lower the cargo ramp, the seals popped open, sounding like an eggshell cracking. This shuttle had never been opened before, not since it was loaded onto the Empyrean back on Earth, and it smelled of ancient glues and sealants. He sat in the pilot seat and patched in to Central Command. Sarek acknowledged him with a cursory grunt, and Kieran listened to him breathing as he waited, tense and quiet.

Kieran watched the radar screen as the blinking point of light showing the New Horizon slowly edged its way toward the center, finally getting near enough to trigger the ship's collision protocol. A light flickered across his screen, and the words "Object approaching" flashed urgently, casting a sickly green light over the cockpit.

"They're here," Sarek said.

Kieran's armpits were soaked. His hands shook as he warmed up the engines, and he rubbed his palms together, trying to calm the mad trembling of his fingers. The shuttle engines purred and the craft lifted off the floor, then slowly he pivoted it around to face the air-lock doors.

"Sarek," he said, but the doors were already opening. As gently as he could, he guided the shuttle into the air lock and waited for the sound of the hydraulics closing the door and then the explosive sound of the air being pulled away until all that surrounded his ship was a vacuum. The doors in front of him opened, and his heart jerked in his chest.

"Oh God," he said. The New Horizon hung right in front of him, hulking and silent and waiting to swallow him whole. Suddenly, he didn't know if he could really do this. But then he found he *was* doing it. The shuttle was pulling out of the Empyrean, poking out its nose like a lizard leaving its hole. Soon there was nowhere to go but into that woman's clutches.

"Sarek," Kieran said with a nervous chuckle. "Just tell me I'm not a human sacrifice, will you?"

Sarek laughed grimly. "You know, Kieran, maybe it's true, what they say."

"Oh yeah?"

"You do have a messiah complex."

Kieran smiled and finally said what he hadn't been able to say before. "I love you, my friend."

There was an awkward pause. Sarek wouldn't meet his eyes in the vid screen, but then a smile seemed to lighten his face. "You're not my type."

Kieran laughed. "I'll take that as an 'I love you, too.'"

Sarek's smile wiped away, and he blinked away tears. "Be careful, okay?"

Before he could answer, Sarek severed the com link.

Kieran was on his own.

The Party

Kieran guided the shuttle into the air lock on the New Horizon, holding his breath until he heard the outer doors close behind him. When the inner door slid open, he was surprised to see a crowd of people clapping and cheering as he nervously set the shuttle down on the floor. He looked at them through the porthole, flabbergasted. They were all wearing simple white tunics and black pants, with sandals on their feet. Many of the women held wobble-headed infants and lifted their tiny hands to wave at Kieran. Anne Mather stood at the center of it all, smiling as though welcoming a wayward son.

Kieran walked down the shuttle ramp and into Mather's waiting arms. She was surprisingly small for such a formidable woman, with a pigeon figure and rosy cheeks. Her skin was smooth, though he could see a webwork of capillaries just under the surface. Her nose was shiny with oil, and her teeth looked like they'd been stained by tea or coffee. He was surprised, not just by her short stature, but by her obvious human fallibility. *She ages. She weakens. One day she will die.* Until now he'd thought of her as a timeless monolith, one who was despised and feared, like a demon-goddess.

She kissed both his cheeks, then took his hand and turned around to face the crowd. "Let's show Kieran Alden a real New Horizon welcome!"

The crowd erupted into robust cheers. Waverly and the girls had described a crew that had been weakened by years of low gravity, but he saw no sign of it now. Everyone here looked healthy and strong. Kieran tried to count the people; the crowd couldn't number more than fifty, but they filled the shuttle bay with their voices. Kieran didn't know what to do, so he waved at them. He felt off balance, and he supposed that's exactly what Anne Mather wanted.

"Can we talk?" Kieran asked her. He was aware of the half-moons of sweat seeping through the fabric of his shirt, and his palms felt sticky. Despite the cheery welcome, he'd never been more afraid in his life. He raised an eyebrow at the woman to show her these theatrics didn't impress him. "The celebration seems . . . premature. We haven't agreed on a treaty yet."

"All in good time. First I wanted to welcome you aboard with a banquet."

He opened his mouth to refuse but was swept up by a crowd of women who drew him across the shuttle bay, chattering in his ear about how happy they were he came, it was so nice to see such a young, handsome man, and already piloting shuttles! How remarkable! He looked for Anne Mather, who walked at the rear of the crowd, a smile creasing her face, though her eyes were narrow and watchful.

They led him to the stairwell and up. Kieran looked behind him to see a long stream of people coming up the stairs. He became aware that they were singing a song of celebration, though with the echo in the stairwell, he couldn't make out the words. The tune was just familiar enough to create a surreal effect. He hadn't expected anything like this, and it made his head swim.

They led him to the central bunker. All the cots had been removed, and in their place were dozens of banquet tables with white tablecloths. The entire room was lavishly decorated with palm fronds and bouquets of Asian lilies, irises, sunflowers, and ferns. Someone took his hand, and he turned to see Mather smiling at him. She pulled him toward a stage set with a long, narrow table, where a dozen aging adults were seated, waiting with austere frowns on their faces. He took his place at the table, just to one side of a podium, and looked up disbelievingly at Anne Mather, who held up a hand for the crowd to settle down.

It had to have been choreographed, because once the room had faded into silence, someone hummed a note, and then the entire crowd took up a melody. It was a three-part harmony with Latin words repeated over and over, sung by voices of all ranges. It was beautiful, but Kieran was filled with a sense of foreboding. There seemed to be a strange disconnect between the reality of the situation and what was happening here. As though none of these people were willing to acknowledge the terrible wrongs they'd committed. How could he negotiate with such people?

When the song finished, Anne Mather took the podium. She smiled down at the crowd—at her congregation, Kieran realized—and said, *"Dona nobis pacem.* 'Give us peace.' I can't think of a more appropriate way to begin this day! Now, let's bow our heads and give thanks for the presence of our friend Kieran Alden."

Obediently, every head in the room lowered. Kieran folded his hands, but he kept one eye on Mather as she spoke into her microphone.

"Peace be upon you," she said to her congregation.

"Peace be upon you," they parroted.

"Lord"—Anne Mather raised her hands over her head as though to touch the divine presence in the air—"it is our fervent wish that you will guide our negotiations with the emissary from the Empyrean, that we may coexist on New Earth for generations. We seek your presence at our table. Help us know what to ask and how to answer, that we may reach an understanding with each other and, if it is not too much to hope, that we might come together in brotherly love and give glory to your name. Amen."

"Amen!" the crowd responded.

The doors at the back of the room opened, and people wheeled in carts filled with trays of food. They offered Kieran fruits both dried and fresh, glazed pastries, breads filled with dates and nuts, chilled shrimp, and pies. He took small portions, but he was too unsettled to eat. The people sitting at the tables below him talked jovially, patting one another's backs. Here and there, out of the corner of his eye, he'd sense someone watching him from the crowd. As soon as he turned to seek them out, they'd already turned to their neighbor, laughing lustily as if sharing a joke.

It's all an act, Kieran thought. *This isn't real.*

He got up from his chair at the long table, and immediately the crowd subsided to a lull as every eye watched him cross the stage to where Anne Mather was seated at the end of the table, talking with an old woman. Kieran saw two large men standing at the back of the room rush forward, and they hovered nearby, watchful. He ignored them and leaned down to Mather, close enough that he could smell the bread she was chewing, and said in her ear, "I want to see the prisoners right now."

"But everyone is so happy you're here!" she said, batting her eyelashes. "I wanted to share this moment with them."

"I'm not here to be shown a good time," he snarled. "You and I have business."

"I'm aware," she said. "But it's customary to show a diplomat the courtesy of a celebration upon his arrival. I suppose you're not familiar with the old customs of Earth."

Why was it so difficult to talk to this woman? "I need to see the prisoners right now, and then I need to get to a com station."

"Oh." She gave a half turn of her head. "Why is that?"

"They're waiting to hear that I've arrived safely."

"All right," she said with a bland smile. "I'll take you to one just as soon as I can."

She placed an olive on her tongue, making no move to leave.

Kieran looked around him, feeling helplessly trapped. This party was insane. Negotiations hadn't begun, yet he had a feeling that in some uncanny way, Mather had already beaten him.

Because she's counting on me to be polite, he realized. *She doesn't think I'm willing to make a scene.*

With a stroke of inspiration, he walked to the microphone at the podium and turned it on. "Hello?" he said, and his voice boomed through the speakers. Immediately the room sank into silence. Even the people serving food stopped what they were doing to look at him.

"If this exercise in insanity is finished, I'd like to be taken to see the prisoners from the Empyrean. Now."

Anne Mather was looking at him, stone-faced, but still she didn't move from her perch.

"NOW!" he yelled into the microphone. The people sitting near the speakers cried out, covering their ears with their hands.

Mather stood up, threw her napkin on the table, and marched up to Kieran.

"These people have worked so hard—"

"NOW!" he screamed at the tops of his lungs. The microphone whistled a piercing tone that seemed to drill through the channels in his ears.

Mather glared at him and took the microphone from the podium. "I'm sorry, everyone, but our guest of honor has to leave."

She turned on her heel and walked out of the room with Kieran right behind her.

"They prepared a good-bye song," she said under her breath. "All that practice for nothing."

"Do you think I'm stupid? That I can be won over with a couple songs and some nice food?"

"I wanted you to feel like an honored guest."

"You wanted me to feel like a fool," Kieran snarled at her.

She gave him an injured look. In that moment, he hated her enough to kill her.

She led him across the corridor to Central Command, which looked much larger somehow than it did on the Empyrean. It buzzed with people rushing around, speaking urgently into headsets. How smoothly things would run on the Empyrean if he had a full crew of reliable deck officers! Even in this, Mather had the advantage.

"Hail the Empyrean," Mather said to a small, tired-looking woman, who nodded cursorily.

"I want to see the prisoners first," Kieran said.

"You said you needed to tell them you've arrived safely," Mather said, wide-eyed.

"After I see the prisoners," Kieran said.

"I have the Empyrean," the woman told Mather.

Mather looked at Kieran, eyebrows raised expectantly.

There was no code word for this, no way to communicate clearly what had happened. He took the headset from the sullen woman and leaned over the com screen to see Sarek's face.

Sarek released a sigh of relief when he saw Kieran. "You're okay."

"I'm fine, but I haven't seen the prisoners yet."

Sarek's expression darkened. "Why not?"

"I don't know," Kieran said, feeling inadequate. A better man, a better leader, could have talked his way in to see the prisoners. He was messing everything up. Already their plan was frustrated. "They're stalling."

Sarek paused as though trying to read Kieran's face, looking for a hidden message. He finally asked, "How are negotiations going?"

"They haven't begun."

"You should come back, then," Sarek said after a pause.

"If you like, Kieran, you and I can go to my office and share a pot of tea," Mather said from behind him.

"This isn't a social visit!" Kieran yelled. The woman at the com station jumped in her seat. "If I'm not taken to the prisoners immediately—"

"But my dear boy, that's not how negotiations work. First you give me something I want, then I give you something you want. This is going to take time."

He pounded the com board with his fist. He had to decide what to do *now*. When he made eye contact with Sarek, the other boy raised his eyebrows.

"Sit tight, Sarek," Kieran finally said. *God, please, let this be the right thing.*

Sarek nodded, then swallowed hard.

Suddenly an alarm from the Empyrean screeched through the com speakers. Anne Mather stood from the Captain's chair and rushed to the screen. Sarek had disappeared from view, but Kieran could see his shadow moving frantically across the back wall of Central Command. Sarek's panicked voice sounded over the speakers, though the words were indistinct. Finally he rushed back into view, panting.

"There's been an accident!" Sarek cried. "Kids hurt by a combine. Oh God!"

"Can we offer assistance?" Anne Mather said.

Sarek looked at Kieran, and Kieran looked at Anne Mather. "We don't have any doctors on board," Kieran said.

"Bring the injured here!" Mather said simply. "Can you get them on a shuttle, or do you need us to come get you?"

"I can get them on a shuttle," Sarek said, "if you can get your medical team ready. It sounds bad."

"I'll send a team down to wait for you in our port shuttle bay," Mather said, and nodded to a com technician, who spoke quietly into her mouthpiece.

"Thank you," Kieran said, pressing his cold palms against his thighs. "It's been really hard without a doctor."

"Now, maybe we can go someplace to talk," Mather said, and drew him out of Central Command and into her office next door.

The room configuration was identical to his own office, but the decor was very different. She had tapestries hanging on the walls, giving the room a warm feeling. There was something odd about the way the items on her desk were arranged—a blotter pad, a notebook, a diary, a picture frame—each item perfectly aligned, books precisely angled in harmony with the corners of the desk, pen neatly resting at the center top of the blotting pad. Everything calibrated, considered, perfect, as though a machine worked here, not a person.

"Can I offer you tea?" Mather asked.

"You can offer me access to the prisoners," Kieran said.

"First I want to talk about your proposal. It's simply not acceptable."

"It's not negotiable," Kieran said.

"You can't expect me to guarantee that my crew will stay on a separate continent from yours. We have only a vague idea of the climate of each geographic region, as I've said before. It's possible that there's very little habitable landmass on New Earth."

"I don't want you anywhere near us."

"We have another forty-two years to get over past wrongs before we get there."

"You say 'past wrongs' as if you had nothing to do with them."

"I've made mistakes, Kieran. As a fellow leader, I'm sure you understand how easily small miscalculations can result in catastrophe."

He stared at her. At some point, his fear had left him entirely. Now all he felt was a bottomless rage. "If you don't take me to see the prisoners *now*, I'm going to leave."

She stared back at him, her eyes narrowed to flinty gray pinpoints. "You'll forgive me, Mr. Alden, if I want to see what your friends do first."

"Friends?"

"The landing party you just ordered? They're on their way. What they do will help me decide whether to let you see your mother or not."

"They're injured," Kieran said. He tried to sound indignant, but he knew his voice was damp with fear. "They can't do anything."

"We'll see about that," she said with an amused grin.

Best-laid Plans

Waverly leaned over Sarah's gurney and tucked the bed linens around her legs. The shuttle bay was filled with a buzzing expectancy as the members of the Central Council loaded their guns.

"Alia put on makeup," Sarah said under her breath. She cocked her head to where Alia was standing by the shuttle. Her eyes were outlined with thick smudges of charcoal, which made her huge dark eyes seem like two black holes. She looked beautiful, and frightening.

"War paint," Waverly said to Sarah, who chuckled.

"Do I look wounded?" Sarah asked, squeezing the reddened bandage to the side of her head.

"Let's see your game face." Sarah squeezed her

features into a mask of pain. "Good enough," Waverly told her. "We don't need to fool them for long."

"Is it wrong of me to say that I've been looking forward to this?" Sarah asked with an evil grin.

"Yes, it is," Waverly said quietly. "Where's your gun?"

"Sticking in my thigh."

Waverly wheeled Sarah into place in the cargo hold and strapped her gurney to the wall between Debora Mombasa and Randy Ortega, who also wore bandages that had been soaked in chicken blood. Debora seemed coolheaded, but Randy was panting with fear.

"Doing okay?" Waverly asked him.

He gave her a steady nod.

Waverly went into the cockpit and took the copilot's chair next to Arthur, who was nervously fiddling with dials and knobs. Waverly wondered if he was really adjusting anything or if he was just making himself busy to take his mind off what they were about to attempt. "Ready?"

He licked sweat from his upper lip and nodded. He tapped his headset and instructed Sarek to open the air lock for the shuttle. Waverly watched him carefully, ready to take the controls if he made a mistake, but his performance was exemplary. She would have thought he'd flown a shuttle many times before.

Once the outer air-lock doors opened, Arthur eased the craft out of the bay and turned it around. They'd chosen the port side to launch from because it was nearer to the infirmary and would make their ploy seem more real, they hoped. The deception felt rather thin to Waverly, now that they were on their way.

Arthur flew the shuttle over the curve of the Empyrean.

The many domes covering the hull reminded Waverly of the pictures of sand dunes she'd seen from Earth. Amanda, the New Horizon crew member who had taken Waverly into her home, had shown the pictures to her and had tried to describe the ever-changing desert landscapes of Old Earth. Waverly wondered what had happened to Amanda, and to Jessica, Mather's personal secretary, after they helped Waverly escape. Anne Mather might have imprisoned them, or worse. She realized she hadn't let herself think of them at all. They were part of that horrible past she'd wanted to leave behind, so she'd banished them from her mind, though in truth, she owed her life to them.

The New Horizon rose like a misshapen moon over the hull of the Empyrean. It dominated the black sky with bubbling gray metal. As they approached, Waverly could see the outlines of people passing by portholes, none of them turning to notice the approaching shuttle.

It made her sick to look at that ship. It was identical to the Empyrean; why then did it look so evil to her? Everything about it—gray skin, misshapen hull, the light emanating from its hundreds of portholes—all of it was forbidding and awful to her. She concentrated instead on Arthur's progress as he piloted the shuttle to the enormous bay doors, which slid open before he could even request to dock.

This is it, she told herself as the shuttle eased inside the New Horizon. Her heart felt as though it were skipping beats, and her hands felt like ice carved into the shapes of brittle fingers.

The inner air-lock doors opened to a group of medical personnel wearing scrubs and white gloves. Strangers

with strange faces. She hated them all. She scanned the
rest of the shuttle bay for armed guards, but saw none.
Could it be this easy?

No, she told herself. *Nothing is easy with Anne Mather.*

Arthur looked at Waverly nervously before he pushed
the button to lower the shuttle ramp, and Waverly heard
the gush of air as the hydraulics engaged. She went to
the passenger section of the ship, where already the
assault team had stood up from their seats. Sealy was
clicking off the safety of his gun and peering through the
sights. Harvey Markem held his gun across his chest,
squeezing the metal with his hands until his knuckles
turned white. As the largest team member, he'd been
chosen to carry the bag of extra guns, which was strapped
tightly to his back in a compact mass. Melissa Dickinson
had already taken her position at the top of the stairs, the
muzzle of her gun pointing down, ready to cover the
team as they descended the stairs.

"Let's go," Waverly whispered to them, and started
down to the cargo hold, where already doctors and
nurses were entering to look at the patients. A small
male doctor leaned over Sarah and peered into her eyes,
only to find the muzzle of a gun jammed into his face.
Two nurses screamed when Randy sat up, pointing his
gun at them. The rest of the medical team, about six in
all, stood staring, their mouths hanging open.

Waverly jumped down the last few stairs and grabbed
one of the nurses by her collar. "Where are the guards?"

The woman only looked at Waverly, working her jaw
but unable to speak. Waverly pointed her gun at the
woman's neck. "I said, where—"

"There are no guards," the woman said, breathless.

"Bullshit!" Waverly yelled in her face.

"It's true," one of the doctors piped up from behind her. "Pastor Mather didn't order guards to accompany us."

Waverly looked from the doctor to Sarah, who had stood up from her gurney and was eyeing the man suspiciously.

"Everyone grab your hostage!" Waverly shouted. She pulled the male doctor by the collar, making him walk in front of her, pressing the muzzle of her gun into the hollow of his back. His dark hair was shorn close to his head, and she could see sweat trickling between the hairs and soaking the collar of his shirt. His fingers were trembling, and she heard his shallow, jagged breaths as he stumbled ahead of Waverly down the ramp and onto the shuttle-bay floor.

"March!" Waverly yelled, though it hurt her throat, and they were off.

Each time they passed a shuttle, Waverly turned, expecting to see guards hiding there but finding no one. She hadn't thought about her emotional reaction to being back on this ship. She felt claustrophobic, hemmed in, and panic threatened to overtake her. This was where they'd done it to her. She shouldn't have come. She gulped air, fought down the panic, and tried to focus on the task at hand.

They reached the shuttle-bay doors without incident, and Sarah went ahead to open them. Waverly braced herself, expecting guards to burst into the room, shooting away, but the doors opened to a peaceful corridor.

It was the same the whole way. Around every corner, at every doorway, the team took positions, shielding themselves with their hostages, but they met no resistance whatsoever. They didn't even find regular maintenance workers. The corridors were deserted.

Waverly knew this was a part of the ship that would be rarely visited by crew members. On the Empyrean, few people went to the sewage plant unless something had gone wrong and repairs were needed. Otherwise this entire area of the ship was fully automated. Still, Waverly had a sinking feeling. Her heart thrummed in her chest so hard she wondered if her hostage could hear it. She could hear his breath, the way air rasped through his throat like rough yarn. His steps were halting, but he let her steer him through the turns in the corridor, keeping his hands at shoulder level.

When the doors to the sewage system came into sight at the end of a long corridor, the team paused to listen for signs of life. The corridor was eerily silent.

"What do you think?" someone said right next to Waverly, making her jump.

She turned to see Alia next to her, holding on to the tunic of a medic, her gun jammed under his shoulder blade. Her dark eyes brimmed with concern.

"I don't like it," Waverly said.

"Are we walking into a trap?" Alia asked, her voice low.

"If we are, we're already in it," Waverly said.

"Where are we going?" asked the medic being held by Randy. "Where are you taking us?"

"Shut up," Randy snarled.

"But this doesn't make sense!" the man cried, near panic.

"I recognize you," Alia said to him with a deadly tone.

"You sedated me so they could steal my eggs. Give me a reason to shoot you."

At this, the man quieted.

"Come on," Waverly said softly to the team. "Let's move."

The team members took their positions outside the doorway to the sewage plant, and Sarah stepped forward to work on the lock, only to find the doors unlocked. She looked at Waverly, surprised.

"What does this mean?" she said under her breath.

Waverly shook her head.

Sarah pressed the button for ingress, and the doors slid open. Waverly was assaulted by the sickly, moist air of processing sewage, the deafening thrum of the pumps and filters, and the sound of gushing water.

The team walked into the room, fanning out, pointing guns into every corner.

There was no one here. The room was empty.

"What?" Waverly heard someone say. *"What?!"*

"No!" cried Sarah. She pushed her hostage away from her, and the woman fell onto the floor.

Waverly turned on the doctor and pointed her gun in his face. He whimpered, his hands high above his head. "Where are they?"

"Who?" he asked, tiny-voiced. "Who do you want? I'll tell you what you need to know."

"Where are our *parents*?!" Waverly screamed, and took two steps forward, forcing the man back against the wall behind him.

The doctor shook his head, mouth hanging open. "They're not here. They were never here."

"Then why would Jake—" she began, but stopped herself.

"Waverly." Sarah stepped forward. "What now?"

"They recorded you coming here," one of the nurses piped up. She was of medium height, and she held her shoulders square as she looked at Waverly defiantly. "Security forces will be on their way."

"Where are they?" Waverly yelled at the doctor she held at gunpoint. "Tell me, or I'll make an example of you."

"Oh God," he said. A spot of wet formed on the front of his scrubs, and a puddle spread under his feet. "They're in the brig, I think."

"The *brig*?" Sealy whined, and slammed the butt of his gun on the floor, making a booming echo in the large room. "We'll never make it there!"

"We have to go," Alia said, defeated. "Waverly, we must go."

"She's right," Sarah said, looking grave. "They're on their way."

Waverly screamed in frustration and fired her gun again and again into the wall right over the cowering doctor's head. Her ears rang with the sound of it. The doctor hid under his arms, his entire body in terror-stricken spasms, until she finally stopped. She had that same feeling as when she woke from her nightmares— that awful satisfaction of having punished someone. But along with the satisfaction came a sour taste in her mouth, and she looked at her trigger finger, which twitched against the hot metal.

"Okay," Waverly finally said, her voice hoarse. "Let's go. Leave your hostages. We'll be faster without them." The terrified doctor closed his eyes with relief, until she added, "Not you. You're coming with us."

His face crumpled, but he let her push him in front of her. Crescents of sweat had soaked through his scrubs, and he emitted a musky, fearful odor. He trembled, and his hemp shoes, sodden with urine, made a squishing sound as he walked.

Waverly and her hostage led the way out of the plant, but once in the corridor, she pushed him against the wall and stood aside until the last of her friends made it out of the room, then she closed the doors and shot the lock with her gun so the other hostages couldn't leave. Dragging the man along helplessly by his collar, she ran after the team, which was already way ahead of her. "We're too spread out!" she called to them, and Randy Ortega, who was in front, stopped to wait near a turn in the corridor that led directly to the shuttle bay.

A shadow passed over Randy, and Waverly pushed her hostage in front of her. "Look out!" she cried.

Randy whirled around, but from around the corner a hand grabbed the barrel of his gun and twisted it away. Randy fell backward but struggled onto his knees until he found himself staring into the muzzle of a black gun. A scrawny man wearing a shirt and pants a size too large for him emerged from around the corner. His gray eyes met Waverly's, and with a deep voice he said, "Drop your weapons."

Waverly tightened her hold on her hostage, and she pushed the muzzle of her gun into his throat.

Cat and Mouse

"I wish that hadn't been necessary," Anne Mather said to Kieran from across her desk. His eyes were on the video screen between them, which showed Waverly and her assault team in a standoff with a single armed man.

"Around the bend in the corridor are eight more men, Kieran. I hope Waverly chooses well."

Kieran watched the way Waverly massaged the metal of her firearm as she looked at the man, who jammed his gun into Randy Ortega's temple. *Please, Waverly, don't do anything stupid.* He'd known something like this might happen. He'd been almost certain she would fail, but he'd capitulated to her plans because he wanted to show Mather that he was willing to fight her. Now he realized he'd only weakened his position. Never more than now did he and his crew look like a bunch of amateurish kids who had no idea what they were doing.

Anne Mather turned off the video feed. Kieran looked up from the screen to see her enjoying his expression. "Why would you risk your doctors that way?" he asked her.

"There was no real risk," she said, shifting in her seat uncomfortably. She was lying, clearly.

"Were you hoping to get rid of a few enemies?" he spat.

"I know you must be angry," she finally said. "I would be, in your place."

"If you hurt them . . ."

"As long as they cooperate, they'll be fine. They're being led back to their shuttle right now," Mather said, and picked up a delicate antique teapot to pour two cups of chamomile tea. She held one of the cups in his face until he finally took it and dropped it with a clatter on the desk between them, sending a gush of tea over the surface. "I may use little tricks here and there," she said humbly, ignoring the spilled tea, "but I was never dishonest about what I want. Peace is my goal, and it should be yours, too."

"Then why have you been stalling?" He slapped her desk, making his knuckles ache.

"To force your hand." She smiled dimly. "I knew you might be planning something. I wanted to neutralize the threat before I started conceding anything to you. Now we have an even playing field."

"No, we don't. You've had all the advantages from the start."

She looked at him appraisingly. A wisp of gray hair at her temple oscillated in the draft from the air duct behind her, distracting him with fantasies of ripping it out of her head.

She's making me angry on purpose, he realized. *She wants me furious so I can't think.*

"I want to see the prisoners now," he said, and stood up from the desk. "Otherwise I'll assume that you've harmed them."

"First I want to discuss the terms of our peace agreement."

"No," he said, and stared at her, waiting.

"Mr. Alden, you've given me no reason to trust you."

"After you kill most of our crew, hobble our ship, kidnap our girls, medically rape them, and imprison our families, you expect *trust?*"

"Trust is the backbone of peace," she said piously.

"Then give me a reason to trust *you.*"

The air was heady with the impasse between them. Finally she slapped her palms on the desk and heaved herself up.

"Fine, Mr. Alden. I'll take you to the prisoners now."

And to his surprise, she walked out the door, beckoning to him over her shoulder. Before, he might have thought he'd gained some ground, but now he knew what he was dealing with, and he followed behind her, flanked by two guards, aware he was likely walking into another trap.

In the elevator, Mather pressed the intercom switch. "We're coming down," she said to someone, who answered, "Yes, Pastor."

"Where are we going?" Kieran asked her. He was painfully aware of the two large men standing behind him, and even more aware of the guns they held across their chests. They did not speak or even indicate that they were listening to his conversation with Mather, but that made them all the more present and menacing.

"To the brig," Mather said. "We've wanted better

accommodations for them, but we can't offer them any kind of security on the habitation levels."

"Don't you have that backward?" Kieran said angrily.

"No, I'm afraid I don't. There are members of my crew who are still furious about the way the Empyrean undermined our fertility. Many of them would shed blood over it. I think you've met one of them, haven't you? Jacob? Is he well?"

"More or less," Kieran said. "If you don't count insanity."

"Oh, he's not crazy, Kieran," Mather said, shaking her head prettily. "He's a man who has been broken. There's a difference."

"Poor little child murderer."

She looked at Kieran sharply. "What are you talking about?"

"He poisoned Max Brent. He was fourteen years old. And he turned Philip Grieg's brains into spaghetti. Philip might not live to see his tenth birthday."

Her lips formed a small almond-shaped hollow that showed the glint of her incisors. She leaned on the wall behind her, and one of the guards reached out to steady her. "I didn't know."

"Yeah, right," Kieran said bitterly. "He was in contact with you the whole time."

"I didn't order any killings, Kieran."

"But you sent him to our ship?"

"No. I promise you, I did not. He acted on his own."

The elevator dipped to a stop, and the doors slid open. Mather beckoned Kieran down the corridor to the brig. Even yards away from the doorway, Kieran could smell a foul odor, and he heard the soft murmur of voices. He didn't recognize any single voice, but together they sounded like home.

A couple of guards stood aside for Mather, and she walked through the doorway and gestured down the corridor. Kieran entered, and immediately a whoop and holler broke through the air. The brig was designed to hold no more than a dozen people at a time, one to a cell, but here the prisoners were crowded in four to a cell. Bedrolls littered the floors, and drying laundry was spread over every surface. The smell was dank and feral.

Kieran felt hands patting his back through the bars, jostling him, shouting questions at him, so many questions he couldn't answer. "Have you seen my daughter? . . . My husband? . . . Are my kids safe?" Endless, desperate questions from so many familiar faces, beloved faces, though haggard and graying. He wished for time to stop and kiss each hand, answer each question, but the guards prodded him along.

Regina Marshall grabbed at him halfway down the corridor. She was cadaverous, thinner and weaker than the rest, but she gripped Kieran's hand with surprising strength. "Kieran, it's so wonderful to see your face. How is Waverly? Did she make it back to the Empyrean?"

"Yes," he said, bewildered by her wasted appearance.

"Give her a kiss for me," Regina said with a needy smile. "Tell her I'll be home soon."

"I will," Kieran whispered.

He saw Kalik Hassan in the next cell over, standing a little back from the crowd. Near him stood Gunther Dietrich, his beard so overgrown it brushed his barrel chest. Both men watched Kieran as he passed, and Gunther raised his eyebrows in a question. Kieran managed to call out to them, "Arthur and Sarek are fine!"

Kalik folded his hands and kissed them. Gunther seemed woozy with relief and closed his eyes as a smile brightened his face.

"Where's my mother?" Kieran asked one of the guards, who shrugged. But then Kieran saw her bony red hands sticking through the bars at the end of the corridor, and he began to run. "Kieran!" he heard her call.

"Mom!" he answered, and ran to her, grasped her dry hands, kissed her cheek through the bars.

Her golden curls had grown out and made a high crown around her head, drooping down to brush the tops of her shoulders. Her cheeks were hollow, and her amber eyes were shadowed by blue circles. Spider veins crawled along the sides of her nose, and she had a red dot of burst vessels in the corner of her left eye that Kieran guessed must be a vestige of the decompression she'd suffered during the attack. But she was alive. She was whole.

Kieran placed a hand on either side of her face, a gesture that, before, would have seemed uncomfortably intimate. But now all he wanted was to touch her, because he could scarcely believe she was really standing before him. Her skin felt papery and dry under his fingers. She seemed so fragile.

"Why did they send *you*?" she asked him as she grasped his wrists in her hands and squeezed. "This is too dangerous for a boy your age."

"Mom—"

"How's Dad?" she said, cutting him off. She bit her lip with chipped front teeth. "He must be so worried."

Kieran pulled his hands away from her. She didn't know. None of them knew. He looked down the corridor at the eyes and hands edging from between the bars of the brig. How could he tell them? What could he say?

"Mom, Dad . . ." He swallowed. The words were impossible.

She watched his face, her eyes working over his features, reading them, interpreting, and she finally nodded wearily. "You don't have to say it."

"I'm sorry," he whispered, and leaned his forehead against the frigid metal bars.

"I was hoping," she said, her voice raw. "But I knew."

"Because he was in the shuttle bay when—"

"Shush." She pressed her fingers against his lips. "Don't speak."

"Mr. Alden," came Anne Mather's voice from behind him. "I've given you what you asked for. Can we resume?"

"Pastor Mather," Kieran's mother said, her tone low and respectful. "Did *you* bring Kieran here?"

Kieran looked at his mother, surprised. She was gazing at Mather hopefully, a light in her eyes. He took a step away from her.

"He wanted to see you very badly," Mather said. To Kieran's utter amazement, she reached through the iron bars and took hold of his mother's hand. "He's a loyal son."

"I know." Lena Alden smiled bashfully. "Thank you."

"Mom . . ." Kieran began, but when she looked at him, he realized the question he wanted to ask wasn't one he could put into words. She'd changed. Something was new in her, and frightening. "I want my mom present at the talks," Kieran said, studying his mother, who beamed at him.

"Lena," Mather asked, "what do you say to that? Would you like to sit with your son in my office?"

"Oh yes!" Lena said eagerly. She stepped back while the guards unlocked her cell, and she slid into the corridor. Her light frame seemed infused with girlish glee as she followed Anne Mather back down the corridor. She smiled at her fellow prisoners, who smiled back at her, even as they begged Kieran for news of their kids.

On impulse, Kieran turned at the last moment and said loudly, "Your kids are safe on the Empyrean!"

The room erupted into applause, and Kieran turned to follow Mather out but was stopped by what felt like a punch to his sternum. He'd caught a glimpse of Harvard Stapleton, Samantha Stapleton's father, sitting on the floor next to the bars of his cell, weeping with relief. Harvard had been with Kieran on the day of the attack and had called the adults to the shuttle bay, where so many of them were shot. That day he'd been so strong and brave, but now the man looked folded, and very small—frail enough that the truth about his brave daughter's death might kill him.

Kieran slipped out of the brig behind Mather, careful not to look directly at Harvard. He didn't want the man to see the sorrow on his face.

Lena Alden held her son's hand the entire way back to Anne Mather's office. She accepted a cup of tea from Mather with a deferential nod, and sat back in her chair, seeming content to listen to the conversation. Mather smiled warmly at her, and Lena smiled back, glad to be noticed.

She's taken over Mom's mind, Kieran realized. For a moment the room went gray, and his lips felt numb and unusable.

"Kieran," Mather said, picking up a portable reader. "I've been looking over your terms—"

He held up a hand. "I have a question first."

"Okay," Mather said, and set the reader down on the desk, looking at Kieran with a bland smile.

"Why are you negotiating with *me*?" Kieran said.

Mather opened her mouth in surprise. "What do you mean?"

"There are plenty of adults on board this ship you could be negotiating with, but you chose to talk to me. Why?"

"Well, because . . ." she blustered. "You're acting Captain of the Empyrean! Who better? You're obviously a very capable young man."

He leaned back in his chair, eyes narrowed. He didn't know what he expected her to say, but this paltry bit of flattery put him on edge. Waverly had tried to warn him about this woman, and she'd been right, as much as he hated to admit it. Everything that had happened today showed how profoundly outmatched he was.

"This isn't going to work," Kieran said, and stood up from the desk. "I'm not qualified for this."

"Mr. Alden, you might have said something sooner . . ."

"I'm not a lawyer. I don't know the first thing about treaties, or—"

"Don't listen to him, Pastor Mather," Lena said with a wave of her hand. "My son is capable of anything!"

"No. I'm not. I'm too young for this." Kieran spoke to Mather. "You need to negotiate with one of the adults."

"Kieran." Mather stood from her desk, exasperated. "Weeks of planning have gone into this meeting."

"You want me to do the negotiating because you think I'm a stupid kid, and that I'll sign anything to get our parents back."

"You've shown you're not stupid," Mather cajoled. "You should trust yourself."

"I do trust myself. And my judgment is that these talks can't go on." He was about to help his mother stand up when a flash of light blinded him, knocked him off balance, and forced him back into his chair.

Flash

The skin of Waverly's scalp crawled as she watched the man screw the muzzle of his gun into Randy's head. *Don't kill him,* were the tiny words in her mind, but she knew pleading wouldn't work.

She pushed her gun into her hostage's neck, and he whimpered.

"Let Randy go," Waverly said through her teeth. Her finger tensed against the trigger of her gun. "I'll kill your precious doctor."

"If you kill him," the man said with a cool smile, "you'll never get off this ship alive. If I have to kill this young man here, all that'll happen is more of you die. See how it ain't much of a trade?"

"You shoot him, and I'll kill you," Sarah said bitterly.

"Wait," the man said to someone around the bend in the corridor. He found Waverly again with his eyes and spoke slowly. "There's a force of eight sharpshooters behind me, but I'm holding them back because I don't want a shoot-out this close to the outer hull. Make sense to you?"

Waverly didn't answer; she could only watch him distantly. He was cloaked in unreality. She was supposed to be standing next to her mom right now, not some piteous, terrified doctor. She was supposed to be walking to the shuttle to take her mom home.

"Waverly," the man said. This time his voice was gentle. *How does he know my name?* she thought distantly, but of course he knew it. She was famous on this ship. "We already have your shuttle crew at gunpoint."

"If you hurt them—" Waverly began.

"We're under orders from Pastor Mather not to kill a single one of you if we don't have to. She's in peace talks, and this could put a crimp in them, don't you think?"

Waverly watched him, her fingers twitching against the trigger of her gun.

"So each of you is going to drop your weapons, okay?" the man said, eyebrows raised.

"Where are the prisoners?" Debora asked from behind Waverly. Her voice sounded smooth and steady, and Waverly wondered how she could be so calm.

"From the Empyrean?" the man said, and shrugged. "Not here."

"When were they moved?" Waverly asked him.

"You drop your gun, honey, and I'll tell you."

Her hands felt cemented to the metal handle of her rifle, and her joints were immovably stiff, as though she'd been standing in this position for millennia. If Arthur was captured, they'd already lost. She could terrify this doctor, who stood trembling so hard his knees buckled; she could even shoot him, get revenge on him for all the girls he violated. But then what? Surely she would die. And so would her friends. There was only one choice.

She let go of the doctor, who collapsed against the wall. She crouched down, eyes on the man who had Randy, and placed her gun on the floor.

"Kick it away," the man said, and pushed his gun harder into Randy's head.

She did as she was told.

She could hear the exasperated gasps of her team behind her, but she saw the look of gratitude in Randy's eyes. He knelt in front of the man, his trembling hands reaching toward the ceiling. *How foolish this was,* Waverly thought. *How stupid to think we could pull this off.*

"The hostages were never anywhere near here," the man finally said to Waverly. "Is that what you wanted to know?"

So Jacob had lied. She'd tortured him until he'd screamed, and still he'd lied to her.

"Now, kiddies. My orders are to escort you to the shuttle bay and send you back to your ship. I think this can be done without bloodshed, don't you?"

Waverly saw Harvey nod like a humble young boy being taught a lesson.

"So, very slowly, I want each of you to put your weapons on the ground and back away from them five steps."

"And if we don't?" Debora said.

"Then you'll learn what it's like to get someone killed," the man said, and took hold of Randy's shoulder to give him a rough shake. Randy whimpered and closed his eyes.

Waverly heard the *thunk* of metal landing on the floor

behind her, and turned to see Sarah backing away from her gun, a murderous glint in her eyes. She met Waverly's gaze, communicating only rage. They were beaten, and both girls knew it. But did everyone else?

Another sound of a gun hitting the floor, and another and another, until Waverly's whole team stood unarmed, looking at the man, helpless.

The man nodded, and suddenly the corridor was filled with armed men, each of them moving with frightening efficiency. They darted around Waverly and her team and stood several paces behind them, guns pointed at the small of their backs. Waverly's spine felt like liquid as the man in charge helped Randy to his feet.

"Let's go," the man said. "No sudden movements. My guys are awfully twitchy."

Slowly, the men led Waverly and her friends down the corridor to the shuttle bay. The doors were open, and Waverly saw Melissa and Arthur standing outside the shuttle, their hands behind their heads, looking grim. Waverly recognized a woman who had participated in the original raid on the Empyrean; her ruddy cheeks and strange, puffy features were burned in Waverly's brain. The woman refused to look at her as she approached.

"I'm sorry," Arthur said to Waverly when she was close enough to hear. "They were hiding in another shuttle all along. They stormed us as soon as you left. We never even got a shot off."

"Don't worry," Waverly told him.

"Keep it quiet," the man behind her said.

The men stood aside to let the assault team onto the shuttle, keeping guns pointed at them as each team member slowly walked into the cargo hold and then up the stairs to the passenger area. Sarah looked angry and disappointed, but she held Randy's hand as he shook his head. Debora savaged the fingernails on one hand with her teeth, her eyes fixed on the floor. Alia was quiet and distant, her face blank. Sealy looked somehow very young, like a ten-year-old boy who had been punished. Harvey's cheeks burned fiery red under his freckles, and his lips trembled as he took a seat.

The man in charge ascended the steps into the passenger area. "I don't expect you'd like one of us to pilot you back to the Empyrean?" he said.

"No," Waverly said.

"Okay, then," the man said. "Now you're not going to try anything else like this, are you?"

Waverly shook her head, her eyes on his shoes. She felt chastened and small. She felt stupid. She should have listened to Kieran. She should have known this couldn't work. The plan they'd thought was so masterful had turned out to be a childish exercise in futility.

"And I probably don't have to remind you, if you try anything fancy once you're off the ship, like trying to damage our hull, you'll only get your parents killed. Right?"

He waited expectantly until Arthur said, "We'll go straight back to the Empyrean."

"All right then. Now maybe we can put this behind us one day and be friends."

"Go to hell," Sarah said to him. Randy stiffened and looked at the man fearfully. Gone was that steady look in his eye, that determination. Waverly could see how Randy had changed from having a gun held to his head. It was the kind of terror that makes you into a different person. She'd done that to the doctor when she shot at the wall over his head, she realized. The memory gave her no satisfaction. It was all so ugly, what they were doing, what had been done to them. All of it, just ugly and sick and wrong.

"Just for insurance," the man said, "I'll be piloting a shuttle right behind you. If you make a wrong move, we'll ram you."

"That would kill you, too," Sarah said.

"Nope. Our nose cone can take it," the man said. "We'll choose a nice soft spot in your hull. Be over before you know it."

Waverly looked at his wry expression. He'd never been afraid of them once. *In his eyes, we're a bunch of little kids playing with guns. We're no threat to him at all.*

Arthur went to the cockpit and Waverly followed, taking the copilot's seat.

"Did you see them?" Arthur asked eagerly. "Were my parents there?"

Waverly shook her head.

"They weren't even in the sewage plant, were they?" Arthur said.

"He lied to us. Even with how much I was hurting him."

Arthur switched the engines on. "Or maybe he told us the truth."

Waverly looked at him, surprised. His cheeks were pale, and his hair was greased with sweat, but he had a grimness about him that seemed somehow dignified. She thought she could glimpse the man he would become, just barely, hovering around him like an aura—a brave, intelligent man.

"At first, remember, Jacob said he didn't know where the hostages were being kept." Arthur said. "That was probably the truth."

"But I kept hurting him."

"*Then* he lied, told you what he thought you wanted to hear."

She closed her eyes as the air-lock doors opened in front of them and Arthur lifted the heavy bird off the ground with a gentle pull on the controls. She felt her weight shift in her seat as the shuttle moved forward, and then she heard the hissing of the air lock as it expelled the air inside it. When she opened her eyes, the outer doors were opening to the spangled black curtain that had folded itself around her home since she could remember. Looking at all those stars was the same as looking at nothing.

"And now here we are," Waverly said grimly.

A sudden wave of emotion overcame her, and she cried, fat tears sliding out of her eyes and clinging to her cheeks. She wiped at them with her palm, and they floated away, perfect spheres hovering in the air. Arthur pretended not to notice. *I'm a failure,* she thought. *Everything I try to do, I fail at it.*

"There they are," Arthur said, nodding to the video screen. Waverly saw the shuttle from the New Horizon directly to their starboard side. She could even make out the shape of that scrawny, smug little man in the pilot's seat.

"I hate him," she said under her breath.

Arthur was silent as he guided the shuttle over the curve of the Empyrean toward the port-side shuttle bay.

Suddenly the shuttle rocked forward violently, throwing Waverly into the windows in front of her. She knocked her head on the cold glass and rubbed her bruise as she struggled to find her seat.

"Watch what you're doing!" she yelled at Arthur. "Jesus!"

"I didn't do anything!"

"Did they ram us?" she cried, looking at the rearview video screen.

She didn't recognize what she saw. Thousands of shapes—triangular, square, jagged and twisted—twirling and flying through space. It looked like confetti, floating away from the Empyrean, silvery, glowing yellow.

"What is all that stuff?" Waverly asked. As she watched, a blinding flash engulfed the screen, and even more shapes flew away from the Empyrean. A spattering of metallic pings pattered across the hull of the shuttle, and she heard the passengers in the back cry out.

"No! No!" someone was screaming over and over. "No! No! No!"

She unhooked from her seat and propelled herself to the passenger area to find everyone looking out the port-side portholes. Sarah was hysterical, her body trembling violently, tears streaming from her eyes.

"They've done it! They've done it!" Sarah screamed as another flash whitened the room.

Waverly blinked, her eyes searing. When she opened them, the shuttle was dark. Or had she been blinded? "What's happening?" she cried, reaching for Sarah, holding on to her friend's shoulder.

"I can't see! I can't see!" she heard someone screaming. Harvey? Sealy?

"Don't look at it!" Debora Mombasa screamed. "Turn away!"

"What is it!" Waverly yelled into the din. "What's happening?"

"They're killing us!" She heard Sarah, her stoic, stalwart friend, sobbing. "They're blowing it up! The Empyrean!"

Blind

Kieran shielded his eyes from the light that flooded through the porthole into Mather's office, but it made little difference. When he looked around the room, it seemed filled with shifting shadows, like Plato's cave, which he once read about in philosophy class. His eyes stung and watered. *I'm blind,* he thought with detachment. The slight shape of his mother walked toward the porthole.

"Mom, look away!" he screamed as another flash came, and another, searing the room with a hot white light. He buried his face in his hands.

Mather was calling out to her guards, "Donald! Merin! What's happening?"

"I don't know, Pastor," came a woman's voice from the corridor.

Kieran heard Mather groping on her desk for something, then the buzz of an intercom. "Command, report!" Mather called.

"It's the Empyrean, ma'am," came a frantic man's voice over the signal. "There's been an explosion!"

"Oh God! They'll never forgive us!" Mather's composure was completely gone, replaced with a frantic shrieking. "Is it their engines? Move away from them!"

"Not the engines! I think the explosions are along their starboard hull, around the shuttle bay and laboratory levels!"

"Hail them!" Mather screamed.

Kieran blinked. He could just make out her outline, and he lunged for it. By pure luck his hands found her throat. He felt the pliant flesh of her neck beneath his fingers, and he squeezed. Her fingernails clawed at his hands, and he felt blood dribble down his wrists, but he held on until an iron grip pulled him off her and threw him to the floor.

"No!" Mather screamed. Kieran looked up to see two shadowy forms struggling over what looked like a gun. "Don't shoot him, Donald. He's in a panic!"

"He was choking you!"

"Tie him up and put him on my divan."

Kieran felt his arms being bound behind his back, and then he was lifted by two strong pairs of hands and set down on a firm bit of furniture. He felt gentle fingers, his mother's, on his face.

"Why did you attack the Pastor like that?" his mother asked him.

He blinked his eyes open and saw his mother's outline leaning over him. "Mom? Can you see?"

"Not too well."

"What did you see out the porthole?"

"I saw the New Horizon being blown up."

"The New Horizon? Mom, *this* is the New Horizon."

"No, honey, we're on the Empyrean," she cajoled.

"No. Mom. We're on the New Horizon. The Empyrean is—" His voice broke. The reality finally hit him, and he felt as though the cushions under him dropped ten feet. For a minute, all he could do was try to catch his breath. He felt a slick of oily sweat coating his skin, and a strange heat entered his face, burning his ears. He thought he might pass out, but he bit his lip until the iron taste of blood settled on his tongue. When he thought he could speak, he opened his mouth and found himself howling. "You bitch! You crazy bitch! You killed them!"

Someone slapped him across the face, and Kieran saw the shape of the male guard standing over him.

His mother said nothing. She did nothing.

"Leave him be, Donald!" Mather said. "The boy's traumatized!" He felt a hand on his knee and heard Pastor Mather's voice right in front of him. "Kieran, I swear to you. I did not know Jacob was planning this!"

Kieran's entire body was taken over by a shapeless rage. Without thought, he threw himself at the sound of Mather's voice and rammed his forehead into her. The impact numbed his forehead and jarred the bones at the back of his neck. The room filled with the panicked voices of Mather's guards. "Pastor! Pastor Mather!"

"Kieran," came his mother's horrified voice. "My God, what have you done?"

He heard the pastor groaning on the floor and tried to kick at her. The guard's shape loomed over him, and a powerful fist rammed into the side of his head. A burst of light exploded behind his eyes, and the room went completely dark.

"Stand down, Donald," came Pastor Mather's breathless voice. "I'm fine."

"You're not fine!'

"He just knocked the wind out of me."

"He's dangerous."

"Leave this room, Donald."

"But why are you coddling him?" the man asked, sounding dumbfounded.

"He's the only hope we have left, you fool."

"Pastor Mather," came a voice over the intercom. "I have Central Command of the Empyrean for you."

He heard Mather's breathless voice. "What's going on over there? Are you all right?"

"I want to talk to Kieran! Where's Kieran!" Sarek sounded hysterical.

Kieran sat up. "Let me talk to him."

He heard Mather's footsteps and felt her presence as she bent down, or knelt, in front of him. "I'm going to put a remote headset on you, okay?"

"Okay," he said through his teeth.

"Are you going to attack me again?"

"No," he said, though he wasn't sure he could control himself.

He endured the feeling of her fingertips gentling the curve of his ear. She fitted the listening device into it. It was repulsive to be touched by her; he'd have preferred she slap him. When she was finished, he spat at her, but he felt the spittle hit his knee.

"Kieran?" came Sarek's frantic voice.

"What's happening?"

"Decompression all along the starboard side!"

Kieran nodded while he tried to think, but his mind was paralyzed.

"Kieran?! What do I do?" Sarek shrieked.

"I don't know," he said, knowing he was letting his friend down.

"You have to get them off that ship." Mather was sitting in front of him, he thought, judging from the direction of her voice. "The whole ship could decompress."

Kieran trembled like a leaf. "Did you close off all the bulkheads that you could?" he asked Sarek.

"I closed all the ones where I'm pretty sure there are no people."

"He has to close all the bulkheads," Mather said. "He can't wait."

"I don't trust anything you say," he snarled at her. "Sarek, try to locate anyone who might be in that part of the ship."

"For God's sake, Kieran!" Mather cried. "You'll sacrifice them all to save one or two! Close the bulkheads!"

Kieran felt the headset being pulled off of him, and he reached out, groping for it, until he heard his mother's voice. "Sarek? This is Lena Alden, Kieran's mom. Do you recognize my voice?"

"Yes," Sarek said hesitantly.

"You must close all the starboard bulkheads immediately, or you'll kill everyone on the ship. Close them now."

"Okay," he said, but he sounded unsure.

"Then he can look for pockets of survivors," Mather said in a soft voice.

"Shut up." Kieran tried to stand, but he felt a sudden weight on him. One of the guards was pushing him down so he couldn't move. "You have no right to call the shots."

"I know that," Mather said.

"Did you close the bulkheads?" Lena asked Sarek.

"Yes." He sounded tearful.

"Okay, now go compartment by compartment with the video system and look for survivors," Lena said. "Call everyone else to the central bunker, okay?"

"Good, Lena," Mather said.

"Why did you do this?" Kieran broke down. "Why do you keep killing us?"

No one in the room answered him.

Trapped

The brig was quiet. Seth lay on his cot, listening to Jake's snoring. Seth had a large, rough, bloody patch on the inside of his cheek, and he worried at it with his tongue. When he was tense or afraid, that's what he did: He bit his cheek, sometimes until the blood came. It was a horrible habit, and painful, but when he was a kid and needed to hide his pain or anger or humiliation, it helped him stay steely. He'd abandoned the habit when he started kissing girls, but now it was back because he knew something terrible was about to happen. He knew it for sure, like he knew his mother was dead that day the ship's emergency alarm sounded. Jake had something planned, and people were going to die.

With a pang, he let his mind turn to Waverly. She

hadn't come to see him. Not once. Had he made her angry when he tried to stop her from torturing Jake? He closed his eyes, tried to erase from his mind the image of her screwing that Taser into Jake's spine, and the way she grimaced, nose wrinkled and lips pulled back over her teeth, making the man scream and writhe. It wasn't that Seth didn't understand the impulse. He understood it too well, so well that he knew she'd never be able to forget what she'd done. She'd learned something about herself she'd have been better off not knowing.

And he didn't like seeing her that way, either. He wasn't so naive as to believe that she didn't have any darkness inside her. Of course she did. Seth lived his life believing that everyone had a dark side; everyone could be pushed past the limits of their own humanity. It had happened to Seth many times. He'd watched it happen to his father, not in any kind of outward way, but in a slow, insidious cancer that grew within the man until the light behind his eyes turned to shadow and he lost the capacity to smile, even at his own son. But Waverly—it shouldn't have happened to her. He'd give anything if he could take it away, make her the way she was before. Help her learn to be simple again.

"But those days are over," he said, and woke himself. He'd been half-asleep, he realized, dreaming of her. Brown hair, brown eyes, light brown skin—she was all one color. She had no flash. Her beauty came from the shape of her, and the way she moved, the expressions on her face. Her beauty was quiet and mysterious. He could spend his life studying it, learning the nature of it.

Or maybe he was just being a romantic idiot.

"It's not love," he told himself, out of habit more than anything. Really, he was just trying to cover up the pain he felt at her abandonment. Because where was she? If what he felt from her that night in her quarters had been real, where was she now?

It's all one way, buddy, he told himself.

When he looked over at Jake's cell, he found the man watching him with a smile on his face.

"Hi," Seth said. He'd become afraid of Jake and how unhinged he was. He'd given up trying to talk to him. Reason was ineffectual, and his quest for information only resulted in nebulous threats that hardly made sense at all. "How long have you been awake?"

The man shrugged. "You were talking in your sleep."

"Yeah. I do that."

"They say it's a sign of creativity," Jake said. "Are you creative?"

"No," Seth said.

"Too bad," Jake said. "I'm not creative, either."

Suddenly, a shudder wriggled through the metal of the floor below Seth, and he heard a distant boom. It sounded like the night the engines misfired, but more percussive. Then came another, and another, and another, each boom closer than the last.

Jake stood up from his cot and gripped the bars of his cell, smiling eagerly.

"What is that?" Seth asked, standing, too.

"I told you it was coming," Jake said. "And here it is."

"What is it?" Seth yelled. He catapulted himself across his cell and jammed his body against the door. If he could only push hard enough, he could bend the metal and free himself. But it didn't give, not even a millimeter. "Jake, God damn it, tell me what you did!"

"You'll find out." Jake tilted his massive head, peered down the corridor expectantly. He looked like an ancient primitive, the kind of being who belonged at a campfire, not on a spaceship.

"What's going to happen?" Seth asked. He felt as though the blood were draining out of his body through a hole in the floor.

"I don't know," Jake said absently, his small eyes alight with anticipation.

"What do you mean you don't know?" The emergency lights came on, casting weird shadows over everything Seth saw. "How can you not know?"

"I didn't set this up," Jake said.

A deep groan moved through the ship—a beast with a will of its own. Seth felt it move through the steel under his feet, and the bars of his cell creaked with the strain. The ship was changing shape, bending into itself. *Where is Waverly? Where are the little kids?*

The intercom crackled, and Sarek's shrill voice whined through the speakers. "All hands report to the central bunker!"

"Hey!" Seth screamed down the corridor. "Hey! You have to let me out of here! Guard?"

He listened, but he heard nothing from the corridor outside. Had the guards abandoned their posts? Was he going to die down here, trapped all alone in the brig with this lunatic?

I don't belong here, he realized. *I've paid enough, and now I want out.*

"Do you hear me?" he yelled. "I want out of here! You can't do this to me!"

He heard the door to the corridor open, and he sank to his knees with relief. Footsteps came toward his cell, and he made himself stand again. "Thank God . . ." he began, but when he saw who had come, his voice died.

A small woman with rodentlike features and stringy brown hair was struggling down the walkway between the cells. She was thin and bony, and her eyes darted around her as though she expected to be flanked by some invisible force. She carried a huge saw that was almost too much for her, and every few steps she had to set it down and rest.

"Honey, what did you do?" Jake asked gently.

"Never mind," she said. "I'm getting you out of here. That's what matters."

He leaned down and kissed her forehead through the bars, but she hardly seemed to notice. "Stand out of the way," she told him.

She never even looked at Seth, who stared at her, aghast. She was spectral, unreal. He swallowed, but his mouth had gone dry. What an idiot he'd been. An absolute idiot.

Jake stepped back, and his wife—the one who was so bitter and angry, the one who despaired of her unborn children, the woman Jake mourned—turned on the saw.

It made a piercing sound that seemed to bore through the tender flesh inside Seth's ear canal, and he covered his ears with his palms while he watched the sparks fly. It took her five full minutes to saw through the first bar, then she had to change the blade from a small bag she had slung over her shoulder. She made four cuts in all, cutting away sections of two bars until Jake could wriggle through the hole she made.

"Now, Seth," Jake said to her. Seth could hardly hear him speak through the ringing in his ears, but he saw the gentle way Jake turned her to look at the bewildered caged boy standing behind her. She looked Seth up and down.

"No time," she said coolly.

"Honey, he's just a kid," Jake said.

"So?" she squawked. "Is his life worth more than ours? Come on!"

She dropped the saw where she stood and pulled Jake down the walkway.

"Someone will come," Jake said to Seth.

"No they won't," Seth said calmly. "They're in a panic. They'll forget."

"Nah," Jake said, but he turned away to run after his wife.

"Hey!" Seth yelled after them. "I'm seriously going to *die in here*!"

He heard the door at the end of the walkway open and close, and he was alone.

But they had left the saw. It was just out of reach. Seth forced his leg through the slim opening between the bars and, with his toe, was able to barely touch the blade of the saw. Maybe with his other leg, and if he pushed harder.

It took twenty agonizing minutes of jamming his thigh between the bars of the cage until the circulation was cut off, and then dragging his toe across the smooth metal of the blade, edging the saw closer, millimeter by millimeter. He could feel the flesh of his thighs bruising painfully against the bars, and every muscle in his body ached. But finally the saw was within reach, and with his index finger and his thumb he was able to pinch the blade hard enough that he could drag it closer and finally pick it up.

The bulky saw wouldn't fit through the bars, so he'd have to hold it awkwardly on the outside of his cell. He leaned against the bars, holding the heavy saw up with his right arm, and turned it on.

The whine of it drilled into his ears, gave him a headache, and it was next to impossible to hold the saw still as it bit through the steel. But when the sparks flew, he took heart and held it to the metal until he could feel and see a groove forming. He sawed on the bar for five minutes, ten, and he'd made it halfway through.

The blade is too dull, he knew. She'd used a new blade for every bar.

He eyed the bag she'd dropped, halfway down the walkway and hopelessly out of reach. Anyway, it might be empty. So he tried to put it out of his mind.

He'd broken into a sweat with the exertion of holding the saw up, and paused when he felt a cool breeze drying his cheek.

The air was moving over his skin, nowhere near a ventilation duct. That breeze was moving toward what must be a hole in the hull of the Empyrean.

"Oh God," he said, and pressed the saw harder against the metal bar, but the saw suddenly bucked out of his hands. Pain crippled his hand; two of his fingers were twisted into unrecognizable lumps. He screamed as pain seared through his arm. For a time all he could do was blink back tears, moaning, but when he came back to himself and looked at the groove where he'd been sawing, he realized what had happened. The blade of the saw, overheated from the friction against the steel, had suddenly bunched up like a ribbon and jammed itself into the groove in the bar. There was no blade. The saw hung useless. And he was as trapped as ever.

He screamed. He screamed and screamed through his damaged throat, hoping that somehow someone might hear him. But then his voice seemed to burst in two, and he collapsed on the floor.

He'd felt afraid before, but it was nothing to this terror. He was an animal. He was trapped. He was going to die.

Panic

"Where do I go? Where do I go?" Arthur kept screaming. Waverly could see almost nothing out of her right eye, but with her left she could see well enough to pull herself back to the cockpit. Arthur sat shaking at the controls, panting, his eyes shocked wide.

"How does the rest of the Empyrean's hull look?" Waverly asked him. She thought she could still see the hulk of the great ship sliding under the shuttle, but she no longer trusted her vision.

"This side looks okay, but that was a massive explosion." Arthur's voice cracked.

"We have to help the little ones get off."

"But what if they're already—"

"Don't even say it!" Waverly screamed. "Just shut up and get us there!" Arthur wiped a tear from his cheek, and Waverly took a deep breath. "I'm sorry."

"The port shuttle bay is probably still intact," Arthur said. He sounded calmer now, and when he pressed the accelerator, the flight felt smooth and confident.

"Can you see?" Waverly asked, blinking. All she could see were dark shapes, but slowly they were resolving into color and texture.

"I saw the explosion in the video display. My eyes are fine."

"Where's the other shuttle?"

"I think they're gone," Arthur said. "It looked like the explosion swallowed them up."

That other shuttle had been a few hundred yards to their right. With a jolt, Waverly realized their own shuttle had narrowly escaped the same fate.

She picked up the com headset and hailed the Empyrean Central Command. "Sarek?" she called.

"Where are you?" came Sarek's frantic voice.

"Are you okay?" Waverly asked. "What's going on there? Where's the crew?"

"I'm fine, and I've called everyone to the central bunker."

"Has the port shuttle bay suffered any damage?"

"I don't think so. The explosion happened along the starboard side."

The brig was on the starboard side.

"Sarek!" Waverly shrieked. "What about the brig? Is it intact?"

"I can't tell for sure. The ship is very unstable."

"You've got to let Seth out of there!"

"I've sealed all the bulkheads, Waverly. There's no way to let him out."

"Unseal them!"

"Then what? He's locked in a cell, and there's no one down there to let him out."

"Someone's got to go down there!"

"Who?" Sarek said bitterly.

"I'll do it, then. Just send everyone else to the port shuttle bay. We need to get the kids off the ship." She said this with a sinking feeling. There was only one place to go: right into the clutches of Anne Mather.

"Okay," Sarek said doubtfully.

"This must have been part of Mather's plan all along," Arthur said grimly.

"And we walked right into it." Waverly punched the seat of her chair. "Now she's got everyone under her control."

"No," Arthur said. "She's going to get the fight of her life. Right?"

Waverly studied his profile. Everything still looked dim to her, but she could see the way his lips were bunched together and how his fists gripped the controls. "You're right, Arthur."

"We're going to get that evil woman."

"And I'm personally going to kill her," Waverly said, making a fist.

Arthur glanced at her but said nothing.

Arthur followed the curve of the Empyrean until the shuttle bay came into view. He looped the craft around and aimed for the huge doors. Waverly saw that his fingers were trembling, and he bit his lower lip until it turned white between his teeth, but he guided the shuttle into the air lock with the assurance of an experienced pilot. Once the shuttle touched down inside the bay, Waverly leapt out of her seat and skidded down the ramp into a scene of chaos.

Already many of the children had been evacuated from the central bunker to the shuttle bay. The littlest boys and girls were huddled in bunches, crying. Some of the older kids were kneeling next to them, trying to keep them calm, but almost all of them seemed to be in shock. Several had trickles of blood coming from their ears. Though the explosion had been inaudible in the vacuum of space, it must have been deafening aboard the Empyrean.

"I want to get my diary!" a little girl wailed—Maysie Fisher, a nine-year-old who'd been orphaned in the attack. "My pictures of my mom and dad!"

Sarah appeared at Waverly's side, her face pale. "Do you feel that?" she asked with dread.

"What?" Waverly asked her.

"That breeze," Sarah said distantly.

Sarah was right. There was a slight motion to the air, brushing gently by Waverly's face. There were no wind turbines in the shuttle bay, and they weren't standing near a ventilation duct. If the air was moving it was escaping out of the Empyrean. The ship was dying.

"Oh God," Waverly said. "I have to go."

"*What?*" Sarah shrieked after her as she ran toward the door. "Where are you going? Are you *crazy*?"

"Seth is trapped!" Waverly screamed over her shoulder, and ran in the direction of the rushing air. "Don't wait for me!"

"I won't!" Sarah yelled, furious. "Idiot!"

The floor shook under Waverly's feet as she ran for the elevators. She pushed the call button again and again, but the elevators were stuck where they were, wouldn't move. *Must be some kind of emergency protocol.*

The stairs, then.

She sprinted for them and started down, taking two at a time. She ran faster than she ever had, making her bad leg sore. She ignored the pain. All she could think was that Seth was trapped and alone, and she couldn't let him die like that.

Her heart wanted to crash through her rib cage, and her legs felt shaky, as though every nerve in her extremities was being fed electricity. She couldn't breathe fast enough to keep up with her feet, but she kept on until she met the first bulkhead. Two steel doors had slid closed to create an impassible floor beneath her feet. She found the emergency intercom display by the door and pressed the call button. "Sarek?"

"What?"

"Open the bulkhead on level twelve."

"No."

"Just for a second so I can slip down?"

"Waverly, you'll endanger the entire ship."

"Endanger? Seriously? This ship is sunk, Sarek. It's over. You didn't see the explosions from outside, but I did, and I'm telling you there's no way to repair the hull. All we can do is save as many people as we can."

She heard him sigh, but then the metal bulkhead doors creaked open and slid away to reveal more stairs beneath them. The breeze was stronger now, and her ears popped, but the air was still good.

She had the same conversation with Sarek five more

times. At every level, he protested, and at every level, she begged until he'd reluctantly open the bulkhead and let her through. Each time, the doors closed above her with a chilling finality, and she realized what a risk she was taking. The deeper she went into the ship, the harder her breath came, the more her head swam, the dizzier she felt. The air seemed thinner, and it was much colder.

What if he's already— She wouldn't let herself complete the thought.

This made her run even faster, but she could hardly focus her eyes. Just above the last bulkhead, she tripped over her own feet and fell down half a flight of stairs. She lay on top of the bulkhead doors, dazed. The trickle of blood running down her forehead stirred her, and she sat up. She had a bad gash on her knee from the sharp corner of the metal stairs, and when she reached up to her forehead, she was surprised to feel a deep cut right at her hairline. With trembling hands she felt her limbs, her trunk, her spine. Nothing was broken.

It took her so much time to stand up and limp over to the intercom.

"Sarek," she said breathlessly. "Open the last bulkhead."

"Waverly," he said, "I can't."

"Do we have to go through this every damn time?"

"No. You don't understand. This time I really can't."

"What do you mean?"

"There's a short between here and the lower levels. The sensors aren't operating."

"But you can move the doors?"

"I can't tell if there's any air for you on the other side."

Blood dribbled into her right eye, and she slapped angrily at it. "Can't you just open them and we'll see?"

"I don't want to kill you."

"Sarek. As a member of the Central Council, I am ordering you to open these doors." Blood blinded her again, so with her fingernails she tore into the gauzy fabric of her tunic and ripped a strip from the bottom. As she tied it around her head, she yelled, "Sarek, I'm not kidding. Open these damn doors!"

"Waverly—" Sarek's voice broke. "The shuttles are leaving."

"This is the last thing I'll ask you to do."

"How will you get back up if I leave?"

"Open all the bulkheads before you go."

"I can't do that."

"I'll close them as I go."

"Waverly, you're sacrificing this ship for one guy."

This stopped her. She was wrong and she knew it. Nothing was more important than the mission, and so nothing was more important than the variety of life-forms on the ship, many of which would not be duplicated on the New Horizon. Not to mention all the chickens and goats, the bees and ants and fish. All of them would be doomed. But it was Seth down there. He might be dying right now. "He's an important guy," she finally said.

"No one is that important."

"They are if the ship is already done for, and it is, Sarek." She punched the keypad of the intercom with her fist, nicking her knuckles on the buttons. "Open the damn doors!"

There was nothing but silence from Sarek's end for the longest time, so long that Waverly began to think he'd left her to die. But finally the doors began to edge open. At first she thought they were opening to a vacuum because the air rushed at the widening crack with furious velocity. But she could breathe. The air was whisper thin, and frigid, but it would keep her alive.

She started down the final set of stairs, heading for the entrance to the storage bays. She opened the door to the enormous room, where the huge shapes of the storage containers, stacked on top of one another, made tall, deep canyons. The emergency lights blinked on and off, casting the containers in an ethereal, unreliable light. She started across, limping as quickly as her pounding heart would allow. She could feel the blood from the gash on her knee soaking into her sock, but she paid no attention. It didn't matter how badly she was hurt. Once she got to Seth, it would all be okay.

The closer she got to the starboard side, the closer she was to the gaping hole in the hull. She could feel it in the distance, waiting to swallow her up.

It felt like an eternity crossing the huge bay. She wanted to run. She tried once, but black spots fizzed and popped before her eyes. She had to stop and rest. If she pushed her heart and lungs any harder, she'd faint, and then she'd be no help to anyone. So she took it slow, keeping her eyes focused on the place where the rows of shipping containers seemed to meet at the end. What was the word for it? From art class?

The vanishing point. She kept her eyes fixed on the place where space seems to disappear into smallness.

I'm not thinking clearly, she told herself. *My mind is running in loops.*

One foot, then the next, then one foot, over and over.

Her steps were so small. The room was so big. She just had to make a lot of steps.

She fell once and rolled on the floor. Her tongue was numb; it felt like a sodden lump of cloth in her mouth. She licked her lips, which had gone dry and crusty.

Next thing, she was walking. Back on her feet and walking. The vanishing point had widened. She could see the place between shipping containers where they divided. She was almost there.

The end of the canyon came before she expected it. She stood looking at the wall. *I'm there,* she thought vaguely. *I made it.*

She didn't know for sure which door led to the brig, so she headed for the nearest one to get her bearings. When she opened it, she got such a blast of cold, for a moment she thought she'd opened it to outer space. It was the starboard side stairwell. One flight down ought to open to the corridor that led to the brig.

It seemed so far away, but her feet stumbled down the stairs, then her hand was reaching for the door latch and she walked through it. The door opened to a corridor. The empty guard post at the entrance to the brig seemed endlessly far away.

"Can you hear me?" she whispered into the darkness, and started forward.

She had to prop herself against the wall as she walked. She looked at the ceiling just ahead of her because she was afraid if she looked at the floor she would fall onto it. When finally the door to the brig appeared to her right, she blinked, unbelieving. How could she have done it? It was impossible, she realized, now that she knew the thinness of the air and could feel the lightning-fast beating of her heart. How could she ever get back up to the shuttle bay like this?

Seth first.

"Can you hear me?" she murmured again. She'd meant to yell. The brig looked ghostly and abandoned, like a mausoleum, and she was afraid she was too late. But then she was standing outside of Seth's cell, looking into it. She couldn't see him.

"Seth," she whispered.

A shape unfolded itself from the far, dark corner of the cell. She was looking at Seth Ardvale. He'd been huddled in a tight ball.

"Waverly?" he said. "What the hell are you doing here?"

"I came here," she said with someone else's voice, someone who was papery thin. "I'm here."

"You idiot," he said, but he was laughing. He jumped to his feet and rushed to her. "You stupid idiot."

"You're welcome, you jerk," she managed to say before she finally passed out.

Blade

He couldn't believe his eyes. There was Waverly Marshall lying on the floor at his feet. She looked like she'd been beaten up, and there was a rough bandage across her forehead from which trails of brownish red oozed down her face. She'd exhausted herself coming here. "The air is thin," Seth said under his breath. He hadn't realized how bad it had gotten until he'd stood up and crossed his cell. His head swam. No wonder she'd passed out. "Waverly! Wake up! Hey!"

She didn't stir.

He reached for her through the bars, but he could only touch her lower leg. He patted it, then slapped it, but she didn't seem to feel a thing. Finally he went to the small sink in the corner of his cell, filled a tumbler full of cold water, and splashed it on her face.

She sputtered and looked at Seth, surprised. "What?"

"What are you doing here?" Seth asked breathlessly.

"I came to . . ." She rubbed at her forehead as though she had a splitting headache. "To get you."

"Where are the keys?"

"Keys?" she said, blank.

"You need a key," he said with a sinking feeling.

"It's not electronic?" she said vaguely.

"You don't have keys?"

"I didn't think . . ." Seth thought that if she wasn't so exhausted, she'd break into tears.

"Jesus, Waverly!" He punched the air, and the motion nearly made him fall down.

"I'm so stupid," she said wearily.

Seth shook his head and sat down on the floor, head slumped against the bars of his cage. "You better get out of here," he said. He should be mad at her, but the air was too thin. Besides, he'd already resigned himself.

Waverly looked around her, noticed Jacob's empty cell. "How'd he get out?"

Seth smiled at that. "His wife busted him out."

"*Wife?*" Waverly shook her head, dazed. "How?" she panted. "He came on my shuttle but . . ."

"Maybe she was part of the original attack," Seth said, and had to take a few breaths before adding, "and got left behind."

"I never even thought of that," Waverly whispered.

He thought Waverly would be much more upset, but he supposed with the lack of oxygen she'd entered an altered state. She blinked her eyes lazily and seemed to have trouble focusing.

She struggled onto her feet, favoring a bloodied knee, and limped over to the saw where it hung from the groove in the bar. "They used this?"

Seth stood up, making his head swim. Maybe he was in an altered state, too. He'd completely forgotten about it. With a surge of hope, he said, "Check that bag."

"This one?" She limped over to the small satchel and picked it up. From inside she pulled a single, shiny disk. "What's this?"

"A blade! Change it! Can you put it in the saw?"

She knelt in front of the saw where it hung from its mangled blade, wincing when the bloody mess of her knee made contact with the floor. She worked slowly and clumsily at the blade, which had torn partially free of the saw in a twisted mess of metal. She cut her fingers on the sharp edges and swore under her breath as she worked and pried at it, until finally it pulled free from the saw casing. She tried to pull the wedged saw blade free from the groove Seth had made in the bar, but it wouldn't pull free.

"Never mind that," she muttered to herself, and fitted the fresh blade into the casing.

"What do you mean never mind?" Seth said.

"Why didn't you just cut the lock?" she asked simply. She heaved the saw up, leaning it on her hip, and stumbled over to the locking mechanism by the keyhole. "I mean, it's got to be just a tumbler, right?"

"Right," Seth said, feeling like an idiot.

Waverly held the heavy saw against the lock and turned it on. The saw jumped to life as it bit into the metal. She squinted into the flying sparks, grunting when the sparks speckled her skin with black singe marks. It was horribly loud, and Seth put his hands over his ears as he watched her.

She swayed as if she were drunk, panting, her breathing out of control and desperate. She was pale, and he thought he saw the slightest hint of blue around her lips. He didn't know what was holding her up.

When her strength gave out, she dropped the saw on the ground, narrowly missing her foot. Seth got up and reached awkwardly through the bars to help her support the weight. It was risky, because if she dropped the saw again she might cut his arm, but it was the only way to hold the saw steady.

When finally the saw burst through the last of the lock, Waverly dropped it on the floor without ceremony and tentatively pushed on the door of Seth's cell. It slid open, and Seth had her in his arms in an instant.

"Thank you," he said into her hair.

"Don't thank me," she slurred.

He held on to her, feeling the rhythm of her heartbeat and the rapid rise and fall of her rib cage as she breathed. They leaned on each other that way for a moment, until he took hold of her hand and pulled her down the walkway to the corridor.

"I don't know if I can," she said breathlessly. "It's so far."

"Shut up," he snapped at her.

"I'm so tired."

"I don't want to hear it. March!"

He pushed her up the frigid stairwell, which was lit strangely by the emergency lights, and then pushed her farther to the storage-bay door. When he opened it, he couldn't believe how cold it was, but he guided her into the cavernous room. He would carry her if he had to, though he wasn't sure he had the strength for it. There was very little oxygen left, and it was achingly cold. Desperately he looked down the rows of storage containers, wishing he knew if there were oxygen tanks stored somewhere down here, but it would be foolhardy to even try looking for them.

He entered a strange state where the only thing he was aware of was the squeak of Waverly's shoes on the floor. Eventually the periphery of his vision grew dark, and there was only one bright spot, directly ahead, at the end of the corridor between containers. So far away. So incredibly far. At one point he realized he'd taken hold of Waverly's waistband and was holding her up. When she finally fell over he laid her out on the floor and picked up her ankle with his good hand, dragging her along the metal flooring toward the far wall. She was immensely heavy, or he was immensely weak.

In his mind he began to hear a song that his mother used to sing to him about an itsy-bitsy spider. The first line ran through his head over and over in a loop: *Itsy-bitsy spider crawled up the water spout . . . Itsy-bitsy spider crawled up . . .* It was infantile, cloying, nagging, horrid. He hated it and wished it would go away, but he found himself walking to the rhythm, and eventually stopped fighting it.

How long did it take him to drag her across the bay? He could never guess afterward. It might have been ten minutes or two hours, but finally he found himself looking at a door, and when he opened that door, he was in a stairwell.

"Waverly. I can't carry you. My hand . . ." he said, on the verge of tears. His fingers were turning blue, and the knuckle joints were swelling horribly. "You've got to wake up. Waverly?"

He knelt by her, tried to rouse her, first with gentle pats to the cheek, then with a full-out slap across the face with his good hand, but she was out, and her breath was thready.

"Okay," he said breathlessly. "You're skinny, right?"

He pulled her up by her wrists, then, leaning her against the wall, laboriously lifted her until he could drape her over his right shoulder. He braced her with his good hand, hoping that would be enough. "God," he whimpered, his cracked ribs screaming under her weight, but he started up the stairs. He took one at a time, pausing to rest after each. The spider song was so insistent now he thought he could almost hear it with his ears—*Itsy-bitsy spider . . . Itsy-bitsy . . .* his mother's voice woven into the wind.

After what seemed an interminable struggle, he knocked his head on something hard and looked up to find that he'd walked right into the bulkhead. He was so surprised he dropped Waverly on the stairs. She landed hard and groaned softly.

"Sorry," he whispered. He dragged himself to the intercom and pressed the button. "Open the lower bulkhead," he said weakly. "Please."

No answer came.

"Please," he said again. "We're trapped."

"Hello?" came Sarek Hassan's voice. "Waverly?"

"She's here," Seth said. "Open the lower bulkhead."

"I can't believe you're still breathing," Sarek said, incredulous.

"Hurry!" Seth tried to yell, but the effort gave him a sudden, severe headache. If he passed out here, they'd both die, so he forced himself to take deep breaths until the headache lessened.

"Get ready for some wind," Sarek said.

The doors eased open, and a burst of warm air blasted Seth in the face. He pulled Waverly up by the wrist. Her head banged on the stairs, but there was nothing he could do. He just had to get her above the bulkhead. When they were clear of it, he pressed the intercom switch on the other side. "Okay, close them," he said.

The doors slowly eased closed, and the wind trickled from a gale to a breeze, back to almost nothing.

The air here was better. Not by much, but Seth felt his heartbeat slowing down incrementally, and his headache lessened slightly. After a few minutes, Waverly's color was improved, and she was taking deeper, slower breaths. He patted her cheek again and tried to wake her. "Honey, Waverly. Can you wake up?"

She smacked her lips, but she didn't answer.

He looked up to the next bulkhead, about ten stories above. "That's nothing," he said ruefully, and heaved her up over his shoulder.

His muscles screamed. His headache came back full force, pounding against his skull like a fist. He groaned with every step. He'd never been pushed this far in his life, but he knew what would happen if he stopped. So he didn't stop.

When finally the next bulkhead hung over his head, he set Waverly down and jabbed at the intercom again. "Sarek? Next bulkhead."

Without a word of answer from Sarek, the bulkhead doors slid open, and another fresh burst of warm air assaulted him. This time the wind was much stronger, and he had to fight hard against it as he pulled her up the stairs. But this air was nearly normal, and he sucked it into his lungs greedily. "Close them," he said as he pulled her the last few inches, and the doors slid closed.

He lay down in the stairwell. The only thing he could do or think about was breathing in and out, that beautiful air, full of oxygen. His headache didn't diminish, nor did his muscles stop their mad quivering, but his thoughts cleared, and he felt that he could go on.

He heard Waverly groan, and he sat up to find her hiding her eyes from the lights.

"Waverly," he said, "you okay?"

"How did I—" She looked around, getting her bearings. "Did you *carry* me here?"

"Yeah," he said.

"I'm sorry. I tried."

"I know." He struggled onto his feet, his legs shaky and unsure, and held a hand out to her. "Come on."

She pulled herself up, leaning heavily on the railing. "How much farther?"

"I think we're about halfway there."

"Okay," she said, and started up the stairs with Seth right behind.

The two trudged on in silence, the only sounds their footfalls and heavy breathing. Seth could feel his pulse in his neck, beating impossibly fast. The moons under his fingernails were blue, and his mouth was dry and sticky. Waverly was unsteady on her feet, and her breathing was rapid and shallow, but she seemed strong enough.

At the next bulkhead, the wind was even stronger, and the air tasted dewy and velvety. He sucked it in like nectar as the bulkhead doors closed underneath him, and Waverly smiled at him. "That's better," she said.

They stood side by side on the landing, resting. Seth felt the strength coming back to his limbs, and his headache seemed a little better, too. He could think.

"Why did you come for me?" he finally asked her.

"What do you mean?" She looked at him quizzically.

"I mean you risked your life to come get me. Why?"

She looked away, discomfited. "You'd do it for me, wouldn't you?"

"I know why I'd do it. I'm asking you why you did it."

"Why would *you* do it?" she challenged.

They stared at each other in a standoff, until finally Seth had to look away.

"Fine. Just say you don't want to talk about it, then," he said, and started up the stairs ahead of her.

"A simple thank-you would suffice," she snarled.

"No it wouldn't, and you know it," he said with a dark look over his shoulder. Her mouth got small, and two lines appeared between her eyebrows.

"You know," she said, starting up the stairs behind him, panting her words, "this whole antisocial thing you've got going? It gets old."

"You seem to like it well enough."

"What's that supposed to mean?"

"You know exactly what it means," Seth said, out of breath. "You just don't like that I said it."

"That's right. I don't," she said, sounding like a spoiled,

haughty little girl. "You're arrogant, and you don't listen, and you make people want to lock you up and throw away the key!"

He whirled on her. "What do you think? That it's your job to tame the savage beast? I'm not into fairy tales."

"Neither am I," she said, looking him up and down, her arms crossed over her chest. "And I'm not into rehabilitating delinquents!"

"Oh, don't pretend like you've never crossed to the dark side," he said. "I've seen you do it."

He watched her shrink down to a small, withered creature, and wished he could unsay it. She ducked her head as if she didn't want him looking at her. All he could do was turn around and start up the stairs again.

He heard her climbing behind him, but even her huffing and puffing sounded diminished by what he'd said. *Bastard,* he called himself with every step. *Bastard. Bastard. Bastard.*

At the last bulkhead, Waverly ran to the intercom and pressed the button for Central Command. "Sarek? Open up."

"Okay," came the response, and the doors eased open. Here there was no difference in pressure, no change in the air.

When the bulkhead doors closed under them, Waverly went to the upper intercom switch and hailed Sarek. "We'll meet you in the shuttle bay, Sarek, okay?"

There was no response.

"Sarek?" Waverly said.

When no answer came she turned to look at Seth. "He must be on his way."

"I wish we could go to the habitation levels and get

some stuff," Seth said wistfully. There was a picture of his mother he wished he could have.

"I know," Waverly said, the anger gone from her voice. The two looked at each other.

"Waverly," he started.

She held up a hand. "Don't."

"I just . . . I'm sorry."

"I said don't," she snapped, but she looked at him with remorseful eyes. "I should have listened to you."

"That guy. He was a kid killer. He deserved it."

"Maybe," she said, but her eyes were still troubled. Because she knew, like he did, that's not really the point, whether they deserve it or not. "I told myself I was doing it for information, but that's not really why."

"Why then?" he asked.

Her lips quivered, and she dropped her head, letting it hang on her spine like dead weight. Her voice was brittle. "Because it felt good at the time."

He put a hand on her shoulder, a small gesture that wasn't enough. But he couldn't think what to say.

She said nothing, nor did she look at him, but he felt her soften under his hand as the hardest part of her gave way a little.

When they got to the shuttle bay, it was quiet. Two shuttles were gone, but there was one lined up at the airlock doors, ready to go. That little spitfire Sarah Hodges stood at the base of the ramp, her arms folded over her chest, tapping her toe angrily. Waverly started toward it, and Seth followed, for the first time able to think about what came next.

"So I guess we're all going to the New Horizon, then," he said.

Waverly shrugged. "I'd almost rather kill myself, but I think this ship is finished."

"Yeah," Seth said. "But I guess from now on that lunatic Mather woman will be calling all the shots."

"She'll probably throw me in the brig."

"Oh yeah?"

"Maybe I'll see my mom there. Or Amanda."

"Amanda?"

"She's one of the people who helped me escape."

"You think that's what will happen, then? You and anyone dangerous will go in the brig, and everyone else will have to—"

"Act like good little puritans," she said angrily. "You'll last about five minutes."

"Then I guess I'll see you in the brig," he said, but he slowed down. They were almost to the shuttle, but he was starting to get an idea. Waverly broke into a staggering jog, and he sped up to keep pace with her as she crossed the huge shuttle bay.

"I thought you weren't going to wait," Waverly said to Sarah, who shook her head furiously.

"I almost left about a dozen times," Sarah said disapprovingly. To Seth she said, "I hope you're happy. I almost died so she could come get you. Not that you deserve it."

"It's nice to see you alive, too," Seth said.

Waverly started up the shuttle ramp, but Seth grabbed her by the elbow.

"What?" she said angrily.

"I've got something to say to you," he said through his teeth.

"Say it on board, then!" Waverly tried to pull away

from him, but he laid his hands on her shoulders. She felt solid, but small, and when he pulled her closer, she stumbled into him.

"Now is not the time!" she started.

"I've got something to say to you, and you're going to listen."

"What!" she shouted, looking at Sarah, at the staircase leading to the passenger area of the shuttle—everywhere but at him. "Seth, we have to go!"

"I don't care anymore that I'm not good enough for you," he said.

That got her attention, and her eyes finally landed on his. "What are you talking about?"

"I said"—he pulled her closer, until his breath rustled the fringe of hairs at her brow line—"I don't care that I'm not good enough for you."

She stared at him, openmouthed, speechless for once. So he kissed her.

It didn't start out the way he'd imagined it. It wasn't tender or loving or gentle. It was angry and needy and desperate. At first she stiffened, but then she gave in little by little, until she was leaning entirely into him, letting him breathe her in.

"For God's sake," Sarah said. "Let's *go!*"

Waverly broke away from him, looking mussed and bewildered. Beautiful. She took two backward steps, and he backed away, too.

"I'm not coming," Seth said as he stepped off the shuttle ramp.

"What?!" Waverly screamed. "What the hell are you talking about?"

"I'm not coming, Waverly," he said.

"Suit yourself," Sarah said, and pressed the button to close the ramp.

Waverly dropped to her knees as the ramp began to rise. "What the hell are you *doing*?"

"I don't know yet," Seth said. "You're better off not knowing anyway."

"This is crazy!" she screamed, and lunged toward the controls for the ramp, but Sarah wrapped her wiry arms around her and pulled her back from it. "Seth! What the hell is this?!"

"I'll see you soon," Seth called.

She dropped onto the floor of the ramp, which left only enough room for him to see her face, florid with rage. "You get yourself killed, Seth Ardvale, and I'll never forgive you! You arrogant son of a *bitch*!"

If there was anything else to say to her, now was the time as the shuttle ramp edged closed between them. But he couldn't make the words. So he held up a hand, and tried to smile at her. Her mouth dropped open, and she just looked at him, her eyes brimming, brow wrinkled with anger and hurt.

The ramp closed and the engines sputtered to life, lifting the shuttle off the floor and into the air lock. The doors sealed behind it with a ringing finality, and Waverly was gone.

Arrogant, she'd said. He liked the sound of that.

Seth turned and, with one last look at his home—the empty OneMen hanging on the walls, the shuttles perched like prehistoric birds on the floor, the flickering lights overhead, and all that quiet—he headed for the nearest OneMan.

ACKNOWLEDGMENTS

Sincerest thanks to Victoria Hanley and Michael Ryan, who gave valuable feedback on the manuscript. Thanks to Kathleen Anderson for being such a terrific agent. Thanks to Jennifer Weis, Mollie Traver, Rachel Ekstrom, Sarah Goldstein, and the entire team of wizards at St. Martin's Press.